VAMPIRE EMPIRE

BOOK ONE: THE GREYFRIAR

CLAY GRIFFITH & SUSAN GRIFFITH

VAMPIRE EMPIRE

BOOK ONE: THE GREYFRIAR

an imprint of **Prometheus Books**
Amherst, NY

Published 2010 by Pyr®, an imprint of Prometheus Books

Cover illustration © Chris McGrath.

Inquiries should be addressed to
Pyr
59 John Glenn Drive
Amherst, New York 14228–2119
VOICE: 716–691–0133
FAX: 716–691–0137
WWW.PYRSF.COM

14 13 12 11 10   5 4 3 2 1

Library of Congress Cataloging-in-Publication Data

Griffith, Clay.
    The Greyfriar / by Clay Griffith and Susan Griffth.
        p. cm. — (Vampire Empire ; bk. 1)
    ISBN 978–1–61614–247–6 (pbk.)
    1. Queens—Fiction. 2. Kings and rulers—Fiction. 3. Steampunk fiction.
I. Griffith, Susan, 1963– II. Title.

PS3607.R5486G74 2010
823'.6—dc22

                                                                2010029653

Printed in the United States of America

ACKNOWLEDGMENTS

To our parents, Melida & Larry and Anne & Motte, who always believed and supported.

Tremendous gratitude to our initial audience who provided valuable insight: Vivian, June, Sean, and Victor. May we all fondly remember Ol' Thomas. Also, thanks to Ann Collette of the Helen Rees Agency and Lou Anders of Pyr Books.

CHAPTER

"**Y**OUR HIGHNESS WOULD be safer below. It's getting dark. Vampires are very unpredictable."

"Thank you, Colonel. I believe I'll stay on deck a bit yet. It's quite warm. That should keep the beasties quiet. Yes?"

Princess Adele noticed a slight smile on the dark, chiseled face of Colonel Mehmet Anhalt, who stood close to her, as was his habit. Under her gaze, the short but powerfully built Gurkha officer covered his bemusement by clearing his throat and offering his brass telescope. "In that case, Your Highness, would you care to have a look?"

"Yes, I should. Thank you, Colonel Anhalt." Adele crossed the quarterdeck of HMS *Ptolemy* and leapt with girlish pleasure down three steps to the ship's waist. A crowd of redjackets from her household guard parted to make a path to the port rail. A stiff breeze rolled the heavy skirt around her calves and whipped the ends of the scarf that struggled to restrain her long auburn curls.

Adele snapped open the telescope and steadied her booted feet expertly against the airship's sway. The distant clouds were turning brilliant orange and bruise purple in the darkening eastern sky. Five miles off the port beam Adele spotted two figures floating silhouetted in midair.

Vampires.

The young princess felt a delicious thrill spread through her. Vampire cadavers were displayed occasionally in the streets of her home, Alexandria, and she had even viewed the purported preserved head of the clan chief of Vienna, but she had seen only a few living specimens in her days. These two lay spread-eagle on the air, vibrating in the drafts that buffeted their nearly weightless frames.

Adele felt a tingle of horror when one turned its head and, she thought, stared at her, looking in her eye with its cold glare. She closed the glass with a sharp breath, going pale. Frustration swept through her that the creature should startle her so. It was not as if the beast had truly been looking at her. It merely had looked toward the ship. Struggling to regain her composure in front of her guardsmen, she resumed strolling the quarterdeck.

A young boy suddenly exploded up out of the main hatch. His face was red from the exertion of racing up the companionways, as indeed he raced everywhere he went. He was barely twelve years old and still round-faced as a baby, with darker hair than Adele's, cropped short. A flowing striped cotton Bedouin robe over breeches and sandals made him look like a ragamuffin from the alleys of Cairo.

He scampered to Adele's side, shouting, "I heard there are two of them out there!"

Princess Adele cut a very different figure from her wild younger brother, Simon. She was the heir, the future empress, and her very proper traveling garb was chosen for reasons of state. Today she wore a heavy cotton shirt, a leather jacket with a Persian sash, and a long velveteen skirt covering high leather boots. In the sash, she had her prized weapon, a jewel-hilted khukri, a broad-bladed dagger that had been a gift from her mother. More, it was a Fahrenheit blade, with chemical additives in the scabbard that gave the steel an intense chemical heat when exposed to air, making it more destructive than a normal blade.

The blade was not all Adele had received from her Persian mother. A light veil wrapped her head and shoulders to protect her against the sun and wind. Unlike her brother's red-cheeked visage that he got from their father, Emperor Constantine II, Adele had olive skin and the distinctive nose of the late empress. Her appearance was a subject of murmured derision among the northern-featured courtiers who dominated the imperial court in Alexandria.

"They're very far away, Simon." Adele put an arm around her brother's shoulders. While two lone vampires posed little threat to a heavily armed *Ptolemy*, she still would have preferred her brother locked safely below.

Prince Simon looked disappointed. "Can I look at the vampires, Colonel Anhalt?"

"*May* I look at the vampires," Princess Adele corrected with a light cuff to the boy's shoulder.

Anhalt was perspiring in his tightly buttoned uniform. "Unfortunately it's grown too dark for observation, Prince Simon. And *Khartoum* has blocked our view." He bowed stiffly to the eager prince, indicating a thirty-two-gun frigate maneuvering through the gathering clouds four miles off the port quarter. HMS *Cape Town*, *Mandalay*, and *Giza* were putting on or taking off sail, struggling to answer the signals to form the nightly cordon around the flagship.

"And you've seen vampires before," Adele argued to Simon.

"So?" The boy craned his neck, straining to peer into the east through the billowing sails of *Khartoum*. "It's probably the most interesting thing that will happen on this trip."

Adele noticed a stony glare on Colonel Anhalt's face as he looked in the direction of the vampires. It was unusually harsh and uncharacteristic of the man.

"Something, Colonel?" she asked, handing the spyglass back to him.

The Gurkha blinked in surprise, then flushed with embarrassment. He studied his polished boots. "No, Highness. Nothing."

"Your expression said otherwise." She stepped closer to him. "Feel free. Have I done something wrong?"

The colonel looked up suddenly, mouth agape. "No! I would never—never—"

"Easy, Colonel." Adele smiled warmly and laid a hand on his forearm. "You merely looked angry. Is there something wrong?"

He wrestled with his thoughts for a moment, and then said, "Forgive my bluntness, Your Highness, but I think it unwise to send you so far north on tour."

Adele nodded in consideration.

Anhalt continued. "And to send both heirs. I don't know what the court was thinking. It's irrational."

"Politics aren't always a matter of the most rational path. I am happy to be here, forging goodwill." Adele, in fact, was thrilled to be away from Alexandria, on board this tossing ship. The alternative was to be at home, immersed in court tedium. When Lord Kelvin, the prime minister, had suggested the tour, Adele had leapt at the opportunity. But she couldn't just make the argument that she enjoyed the adventure. There was a purpose, and it was one that was important to her aside from escape. "It's imperative that the independent city-states on the frontier, such as Marseille, see the future empress of Equatoria. The connections I can make on this tour could be very helpful. There is a war coming."

This was a fact both Adele and Colonel Anhalt knew well. Within a year, conflict would begin that would reshape the world in blood. Adele was no warmonger, but she knew the fight was necessary.

It had been 150 years since the vampires rose. The monsters had lurked quietly among humanity from the beginning of time, but one dark winter night in 1870 they came en masse intent on subjugating human society. It was not known why they chose that moment to attack. Perhaps a great leader had inspired them. Perhaps they sensed a particular weakness in human culture as it teetered between faith and science. And clearly, humans were not prepared; they were taken totally by surprise. Most people had even given up their beliefs in the existence of such creatures as vampires.

The vampires struck at the hearts of the Great Powers of Europe, America, and Asia. They decapitated governments and armies, and destroyed communication and transportation. Order was replaced by horror, panic, and collapse. Within two years, the great industrial societies of the north were cadavers and the vampire clans divided the old world between themselves.

At that time, no one had understood the true nature of the vampires. Few enough did, even today. Adele, however, had the benefit of the dons of the Imperial Academy of Sciences in Alexandria to teach her what was known, or thought was known, of the biology and culture of humanity's greatest enemy. Myths about these creatures had grown up over the centuries—myths that were based on truths, but not the truth. Vampires were far more dangerous than the old legends could have imagined.

Most respected men of science stated with certainty that vampires were not the resurrected corpses of humans. The creatures were now classed as a parasitic species that thrived on human blood, and they had been categorized *Homo nosferatii*. Vampires and humans had disturbingly similar anatomies and physiologies, except that vampires had sharper teeth, retractable clawlike fingernails, and eyes acutely adapted to nocturnal hunting. Four of their five senses were magnificent; sight, smell, hearing, and taste were well beyond the level of a dog or cat. However, vampires had a stunted sense of touch, making it difficult for them to manipulate objects or use simple tools. Anatomy lessons conducted in the gaslit chambers beneath the Imperial Academy of Sciences in Alexandria had demonstrated that vampires seemed to feel no pain and rapidly healed from even the most horrific wounds.

It had never been demonstrated convincingly that vampires created new vampires by infecting humans. Scholars debated with great vigor how, or even if, vampires propagated. There were many theories, but the current dominant belief among the learned was that the creatures lived forever and that there were as many now as there had ever been or would ever be.

Vampires had never been seen to transform into bats or wolves, but they could travel on the wind by amazing control over their density, which was not yet fully understood. Specimens rarely lived long enough in captivity for satisfying experimentation. Sunlight did not turn them to dust, but they were pathologically susceptible to heat, which made them weak and lethargic. Hence, their tendency to come out at night and haunt northern climes.

Certainly none of this latest scientific knowledge had been available to the terrified victims of the Great Killing in 1870. After those attacks, hundreds of thousands of humans had fled south toward the equator, where they sought refuge in colonial possessions and fought savagely for land in a great frenzy of cultural collapse and coalition. Eventually the shell-shocked remnants of northern humanity blended with local people and set about trying to re-create new versions of their beloved societies based on steam and iron in the wilting tropical heat where vampires rarely trod.

Prince Simon scrambled to the rail again. "I think I see them!" He looked back at Colonel Anhalt with a pleading gaze.

The Gurkha offered the young prince his spyglass before turning his attention back to the princess, his hand resting on the hilt of his Fahrenheit saber, an officer's weapon. "I still think it's foolish to waste your time currying favor with the border states. There are only two sides to this war: human and vampire. What's the purpose of diplomacy with those who will need us once the fighting starts?"

Adele sighed cheerfully. "You're just argumentative. You know it isn't that simple. We will need the independent states on the frontier as much as they need us. We will want their ports and facilities to move our armies into Europe. Isn't it better to have an understanding beforehand? No one expects a human state to side with the vampires, but the border states have self-interests too. And there will be opportunities for the Empire to expand as we roll back the vampires. Our world is about to change forever."

Adele's world was very different from the one her great-grandfather would've known, and which she had read about in history books. There were new Great Powers that were like the resurrected corpses of the world powers at the time of the Great Killing. Her own Equatorian Empire was built on the ruins of the British Empire. It stretched from India to South Africa, with its great capital set amid the dusty mosques of Alexandria. The American Republic was a republic in name only. It was ruled by an oligarchy of wealthy families from its center in the torrid quietude of Panama with firm control over most of Central America and the West Indies, and growing hegemony over the southern region of the old United States. When the vampires attacked Japan, that emperor removed himself to Singapore and spread his power over the green temples of Malaya and much of Southeast Asia. The world over, a dizzying array of semi-independent city-states struggled along the vampire frontiers, where warm summers made it difficult for the monsters to extend their power on a permanent basis.

Those who traced their heritage to the north remained galled by the vampire clans' continuing domination of the old lands. They always talked of returning "home" and driving the vampires back into the darkness.

Now that moment was at hand.

The human states believed they were sufficiently reorganized to strike and had the proper technology to counter the swift, savage hordes of the vampire clans. A brutal War of Reconquest would begin with the coming of spring in the north.

And Princess Adele, standing windswept on the deck of *Ptolemy*, was a linchpin in the strategy. It was her birthright to be part of the bloody struggle for the future of the world. She was the matrimonial prize that would unite the two greatest human states into an allied war machine.

Adele regarded the imposing figure of Colonel Anhalt and laughed at his worried scowl. "Thank you for your concern, but surely nothing will happen. We are far south of clan territory. Marseilles hasn't been attacked in—what—fifteen years?"

"Seven, Highness."

"Seven then. And the weather is quite warm. As our meteorologists predicted."

Anhalt grunted in tepid acceptance of her logic.

"And I have my White Guard around me." Adele smiled at the furrowed brow on the dark face before her. "You'll keep me safe, won't you, Colonel Anhalt?"

There was a sudden and surprising glisten of moisture in Anhalt's hard eyes. "With my life, Your Highness."

Adele replied, "Dear Anhalt. Where would I be without you?"

"I pray you never have to find out."

"I as well."

A nervous young naval officer stopped and bowed. "The admiral's compliments, Your Highness. He says we will have chemical lights momentarily, and perhaps you should consider moving belowdecks."

The princess replied with proper formality, "Thank you, Lieutenant Sayid." And she noticed his surprise and pride that the imperial heir recalled his name. "I think that two vampires would hardly dare attack an imperial capital ship of one hundred guns."

"One hundred and fifteen guns, Your Highness," the boy responded stiffly.

"Indeed?" Adele smiled. "Impressive. But in any case, since vampiric vision is reputed to exceed a cat's, surely they could easily perceive the better part of a regiment on deck."

Lieutenant Sayid raised a knuckle to his brow in salute and immediately turned to pass orders to the bosun's mates with a less nervous voice. Then he pulled appropriate signal flags and stuffed them into hardened gutta-percha cylinders. The foot-long cylinders went into shining copper pneumatic tubes and were shot to the platforms high in the ship's rigging.

Princess Adele watched as gangs of sailors clambered up the shrouds and ratlines toward the gigantic, gas-filled dirigible overhead. The dirigible was encased in a tightly crosshatched metal eggshell designed to protect it from enemy cannon fire. A row of three wooden masts extended laterally from each side and also along the top spine of the steel frame. Sails were set in concert with filling and evacuating parts of the multichambered dirigible, to propel and steer the massive airship. It was an intricate ballet, a wonder to watch.

Simon glanced at his big sister. "You want to be up there with them, don't you?"

A startled Adele began, "Don't be silly. . . ." Then she stopped and responded honestly, "Yes. And so do you."

The boy laughed and nodded his head vigorously, craning his neck to get a glimpse of the fearless sailors. Adele dropped her arm around her brother's shoulders and followed his gaze upward, feeling a powerful desire to climb the quivering lines alongside the sailors and scale the dizzying main topmast swaying high above the airship to feel the clouds on her face. She envied those simple men who shouted, laughed, and even sang in the wind-ripped tops with only the sureness of their grip separating them from a long but certain death.

On the blustery quarterdeck, Lieutenant Sayid interrupted her thoughts by touching the brim of his cap politely. "Your Highness, if you would please step to this spot between the carronades. I would be loath for you or the prince to be struck by an inconsiderate falling airman."

Simon immediately planted himself and stared up at the swelling sails, forcing Adele to tow his rigid form against the rail. She began to say something to the young officer, but he was already engaged in another duty. With a heavy sigh, she leaned against the hard mahogany gunwale, content to monitor her restless brother in the gathering darkness.

A maid appeared from below with Adele's heavy cape and a coat for Simon. The weather was too warm for a cloak, and Adele would have refused, but the maid was only following orders. If the poor girl returned below with the cloak still in her possession it would create a crisis that would envelop Adele's entire staff. The maid confidently informed Adele that dinner was in exactly twenty minutes. Then, on her way below, the servant exchanged light, bubbling words with the handsome Lieutenant Sayid. Adele watched them, fascinated by the mix of hesitance and boldness; a young woman, a handsome officer. Such charming simplicity.

A sudden flash of moonlight reflected in the ostentatious diamond ring on Adele's left hand and forced her to remember her wedding was barely a month away. It wasn't so much a wedding as the starting gun for the war, the signal that Equatoria and the American Republic were one. All the linen, china, and warships would be bound to the same household. Adele thought of the beautiful gold locket that held a picture of her Intended, Senator Clark. War hero. Vampire killer. Scion of a great American house. Undeniably handsome. He had the open brashness of an American, which in another situation she might have found attractive.

Still, the young woman had generally refused to think about the Impending Event because the thought of a stranger's weight on the other side of her bed caused many sleepless nights bathed in a frightened sweat and with a shortness of breath. She couldn't conceive of how her Intended's war-roughened hands would feel on her skin, nor did she want to. Her spy inside the Office of Court Protocol had confided to her that the issue of sexual commerce was still under negotiation and, although it probably could not be eliminated completely, it would at least be kept to the minimum necessary to conceive an heir. The marriage was a political necessity and, therefore, Adele's duty, but she doubted it would ever be more than that.

Adele reached up absently and through her heavy blouse damp with perspiration she felt the small stone talisman hanging around her neck. She wore it instead of the beautiful gold locket with a photo of her Intended, which was buried deep in her luggage. Her revered mentor, Mamoru, had given her the religious stone talisman for protection, and it gave her a sense of solemnity and calm. But Adele kept it hidden; no one could know that their princess wore such a superstitious item. Members of court already suspected that her youthful exuberance was a dreadful portent of her failure as empress. Surely they didn't need to know that she had a penchant for the occult and miraculous. The "better" class of people in Equatoria put religion and magic in the same category. Churches and mosques and temples still existed, and services were still held, but those who attended were viewed as quaint at best and deranged at worst. Mamoru was a very spiritual man, and Adele found that part of him fascinating. He claimed that spirituality and naturalism, as much as steel and steam, would destroy the vampires. It was only a matter of firm belief and correct practice.

Ptolemy began to glow with the quavering blurs of chemical bulbs. The other ships in the fleet appeared as vague yellow smudges in the night sky. Far beneath the ship the earth was hidden in a swallowing blackness that had fascinated and terrified Adele since they had left the civilizing lights of the Empire for the vampire frontier of southern France.

Prince Simon's urgent voice interrupted Adele's thoughts. "Do you think we'll meet the Greyfriar out here?"

Adele shook her head with confusion. "What? The Greyfriar? What in the world are you talking about now?"

"The Greyfriar! He's a hero who fights the vampires in the north."

"Oh, yes. No, of course not. He's not even real, Simon. Just a story to make people feel better."

Simon narrowed his eyes at his sister's ignorance. "He's not a story. He's real. I saw pictures in a book. He carries swords and guns and wears a mask. People say he killed a hundred vampires in Brussels. A hundred!" The young prince began to wave his arm around as if he had a sword, striking and slashing. "He's a master fencer with all blades! His swords move so fast vampires can't see them! Whoosh whoosh whoosh! Their heads are rolling before they even know the Greyfriar is there! Hah! Colonel Anhalt, you believe in the Greyfriar, don't you?"

The soldier said over his shoulder with mock solemnity, "Indeed I do, Your Highness. I heard he killed a hundred vampires in Brussels too."

"You see, Adele! I told you!"

Adele replied, "Simon, be still."

"Why can't we meet him? I'll bet if we told him we were coming, he'd meet us. We're the royal family of Equatoria."

"We can't see him because he's not real! Now stand still and mind me!"

Simon huffed. "Well, then, will they let me command the ship?"

"No, of course not," Adele snapped irritably. Then she blinked and said more softly, "Not now. Perhaps tomorrow when it's light."

Adele wanted to nurture Simon's youthful curiosity and excitement, not stifle it. His enthusiasm was important. The Empire needed men like Simon, brazen and curious. Currently at court, to her dismay, there already were far too many of the venal type of man he would become if the palace drudges got their talons on him.

"Why not?" Simon wandered from her side, intent on exploring the ship's wheel, where blazingly bright copper pneumatic tubes gathered to form something like a Baroque organ. Prince Simon was due to become an officer in the Imperial Navy, and this idea excited him.

Colonel Anhalt coughed commandingly at the young prince as small hands played over the pneumo tubes.

Adele darted from the rail and grabbed her brother's arm. "Simon, don't get in the way!"

"I'm not going to hurt anything!" the boy retorted.

They were interrupted by the clack of a pneumo arriving from the tops.

With his back straight, Colonel Anhalt said to Simon, "Would Your Highness care to retrieve that signal from the chief of the top mizzenmast?"

With a yelp of joy, Simon lifted a round copper flap, and a rubber cylinder dropped out into his hand along with a splash of dark liquid. "Ew. What's this?" He lifted his stained fingers into the yellow light.

Oil or grease, Adele thought with mild exasperation, automatically reaching into her pocket for a handkerchief. Anhalt stared at Simon's hand with furrowed brows. He pulled the pneumo cylinder from the boy's grasp and sniffed it.

"Blood," the rough soldier murmured. Abruptly his stern visage turned on a horrified Princess Adele. His voice was firm and demanding. "Your Highness, take your brother below, if you please."

Adele put one hand instinctively on the hilt of her dagger and with the other tugged Simon toward the main hatch as Colonel Anhalt gazed up at the vast dirigible one hundred feet over his head as if trying to see through it to the invisible topmasts above. Several naval officers on the quarterdeck stopped chatting among themselves and watched with growing interest.

Suddenly the airship lurched. Adele grabbed a pneumatic tube for support and pulled her brother back to his feet. In the rigging high above, she saw a figure tumble sickeningly, flipping this way and that, unable to grasp a safe hold, until he shot past the deck into the black atmosphere below the ship. Before Adele could understand that sudden tragedy, another man fell and then another. Then she saw strange shadowy things moving with unnatural agility down through the lines, pulling hand over hand toward the deck.

Two dark cadaverous figures settled to the deck amidships with no sound and lifted their bloodstained faces into the light. Adele saw true savagery for the first time. These vampires were not stories or frightening figures in the distance; they were real, covered in blood that glistened in the lamplight. She clutched her brother close.

Sailors stared at the horrific intruders. A squad of redjackets raised their rifles and opened an erratic fire. One vampire was blown off his feet. The other streaked forward, a blur in the half-light, and two soldiers screamed. The wounded vampire then bounded to his feet and also rushed into the fight. It was a short, bloody affair.

Two other vampires dropped onto the quarterdeck, hissing like cats, only yards from Adele and Simon. One leapt at Simon, too fast for Adele to scream or react.

The vampire's head exploded and the body tumbled.

Anhalt appeared at Adele's side with a smoking revolver extended and Fahrenheit saber in hand. "Get below! Quickly!" He fired twice, hitting the second vampire in the head, and it dropped palsied to the deck.

"Form square!" Anhalt bellowed over the staccato gunfire erupting across the deck. "Fix bayonets! Up and out! Up and out!" Soldiers scrambled for the quarterdeck and gathered into a ragged square around the main hatch. The men fumbled with bayonets and tried to work their rifles as they'd been drilled, each trooper alternating his aim out or up to cover both ground and air. Some young faces were blank, others stained with horror and blood.

Adele sent her brother down into the companionway. She saw the rigging over her head was full of vampires, perhaps a hundred of them squirming and crawling, like a dead tree full of caterpillars. Then the two royals were below, where soldiers and sailors raced frantically through the corridors. Officers shouted orders and counterorders that were lost in the din of tramping feet. Anhalt dropped quickly through the hatchway and detailed five soldiers to accompany Adele and Simon into the bowels of the ship.

They went down and down, past the acrid-smelling chemical room, into the reeking orlop deck. They were taken to a small dark chamber, fore or aft Adele could no longer say, inhabited by goats, pigs, and crates of chickens.

"You'll be safe here, Your Highness." A soldier shoved the royal siblings into the manger, then slammed the door shut.

For a long time, neither Adele nor Simon spoke in the blackness. She hugged her brother, noticing that he was shivering, his unblinking eyes staring at a small goat that stood in the straw nearby. They strained to hear traces of the battle, hoping for hints of victory. Surely, the finest troops of the Equatorian Empire could defeat vampire raiders. The vampires would flee like vermin once they realized that this was not a lazy merchant vessel that had strayed too far north.

The room shuddered and made a heart-sickening lurch to starboard.

Simon screeched and squeezed Adele as they tumbled across the manger. Trying to cushion Simon's body, she hit the bulkhead amid a pile of chicken crates. Adele lifted a crate off her brother and brought him closer.

After several frightening minutes in the dark, the door flew open and Colonel Anhalt appeared with a horrid gash marring his dark face, his tunic torn and drenched in blood. He carried a trooper's carbine and his saber, smoking with boiling blood. "Highness, quickly if you please. The ship is going down."

Adele climbed to her feet. "Lifeboats?"

"No." Anhalt shepherded the royal pair from the room. "Too unsafe." Airship lifeboats were small gondolas attached to chemically inflated balloons; easy prey to vampires. Three soldiers moved ahead and four fell in behind. As the group climbed to the gun deck the chemical lighting went out, plunging the ship into pitch black. The hallway was listing at a rough angle, and footing was treacherous. Ahead, sailors were filling a room with mattresses and rolled hammocks. Anhalt indicated for Adele and Simon to go inside. "Stay here, Your Highness. And don't worry."

Adele pushed Simon to the floor, where he stayed compliantly. Sliding her hand off her brother's stiff shoulder, she moved back to her trusted Gurkha colonel and whispered, "What's our situation?"

Anhalt hesitated, but after staring into the steady eyes of the young woman he admired, and again realizing why he admired her, he said, "The vampires have destroyed most of the sails and damaged the dirigible. And we can no longer stay aloft. The White Guard is losing the deck."

"How is this possible?" she asked, incredulous. "Raiders don't—"

"These aren't raiders, Your Highness. This is a full-scale attack by clan packs. They mean to destroy this ship. Perhaps the entire convoy."

"That's incredible! Surely we have the firepower to stop them."

"I hope so. Vampires are desperately hard to kill. The monsters do not know they are injured until they are in pieces. Even with a Fahrenheit blade, you have to destroy a vital organ or sever the head."

"How many are there?"

He shook his head and hefted his red saber without outward emotion. "Fewer now."

"How many men have we lost?"

"Many," Anhalt answered, and turned to leave.

Adele noticed the bloody footprints left by the colonel and his four White Guardsmen, and anger raced through her. The door closed and she knelt beside Simon, dragging a mattress over them. She sang softly to her brother, a lullaby she used to sing to him when he was a baby. They waited.

Adele heard a strange sound mixed with her own voice.

But there was so much noise enveloping the ship that at first Adele dismissed the sound as just part of the battle. Then it came again from just by her ear. It was coming from the other side of the bulkhead. She strained to hear. Men running? The creaking of stressed timber? Rats scurrying for safety? There was something about it that didn't seem to fit any of those.

"What is that noise?" asked Simon in a small voice.

"Nothing," Adele responded. "It's nothing." But the anxiety inside her wouldn't go away. She shifted and eased Simon away from the wall. From within her cape emerged her Fahrenheit khukri dagger. The glow from the blade gave her some small comfort, but couldn't stop the wild pounding of her heart.

Then the wall started to break apart.

CHAPTER 2

ADELE AND SIMON were showered with splinters as a hole was punched in the wall and a thin object snaked through. Something sharp dug into the young woman's side. There was a horrible hissing noise, almost one of pain as it grabbed her. Arching back with a cry, Adele instinctively slashed at what held her. Her blade came into contact with something long and bony. An arm!

Simon was shouting. The pale arm of another vampire had reached through another hole and was dragging him toward the bulkhead.

"No!" Adele grabbed Simon and stabbed the arm holding him. There was no satisfying screech of pain from behind the wall, only the smoldering stench of burning flesh from the khukri's chemical, which would continue to burn for some time.

A skeletal hand slapped the dagger from Adele's trembling fingers, sending it skittering across the floor. Simon was yanked away from her, and he crashed against the splintering bulkhead. Claws tore at the wood, widening the hole behind Simon.

Adele staggered to her feet and tore through debris for another weapon. Without one, she and Simon would be lost. Her hand landed on something metal, slender, and over two feet long; it was a marlinspike. She spun it around and jabbed the closest vampire arm. The small grunt that echoed gave her hope that she could hurt them.

"Adele!" Simon shouted in a panic as he struggled to keep himself from being pulled through the ever-widening hole. The vampire on the other side didn't seem to care that he didn't quite fit. It was desperate to have him.

Adele struck again at the hand gripping Simon's shoulder. "Hold on, Simon!" There was less than an inch of space between her brother and her target, but the steel tooth hit its mark and plunged through the thin wrist. The claw released Simon, and the boy scrambled around his sister.

Adele held onto the spike like she had gaffed a thrashing fish. The hand twisted unnaturally and grasped the tool, ripping itself free of the spike and tearing its own wrist to shreds before pulling its arm back through the wall to safety.

Glancing wildly about for the direction of the next attack, the royal siblings backed away, though there was little space for them to go.

Then a wide portion of the weakened bulkhead close to the deck shattered in a cloud of dust and wood splinters. Through the haze of smoke and dust Adele was looking at the female vampire face that she had seen through the spyglass while on deck earlier. Now there was nothing to stop the vampire from coming in.

Adele dragged Simon with her as she retreated. He was softly crying against her. She could feel her brother's fear mixing with her own. But there was no time for comforting words, because the face of death appeared in the hole, head and shoulders visible as a long bony arm clawed for purchase.

Determined to protect her brother, Adele reared back with the spike and stabbed again. The spike sank through ribs and flesh and embedded deep into the wood, pinning the female to the deck. The creature bared her teeth and hissed, thrashing in anger, but she couldn't free herself.

The ship shuddered and threw Adele and Simon to the deck. Their stomachs lurched as the big vessel dropped sharply. Everything in the cabin started a slow slide. Adele grabbed a mattress and tried to use it to shield them.

"We're going down!"

HMS *Ptolemy* hit the ground.

The impact tore Adele and Simon from under the mattress, throwing them into the air and slamming them against bulkheads. Adele tumbled for what seemed hours. Her world was noise and pain. She no longer knew up or down.

When everything finally stopped, Adele lay still in the flickering dark and choked, "Simon! Simon! Are you all right?" There was no answer. She heard nothing—no screaming, shooting, or explosions. Clawing at the mattresses and rolled hammocks around her, she struggled to stand but was unsure how or where to put her feet. She could smell smoke; the ship was on fire. They had to get out.

Adele saw a small leg sticking up awkwardly into the air. The frantic girl scrambled to it and grabbed the ankle. Tearing at the wreckage, she reached down, feeling along her brother's torso, and gathered the front of his robe. With all her strength, she pulled Simon up out of the maw. She stared at his face; his eyes were open.

"Are we dead?" he asked her, coughing against the smoke and dust.

Adele pressed her face against his heaving chest. "No. We're fine. We made it. Now we just wait for another ship to come and pick us up." It was a pale attempt to reassure him, and her eyes darted around them. But no frightening faces stared back at her.

Together, the imperial siblings took unsteady bouncing steps across the jumbled mattresses to the door of the cabin. A glint of light caught Adele's eye, and she saw her dagger lying amidst the debris, the chemically heated blade now cooled into a normal weapon. She snatched it up with a small yelp of triumph and slipped it back into the scabbard at her belt to be charged once more. Adele's shoulder and legs felt hot, but she didn't pause to look for injuries. Better not to know for now. They kicked wreckage away from the door, which she then wrenched open. The corridor outside was a world of debris. Wooden planks and metal rods, barrels, and broken beams created a jagged landscape. Redjackets who had been standing guard outside the door were trapped in the chaos. All were dead. Adele shielded Simon's eyes.

As quickly as they could, the two made their way from the remnants of the cabins into the open gun deck. Massive iron cannons on their huge wooden carriages, each weighing several tons, had broken loose and were scattered like toys or carelessly thrown pieces of driftwood. Sailors stumbled through the wreckage, some helping comrades who were trapped or injured. The hot dusty air was filled with muted moans of pain and anguish, and the smell of smoke and blood.

Adele saw the night sky above through a long fissure in the ship's bulkhead. "Up there," she told Simon. "Let's climb." She helped the boy clamber his way up the tilted deck. They grabbed whatever handholds they could find. Wreckage shifted suddenly, threatening to throw them down, but they finally reached the jagged hole and emerged onto the sloping hull of the overturned hulk.

Taking in great breaths of fresh air, Adele turned to her silent brother. "Are you hurt?" She touched his limbs and head. She wanted him to talk. She wanted him to react.

The young prince flexed his elbows and knees, then shook his head. "No. Everything works."

"Me too." Adele laughed and kissed the top of her brother's head. "We'll be okay."

The gem of the imperial fleet had smashed through a Provençal forest, leaving behind a wasteland of uprooted trees. The airship was heeled over on her starboard side with the dirigible and its metal shell shredded. Masts were snapped and scattered across the great mounds of earth the crashed ship had gouged up. Men crawled out of gashes across the length of the hull and wandered over the vast beached wooden whale. Adele helped several of them while speaking calmly and encouraging them as best she could. It was her duty in a crisis. Men also moved around on the ground. She saw surviving White Guardsmen among them and searched unsuccessfully for Colonel Anhalt and members of her household staff. She prayed that Colonel Anhalt was still alive.

Adele turned her gaze up to the cloud-filled sky, searching for the glows of the other ships in the fleet. She thought she saw a faint yellow blur, but couldn't be sure. Then she noticed tiny, wavering shapes flitting over the face of the grey clouds.

How was this possible? It was even warmer on the ground. Why were they still coming? What was driving them?

Adele tried to push Simon back inside the ship's hull as a vampire landed near her. The creature seized Adele's arm, but immediately released her with a screaming hiss. He stared intently at the young woman with his head bobbing like an animal. The vampire wore a mixture of military uniforms, including a general's jacket replete with tarnished medals and badges of honor. But the weird uniform meant nothing; vampires wore what clothes they could loot from cadavers or wrecked homes. He continued to hiss in that language that no human had ever penetrated. Adele realized, without understanding how, that the thing was talking about her. She couldn't distinguish specifics in the horrid language, but she suddenly perceived that this entire attack was about her. The vampires were searching for her.

Even more incredibly, this vampire "general" was afraid to approach her. Adele could sense his fear, and she used it. She came forward aggressively, and the thing shuffled back, brandishing his claws. Then Adele heard a short but recognizable grunt from behind. She whirled to see another vampire wrapping his pale, bony arms around her shell-shocked young brother. She lurched toward them as the thing leapt from the ship's hull with Simon in his grasp. Adele choked a scream as she watched them plummet to the ground. The vampire landed hard on his feet and carried Simon off through the high grass into the dark forest.

Adele climbed down the airship's ruptured hull. She ignored the vampire general as he continued to hover threateningly. She missed holds and slipped several times, but didn't panic. The hard-minded princess didn't notice her bloody hands as she dropped to the ground and sprinted after Simon, racing headlong past dazed soldiers and sailors who were trying to fight the descending vampires. Pausing only long enough to wrest a saber from a dead trooper, she plunged into the forest, heedless of branches and thorns that scratched her face and body. Her breath tore from her throat and her heart pounded.

The princess came to a stop in a grassy clearing. On the far side of the glade stood a female vampire dressed in black knee breeches and black silk stockings with no shoes, bare-breasted under a dark swallow-tail coat with gold ribbons festooning the shoulders. The female was tall and statuesque, but pale and blue-eyed, like all of her kind, and wore her ebony black hair in a braid that hung long down her back. Simon lay at her feet with his abductor kneeling nearby.

The tall female hissed and pointed with her well-formed hands. Her clawlike nails, which Adele knew vampires could deploy like a cat's, were retracted to display her lack of fear. The female smiled and said with harsh sibilance, "Princess Adele."

Adele was shocked to hear a vampire speak English, particularly her own name. She stared at this vile parasite, so much like a beautiful woman.

Then she heard human voices, and two of her White Guardsmen ran into the clearing beside her. The vampire who had abducted Simon was already on the attack. Both soldiers fired, and his torso exploded.

The tall female vampire with the long black braid snarled and moved. The dark creature seemed to appear in front of the two soldiers as they frantically worked their rifle bolts. The two men disintegrated into a shower of viscera and bone without another shot or sound. The female paused to lick the hot blood off her hands.

Adele heard a sound just over her left shoulder and wheeled, catching the image of a pale figure with no splash of soldier's red or sailor's white. She cut through the target, feeling a brief tug on the saber blade, and completed the spin to face the tall female vampire with the saber already back to attack position. A vampire's head rolled on the ground; the body made a slight sighing noise as it slumped to the dirt behind her.

The princess felt neither exhilaration nor disgust—only duty, and the weight of the sword in her hands. She was naturally aggressive, bursting with relentlessness unexpected in a small girl, which had always served as an advantage. But she had never mastered defensive skills, earning her many a thumping from her tutor during fencing matches.

She charged the tall female vampire, three strokes already mapped in her mind. In the fleetest part of her brain she saw the female moving at the same time.

Adele looked up from the dirt. Her hands were flat on the ground. The saber was gone. Standing over her, the female vampire inspected a raw stomach wound and a slash in her brocade coat.

The female said, "You struck me. No human has struck me in a hundred years." The creature was impassive, showing neither anger nor desire for retribution. Still, she eyed Adele curiously.

"Please," Adele breathed, "take me if you wish. But release my brother. He's just a boy."

"We will take you." The female strolled away from Adele and continued observing her wound with the minor annoyance of someone who has lost a button from her coat. "But he's not just a boy. He is the heir when you're gone." She raised her head and emitted a piercing cry like the screech of a rusted cemetery gate, a scream that seemed to slice across the countryside.

A male vampire slid into view between trees and reached for Simon. Then the creature's head suddenly parted from his shoulders.

A booted foot shoved the decapitated carcass into the dirt.

A man stood over Simon. He was tall and thin, and his face was covered by a head wrap similar to that worn by the high desert Bedouins. Over his eyes he wore smoked, dark glasses. His clothing was dark grey, almost black, a short military-style jacket and cavalry pants with a red stripe, and knee-high, black riding boots. Over it all he wore a long cloak with a hood thrown back. He had a gun belt with two holstered pistols. In his left hand was a basket-hilted longsword; in his right was a well-blooded scimitar.

The man bounded toward the tall female vampire. "Take the boy and run!"

Adele realized the mysterious swordsman was shouting at her. She scrambled to her feet and ran to her prone brother, already hearing the ringing of steel against claws. The stranger in grey seemed eerily familiar. Inexplicably, she was afraid for him and afraid of him at the same time.

Adele gathered Simon in her arms and ran. A group of vampires dropped to the ground in front of her, but they were staring beyond her to the fight. As she stumbled past, two of them recovered their senses and flashed over to block her. Their movements were no longer blurs to her. Adele could see their actions with a clarity and purity that surprised her.

She had no purpose other than to protect Simon. Holding him awkwardly with one arm, she landed a staggering blow on the jaw of one vampire. She then drove curled fingers into the face of another. The princess blocked a swipe, locked the arm, and drove a foot into the vampire's knee. It would've been devastating against a human, but she instantly realized that she'd made a mistake, because the vampire showed no pain. The thing seized Adele's neck, but instantly yanked his hand back with a screech.

Clawed hands surrounded Adele and wrenched Simon from her grasp. He was lifted into the air. The boy screamed. The vampire reared back and threw Simon with all its horrible strength. The boy's little form flew through the air as if shot from a cannon and smashed sickeningly against a tree.

Adele's legs nearly gave out as she stared at the sight of her little brother lying motionless. The seemingly endless moments they had shared flashed in her brain, crowding out any conscious thought. All Simon had been, all he could have been, come to this? This was his end? A lifeless body in a forest in France. She started to move toward her brother, but slavering vampires crowded her way, reaching out, slapping sharply at her but hardly daring to touch her.

The swordsman drove his scimitar down through the tall female's shoulder. The force of the blow staggered her to her knees. He left the scimitar embedded in the vampire as he wheeled toward Adele. Three vampires moved to intercept the charging swordsman. Without breaking stride, he pulled a pistol with his free hand, aimed, and fired. One vampire spun from the impact and collapsed. The swordsman then shot a small female in the stomach and battered the other creature with the basket hilt of the longsword, knocking him onto his back. His foot pressed against the supine vampire's throat, he plunged the sword into his heart and then fired a shot into the head of the wounded small female, who was rising to her feet.

A clawed hand raked the swordsman's shoulder, tearing his cloak.

He blocked the next swipe, kicking the attacker away. He aimed for a debilitating head shot, but he sensed something behind him and twisted to dodge a savage blow from the tall commanding female that would have torn off his head.

"You will die," the female told him, with one arm hanging limp.

He wasted no words but drove the palm of his hand flat against the female's bare chest, sending her airborne back toward the treeline. Midway she changed her density and hit the trunk of a tree with no more than a subtle bounce. Righting herself, she stepped to the ground.

The swordsman was already running toward the princess. He swung his blade and severed the top of a vampire's skull. With one hand he reached down to pluck a Guardsman's saber from a motionless body at his feet and flung it end over end toward the tall female. The blade plunged into the female's chest and into the tree behind her. The hilt of the vibrating blade stuck in her ribs. She screamed and clawed at it in a rage.

The swordsman grabbed Princess Adele roughly by the arm and dragged her into the dank forest.

CHAPTER

ADELE STUMBLED ALONGSIDE her rescuer.

"This way," he commanded.

"Simon . . ." Adele gasped. "Go back . . . my brother."

"Impossible. He is lost."

Her face immediately locked in an expression of horror and anguish.

"I'm sorry, Princess. I must keep you safe."

Tears grew in Adele's eyes, though her words were angry and sharp. "Why won't you help him? I don't care about me!"

"You are next in line. Your brother is most likely already—"

"Don't you dare say it!" Adele stopped running, forcing the swordsman to turn back to her. The top of her auburn head barely came to his chin, but her eyes snapped defiance. "He could be alive!"

"They want you."

"I demand we go back for him."

"No."

"My father will hear of this!"

He nodded without great interest. "We must go. Quickly. They're coming."

Adele took an involuntary breath of fear.

The swordsman stared at her, the glass lenses covering his eyes hard and cold. "Once we get you to safety, I will go back for your brother, if possible." Then he added without conviction, "With any luck your troops will have rallied and repelled the attack."

Adele squeezed her eyes shut and forced her emotions down. She needed to think clearly. She could hear the logic in his words; they echoed in her ears, especially what he wasn't telling her. It was better Simon die than fall into vampire hands. The swordsman crackled with a compelling urgency, and she knew she was slowing him down in more ways than one.

"Please, Princess, no more discussion."

She gathered her skirts again. "I'm ready."

The swordsman turned and was off, sprinting, practically flying over rocks and mossy, fallen trees.

———

A squad of determined White Guardmen broke through the trees in ragged formation. Colonel Anhalt was in the lead, a pistol and saber at the ready and two more pistols jammed in his waistband. The sturdy Gurkha had one objective: protect the royal family.

Laid out before him was a sight from his deepest nightmares. A clutch of vampires surrounded the tiny body of Prince Simon with their claws raised and teeth bared. Anhalt fired with a retort that silenced the triumphant cackle of the vampires. The head of the creature closest to the unconscious prince snapped back with a bullet lodged in his fore-head, and he slammed to the ground. Anhalt shouted and ran toward his objective. He didn't know if his men were still behind him or not.

The pistol fired again, accurate to a fault, shattering the jaw of another vampire near the boy. Anhalt blasted the temple of a third vampire as he reached the prince, sweeping his Fahrenheit saber to knock aside a lifted claw coming from his right. A second later the creature was on the ground and two White Guardsmen were running it through with bayonets.

"Form square! Protect the prince! Or die trying!" Anhalt shouted with his feet firmly planted on either side of motionless Simon. His men quickly complied. There weren't nearly enough soldiers to form a proper barrier, but it didn't stop them from creating the barest of defense around the remaining heir to Equatoria.

More vampires descended from above, and the White Guardsmen lifted their rifles to the sky. Every man on the line fired, and the air filled with white smoke and blood. The front wave of monsters fell. Colonel Anhalt knelt low over his charge. When the next surge came from the vampires it too was a gruesome slaughter.

For the first time, the creatures faltered. But the male creature festooned like a general screeched in rage behind his brethren, and they came again swiftly and without mercy.

"Fire! Fire! Fire!" Anhalt shouted.

A cacophony of shrieking, hissing, and rifle discharge deafened the colonel. Then suddenly the vampires were among them. Bayonets slashed flesh to the bone; pistols shattered skulls to pulp. The fighting and dying all screamed.

Anhalt moved not an inch from his position and hacked relentlessly with his saber. It was not elegant or superb to see, merely effectual and lethal. A vampire came in low under his blade and slashed him on the left leg. Anhalt actually felt it strike bone. He grunted, and the whites of his eyes flashed at the agony, but he twisted his saber and drove down deep into the back of the vampire's neck, twisting and severing the spinal column. It slumped at his feet, tendrils of smoke rising from its mutilated neck.

Anhalt raised his head, searching for another target, but saw instead the vampires holding back. There were only a few of them now. All bloodied, with gaping wounds, some without arms or legs. They staggered and then took to the air. The Gurkha thought they were gaining altitude for another run at his ragtag squad, but instead they veered off toward the north.

It was over.

Anhalt regarded his men. Most were dead, but seven were still standing, soaking in blood and gore.

"Well done," he rasped as he knelt to find whether they had been defending a dead boy or a live one.

The youngster stirred. His face was covered in blood. "Where's Adele?"

"Stay still, Your Highness," the soldier answered, laying a calming hand on the boy's small shoulder. The vampires were gone, and Anhalt could only assume they had what they wanted: the heir to the Empire. He feared the worst for the princess, but could not tell her brother yet.

"I want to see her," Simon gurgled.

"You can't."

"Where's our ship?"

"Don't worry about the ship." The colonel didn't know where the remainder of the fleet was or when they might come. Or if they would come at all. The frigates could well have been destroyed in the attack.

Anhalt knew the boy was gravely injured, but his cursory examination of the prince didn't show any mortal wounds. Still Simon had to receive medical attention soon. The ship's surgeon was lost, and none of his aides had been found in the hours since the crash. Marseilles was not far; reachable by foot. Although Anhalt was loath to strike out overland with so many vampires abroad, it was an even greater danger to stay where they were. The prince's life was even more crucial now, particularly if the princess was lost to them.

His princess lost. That fine young spirited woman. That magnificent heir to the Empire. Gone. Taken by those animals. Subjected to such horrors and degradations. All because of Anhalt's failure. He smelled the blood soaked into his tunic and felt shame in his gut. He had to bite his lip to prevent utter despair from welling. The gash across his face burned. He touched the butt of his revolver.

The colonel quickly shoved down the dishonor. Plenty of time for that later. He had to see through his duty to Prince Simon. He collected a squad of ambulatory men. There were only twelve, but that would have to serve. He couldn't ignore the searing pain in his leg where the vampire had slashed him. He bound the wound as best he could, and it would have to do until the young prince was safe. The colonel gently gathered up the boy in his own red-jacketed arms and started off to the west.

—⟨∾⟩—

It was hours later when Adele and the swordsman came to the base of a small cliff. Adele couldn't speak; she only slumped beside the kneeling swordsman with loud, painful gasping. Her quivering fingers gripped his cloak, as much for comfort as for physical support. His back stiffened as she dropped next to him. With eyes tearing in the harsh wind, she could barely see the outline of a tiny hovel embedded in the face of the cliff. Immediately she tried to stand. The swordsman grabbed her arm and yanked her down. Too fatigued to respond, her breath hissed through her lips with harsh gasps.

Why was he so unaffected? She could only wonder, and wish she were a man instead of a feeble girl as she lay muffled by her exhaustion. Staring at him through burning eyes, she wondered again why he seemed so familiar.

Then it came to her in a rush. He was the Greyfriar. Like everyone, she'd seen a picture of this man: a blurry photograph of this grey-clad figure standing over vampire cadavers on a cobblestone street. The photo had been smuggled out of the north as proof of rumors that there was an active human resistance inside clan Europe. The Greyfriar's exploits were legendary, but as Adele told Simon, his exploits were so legendary she believed him mythical, the photograph merely fabricated to create hope. The stories, she felt, were born of more than a century of subjugation and frustration, a resurfacing of the legends like Rostam, King Arthur, or Robin Hood. It was an understandable desire for a hero to deliver humanity from horror.

Then he was in her ear, a slow low voice as if it were a mere spirit on the back of a wind.

"I will make sure the way is clear. Stay here."

Adele could do nothing but comply.

He melted away before her eyes, dissolving into the predawn twilight that leaked across the European nightscape. She huddled and tried to hear his passage over her harsh breathing. It took effort, but soon her ragged gasps slowed into rhythmic deep breaths.

Several minutes went by, and the swordsman had not returned. The shadows became large patches of pitch that could hide an army. Adele slid her hand to her scabbard, where her fingers clenched the hilt of her jeweled dagger as she pulled it to her chest for protection. She didn't dare draw it because the glow of the blade might give away her position.

The woods were silent around her. Nothing stirred, not even insects or creatures of the night. Her heart thudded harder against her breastbone, and she struggled to still it. Could the vampires have gotten here before them? Their path had been erratic. No one should have been able to predict or follow their route.

To her left the thicket shifted with a hiss. She spun and her blade struck.

The long steel of a sword pressed her dagger aside. The swordsman eyed the girl, but said nothing and motioned for her.

"Sorry." Adele laughed weakly and lowered her small luminous weapon, slipping it back into its sheath.

The cabin was nestled at the base of the cliff. It was small and sparse, but seemed a godsend. The swordsman opened the rough-hewn door, and they went inside quickly. It was hard to see through the murky gloom that permeated the room. Still, the swordsman moved through the house and its furnishings as if it were his own home.

Adele stumbled against a chair and took it as a sign. She flopped between its cold padded arms, watching the Greyfriar make their meager sanctuary secure. Before she knew it her eyes had closed. She awoke what seemed like seconds later. The cabin was suffused with pale sunlight. She tightened her grip on her dagger.

Her protector wordlessly offered her a meager meal of hardtack. She took it gratefully and choked it down, followed by a few swigs of water from a tin cup.

A nod of his head indicated clean linen and herbal antiseptic on the table. "For your wounds."

Adele's eyebrow rose when he just moved to stand at the window. No offer of assistance came, so she doctored her hands and various other scratches. Perhaps it was more prudent that he keep watch for their enemies.

From his place leaning against the far wall, the swordsman said, "Drink as much as you can while you can, Princess. Our flight took a lot out of you."

"And you too."

His forehead crinkled with what Adele could only perceive as humor. "I ate and drank while you slept. Refresh yourself now. We'll leave soon."

"Leave? Why? We're hidden here." She leaned back in her seat, taking another long draft of water. It had never tasted so good.

"The enemy can find you here," the swordsman pointed out. "Flay is proficient at such things."

"Who?"

"Flay led the vampires who attacked you. The tall female."

"You know it by name?"

Greyfriar hesitated a moment, then nodded. "She is renowned. The most brutal warrior I have ever seen."

"You sound as if you're afraid of this Flay."

"I am."

That admission did little to comfort Adele. "Where will we go now? Back to the ship?"

"No. Toward the nearest human settlement."

"How far will that thing follow us, this Flay? For how long?"

"As long as it takes. She won't dare return to face her master without her prize."

Adele gazed at her companion for the first time with real scrutiny. His face and eyes, mainly covered, revealed little. She relied more on his body movement to detect what little emotion she could.

His garb hid most of his details, save his height. He was a very tall man and thin, but made a dashing figure in his peculiar uniform. And though he tried to hide it, there was a noble way about him. Something only a princess would be able to see, despite the fact that he hunched his shoulders or stooped a bit lower when he walked. There remained poise and reserve and a touch of arrogance. Traits she knew too well.

Adele's brain cast about through the various families of noble birth in an effort to place him. She leaned toward him and tried to look into his glasses again, desperate to see something familiar about him.

"You are the Greyfriar, aren't you?"

He glanced quickly at her. "You've heard of me?"

"Of course. Everyone's heard of the Greyfriar, although honestly I thought you were just a fable. You're very famous back home in Equatoria."

The swordsman considered her words. "Do they . . . do they make books about me?"

Adele laughed softly. "Oh well, yes, I believe so. You're certainly the talk of the ladies in court. They'll be so jealous of me."

"These books . . . have you seen them?"

Adele replied, "Sorry, no. I don't have time for popular reading. The life of a princess, you know. But believe me, you are a great hero to the free humans."

"I see." Greyfriar appeared to smile, although his features were draped, and Adele could hear the pleasure in his voice. But then his tone became sharper. "Your future husband is a great hero too."

This jolted the princess with surprise. "My future husband? How do you know about him?"

"The coming marriage of the Equatorian heir to the greatest American warlord is common news. Even in the north. The vampires fear him, and your union."

Adele felt the first pulse of pride she had ever taken in her Intended. "Well, he is a soldier of note, that's true. It's a rare man who takes the fight to the vampires."

Greyfriar nodded and turned back to the window without another word.

Had she offended him? Adele wondered suddenly. "Why do you dress like that, so mysteriously?"

The swordsman touched his swathed chin. "To hide myself from my enemies. And from those whom my enemies might exploit."

She couldn't fault that logic, but still she offered quietly, "There's no one here but me. I would keep your secret."

His shoulders bobbed with a bit of mirth as he turned toward her. "You are a hairsbreadth from being captured. It would be foolish to take such a risk."

Her face fell, not only with disappointment but also with fear. "That doesn't exactly fill me with confidence."

He added, "Perhaps someday when the world is not so harried, I may reveal my identity."

Adele drew in a deep breath, but her voice did not crack. "I would like that very much. I owe you a great deal."

Greyfriar said, "Flay's attack was both flawless and uncommonly large. It's been years since I've seen such a gathering. I'd wager she threw five packs into that meat grinder. All after a single prize—you—and she risked much to seize it. The weather was against her, but she attacked anyway. She drove her army where it shouldn't have been. Her losses were great, and she still doesn't have what she desires." He seemed to smile again as he approached Adele to refill her cup.

"But how did you know about the attack?" the princess asked sharply.

"It's my business to know." He tugged gently at his mask to adjust it. "And I tried to prevent this disaster. I sent a warning to the Empire that Flay intended to attack your fleet. My message was lost or ignored."

"I'm sorry. I didn't mean to doubt you. I'm not blaming you." Adele laid a hand on his. He was chilled. She could feel it even through his glove. It made her guilt even more acute.

He jerked his hand back a bit too abruptly and stepped away. "You have every right to question me. I am nothing but myth and hearsay. I wear a mask to hide my true self."

Why did he wish not to be touched? she wondered in dismay. Was it merely because of her nobility? Was she wrong about his birth? Was he a common man?

Adele said, "My mentor told me once that only a fool would reveal himself to his enemies out of arrogance or for glory's sake. I don't see any of that in you. You want to help push the vermin back, not for accolades and riches, but because you want to see justice done." She rose and stood beside him. "Don't ever doubt that you are appreciated by all humanity."

"Thank you. Now, we should go."

Adele replied quickly, "I still think we should stay here. We're hidden and the house has the mountain at its back. We can defend ourselves here."

Greyfriar paused, studying his charge. "Princess, scent is a vampire's tool. They can smell the blood of their victims from quite a distance. There is no way to mask it. Flay will have hunters on your trail. The only possible safety is to get you beyond her reach."

Adele drew a deep breath and shook her head in apology. "Of course. You're right. I'm just scared. But why should I be? I'm with the Greyfriar. My brother would be jealous. . . ." Her words trailed off as once again little Simon's death became real. For a brief moment she had actually forgotten. But now that she had remembered, the pain was that much more acute.

"Princess, I will see you home. Trust me."

Several seconds went by before Adele nodded with a pale smile. "My life is in your hands."

CHAPTER

ANHALT WEARILY REACHED a rocky pinnacle where he saw the sun setting behind the distant towers of Marseilles. Airships floated over the city, some small and barely flyable, others fat merchant vessels. Marseilles was one of the richest trading cities on the vampire frontier.

The air was cooling, and Anhalt smelled the sea in the wind. He glanced down at the drawn face of the young prince, who was asleep nestled in his powerful arms. When he attempted to hoist his pack into a more comfortable position, the boy's eyes fluttered open and he looked up groggily at the blood-flecked face of his savior and smiled.

"How do you feel?" Anhalt asked.

"Okay, I guess," the prince replied thickly.

Anhalt pinched the boy's calf between his thumb and forefinger. "Do you feel this?"

"Feel what?"

The colonel didn't answer.

"Where are we going?" Simon asked.

"I'm taking you to the free city at Marseilles. They'll get word to the Empire . . . to your father."

"Where is the rest of the White Guard?"

How could he tell the boy that most of them were dead? "Some are here beside you. The others are dealing with the remaining vampires."

Simon narrowed his eyes angrily. "The White Guard will handle them! They won the Battle of Cape Town!"

Anhalt fumed again at the stupidity of the court sending both heirs so close to the frontier.

Simon breathed out sharply through his nose. "What will they do to Adele?"

Anhalt's mouth was a hard slit as he crushed his emotions again. "Nothing. I'll get her back."

"You will?"

"Yes, Your Highness." The soldier started off again toward Marseilles over rocky ground. His legs ached, but he forced himself onward. He did not take his eyes off the path as he muttered, "Or die trying."

Prince Simon felt enormous strength in this man's arms. He had been carried by servants and tutors, and even once, at the earliest tip of his memory, by his father, but none of them had radiated this same unbending support. It was like resting in the saddle of a steady horse or in the limb of a favorite tree. He heard the comforting squeak of leather from scabbards and holsters as the soldiers ran. Simon wanted to reach out and touch Colonel Anhalt's face despite the blood of battle dried hard on his cheek, but he knew true warriors would not permit such things.

Several farmers, returning to town from their fields and orchards, some on foot, some riding in an oxcart, spotted the approaching soldiers. They exchanged confused glances but waved and waited, offering them room in the cart. Anhalt accepted but kept Simon in his arms.

The farmers offered Anhalt wine. He declined, but handed the bottle to Simon. The boy turned it up greedily, spilling red liquid down his chin. It was warm, but good; stronger but not as sweet as the diluted date palm wine he drank at home. When Anhalt finally pulled the bottle away, Simon heard the farmers laughing. He sneered at them and prepared to shout a reprimand, but the soldier touched Simon on the face with his gloved hand, shaking his head once. These were not people who needed to know royalty rode with them. Soon the farmers stopped laughing and offered Simon blocks of delicious cheese and some bread.

"Vampires? In force near our city?" The face of Mayor Comblain of Marseilles was red with consternation. "Monsieur le Colonel, are you sure?"

Anhalt nodded with assurance. The councilmen and civic leaders simmered with concerned murmuring and arguments. They were dressed in bourgeois finery, top hats, pearl grey spats, most with beards and great muttonchop sideburns. The opulent Second Empire architecture surrounded them, remnants of a time when humans on the continent had only themselves to fight.

The mayor, an overworked and underqualified official, stood wearily. He was marked as a leader only by his conspicuous red sash and spray of flowers on the front of his top hat. He raised his hands for quiet. "Please, messieurs, please. Let's remain calm. Vampires are not new in this vicinity. We are prepared. I shall call out the militia immediately." His ruddy face quivered as he turned to Colonel Anhalt, who sat ramrod straight in a chair on the dais. "This is most troubling. We haven't had such a major attack in many years."

The imperial commander raised his hand slightly. As the room quieted, he stood with a painful slowness, purposefully exuding a sense of calm, a stillness that these people craved. He said in excellent French, "The vampire army has retreated north. They had a mission, and the mission is complete. These were not winter raiders. I fully agree that it would be wise to alert your citizens. And send word to the outlying towns and villages to be on watch. There may be stragglers in the area over the next week or two."

"Colonel Anhalt," boomed a voice from the floor, "what was the purpose of these vampires?" The voice belonged to a large and loud prominent trader. The room grew relatively silent out of respect for the mercantile colossus, who stroked his gigantic mustache and tugged on the gold chain of his watch that emerged with playful impertinence from the pocket of his silk waistcoat. He ostentatiously twisted small knobs on his intricate watch, consulting its complex readout.

The soldier waited until everyone had turned their eyes from the large man back to him. Once he had retaken the center of attention and authority, he said, "They attacked an imperial fleet."

The room erupted in rambunctious dismay. Mayor Comblain flushed even brighter red, his mouth gaping as if verging on apoplexy. "They attacked imperials? Openly! How outrageous! How horrible! If they dare that, what's to stop them from ravaging our city? Is it war now? Which clan is responsible? Geneva? Paris? What should we do?"

"Colonel," the rotund merchant shouted, "do you know the names of the ships damaged in the battle?" He owned the vast majority of the shipping into Marseilles from the imperial depots in Alexandria, Cyprus, and Malta. The thought that his goods were left scattered across the countryside by vampires who cared nothing for a man's hard work terrified him. He clicked over the display on his watch again, checking the list of his convoys that may have been in the area at the time.

Anhalt squeezed his eyes tight out of exhaustion. The stench of sweat and fear in this chamber was giving him a headache. He again raised a hand for quiet while the mayor prattled orders to his secretary about conscripting more men into the militia and enforcing war emergency orders on local manufacturers.

"Please, calm down," Anhalt said. "This was not a merchant convoy." The merchant took a deep breath of relief, but to his credit maintained a concerned look on his face as the soldier continued. "The prize the vampires sought was Her Imperial Highness, the princess Adele."

The fearful murmur in the room eroded into confused silence. Some were overwhelmed by the sadness of a tragedy befalling someone powerful and supposedly privileged. With thoughts of a now bloodless Princess Adele swirling about the room, several men in the room crossed themselves. Others sneered at those who did.

Councilmen were trying rapidly to calculate political angles of the shocking news. Marseilles was not a part of the Equatorian Empire; it was an independent city-state, so it wasn't the case that they had lost their own future empress. However, Equatoria was a massive state with a long reach, and Marseilles relied on imperial trade and sometimes firepower. Many feared the great Empire was also deceptively fragile. A succession crisis created by the heir's death might precipitate a struggle that could shatter the Empire and destabilize the entire hemisphere.

Continental city-states such as Marseille had reason to want a generally beneficent Equatoria to remain powerful. For instance, many of the cities of the French homeland feared the Algerian-based kingdom of OutreMer, which was ruled by the mad Louis Napoleon IX and controlled by the descendants of Foreign Legionnaires. Marseilles' city fathers jealously guarded their independence against the fanatical Legionnaires, who believed they had the true Bourbon king in their sun-cracked grip, and they counted on the threat of Equatorian power to keep the Legion behind their Algerian walls.

Even farther south, the major African kingdoms of Bornu and Katanga had shown signs of expansionism in the last two decades. An imperial collapse would invite powerful King Msiri of Katanga to seize the Nile watershed and reopen the bloody wars for the Zambesi gold and copper fields. And many felt that the Zulu in the Empire's mineral-rich but fractious Cape Province could easily rebuild an independent military machine and swallow up a weakened Equatoria and much more territory besides.

The mayor said, with a sense of relief, "Well, Emperor Constantine has a son. So although we grieve for this poor, poor girl, thankfully the imperial succession hasn't been endangered."

Anhalt said, "The young boy I brought here is the emperor's son." The council room dissolved tiresomely again into panicked conversations dominated by anger and fear that a vampire force pursuing the imperial prince would now fall on Marseilles. The colonel said in a louder voice, "Messieurs, there is nothing to fear. The vampires are not searching for the boy. But the Empire *will* be searching when news of the disaster reaches their borders. If political stability concerns you, it would be in your interest to avoid a situation where the emperor appears bereft of heirs. I would ask you, please, to forward my message to the imperial base on Malta. I need a ship to return Prince Simon to Alexandria. Then I will form an armada immediately to pursue Princess Adele's captors."

"But surely she is already dead," Mayor Comblain argued.

A tall man in the front blurted out, "We should organize a prayer vigil across town. Perhaps the archbishop could—"

He was drowned out by groans and derisive catcalls.

The querulous merchant boss bellowed from the floor, "Messieurs, I propose that we appoint a committee to consider what reward we should expect from the grateful imperial court for the return of the new heir apparent. I would happily undertake to chair that committee."

Anhalt pointed at the bloated industrialist. "You will not use this boy for extortion."

"Who are you to speak to me so? I have the interests of this city at heart."

"Please! Please!" the mayor said quickly. He extended a quivering hand toward Anhalt. "We are all grateful many times over for the assistance the Empire has given, not just to our fair city, but to many free humans across the continent. I am sure that the emperor will shine upon us for assuring him of the safety of his beloved son. We need not be gauche."

"We should expect compensation for services rendered." The merchant grinned and patted his girth. "Everyone has to eat, monsieur." This aroused a chorus of nervous laughter from the room. "I am proud of my work pulling Marseilles from the dark ages. And you will certainly share in the reward, Colonel, if that is your concern. I am a fair man and you've earned it."

Anhalt abruptly waded into the stiff-collared crowd. His robotic motions were frightening in their directness. Men drew back, accompanied by the scraping of chairs. In the back of the room, several beefy teamsters, much out of place in the neoclassical surroundings, detached themselves from the wall and sidled forward. The merchant glanced at them quickly, and they stopped but continued to watch, ready to move.

Anhalt drew up in front of the massive trader, who towered over him. The soldier was assaulted by the smell of wine wafting off the corpulent man. He knew this man before him, or knew his type. Here in the council chamber the merchant could speak the most beautiful classical French, but in his office and in the waterfront warehouses of Marseilles he spoke the harsh mercantile Mediterranean patois that had grown up since the vampire revolution had forcibly mixed European, Levantine, and North African.

The soldier leaned close and whispered, "The boy will be treated with care and returned to his family as soon as possible. I hold you personally responsible, monsieur. Or would you prefer your ships in imperial ports to be seized and impounded?"

The merchant turned pale, eyes narrowing. But he remained quiet. The rest of the room had receded from the contest between these two men. Even the mayor couldn't dredge up further conciliatory things to say. Anhalt snorted derisively and, without a glance at the two teamsters who glared at him, strode out the wide doors of the council chamber.

———

Simon was lying in bed tugging on the clothes he had been given to wear. "They're not very well tailored," he observed without malice. Then he sniffed his sleeve and wrinkled his nose. "Wool." His face was black and blue, and he had been bandaged tightly around his chest. He had hurt very badly until he was given some drops of laudanum. Now he couldn't feel much of anything and the world was pleasantly fuzzy.

Anhalt turned from the window casement, and the lovely moonlit view of the harbor crowded with small sailing ships and a few steam vessels. He was pleased to see the prince had movement in his upper body; it was a good sign. The doctor had said that Simon's back was not broken and that he would likely regain much of the mobility in his lower body, despite his rough and ready conveyance from the battlefield to Marseilles. This relieved Anhalt's burden of guilt considerably on that matter.

Simon asked, "When are we leaving?"

"Soon. Messages have been sent to your father, the emperor." Anhalt carefully eased his full weight back onto his injured leg.

"Won't you escort me all the way to Alexandria?"

"My duty lies with Her Highness, Princess Adele."

Simon's eyes welled with the first sign of tears since the battle and loss of his sister. "If I were emperor, I'd make sure everyone was safe from vampires."

"Do you wish to be emperor someday?"

The boy lay still, but his sniffling broke the silence. He rubbed his cheek against the pillow. "Not really."

"Then don't worry. You won't have to. Her Highness, your sister, will be fine." Anhalt clapped his hands behind his back and straightened. "Is there anything you want me to tell her when I see her?"

Simon thought. "No. I guess not." He grinned. "Tell her she was stupid to get captured." He giggled. "All that training she does with Mamoru and it didn't help." Simon paused, then said, "Mamoru scares me. He was a priest in Java." Suddenly Simon stopped and looked around. "Um . . . I'm not supposed to say anything about that." He bit his lip.

"Don't worry. Mamoru scares me too. But he is a man of honor and discipline. Speaking of discipline, do you have any?"

"Why?" Simon now noticed that the soldier was holding something behind his back. "Yes! I do! I do!"

Anhalt produced a sheathed dagger. He drew it out for Simon to see. It was a nine-inch steel blade with a fine copper and ivory hilt, simple and unadorned. "Do you know how to use this?"

The boy gasped at it, although he had countless fancier ones as ornaments throughout his imperial residences. "Yes!" He reached out. "Here, I'll show you."

The soldier pulled the blade back. "No, no. I want you to have this, but only if you'll be careful with it."

"Have you killed any vampires with it?"

"Yes."

The boy stared wide-eyed at the blade and breathed, "*Deus vobiscum!*"

The soldier slid the dagger back in the sheath and handed it to the boy. "It's yours. It's very sharp. Know this: the first time you cut yourself, I must take it away from you."

Simon carefully slid the blade from the sheath. "Thank you, Colonel Anhalt. I'll keep it forever."

"Long life to you, Your Highness." Anhalt saluted and departed, his boot steps echoing away down the corridor.

CHAPTER

THE MORNING LIGHT had yet to make an appearance over the eastern sky, so Adele kept her hand on Greyfriar's cloak as he steered her through the forest. She prided herself at this point that she was able to see branches and vines, and twist to avoid them. They stayed in densely wooded areas as much as possible, which permitted only the barest of light from the sliver of moon in the night sky.

Adele couldn't help but marvel at the man with her. His abilities were uncanny, practically mystical. Much of what she felt toward him was jealousy, since she craved his endurance, sense of direction, and night vision. But in those small gaps between envy and ragged exhaustion, she wished to know him better. The skills he had mastered, the air of nobility about him, demanded her attention. What had made him the man he was? What harsh childhood had he borne which turned him onto his current path? Certainly it must have been something epic to make someone choose such a life.

Such maddening curiosity made Adele forget her misery, though sadly it sparked little else. To her shame, she was lost. Their direction had changed so frequently that she no longer could tell where they were heading. The brief snatches of night sky through the branches, though brilliant with stars, did not give her the time to check constellations.

She was at Greyfriar's mercy.

To her relief, Greyfriar slowed his pace. His masked face turned slightly toward her. Surprisingly, a sheen of sweat was on his brow and his breathing was actually laboring. She wasn't sure if that was a good sign or bad.

"We're close," he said.

"To what?"

"A human settlement. We should find shelter there."

Relief welled in the young woman. They were safe finally. "How large a settlement?"

Greyfriar paused to listen to something she could not hear. Then he answered her question. "Several hundred souls. They call it Riez."

"Let's go." She strode forward.

"Slowly, Princess," he commanded. "There is open ground between us and the town."

Adele frowned at the swordsman for a split second for his tone, but quickly relented. He had not led her astray yet. Also, she noticed instinctively that he didn't use the proper "Your Highness" as befitted her position, and she found it irreverently amusing. With a gesture of her hand, she said, "After you."

She imagined a flicker of amusement, as if he smiled beneath the mask. "This way."

Adele saw pale lines of smoke rising from numerous chimneys beyond the clearing and smelled the delicious warmth of wood smoke. The small frontier town was a decrepit shell of what it had once been. It was now reduced to overgrown medieval structures and a few poor farmers going to and fro beginning their daily chores. It looked picturesque and peaceful. Adele thought it was the most beautiful sight in the world.

She raised her gaze to the sky as Greyfriar was presently doing, scanning the cobalt blue above them for signs of vampires.

"Clear?" she asked.

He drew his gleaming sword. "If something happens, I want you to run toward the village. Scream."

She raised her eyebrows defiantly.

Bemused at her pride, he added, "To attract attention. Don't look back and don't try to help me. Do you understand?"

Adele's heart raced, pounding with such force it almost hurt. "Yes." She looked around the woods, almost afraid to ask, "Are they here?"

"Possibly. Flay would know this is one of the closest settlements. She could have been here before us. Waiting."

"I'm ready." It was a lie. If it were left to her, she would stay right where she was for the rest of her days. The thought of walking across an open field while malicious vampires waited to strike made her knees so weak she doubted she was going to be able to follow Greyfriar. But she knew that she had no choice.

"Quickly now," he bade her, and they ran.

Greyfriar slipped through the high grass, aiming for a worn path that ran to the village. His eyes scanned about him, watching for ambush. Clouds of dust billowed up at his pounding feet. Adele was beside him with dagger in hand.

People from the village noticed them and paused in their morning toil. Adele lifted her arm, but had no breath left to call out. A few farmers started walking toward them with implements in their hands.

But nothing horrible erupted from the treeline and nothing swooped down from the morning sky. They were going to make it! Perhaps Greyfriar overestimated Flay, Adele thought with excitement. Flay was just a vampire, after all. Cunning, perhaps, but only in the way a savage beast was cunning.

Greyfriar's attention had already turned to the farmers.

"Greyfriar!" exclaimed a tall gaunt man with a scythe in his grasp. "It's the Greyfriar!" he shouted to the others with excitement.

Adele could only watch, stunned by the enthusiastic greetings of these people for the man beside her. A bearded man in rough twill work clothes grabbed her as her legs trembled and finally failed her.

"What has happened?" the thin man asked Greyfriar in French.

"A ship was attacked by vampires," Greyfriar replied in an accent so perfect he might have been born here. "We need shelter."

"Of course you shall have it! Bring her into town."

"I may have been followed."

"Spread the warning, Makepeace," the thin man shouted, and clasped Greyfriar by the shoulder. "We offer you our protection."

"Thank you, Shepherd. It is good to see you again. I wish it were under better circumstances."

"We cannot always choose our moments of reunion. Who is this young woman? A survivor of the attack?"

Greyfriar nodded, letting his friend make his own assumptions and not offering more.

"Not the only one, I hope?" Shepherd inquired with growing horror.

"There were few left alive when I arrived."

"The poor thing. How long have you been on the run?"

"A day or so."

Shepherd tsked. "You need food and rest."

Greyfriar habitually checked to be sure his mask was in place before he turned from the window. "I've sent word that will soon reach the Empire. You will be home before too long. I hope."

"Thank you." Adele was watching him, desperate suddenly to learn something about her rescuer before they parted ways. "What does your name mean?"

The swordsman seemed confused briefly as he slowly paced along the rough plaster wall. "Oh. Greyfriar is a church in Scotland."

"Scotland? Have you been there?"

"Yes."

"So far north? How do you manage it?"

"It's not as difficult as you might imagine. If you're alone."

"Are you a geomancer?" Adele leaned forward. Her mentor, Mamoru, had told her about the skills of geomancy that allowed certain humans to move unseen by vampires. She had always wondered whether it was true. "I've heard stories about them. They travel the north, spying on the vampires. But they can't be seen. Is that right? Can you do that?"

"No. I've heard those stories too. I assume they're just stories. How is such a thing possible?"

"Well, how are *you* possible? I thought you were just a story too. Just a creation by people so sick of living in fear they created a man who couldn't possibly exist."

"Perhaps I am."

Adele didn't appear to hear his soft reply. She had fallen into her own thoughts.

Suddenly she said with great vigor, "I hope they all die. The vampires. My father intends to kill them all, you know. That's why I am to be married." Her hands gripped the chair's arms till her flesh turned white. "I hate them!" Her grief was surging out as anger now that they were relatively safe. "When I'm empress I'll send all my airships to kill the vampires. They're not magic; they can die."

"Yes," Greyfriar said quietly. "They *can* die."

"My army is the greatest in the world. My grandfather conquered India and my father conquered Africa. We intend for all humans to join together and kill the vampires."

Adele turned away from Greyfriar. It wasn't right for him to see her so emotional. She was a princess, and so her voice stilled. "Once I'm married to Senator Clark, all the vampires will be killed so people can live in the north again. And live in the snow. My brother was desperate to see snow." After a while, she said, "I've seen pictures of snow and I've seen it on mountains, but not up close. It's too dangerous; there might be vampires."

"I have seen snow."

Adele looked imploring. "What's it like?"

"It's quiet. And lonely."

"How long have you been fighting?"

Greyfriar took a deep breath. "A long time. Most of my life."

Adele smiled at him. "Amazing. That you're still alive. You must know a great deal about them, about vampires. We could use a man such as you in the coming war."

The swordsman lowered his head and continued pacing, accompanied by the creaking of leather and the clashing of his weapons. "I do what I can from here. These are the people who need me the most."

"But you must have a great deal of intelligence on vampire society.

We have some concept of how it's structured, but you could be very helpful. You must know about how they"—Adele sneered with contempt—"organized themselves into their clans after they conquered the north."

"They were organized before the Great Killing, although not quite so rigidly as now."

"So these things have always lived next to us?"

"Yes. The clans have existed on the fringes of the human world from the dawn of time."

Adele leaned forward with her eyes sharp and bright. "What about now? Where is the center of vampire power?"

Greyfriar shook his head. "It's not that simple, Princess. Each clan has its own king and nobles. They sometimes unite in common cause, as they did for the Great Killing, but the vampire north is not a single entity. And that doesn't even account for the clans in America and Asia."

"America and Asia will come in time. I'm concerned with Europe. If you had an army, where would you strike to cripple them? Paris? Vienna?"

Greyfriar leaned on a table, hands spread wide, as if at a war council, and said to Adele, "Paris is decayed. Their king died decades back, and a power struggle has diminished them. Vienna is a necropolis. Even vampires have deserted it."

"Then who? Where is the heart of their power? London?"

The swordsman paused in thought. "Perhaps. London is strong and unified. King Dmitri has maintained his hold on his throne. His lords are loyal to him. Or loyal to Dmitri's son, Cesare."

"Cesare. I've heard his name before," Adele said.

"I'm sure that would please him. During the Great Killing he took control of the British clan, which he continues to rule through his father, Dmitri. There is an older son, Gareth, but he is of no matter. Cesare is the true ruler. He was the one who ordered every man, woman, and child in Ireland to be slaughtered."

"My God," she whispered. "I've read about that. Could that be true? It seems an impossible act of barbarism."

"It is true. There is no act too barbaric for Cesare to contemplate.

There are nearly no humans in Ireland still." The swordsman glanced up at Adele. He paused before saying, "Then you are not aware that Flay was the vampire who led the slaughter in Ireland."

"The one who is chasing me?" Adele's voice seemed far away.

"The very one. I'm sorry. But rest assured I will protect you." Abruptly, Greyfriar turned. "I have to go."

"What? Where are you going?" She had lost everyone she relied on—Simon and Anhalt—and now Greyfriar was leaving.

"To scout the area."

"But you'll be back, right?" Adele knew she sounded desperate, and she hated it. This fear inside her was like a living thing suddenly, and she had kept it at bay for so long that it now seemed impossible to control.

"Yes, I'll be back."

"Of course." Adele sat up straighter. "I'm sorry. I sound like a lost little girl."

Greyfriar's head tilted a bit as he regarded her. "You have the right. You've been through an ordeal. The fear will ease in time. Never be ashamed of fear. Use it as a weapon. Let it give you strength and resolve. I've seen you manage it these past few days. You are much stronger than you give yourself credit for."

Adele smiled, grateful for his words. It pushed back her anxiety and made it bearable again. "You deserve a reward for your own bravery. I could recommend my father to make you a duke. Would you like to be viceroy of Somaliland?" Her smile broadened with a trace of personal amusement, almost embracing the little girl again. "Or we could give you a palace. We could throw Lord Kelvin out of his. He's terribly annoying, but he has a beautiful mansion on the Rue Victoria. It's got a garden with—"

Greyfriar held up a gloved hand and laughed, a low rumbling in his chest. "Thank you for the offer. But I don't need a palace."

"I wish Simon had been able to meet you, the legendary Greyfriar. He would have been thrilled." The girl looked out through the open window and was cast back to the battle and her poor brother's limp body. "I couldn't save him. I was so helpless," she said quietly, almost to herself.

"On the contrary, I've never seen a human perform so well against vampires."

"You think so?"

"Yes. Your decapitation with a saber was amazing. If I had been in your place, even I would have had trouble hearing that vampire. But you turned and struck cleanly and surely. You were certainly more effective than your soldiers. So whatever disciplines you are studying, the imperial army would do well to study them too."

His words removed some of her dark guilt. Adele stretched and pushed the plate of food away. It had tasted delicious. Amazing how such simple fare could seem so divine after a brush with death. Everything tasted more intense and flavorful. All her emotions seemed stronger and at the same time more sweet.

Adele saw the swordsman arranging several packs that he had left near the door. "What's in the bags?"

"Ammunition." Greyfriar stroked one pack with care. "And a book."

"A book?" Adele's face lit up with curiosity.

"A gift." He opened the pack and removed a leather-bound folio. "I've kept it here. But now I'm going to take it with me."

"What is it?" Adele leaned forward.

"An anatomy text." The man held the book open, facing her.

Adele's eyes widened at the sight of a masterful pen drawing of a cadaver with its chest cavity split open. The princess squinted at the picture. "What is that?"

Greyfriar turned the book away from Adele and studied the dissection plate. "It's Randolph's *Treatise on Homo Nosferatii*. I'm told the finest text on the subject of vampire anatomy. Apparently, Dr. Randolph has dissected more vampires than any other human. At your own Academy of Sciences, by the way. He is a very learned man."

"Sir Godfrey Randolph? Yes, I've met him. He's retired now, but I believe he lives near Cairo. I could arrange for you to talk to him."

Greyfriar leaned forward in consideration. "A gracious offer but impractical. Thank you. His book will have to do for now."

"Why do you care about vampire bodies?"

The swordsman closed the book and replaced it in his rucksack.

"You must know your enemy." He donned his cloak again, apparently eager to go.

"So you like books?" Adele asked quickly.

"Yes. Books are very rare in the north." The swordsman opened the door, but then paused and turned toward her. "Sleep well tonight. I'll return in a short while."

And he was gone. Adele felt an immediate loss that she knew instinctively was silly. Such fondness was only due to the dire circumstance they had shared and his selfless acts to save her life. But still she enjoyed the emotion. It was one she had never felt so strongly before. He made her feel safe. Which was an amazing feat in this day and age.

CHAPTER 6

ADELE JERKED FREE from a nightmare of running barefoot and alone through charnel halls of ships with the screams of the dying ringing in her ears. She sat up in the bed and encircled her knees with her arms. She was fully dressed, feeling too vulnerable to shed her clothing.

"It was just a dream," she whispered. "Just a dream."

The simple house in Riez was quiet, cold, and dark. Adele knew she should rest more. Greyfriar had sent word of her survival to Equatoria, and soon an army would be about her that would rival a full-fledged invasion. Her father would take no chances. Vampires would never be so bold as to attack the huge force he would send to retrieve her.

It made her ill to think of how close they had come.

Suddenly in the dark came a hard thunk. Adele straightened immediately, straining to hear more. Perhaps it had not been the dream that woke her. Someone was awake downstairs. Greyfriar, she thought, back from scouting. She rose to her feet and padded to the bedroom door, hoping to hear whom it could be awake at this hour.

Another loud thump. This time there was a low moan and an abruptly hushed cry along with it. Adele's eyes flew wide, and she threw the lock on the door. She scrambled back to her bed, drawing out the blade she had hidden under the pillow. Something large and dark flew past the window. Flinging herself to the shutters, she fumbled with the latch as her fingers grasped the knife tightly.

They had come for her! They were in the house!

She let out a shrill scream to wake everyone, lest they be caught in their sleep. It would give her position away, but that couldn't be helped. She screamed Greyfriar's name as loud as she could. Abruptly there were screams all around her as the house woke and found themselves facing horrors at their bedroom doors.

Then a sound reached Adele's ears that plunged her hope to the cold ground: terrible hissing right outside her door. She pulled herself back into a corner of the room, silent now. The handle lifted up and down. Then something shoved hard against the door.

Should she wait here, or should she flee? She chose the latter and ran for the window, throwing back the shutters and yanking it open. She looked about for a ledge. There was a balcony just below her, small but manageable. She had one leg over the sill when the wood of the door splintered apart as a vampire clawed its way inside.

Adele slid out the window, dropping a few feet to the balcony below. Her room was only two stories up, so she could reach the ground with one more drop. She climbed the wrought iron rail of the balcony and hung as low as her arms could take her before dropping. It would be only seconds before they were after her.

The princess hit the ground and collapsed, going as limp as possible to absorb the impact of the fall. Her teeth snapped shut; luckily her tongue had not been caught in them. She tumbled twice, scrambled to her feet, and ran. She didn't dare turn to look behind her. It was best to assume the vampires were right on her heels. What she needed was a defensible position until Greyfriar came. She believed he would come. She just had to stay alive long enough for him to reach her.

Adele heard hissing close behind. One of the creatures had found her and was signaling to its brethren, but the hissing also gave its location to her without having to look. She suddenly stopped and spun. Her glowing blade flashed straight across the vampire's throat, and the hissing stopped. The thing clutched the gaping slash with both hands, his eyes wide with surprise. Adele had no desire to stand and gawk. There were sounds of chaos all around her. Screams and shrieks assailed her ears. The village was under attack. She knew she couldn't hide. If there was anything to be done, she had to try. Adele ran along the street to find it awash in blood. Bodies were everywhere. Adele kept to the dark places to hide from watchful eyes above. Every few seconds shadows would slink over the ground as a vampire drifted overhead looking for prey.

A young woman darted in front of Adele, looking behind her in sheer terror. She screamed as a dark form fell on her, bearing her to the ground. Adele plunged her dagger into the creature up to the hilt, again and again, blood and smoke splattering around her. The thing hissed and arched back, more out of aggravation than pain. Adele grabbed him by the shoulder to better anchor herself, and suddenly the vampire began screeching. The vampire writhed and threw himself away from the princess. He rolled and scrambled to his feet, slipping away into the darkness with amazing quickness. Adele helped the poor woman to her feet.

"It's you!" the woman screeched. "You're the stranger! You came with the Greyfriar! They're here for you! You're the reason they've come!"

The accusation bit deep into Adele because the woman was right. She had saved one, but ten more died beyond her reach.

Adele shook the woman to get her attention. "Hide yourself and stay quiet."

She had to find Greyfriar. No doubt he was somewhere protecting those he could. Or he was coming for her. Maybe she should stay where she was so he could find her. Fate took that decision from Adele.

Three people fled their home no more than twenty feet in front of her. In a matter of seconds, a female vampire descended upon them. One man died instantly from her sharp claws. Another man screamed as the vampire turned to him.

Adele ran forward, hoping to do something, anything. The vampire sensed her approach, raising a bloody hand and licking the red as her attention turned to her new victim. The princess didn't slow, but rushed forward, her right arm drawn around in front of her and resting on her left side. It didn't rest for long. As soon as she was close enough to strike she brought it around in a wide arc. The Fahrenheit dagger ripped through the vampire's abdomen, slicing through coat and flesh.

The beast looked down in surprise. Adele was already spinning for a second sweep. But the vampire blocked it. Adele kicked out and struck where her blade had cut. The female screamed as she was flung backward, smoke rising from the wound. As Adele came forward, the creature scrambled away. Then more shadows glided over the street and two vampires lit on the ground beside their whimpering brethren.

Adele knew she was outmatched. She backpedaled, lifting her weapon toward the first creature as it rushed her, trying to see the other one too. The blade cast a green hue to her attackers' faces, making them even more horrific. Her blade blocked the first, but her stance was too awkward to avoid the second. The vampire surged toward her legs.

Then a cloaked shape rushed past her shoulder and slammed the second vampire to the ground in a cloud of dust.

"Greyfriar!"

His tall figure leapt, and he drew his rapier while in the air, the blade falling as he came down. A bloody head lolled to the side. The swordsman didn't stop moving but rushed the vampire Adele was barely holding at bay. The creature withdrew from her and turned to face the cowled vampire hunter. Clawed hands rose to strike the man across the face, but Greyfriar ducked and thrust through the chest of his opponent, twisting the blade to destroy the heart. The body fell to the ground, and Greyfriar turned to Adele.

She wanted to run to him and collapse in his arms. Her breath was ragged with spent adrenaline. Her hand reached out to touch him and he flinched.

"I couldn't find you," she whispered.

"I shouldn't have left," was his pained response. "We must go."

"Princess."

Her title was practically whispered from a dark silhouette along the stone wall. Adele's skin crawled as the word slipped over her.

"You *will* be leaving, but with me." It was a female voice.

Greyfriar shoved Adele behind him as Flay stepped out of the shadows. The tall figure entered the moonlight, her skin almost white in its reflection. Her black braid was still perfect, not a hair on her head displaced.

"No, not this time, Flay," Greyfriar informed her.

Flay's mouth quirked slightly and she regarded the swordsman. "You are only one man." She almost spat the last word.

As if on command, several vampires drifted down on both sides of her, all of them flecked with gore and streaks of crimson across their mouths. Some stood, while others crouched like animals, hissing and licking at the spots of blood on their bodies.

"There is no one left alive to help you." Flay took another step forward. "As if they could or would."

Greyfriar said, "You killed an entire town just to get one girl?"

"They were in my way. As are you."

Flay did not attack, but her minions did. They rushed Greyfriar like rabid animals. Adele was actually shoved aside by the vampires scrambling after their single purpose, to kill her companion. He fought back, blade flashing in the moonlight. Blood sprayed as steel sliced into the pack of vampires.

Flay screeched a command at an underling, and the male stepped hesitantly toward the princess. Adele raised her blade to strike, but suddenly her arms were pinioned from behind amid a horrible hiss of agony. The vampire in front of her lashed out with blurring speed. She braced for the pain, but the thing only ripped open her heavy blouse, seized her stone talisman, and pulled it off her neck. As the thing flung the crystal pendant into the night, the vampire was already screaming and falling to the ground from a pain that wasn't just physical. Adele's arms were released, and she suddenly felt defenseless without her talisman.

Adele surged forward, her blade raised high, but she was seized by her hair and thrown into a wall. Bright light and darkness exploded. Adele tried to get to her feet. Dust from the shattered stone fell over her like pixie dust. Again she was picked up by her hair, her feet dangling. Her wrist was twisted until the glowing dagger dropped from numb fingers.

Adele's eyes focused on the face of Flay.

"You are dangerous no longer, and now you are mine, Princess." Disdain dripped from Flay's lips, and she threw Adele to two vampires who had just drifted down. They pulled the khukri scabbard from her belt, tossed it aside, and started dragging the girl away.

"Greyfriar!" Adele screamed.

"Princess!" Greyfriar struggled to free himself from the mire of pale creatures. His feet slipped in the blood that pooled on the ground. He swung his blade in a wide arc, decapitating one. Leaping high into the air, he twisted around, frantic to come to Adele's aid, but four more vampires surged after him, dragging him down. His rapier hacked and battered in ways most unbecoming to its usual poetic dance. There was no time for finesse.

Gaining only a moment's respite, Greyfriar craned his neck around, trying to see Adele, but she was already gone. Another trio of vampires advanced on him. They were meant to delay him. And it was working. Flay stood behind them, her lips pulled back in joyful satisfaction.

———

Through her haze, Adele saw an airship at rest. It was a small derelict sloop or brig painted black and carrying no lights. A vampire carried her up the gangplank and dropped her roughly onto the grimy deck. One creature knelt next to her, putting a clawed hand sharply against her back and pressing her down. The beast shouted orders in slurred English.

Adele watched human crewmen scurry about. She felt the bile of anger rising in her throat. Bloodmen. Humans who willingly served the vampires. Vampires could not—indeed, would not—fly an airship. That was menial human work, so they had menial humans to do it.

The princess heard the telltale sound of chemical bags filling overhead. The deck swayed and the ship gathered upward momentum. Humans clambered into the rigging to set the sails.

When the ghostly craft was well away, the vampire released his grip on Adele. She immediately leapt to her feet and raced for the rail. Something grabbed her shoulder, yanking her back. Before she could lash out, a pair of strong arms seized her and spun her around. She felt the hot breath of a human on her face. Standing close in front of her was the haunted figure of the airship's captain in a ragged costume that was a mockery of a true naval uniform.

"Don't," he said to her.

Adele spit in his face. He didn't flinch; he was accustomed to derision. He didn't even wipe the spittle from his cheek.

"Don't," he repeated. "You are their prisoner now."

"I would rather die!" Adele screamed the words, knowing that her strength was leaving her and soon she wouldn't be able to shout her outrage.

"They won't let you." The captain stepped aside.

Two bloodmen manhandled Adele below and locked her in a bare cabin. She fell against the damp wood of the deck. In a matter of minutes, her life had stopped. All alone in the dark, she wept, sure that no one could see her.

———✎✎✎———

A hissing of chemicals made Greyfriar glance upward. As the rotting airship passed overhead, the swordsman knew he had failed. Flay hissed orders to those nearby who were still capable of responding. They all floated up into the air like a child's balloons suddenly released from the grip of a small hand. More and more of the creatures began to drift up out of the village, leaving the slaughter where it lay. The breeze caught them, and they wafted away as if they were dead leaves.

Bloody and torn, Greyfriar clutched his longsword. His chest was heaving, his breath ragged. Flay backed away from him, but not out of fear. The vampire stared angrily at the swordsman.

"Someday I will have you." With that, she too lifted from the ground.

As he watched Flay vanish into the dark sky, Greyfriar ceased his harsh breathing immediately, as if it were a mere affectation. He was no more winded than the dead around him. He surveyed the area—five vampires wounded so mortally their recuperative powers would not save them. Using his pistols, he dispatched them without remorse. Now the town around him was dead, silent as the new grave it had become.

He picked up something from the bloodied dirt. Greyfriar replaced Adele's Fahrenheit dagger in its scabbard and slid it into his belt. He would take the time to bury the villagers. He was in no hurry now to pursue the princess. He knew where Flay was taking her.

CHAPTER 7

USS *RANGER*, A twenty-four-gun frigate, was expertly crafted and manned. Cutting through the air like bright American steel, its white sails billowed while the chrome cage containing its sleek gasbags sparkled.

Some of the old-timers of Alexandria grumbled as they shielded their eyes while watching the American ship approach over the green Mediterranean. *Where are their battleships?* they muttered. *A man comes for an imperial wedding and doesn't arrive on the greatest ship in the American fleet? Hmph.*

Still, the vast crowd at Pharos Airport and along the quays cheered with convincing vigor as the frigate hove out of the ceremonial escort of Equatorian ships. Unlike the ponderous imperial capital ships that overshadowed it, *Ranger* was fast and nimble, a swift shark among plodding whales.

The Equatorian prime minister, Lord Kelvin, stood on a reception platform festooned with bunting and the flags of Equatoria and America, and gave a satisfied smile. But not too much of a smile. Not so much that anyone watching him would know he was smiling. That would be bad form for the prime minister.

Beside Lord Kelvin stood two grandees of the Empire. One was Admiral Kilwas, First Air Lord, author of the air campaign that broke the rebels of Zanzibar. Beefy and dark, the admiral was resplendent in his uniform and provided a necessary example of imperial solidarity, being from the rich trading coast of Tanganyika. On Kelvin's other side was the commercial behemoth Laurence Randolph, Lord Aden, master of an incalculable fortune made from timber, coal, and oil that fueled the steam and iron of the Empire. He sported well-tailored formal attire, a singular figure, fit and handsome, appearing much younger than his years, with a rakish mustache and bright eyes that showed he knew more than anyone around him.

The American vessel tacked on final approach to the main air tower. Any slip by the foreigners would become the talk of the city and would injure their reputations in the minds of the Alexandrians. This thought made Lord Kelvin's nearly nonexistent smile vanish. It simply wouldn't do for the new imperial consort to start off on the wrong foot with the people of the capital. The winds at Pharos were notoriously fiendish. Kelvin had begged the Americans to take on a local pilot, but Senator Clark had flatly refused, insisting his "boys could moor *Ranger* to a chestnut tree in a gale."

The pennants on the Pharos One docking tower switched like angry cats' tails. High on the mooring platform, a crew stood stiff-legged in the blustery wind, waiting for *Ranger*'s bowline. They were from the emperor's household, responsible for handling Constantine's flagship on those increasingly rare occasions when His Imperial Majesty went aloft. Although it was a shocking breach of protocol for imperial household staff to serve a mere American senator, Lord Kelvin had sidestepped that embarrassment, and very cleverly he thought, by temporarily demoting the entire crew. Once *Ranger* was secured, they would all resume their duties in the imperial household.

Ranger closed fast on mighty Pharos One. The last of the spritsails luffed, and the airship's prow turned to the tower. The bowline flew. The tower crew caught it and made it fast, securing the line to a massive multigeared mechanism. The center dial burned a luminous blue, and then slowly the gears started to crank the bowline to secure the ship to the tower. The crowd seemed satisfied. Admiral Kilwas breathed out through his nose. Lord Kelvin wanted to let out a breath too, but refused to show such bad form. He watched for the venting of chemical buoyants from the American ship, but it didn't appear. The admiral made a dismaying grunt of confusion as multiple cables dropped from the frigate's gunwales to the ground. He even leaned over to another officer and exchanged a few whispers. Kelvin silently urged him back into place.

Lord Kelvin's hands ached, but he wouldn't flex them for fear of looking less than placid. His red ceremonial sash had worked itself up along his neck and it chafed, but he refused to adjust it. It was bad form to look uncomfortable. He would deal with the rash on his neck later.

Imperial dignitaries on the reviewing stand could see the port side of *Ranger* and were shocked enough to murmur when the ship's gun ports opened and cannons were run out. The crowd below was beginning to seethe. They were surprised by the guns too. And then even more surprised to see men lined up along the ship's rails with the sunlight glinting off their distant accoutrements.

Lord Kelvin was horrified when Admiral Kilwas requested his brass spyglass and placed it to his eye like this was some common boat race on the Nile. The admiral exclaimed, quietly thank God, in his native Swahili, causing Kelvin to snort through his nose in reprimand. The prime minister could make out the men at *Ranger*'s rail taking hold of the cables that dangled down in the wind.

Suddenly a broadside roared from the frigate, first starboard, then port. The cannons' discharge was odd. Some guns belched red smoke, some blue, and some white. The heavy multicolored smoke obscured the ship like garish cotton.

Then men dropped out of clouds trailing wisps of red, white, and blue smoke. Some in the crowd screamed at the sight of men apparently falling to their deaths. The Americans plummeted wildly on the cables, fifty of them in blue uniforms, with white cowboy hats flying madly behind them on long latigos, and one trailing a fluttering American flag. The commandos landed expertly at the base of the Pharos tower.

Admiral Kilwas leaned forward into the spyglass and laughed. Out loud. Lord Kelvin almost flinched.

The crowd experienced a brief moment of confusion trying to under-stand how they should react before a flood of adulation swept over them. They had been taken unawares, and although they could have shown their embarrassment with scorn, instead they threw up their arms and roared with pleasure.

The American soldiers formed rank with their flag-bearer in the lead and began a loose-limbed march along the causeway toward the main quay with the sparkling Mediterranean behind them. Fahrenheit sabers dangled from their hips on one side, and sidearms were holstered on the other. Their dark blue pants ended in high white gaiters and black boots. They wore no jackets, but their heavy blue tunics had epaulettes and a double breast of shiny brass buttons. Jaunty yellow kerchiefs fluttered in the wind. Broad-brimmed white hats shaded their eyes, and their white smiles gleamed.

Lord Kelvin glanced at his leather-bound copy of the official agenda on the podium in front of him. The band was off cue. He turned to page two and eyed his prepared remarks of greeting. Then, with a surge of panic, he realized that the Americans, descending via ropes like common orangutans, would have left their imperial protocol officer behind. Would they remember where to stand? Would they remember what to say?

A disaster, Kelvin thought. *This has become a terrible disaster. Oh God, now Senator Clark is waving to the crowd!*

Senator Clark, who strode just ahead of the flag-bearer, threw his meaty hand about as if he were signaling a barmaid for a refill. His frank grin shone out from behind his full black beard and mustache. All of the rustic commandos had similarly massive displays of facial hair.

Lord Kelvin's stomach twisted. Grooming and dress instructions had been included in the protocol memorandum. Imperial style for facial hair was mustache and perhaps muttonchops, if necessary. Full beards were no longer appropriate, since the emperor had shaved his two years ago. Surely the protocol officer had instructed Senator Clark of this fact. Yet here he was looking like a wild man. And instead of full dress uniforms, the Americans were apparently clothed as some sort of cabaret performers.

The senator leapt onto the stage, drew off his massive white gloves, and stuck out his hand toward Lord Kelvin. His booming voice rang out. "You must be Lord Kelvin. I'm Senator Clark. It's my pleasure, sir."

His Lordship stared at the calloused fingers, weighing rudeness against trying to salvage something of the protocol. The American grinned and leaned forward expectantly. Kelvin couldn't be publicly discourteous. Therefore he forced himself to forget decades of training and abandon the months of careful planning that had gone into preparing for this very moment. This was the meeting of two great nations, two great peoples. And it came down to this, a proffered mitt and a prosaic exchange of bucolic pleasantries. Lord Kelvin slowly extended a hand. Clark crushed it in a vise of friendship.

The crowd roared.

Clark turned back to the mob and lifted his fist into the air, still clasping the hand of Lord Kelvin, who was horrified at being made part of such a barbarous display. But the disintegration of the magnificent ceremony wasn't quite over. Clark released Kelvin's hand, for which His Lordship was grateful, but then the boisterous American actually draped his muscular arm around Kelvin's morning-coated shoulders.

Clark waved his gigantic white hat over his head and guffawed like a drunk at a burlesque.

—◦◦◦—

Clark poured dark liquor for Lord Kelvin, Admiral Kilwas, Lord Aden, and himself. He lifted his glass. "Gentlemen, I give you the alliance of the American Republic and the Equatorian Empire."

The four glasses clinked, and the men drank after the admiral added a "Hear! Hear!" Clark wiped a practiced finger under his luxurious mustache and slammed the shot glass onto the polished teak table. Lord Kelvin took the barest sip and quietly set his glass down.

"Bourbon," Clark announced. "It used to be the American drink. We still get it out of the old South. But there's a lot more rum in America now. Rum's fine. But it's not bourbon by a long shot." He poured again.

Admiral Kilwas raised his glass. "Death to the vampires."

"Damned straight!" Clark barked, and drank it back.

Lord Aden gave a quick charming smile at the American and sipped.

Lord Kelvin wet his thin, colorless lips again and replaced the full glass on the table. In this private room, the prime minister didn't restrict his movement as he did in public, so he felt free to run a hand over his slick black hair. As he opened his mouth to speak, the American was pouring yet again. Kelvin soon saw glasses poised at his eye level.

His Lordship lifted his drink, cleared his throat, and managed a reedy, "To His Imperial Majesty, Constantine the Second. And to Her Imperial Highness the princess Adele and the coming union." He put the glass to his lips.

Clark smiled appreciatively and quaffed again, as if it were no more than water. Even Admiral Kilwas could only slowly down this third blast of bourbon.

The senator gave Lord Aden a lopsided grin and said, "Lord Aden, pleasure to see you again, sir. Did you enjoy your trip to America last year?"

"I did indeed. The capital in Panama City is lovely. I was most impressed by the generosity of the people across the Republic."

"What about our chemical energy program? Impressive, no?"

"Yes. Quite."

"As our alliance progresses, we'll get you Equatorian boys off your filthy steam power. We'll boost your chemical industries tenfold."

"Hm. No doubt chemical power will make a useful addition to our existing systems."

"Oh, trust me, you'll forget all about wood and coal and oil once you see what our chemical engineers can do. You saw USS *Hamilton* when you were in Panama, didn't you? Our first fully powered air battleship. Aluminum bursts. Magnificent stuff."

Lord Aden took another sip from his glass and smiled. "Yes. Interesting prototype. It shows promise for the future. But I note you arrived in a sailing airship."

Clark laughed. "Yes indeed. I love *Ranger*. She's the most beautiful thing aloft. But powered flight is the wave of the future."

"We must show you our steam airships." Admiral Kilwas nodded.

"HMS *Culloden* is moored in Alexandria, I believe. We can certainly arrange a tour."

The senator nodded. "Steam. Limited. We're not sitting on endless coal in the tropics."

"We've done well," Lord Aden said quickly. "Your chemical technologies are fascinating, I grant you. But underpowered compared to steam. And underdeveloped, as of yet. I think our present hopes are best laid with fuels that work now."

Clark laughed a bit harshly. "Spoken like a man who makes his fortune in old energy." He reached into an army pack beside his chair, pulling out a small cypress box that he threw open on the table. Cuban cigars. He took one, applied a long wooden match to the tip, and sat back, crossing his legs. "Your Lordships. Admiral. Shall we get down to brass tacks?"

"Indeed yes," Lord Kelvin replied, quite relieved. Dignified discussion was much preferred over unpredictable and rampant vulgarity.

Clark blew a long stream of smoke. "I'd like to see the emperor."

"Of course." Kelvin consulted the vellum pages of the agenda. "You are scheduled to attend the public audience with His Imperial Majesty the day after tomorrow. With your men." His Lordship glanced up to assure himself that Clark understood how accommodating he was being. "And you have a private conference with His Imperial Majesty and the Privy Council two days after that. If you consult the schedule we provided to you, you will see all that." Kelvin kindly opened the leather-bound copy of the agenda to the page detailing Clark's first audience with His Majesty and slid the book along the table toward the American's dirty boots.

The senator eyed the book, then hummed with dissatisfaction and flicked ash onto the intricate parquet mahogany floor. "Mmhmm. Also, your protocol man was a little hazy on when I would see Adele."

Kelvin aimed his impassive hatchet face at Clark. "The wedding with Her Imperial Highness the princess Adele is scheduled for one month and two days from this day."

Clark grinned. "I know that, Prime Minister. But I'd kinda like to see her before the actual wedding day. I'd like to arrange a dinner of some sort. That seems only right."

"It does?" Though empowered by the familiar walls of the council chamber, Kelvin still felt a bit put off by Clark's use of *Prime Minister* rather than the more proper *Your Lordship*. He was therefore disinclined to be less obtuse than he might normally appear.

The American laughed and stared lovingly at his cigar. "It's customary where I come from to at least see the bride before the wedding."

"Most interesting," Lord Kelvin murmured. "However, Her Imperial Highness the princess is away at the present."

"What?" Clark's chair thumped to the floor as he sat up and stared hard at the eel-like prime minister. "She's not even here when I arrive?"

Kelvin sensed Admiral Kilwas tensing from Clark's outburst. But His Lordship merely flipped a page and said in an even voice, "She is touring the frontier, Senator. She may be your Intended, but she has constant duties of state. She wished to be here, but of course, the state must always come first. You will find Her Imperial Highness the princess Adele embraces that fact completely. As, I'm sure, do you."

Lord Aden spoke again with businesslike precision. "It seemed prudent to shore up imperial goodwill on the frontier, with the coming hostilities nearly upon us. Many of the free cities to the north have never seen a member of the royal family. The court wished to judge their receptiveness, in case annexation becomes a necessary option."

"Yeah." Clark clamped down on his cigar. "But surely a tour of the frontier could have been scheduled for some other time. My arrival here was arranged months ago."

Lord Kelvin smiled without mirth. "There was no slight intended, I assure you, Senator. Her Imperial Highness's tour was scheduled months ago. Before arrangements for your nuptials were concluded."

The massive door opened, and an orderly made straight for Lord Kelvin, handed him an envelope, and then stood back against the wall to wait for a reply. Kelvin was perplexed that a message would come by special courier and not through the multiple ranks of pneumatic tubes that served as the communications array for the palace. Hundreds of such pipes ran through the vast building, and their clunking could be heard echoing day and night. Kelvin opened the envelope purposefully and pulled out a sheet of heavy paper, scanning it. His brow clouded and he read it again.

Kelvin then handed the note to Admiral Kilwas, who read it quickly and leapt to his feet in alarm. Clark stood too, his hand going instinctively to his holster.

"What's wrong?" the senator barked.

Lord Kelvin looked at the admiral's ashen face for confirmation. Clearly he hadn't misread the message. It was, in fact, the end of the world.

The prime minister regarded Senator Clark and said with dour precision, "The court has just received a message from Colonel Anhalt, the commander of Her Imperial Highness the princess's household guard. Her Imperial Highness the princess Adele's ship was attacked. It went down with great loss of life. Her Imperial Highness the princess is missing. It is assumed she was taken by the vampires."

"Oh no," Lord Aden breathed.

"Taken? Or killed?" Clark asked coldly.

"We do not know. We have no idea where she is. Or if she is alive now."

"Well then for now we'll assume she's alive." Clark straightened his saber. "Take me to the emperor. It's time to start a war."

Lord Kelvin nodded sadly and closed his schedule book.

CHAPTER 8

LONDON WAS A charnel house.

Adele smelled the city long before she saw it. Desolate hours had passed locked in the cabin of the squalid airship with only her thoughts of her poor brother for company. With the sunrise, she was allowed on deck under watchful eyes. She wra   pped herself in a stinking blanket to ward off trembling that was only partly caused by the damp chill air.

When the shadow of the airship had passed from the slate sea onto the rolling green of southern England, Adele felt a spark of fascination growing that gratefully distanced her from her situation. The country far below was the land of her father's ancestors, a realm of legends and heroes held in highest esteem by her family. Of course, no one in the royal family had living memory of Britain, but many treasured relics had been spirited away in the chaotic years of the vampire onslaught. The imperial palace in Alexandria held paintings of the English landscape that, to Adele, might as well have been another planet. But here now she gazed down on that mythic landscape. It had grown much wilder since those grand days of gentlemanly squires showing their prize heifers, but the lines of fields and pastures were still visible from the air. However, towns and villages were ruined and largely abandoned, with only rare and infrequent trails of smoke betraying the existence of the vampires' human herds.

Suddenly, a wretched stench overwhelmed Adele. She coughed and covered her face with the disgusting blanket. Nothing she had ever experienced matched the vile odor wafting up toward her—not even the slums of Cairo in summer. The reason for the stench loomed on the northern horizon. A dark shape squatted along the shining line of a river. It was London, the great city. London, the seat of the vampire clan that ruled Britain.

There were many accounts of nineteenth-century London as it had been before the vampires came. The young princess had been amazed by descriptions and pictures of the city's grandeur. It had been the center of art and science and technology, the center of the world. Now it was the heart of a cadaverous kingdom. Centuries before, travelers often complained that London smelled, stinking of smoke and chemicals and compressed humanity. Adele could testify that it still smelled, but now it was the stench of blood and decomposition.

She possessed an intellectual concept of what she was going to see. For years, ghastly reports had come south on the wretched state of the great cities of northern Europe. Adele had experienced chills reading the grisly communiqués in her warm, lemon-scented gardens. But those reports in no way prepared the princess for the visceral reaction she had to the evidence of her own senses.

The ramshackle airship descended, approaching the spires and domes and the horrid slate grey blocks of buildings. Adele saw dark mounds scattered on the avenues, streets, and alleys. A closer examination revealed that the mounds were piles of dead bodies. The city's wide circles and narrow courtyards were heaped with bones. The turgid river Thames was at low tide and, as the airship skimmed over it, Adele saw white femurs and rib cages protruding from the muck along the shoreline. Nearly all the glass windows in the city were smashed, except, amazingly, some of the stained glass of Westminster. Green grass sprouted through the cobblestones while lush vines grew without restraint, hiding edifices and obscuring the statues of the formerly great humans. The airship glided over the collapsed roof of Parliament. Dark figures clung to the outside of the ivy-choked ruins of the Big Ben clock tower and rose into the air like blowflies from a cadaver. Adele's heart raced with terror and despair to see so many.

The airship captain shouted orders, breaking Adele's grim reverie, and the bloodmen scrambled into the rigging. The ship reduced sail, heeling slightly, starting its turn over a large expanse of trees that were just beginning to leaf out with spring. The land below was once a park, but now it was fenced and the ground beneath the trees was brown and worn. Then Adele saw why. Crowds of humans, naked or clad in rags, shuffled aimlessly among the trees—food for the city's vampire lords. Only a few of them troubled to gaze up at the passing ship; then they quickly returned to pacing or drinking from a pond. Their distant, uncomprehending faces were blank like livestock. Adele felt sick.

The airship leveled off over sprawling, decrepit Buckingham Palace. A lone figure ascended from the roof of the palace and seized the shrouds of the airship with amazing grace and swung aboard. It was Flay. Adele was suddenly enraged by the memory of her brother hurled carelessly against a tree like a toy, and the careless slaughter of the people who had thought nothing of sheltering her as Greyfriar's ward. The bloodmen shuffled away from Flay, who was now wearing a man's heavy brocade coat with broad cuffs, garish green, that made her pale flesh underneath even more translucent.

"Princess Adele," the female vampire said. "Welcome to London."

Adele ignored the early evening chill and dropped the blanket, unwilling to accept any comfort from the enemy. She stared contemptuously into the female's eyes without flinching. The imperial heir wouldn't give the vampire the satisfaction of seeing fear. The confident public face that her father adopted during private crises became hers to emulate.

Flay slowly stooped and lifted the blanket from the deck. The creature held Adele's cold stare and deliberately dropped the blanket over the rail. "Princess, I shall no longer burden you with comfort. I am Flay, the war chief of Prince Cesare, lord of Ireland. And you are his prisoner."

———✦———

In the twilight, Adele paced a dingy outer courtyard in the Tower of London, where she had been deposited without further word. Numerous vampires crouched on the parapets, looking down at her with animal curiosity. A bloodman emerged from a dank doorway carrying a large sack over his back. He stared at her too, but surreptitiously, from under downturned brows like a born servant. The miserable drone emptied the sack of skeletal remains into a cart that was already full of bones, and appeared as if he wanted to say something to her, if he was even capable of proper language, but his nerve failed. Adele was grateful not to have to interact with the filthy thing. Two bloodmen put their shoulders to the cart and pushed it under an archway out of her sight. Ravens rose from the crumbling ruins with excited cries and followed the creaking bone cart.

As Adele's eyes lifted with the black birds, she spotted two vampires drifting toward her over the wall. One was the warlord, Flay. The second was a fine-boned male, dressed in a passable formal suit with a long swallow-tailed morning coat. The male was a few inches shorter than Flay, but as they settled noiselessly to the cobblestones, the female showed the deference of distance.

"I am Cesare," the male said as he walked past Adele.

This was the one, the princess thought as she stared at him. Cesare. This creature had every soul in Ireland put to death. He was one of history's greatest monsters. And she was in his hands. She wondered what his game was. If she had been captured for food, surely she'd be a drained husk by now. Perhaps Cesare was saving her for himself. Maybe he intended to torture her slowly to death. There was no way to know the mind of one of these animals. But Adele was sure she would give them no pleasure by pleading or crying.

Flay prompted Adele to follow Cesare. They all entered the doorway from which the bloodmen had just carried the bones. The princess followed the vampire's light footfalls up stone steps into a chilled, dim room that was empty except for a pile of straw in one corner. How thoughtful, she mused grimly as she surveyed the chamber, to clean out the remains of the previous residents.

Adele snapped, "I will need a fire if you want me to survive." Cesare turned quickly from the window, clearly surprised by a demand. Adele was pleased by the reaction and asked sharply. "What do you want from me?"

"Ah, good," Cesare responded, interlacing his fingers in front of his chest. "I want two things. First, tell me all you know about the Equatorian war plans. Second, tell me about your spies in Britain."

Adele laughed, partly in relief that he wanted information, not just the joy of pain. "You know nothing about me, but I assure you I will tell you nothing."

Cesare tilted his head and spoke quickly. "Princess Adele, you are nineteen years old. You were born in Alexandria. Your mother, the empress Pareesa, died when you were seven years of age during the birth of your late brother, Simon, prince of Bengal. Your father is the emperor Constantine, the second of that name and the third of his line. Both he and your government are dismayed at the prospect that you, a mere female, will inherit his throne. They fear that you are not capable of ruling and that under your feeble hand the Empire's fragility will be exposed and it will fly apart in a series of rebellions and secessions. To prevent such a disaster, it has been arranged for you to marry the Butcher of St. Louis, a"—Cesare's lips curled in disgust—"war *hero* from the American Republic. This union between you and the renowned murderer will place a man on the throne and create an alliance between the Equatorian Empire and the American Republic. Thus joined by sacrificing your precious virtue to the bloody Clark, the two greatest human states will start a war to destroy my people utterly. Please correct me if I've made a mistake."

Adele laughed again. "I'm sorry, but watching a vampire talk politics is like putting a gown on an ape and calling it a duchess." But in fact, the vampire had not made a mistake. While some of the information that Cesare had revealed was common knowledge, she was frightened nonetheless by the thought of this vampire being aware of her personal affairs. She was also increasingly disturbed by Cesare's *humanness*. Provided his sharp fingernails were covered, the creature wouldn't attract undue attention relaxing in an Alexandria café with coffee and a newspaper.

Adele's face must have betrayed her uneasiness, because Cesare smiled, revealing sharp teeth. "Apes and duchesses aside, Princess, I am well informed. I know that your heavily armed warships crowd the towers of Port Said and Malta. And likewise, I am informed of a great buildup of American forces in Cuba and the Yucatan. I am also aware that your people have spies in my domain, scuttling about like bugs, hiding in the woods. I have killed several myself—after they told me everything they knew. But I want to know more. Centuries of struggling for survival have shown us the value of intelligence."

"Even mad dogs fight to survive. That doesn't imply intelligence." Adele averted her eyes to the stone floor, to her own feet clad in the boots scuffed in the sandy streets of faraway Alexandria. She couldn't bear to watch the sardonic face of the creature who had butchered hundreds of thousands. The young woman tried to control the shaking of her hands and to steady her voice. Cesare's questions about spies seemed to indicate that *geomancers* might truly exist, or at least that vampires believed there were human agents operating in the dead north.

Cesare's eyebrows inched up again, this time giving him a falsely sincere façade. "A human's opinion means nothing to me. In fact, human opinion in general has meant nothing for more than a century. Tell me, does it amaze your scholars that it took us less than five years to destroy the greatest societies your kind had to offer, societies that had been constructed over many centuries? Five years! A fraction of a second to us. You are nineteen. I am nearly three hundred years old. And I will live to be over eight hundred. I participated in the Great Killing. What you know only as distant history, I remember and savor."

The vampire's smile faded, and he took several clicking steps toward Adele. "I disdain your weak, failed culture. Machines. Books. What good are they? I use your names because it amuses me. I wear your clothes because it amuses me. I speak twelve of your human languages because it amuses me. How many do you yourself speak? One? Two? But I needed no books to learn them. I don't need tools to master the world." Cesare was only an inch or two taller than Adele and, again, he tilted his head with derision when she defiantly matched his gaze. He held up his hand, and razor-sharp nails extended slowly from his fingertips with a faint squishing noise. "These are my tools." Cesare spread his clawed fingertips lightly over his icy face. "And these. From here, I can see a bird over the ocean. I can smell blood spilling miles away. I can ride the wind and become a shadow. I can hear your heart beating. I don't need technology. When we rose up, we faced you humans and your machines. Your guns were not powerful enough. Your ships and railroads were not fast enough. Your homes and palaces were not strong enough. None of your creations could save you from me. I killed all of you I laid my hands on, and I drank your blood. And I will do it again when the time comes."

Adele remained quiet. She would say nothing more to this thing. She had no reason to bandy words or debate. Silence would be her weapon. If it killed her, so be it.

Cesare retracted his claws and said, "Tell me about the Equatorian war plans."

Adele turned away from him, holding her breath, waiting for a blow from behind.

Cesare said evenly, "Tell me about your spies."

She stepped to the window that Cesare had vacated. The sun was sinking, and the city was succumbing to the same cold darkness that killed it every night. She closed her eyes against the unbelievable thought of spending her first night in this terrible place. *First* night. That implied that there would be many. It was worse than the fear of death.

She heard Cesare's footsteps moving to the door, followed by hissing words he spoke to Flay. And Adele could understand. The harsh sounds made some sense to her. She didn't know how, but she had always been good with language. Adele didn't recognize words concretely in the disgusting hissing, but she grasped the sense and the intent.

Cesare instructed Flay to bring the princess "roasted flesh," and Adele knew that the term meant human flesh. It was Cesare's idea of a joke, no doubt. It disgusted her enough that, gratefully, her formerly ravenous appetite was destroyed. If they wanted to keep her alive, they would eventually find bread or vegetables.

As Flay glided down the winding stone stairs, Cesare said to Adele, this time in excellent Arabic, "I am giving you food. And I will arrange for you to have fire. When we talk tomorrow, you will tell me what I want to know and you will go home. This door will remain unlocked. I pray you abandon hopes of escape, if you hold any. There is no possibility. I notice that you wear a garish ring, no doubt given to you by Senator Clark. I have not deprived you of it because it is yours and we respect your peculiar human notions of property. But here in my domain, even the brightest diamond is no different than a common stone you may find on the ground. You can barter nothing with it. It has no value to any vampire, nor, I can assure you, to the humans among us."

Adele continued to gaze out the window at the glistening river and the dark shapes bobbing in it. Her mind cast back to her former world in Alexandria, existing at the same time as this one: Simon climbing trees in his garden, her seat in the library, warm spring days with the air scented by lemon and lilac, warm sand and the endless drum and rush of the surf.

Adele's hands touched cold stone, and her aching shoulders slumped in despair.

"Do rest, Princess," Cesare said with mock kindness.

Adele straightened her back, but her quick recovery was evident. She was angry for showing weakness in front of the thing. Still, she refused to turn, and soon she heard the sound of his retreating footsteps.

Placing her back against the wall, she slid to the floor. The darkness reduced her world to mere arm's reach. She was almost grateful; she didn't want to see what was out there. It was nothing but evil. An evil she despised.

Equatoria would not stand for this. A retaliatory strike was coming as soon as the swift hand of retribution could gather itself. Adele knew this without doubt. And no doubt the Americans would come for those that dared kidnap the future wife of their most renowned vampire killer. Surely Senator Clark was not the kind of man who would suffer such an affront.

There was also Greyfriar and his uncanny ability to emerge from the shadows to pluck her from the encroaching darkness. She missed his stalwart presence, offering hope where there was none to be had. His absence made the time before her seem like a great chasm.

Still, regardless of what actions were being set in motion, or were in motion already, it meant little to Adele's life. Her fate was sealed. Cesare would never free her, and he would kill her as soon as the first human set foot on the shores of England. That was a certainty. After all, she would do the same with a captive of her sort.

Adele had no intention of sitting like a poor little princess and waiting for that moment to arrive. Cesare and his kin would pay a terrible price. She would strike at the heart of the vampire court. Cesare would no doubt come frequently within her reach. Perhaps if she played it right, she might get close to the king, Dmitri. What a dream strike that would be. Adele swore that she would take off the head of this foul clan at this most important time in history. It would send their filthy court into chaos and make them vulnerable to the war machine that would soon roar up from the south.

Adele's heart lifted. Suddenly she wasn't afraid of the path looming before her. Instead a rush of excitement and anticipation filled her, and she welcomed the faint warmth it brought, pushing away the chill of dreadful London.

Her hand went to her sash, which was sadly empty of her mother's dagger.

She needed a weapon.

CHAPTER 9

JUST AFTER DAWN, USS *Ranger* descended on Marseilles at the head of a flotilla of imperial cruisers. As soon as *Ranger* moored and was drawn down, Senator Clark and his second in command, Major Stoddard, disembarked to be met by a clutch of Marseilles city fathers. Clark shook hands hastily, concentrating enough to commit everyone's name to his formidable memory. He then directed a hard squint at a ramrod-straight figure in the torn remnants of an Equatorian uniform.

The man introduced himself in a clipped Gurkha accent. "Colonel Anhalt, Senator."

"Anhalt?" Clark towered over the small but sturdy officer who was bandaged and in apparent pain. "Anhalt? You commanded my fiancée's household guard." It was an accusation.

"I did, and do, sir."

"Then how is it you are still alive?"

Anhalt didn't lower his gaze, but the question clearly wounded him. "Would that I weren't."

"No doubt." Clark turned his back on Anhalt and moved on. The city fathers fell in naturally around him. The colonel limped behind.

Major Stoddard saluted the wounded Anhalt. "Colonel. My name is Stoddard. I am the Senator's adjutant." The young American officer was tall, willowy-thin, and dark; he had grown up around New Orleans on the vampire frontier.

Anhalt nodded curtly, still stinging from Clark's rebuke, but returned the salute and then extended his hand with quiet gratitude. "At your service, Major."

Stoddard shook the offered hand, nodded warmly, and then turned his attention back to his commanding officer, already well ahead of them.

"What's the boy's condition?" Clark asked no one in particular.

"He is quite well, sir," Mayor Comblain offered eagerly, struggling to keep pace with the long-legged American. "We have made him comfortable and offered—"

"What were the losses?"

Mayor Comblain opened his mouth to speak, but it was Anhalt who replied. "HMS *Ptolemy*, *Khartoum*, and *Cape Town* were lost. HMS *Mandalay* and *Giza* are missing. A recovery team is still at the crash site, but we expect at least fifty percent casualties. Something on the order of eight hundred men: army, navy, and imperial staff. Air Lord Admiral Kurtiz was killed in the fighting."

"How many vampires?"

"We estimate the attacking force at two thousand. It was a—"

"No. I mean how many did you kill?"

Anhalt paused, embarrassed but unbent. "I . . . don't know. We've recovered nearly two hundred bodies and destroyed them."

Clark whistled with disdain. "Eight hundred men dead, one battleship and four frigates lost, in exchange for a couple hundred enemy? That's what I call an extravagant battle plan. So you saw Adele taken alive, Colonel?"

Anhalt bristled at the American's familiarity with Her Highness's name. "No, Senator. I did not. But we believe His Highness Prince Simon was the last to see her. He deems she is alive. He was—"

"Then let me talk to the boy. He seems to be the only one who knows anything."

Anhalt wouldn't slow his pace despite the ache from the gash on his leg. The wound reopened, and he noticed a sliver of blood soaking through his uniform on his thigh. The edges of his vision greyed as Clark mounted the broad marble steps to the finest house on the Marseilles waterfront. He desperately hoped he wouldn't pass out from the pain.

The senator threw back the doors—he never merely opened a door if he could throw it back. When he threw back the final mahogany door to the upstairs bedroom, he announced, "Prince Simon! I've come to bring you home."

Prince Simon looked up from a book and furrowed his brow. "Where's Colonel Anhalt?"

Clark maintained his heroic grin. "I'm Senator Clark."

"I know. Where's Colonel Anhalt?"

"I have a gift for you from home." Clark stretched out a hand, and one of his officers gave him a package wrapped in colored paper and tied with string. The American paused with annoyance as Anhalt stepped into view in the doorway. Then he handed the gift to Simon, who waited for the colonel to nod before tearing open the paper. The boy looked at the box beneath without much interest.

"Candy," Clark said. "I'm told they're your favorites."

"Yes." Simon put the box on the floor next to his chair.

The American spun on his heel. "I'd like a word with the lad." He slammed the door shut in Colonel Anhalt's face. Then Clark clasped his hands behind his back. "So we're alone now. How are you, son? You can tell me."

"Fine."

"Any pain?"

"No. I'm fine."

The Senator watched the sullen boy. "So I'll bet you were scared out there."

Simon glared.

"No shame in that," Clark said hurriedly. "Vampires can be frightening."

The boy stayed quiet.

Clark went to one knee next to the boy's overstuffed chair in an awkward pantomime of concern. "Don't worry, Simon. I'm going to see you safely home."

"My name is *Prince* Simon. Or Your Highness."

Clark rose and stepped back, resisting a powerful urge to cuff the young lad. He was about to inform Simon that in America children don't speak so to their elders when Simon continued, "My sister is still alive. And Colonel Anhalt will save her."

"Colonel Anhalt will return to Alexandria." Clark leaned back with a sneer. "I will mount a force to save your sister."

"Colonel Anhalt rescued me," Simon responded defensively.

"You think much of him."

"Yes." Simon lifted his head with pride and confidence that exceeded his age. The boy turned up the hem of his corduroy jacket to reveal the dagger hilt at his belt. "He gave me this."

Clark smiled in a patronizing way. "How nice. He could've used you in the battle. Maybe he could've killed a few more vampires then."

"You weren't there!" Simon retorted.

The American snapped back, "You might wish I had been! I've killed more vampires than you can count, my lad! I know a success from a failure. And this was a failure. Now, pack! You're going back to Alexandria on *Ranger* before the sun sets. And after I deliver you to your father's waiting arms, I will rescue my future wife, and get this war back on schedule."

Clark threw back the bedroom door and said to Anhalt, as if the colonel were a footman, "Get him ready. I'll be back in four hours. I will take your prince to Alexandria. I want your people to see the love I have for the royal family, and they need to see it as fast as possible. Your humiliation has distressed your capital. They need confidence restored." With that, the American cruised down the corridor with his entourage in his wake, leaving Anhalt grimacing in the corridor.

Major Stoddard paused in front of Anhalt, about to say something to ease the man's humiliation, but chose instead to exchange merely a sorrowful glance with the Gurkha officer before following after Clark.

———※———

A slender man walked down a gangplank over the greasy black water of the Nile. Smoke from the steamer swirled around him. It was a warm night in Giza, and the dockhands were busy even this late. Passengers departing the steamer paused to harangue the army of porters for being slow with their luggage. Travelers were met by friends or loved ones with embraces and handshakes. And a few wandered lonely to one of the many pubs or coffeehouses nearby. Herds of longshoremen moved under bright chemical lights, shifting containers of grain and fruit onto boats for the short jaunt to the coast or onto rail cars bound for Port Said. Steel and machine parts forged in the belching factories of Alexandria waited to head inland via river or rail to the booming cities of Luxor, Aswan, and Khartoum.

The man who left the steamer did not wait for luggage nor meet friends nor go for a drink. His plain black suit topped by a modest homburg attracted no attention. He was Japanese, but it was not incredible to see Far Easterners in any imperial city. His walking stick tapped the wooden planks as he slipped through the crowd.

Outside the port gates, he searched for a horse-drawn cab, but without luck. He settled for a steam hansom and settled into a leather seat that smelled of sweat and oranges. The man removed his hat and ran a gloved hand over his close-cropped black hair. He watched the town roll past, but the cab's rocking motion, the sauna of steam and mist, as well as the clacking of the cab's steel wheels along the macadam street was hardly relaxing. Technology for its own sake. It made no improvement on the horse and, in fact, was a distinct regression in the man's opinion.

After only a few minutes, he banged the roof with his stick and paid the soot-faced cabbie. A dry desert breeze accompanied him along the sidewalk as a few after-dinner strollers greeted him with friendly nods, taps on hat brims, or fingers to lips and heart. He returned their kindnesses but kept his head down. His stoic blankness did not betray the thrill he felt every time he glimpsed the Great Pyramid of Khufu through the gaps between the fashionable brick townhouses.

The man took a fifteen-minute ramble to ensure he hadn't been followed; then he climbed three steps to a portico and pulled the bell. The door was opened promptly by an Egyptian butler who took the visitor's hat and stick.

The Japanese man crossed the cool foyer with its lovely inlaid cypress floor and entered the dim library. He didn't pause to peruse the many volumes rising twenty feet to the ceiling. Instead he went quickly to a large golden sarcophagus against the wall and opened it. He gave an empty smile at Sir Godfrey's little conceit. A secret passage hidden in the mummy case. Such typical playfulness.

Inside the sarcophagus he entered another world, descending one hundred narrow steps into a very long, hot gallery carved during the Old Kingdom. The passage was so narrow both of his shoulders nearly brushed stone. Hissing gas lamps bracketed high on the walls provided faint ghostly light.

After ten minutes, a small rectangle of pale light appeared far above. He took a shallow breath and climbed worn stone steps. He tried to keep his footfalls quiet, but when he finally reached the doorway three figures were already watching for him. Two women and one man. Black, and brown, and white. No matter their gender or color, their faces were stern and agitated.

"Good evening." He bowed.

The stone-walled chamber was only twenty by twenty, but the ceiling was lost high in the darkness. The walls were painted with scenes of death magic from the Old Kingdom. A red basalt sarcophagus dominated the floor. It was plain, lidless, and empty. The room deep inside the Great Pyramid was clearly known to ancient tomb robbers, but it had never been rediscovered by archaeologists in modern times.

"Well, Mamoru, is Princess Adele dead?" Nzingu Mamenna was the first to speak. She was a sorceress from Zululand. She wore a fashionable dress with graceful embroidery and beadwork done with her own hand. Only a close examination would reveal that the beads were polished bits of bone.

"Well, Nzingu, let's let Mamoru catch his breath, shan't we?" Sir Godfrey Randolph stepped forward with a pacifying chuckle bubbling out from behind his magnificent white mustache. "Here, have a glass of wine, old boy. It's most excellent, I must say. I've had four myself." The old gentleman with a beet red face stood in a sweat-stained white linen suit. Sir Godfrey had a tendency to mutter and dither like the absent-minded scientific amateur his social circle in Giza took him to be. He was a retired surgeon, long past practicing, and now most famous as the eccentric older brother to the empire's richest man, Lord Aden. But above the bushy mustache, his eyes were piercing and hard. His knowledge of ancient occult texts was unequaled.

Mamoru sipped the offered wine and exchanged a quick glance with Sanah the Persian. Only Sanah's dark worried eyes were visible over the edge of her black veil. She had gathered knowledge and practice from her Persian homeland as well as from Afghanistan and India. She collected arcane religious rituals like butterflies. Her delicate hands, which were her only visible flesh, were covered with intricate henna tattooing and festooned with large silver jewelry. She spoke only rarely, but wrote aching poetry that made men cry.

Mamoru announced, "Obviously you have all heard that Princess Adele's convoy was attacked in southern France during her tour."

"Tour!" Nzingu the Zulu spat. She never cared to bandy words, which was why she had fled to Equatoria when the last independent Zulu king decided to embark on a modernization program including dispatching witchfinders to root out sorcerers. "It was ridiculous to send her! How could they do such a thing? So the princess is dead. What do we do now?"

"No." Mamoru shook his head. "I believe she is still alive. If they had wanted to kill her, she would've been killed after they forced her airship down. They are not shy about killing."

Mamoru knew Sanah the Persian was waiting to meet his eyes with sympathy, but he refused to look up. His fists clenched and unclenched as he struggled to manage his breathing and maintain his calm demeanor. His distress would be clear to the Persian because she knew him well enough to know the tragedy of his own wife and daughter at the hands of vampires. Neither Nzingu nor Sir Godfrey would notice that Mamoru appeared other than the serene and disassociated magi he always was. They could not know the psychic toll this tragedy was taking on him beyond the obvious loss of his young protégé.

Mamoru said, "Apparently Princess Adele fell into the hands of the Greyfriar."

Sir Godfrey hooted. "Well! That's a bit of luck."

"But," Mamoru continued, "I fear this is no longer the case. Information is sparse, but it seems that the Greyfriar was unable to complete his rescue. And the princess was indeed taken near Riez, resulting in the complete devastation of that town."

"Greyfriar!" Nzingu snorted. "Is that what this cabal has come to? Depending on masked lunatics?"

Mamoru went on without reply to Nzingu. "I believe it likely that Princess Adele is in the hands of the British clan—"

"Good God!" Sir Godfrey blurted out against his will. "Cesare!"

The reaction of the women was stunned silence. Even magicians did not know how to respond to the unthinkable.

Mamoru continued with calmness admirable given his distress. "I am currently attempting to find her and determine her condition. Forces are in motion. There is hope. There is always hope. Prince Simon is well and should be home soon."

"Hope." Nzingu shook her head derisively. "All our work and planning in jeopardy. Simon is nothing to us. There is no substitute for the princess. And if she is in Cesare's claws, she is dead. The London clan has always been the worst. Many of the other clans already kowtow to Cesare. And he wants to rule all his kind. Even if the princess is still alive, what are her chances of escaping on her own?"

"Unlikely, I fear." Mamoru swirled the wine in his glass, watching the red liquid in the flickering gaslight. "The distances involved—"

The Zulu sorceress pressed him. "But what of her vaunted skills? Your training?"

The Japanese man looked at her from under downturned brows, his lip curling into a sneer for the first time. "Princess Adele's training has not progressed as you might have wished, it is true. But you must recall that the court's official policy is that anything spiritual is a useless relic of a dark past. We have our own witchfinders here, Nzingu. Transforming the imperial heir into a magician is a very complicated undertaking, and not one that can be rushed."

Sir Godfrey said, "My dear lad, we all understand the difficulties from the technocrats in the imperial court."

"Indeed?" Mamoru replied with cold formality. "None of you have endured as much time in the court as I. In my four years here, I have been watched very closely. I was questioned and disciplined by the court five times, including two interviews and stern rebukes from Lord Kelvin, who was most displeased that I was not reinforcing the official doctrine that religion is worthless superstition, and that the power of science and technology is humanity's sole solution. Only the emperor's personal intervention allowed me to weather the attacks from the court, and that only because the Most Serene Emperor in Singapore is our great patron.

"Only in the last six months have I managed to bring Her Highness to magical practice of any sort. I intended to accelerate her practicum after the marriage to Senator Clark. The court's attention would have been consumed with the war, and the senator would become like the steel-minded male heir that Lord Kelvin always desperately wanted rather than a weak girl like Adele. The princess is the most extraordinary adept our world has ever seen, and properly trained in matters of magic and faith, she will wield prayer like lightning. She will rid the world of vampires. But, alas, I do not think she is yet skilled enough to engage or elude the creatures. I must confess, I had not yet trained her to master such specific skills. I beg your forgiveness for my failure."

Mamoru bowed deeply and already regretted explaining so much. It made it seem as if he needed to justify his actions.

Sir Godfrey smiled and refilled Mamoru's glass. "All unnecessary, I assure you, dear boy. If there is any blame to ascribe, it belongs to the bloody fools at court who sent the princess north. Certainly, no one questions your abilities, my dear Mamoru."

Nzingu remained conspicuously silent. She turned quickly, and the bone beadwork on her gown rattled.

With proper detachment, Mamoru said to the Zulu witch, "Although I have no right, I would ask that you not despair just yet."

Sir Godfrey rubbed his hands together. "Quite. So clearly you have someone in Britain to search for the princess?"

"Selkirk," Mamoru replied. "An excellent geomancer."

Sir Godfrey pursed his lips, trying to conjure a face to the name. Failing, he shrugged with acceptance of Mamoru's characterization.

Nzingu was lost in her own thoughts of ruin. Only Sanah now locked eyes with Mamoru. Clearly she recognized the name Selkirk, and just as clearly she was not pleased.

Mamoru ran his hand along the edge of the basalt coffin, feeling the texts carved into the stone. "I have every confidence that we will have our princess back. Our resources are vast. And despite our animosity toward the Empire, Equatoria's reach is long and can be exploited for our own purposes. I feel certain that once this difficulty is past, our plans will go forward. As they must."

"Hear hear," Sir Godfrey murmured, and tapped his hand on the sarcophagus, filling the chamber with the clang of his gold signet ring.

Sanah closed her almond eyes, revealing on the outside of the lids henna markings that looked like eyes. She turned the eternal sight away from Mamoru, raised her face, and softly began to pray.

———

Two mornings later, Senator Clark appeared on the reviewing balcony of Victoria Palace in Alexandria. He carried Prince Simon in his arms like a loving father. Prince Simon's actual loving father was not present, it having been decided that Emperor Constantine should stay out of the public eye to highlight his concern for the continuing gravity of the situation. The crowd was exalted by the sight of Prince Simon alive and well. And they were stirred by the tableau of Senator Clark as rescuer of imperial fortunes. Now they sensed the vampires would be sorry they had ever resorted to such a cowardly act as attacking the imperial children.

The night that had looked so dark to the Alexandrians now dawned brighter as the rays of the sun sparkled off Clark's brass buttons. After fifteen minutes of roaring adulation, Clark carried Prince Simon inside and deposited him on the marble floor without another thought. The boy naturally sought the side of Colonel Anhalt, who lingered in the shadows of the vast corridor.

Clark said to the properly attired prime minister, Lord Kelvin, "I want two cruisers—forty-four guns at least, but primarily with bombing capabilities. They must be fast. I want them to carry five companies of marines experienced in vampire fighting. No household guards. Persian units if available; I hear good things about those boys campaigning around the Caspian. And I want them ready to move in two days. We've wasted too much time already."

Kelvin didn't blink because that would betray the shock he felt. He looked up at the broad American shoulders towering above him. "Why?"

"Because I'm going to bloody the enemy. I want those monsters worrying about me and what I might do." The senator clamped a cigar between his teeth. He held a flame to the end and drew heavily. "My wedding is only a month away, Mr. Prime Minister. It's high time I killed some vampires, or I might not get to walk down the aisle."

CHAPTER 10

I T WAS A blustery evening when Greyfriar saw a few lights shining in the familiar skyline of Edinburgh with the sharp edge of Arthur's Seat on one end and the brooding castle on the other. He could tell it was cold from the many plumes of inky smoke rising and the cloying ash in the air.

He had made his way swiftly north from France in only a few days. Fortunately the sharp winds of the North Sea had allowed him to fly. Even in a brisk wind, it was difficult to accommodate his heavy sword and firearms, plus the rucksack containing his massive and precious book.

Greyfriar settled to the ground several miles from the center of Edinburgh. He removed the smoked eyeglasses and the cloth that masked his face. He rolled his weapons into his cape and carried the bundle as he walked toward his city. Most people were inside because it was dark, and they craved the protection and warmth of a fire. The peasants who saw the swordsman greeted him with obvious affection. One offered up his lone loaf of bread, but Greyfriar waved it aside politely.

Greyfriar made his way up the rough cobblestones through the open gate of the great castle. There were no lights here. And no fire. He opened a small wooden door set in a massive stone wall and went inside.

The sounds of movement echoed throughout the rambling castle, and a strange stampede of soft padding came closer.

From out of the darkness a herd of cats appeared. They galloped toward him and crashed about his ankles like a furred wave. The mass of yellows and blacks and whites slipped around his legs. He reached down and stroked several of them, even though he could barely feel their small bodies beneath his fingertips.

Then a man entered the room, stepping awkwardly through the flood of cats. The man was tall and wore a heavy brocade shirt with a red-and-green kilt, an old regional fashion. "Did it go well, my lord?"

"No, Baudoin. I failed." Greyfriar opened the rucksack and removed the book. He inspected it for damage.

"She's dead then?"

"No. Flay took her."

"Flay?" Baudoin's face twisted in revulsion.

Greyfriar smiled slightly. "And I had my chance at Flay, but failed that too."

The servant glanced accusingly at the bundle of blood-caked weapons. "You were using those, then?"

"Of course."

Baudoin held up a hand, and his fingernails lengthened into sharp little daggers. "Next time use these."

"The whole point is not to use those." The swordsman laughed as he pulled off his gloves and tossed them aside, adding casually, "The princess killed some of us."

"What? How?"

Greyfriar stared into the distance, remembering the sight. "With a sword. It was perfect. A thing of beauty."

"Just luck, most likely." The servant placed the swords and gun belt on a long wooden table.

"Perhaps. She seemed surprised too." The swordsman sank gratefully into a chair.

Baudoin hung the mask and long grey cape on a peg. "You know where she is, then?"

"No doubt in London. With Cesare."

Baudoin busied himself cleaning the sword to cover his sudden agitation. After a moment, he asked, "So what will you do?"

"Go there."

"And what happens when Cesare has you killed?"

Greyfriar laughed again from his place at the table perusing the anatomy book. He had to be very careful not to tear the pages when he turned them.

Baudoin turned from the basin where he scrubbed awkwardly at the dried blood on the rapier. "That's not an answer, my lord." He struggled to grip the weapon. The sharp blade sliced his deadened fingers, but he gave the gashes only the barest glance of annoyance.

The swordsman grunted noncommittally and continued looking at the amazing plates of dissected vampires. He held up his own hands with their clawed nails and tried to imagine the intricately drawn network of tendons and muscles under his pale skin.

He said to his servant, "Bring some water to clean the blood from me. I have smelled like a human for too long." It was a tedious method of masking his true scent from other vampires, but effective.

Baudoin huffed with disdain and tossed the sword down with as much dissatisfied vigor as he dared given how much his master loved the weapon. Then he left the room, hissing at cats scampering around his feet.

After Greyfriar washed the caked bloody disguise off his body, he returned to the study of the book, unaware of the passage of any time until he heard a throat cleared above him. Baudoin stood with a teenage girl. The girl's eyes were averted to her feet. She trembled.

Baudoin said, "My lord. Dinner."

The swordsman felt a surge of hunger when he saw the young girl, but he fought the urge to leap to his feet. He closed the book and shoved it aside. He stood slowly and said to her, "Don't be afraid. I won't harm you."

The girl nodded, but didn't look up.

"Do you know who I am?"

The girl nodded again.

Greyfriar said, "Tell me."

"Prince Gareth," she whispered with quivering lips.

"Correct. And you know I am your protector. No vampires prey here. And not one of your people has preceded you into this castle and not left alive. You know that too?" She was new to him, perhaps new to his kingdom as well. It wasn't unusual for refugees to seek out his land. There were tales told of safety in Scotland, but it was another matter to stand before a thing of legend and pray the rumors were true.

The girl swallowed, too terrified to respond.

Prince Gareth moved close to her and placed a hand on her shoulder. She shuddered, but stayed on her feet. The swordsman signaled his servant to withdraw.

Baudoin said, "Her brother was delicious. I just dined from him. He's waiting for her below."

"Get out."

The servant smiled smugly and backed out.

"You may choose," Gareth said to the girl in a quiet voice. He removed a steel dirk from his belt. "I can make a small incision with this. Or not."

The girl didn't respond. She breathed harshly through her nose. Eyes shut tight. She was so frightened, Gareth could take no pleasure in this. Sometimes his meals were more engaging. They knew they wouldn't be killed, and some even seemed to relish the honor, or at least the duty they were doing for their lord. Any blood provider was free of obligation for a year. He had even had pleasant conversations with some of them, and they had volunteered to return. He would always refuse for fear of acquiring too much of a taste for them.

Gareth decided to feed quickly and send the girl on her way. He sliced her quickly with the knife and drank. The familiar urge welled up in him. The delicious warm blood slid over his sensitive tongue. He could taste the knowledge of her. Aside from her crippling fear, which gave her blood a pleasant tang, she was quite healthy. And she was only a day away from being fertile, so her blood was very rich. He craved to know more, to learn from every last drop of her. He would feel her most in the paroxysms of the middle flow pumping hard into his mouth as her pounding heart fought to keep her emptying body alive. She would then collapse with her life, and he would relish the delicious liquid drizzling out as she died. That final trickle of memories and hopes over his lips would be the sweetest.

Gareth suddenly saw an image of Princess Adele drooping lifeless in the bony hands of Cesare. He saw his brother moan and his eyes roll in his head as he mouthed the last congealing blood from the princess's still-throbbing throat. Adele's lips twitched, calling an unheard name.

Gareth pulled his face away from the red incision and clamped his hand to stanch the flow. "Baudoin!"

The servant scuttled in and led the unsteady girl away.

Gareth plunged his hand into the dirty water in the basin and washed off the girl's blood. He seized the rapier with his wet hand and squeezed, relishing the hardness of the hilt, then sat heavily and felt the familiar onslaught of empty rage that always followed one of his limp half feedings. The hot, bloated warmth that came from draining a meal was a distant memory to him. There was no pleasure like it. A complete feeding made for a satisfied stupor that left the senses stunned and delivered the feeder into remorseless slumber.

Gareth had not slept so well for nearly a century. Not since the war and the break with his father. And certainly not since Greyfriar had appeared.

CHAPTER II

SENATOR CLARK STOOD on the quarterdeck of USS *Ranger* and watched Mr. Montoya, chief meteorologist, approach trailing a long stream of paper tape. Clark saw a smile on Montoya's face and he relaxed.

"Much improved," Montoya reported with a touch of pride, as if he controlled the weather, not just reported it. "High tomorrow should be over eighty. Winds light."

"Thank you, Chief." Not optimum, but as well as could be expected here this time of year. When fighting vampires, the warmer the better. And light winds cut the creatures' air mobility. Clark turned to the commander of *Ranger*, Captain Root. "Signal the fleet. We attack Bordeaux tomorrow at thirteen hundred." As the signal lights informed *Persepolis* and *Canterbury*, Clark went below to prepare.

Prior to departure from Alexandria, military commanders had debated tactics. The Americans had come equipped with samples of some of their newest weapons, including shroud gas bombs that could envelop vampires and deprive them of natural advantages of preternatural senses of sight and smell, and blood gas that mimicked the scent of blood and was used for misdirection. Clark argued against using the gas in this case. He would open the operation with several solid firebombing runs over Bordeaux, intending to blast the town into rubble, to burn it to the ground along with the clan that inhabited it.

In his spartan cabin on *Ranger*, the senator studied old maps of the Bordeaux area, confirming yet again the brilliance of his planning. The vampires of Bordeaux were a minor offshoot of the Paris clan, small in number, perhaps only two hundred. This clan was not a major military power. They were not the authors of the attack of *Ptolemy*. They did not have Princess Adele.

Clark didn't need her to be there. He just needed vampires to be there. They needed to know that he would respond to provocation with force. Massive. Overwhelming. Force.

The senator had fought vampires too many times to be awestruck by their mystery and lore. Those unfamiliar with vampires frequently went into battle already mesmerized by fairy tales, and it was typical to be stunned when confronted by the creatures' preternatural physical abilities. But ultimately vampires fought like animals, driven by instinct and conquering by cunning and prowess. Against a disciplined and well-armed force, these monsters once thought unbeatable could be destroyed. Clark had done it. Five years ago, he had led the army that drove them from St. Louis. Of course, the next winter the vampires returned and took back the city, but by then Clark's myth had been made and could not be unmade.

This mission would be the first tile in a new mosaic of his legend. The kidnapping of Princess Adele, or the "Ptolemy Disaster," had come as a surprise and had thrown Clark's plans into disarray. Still, the senator was a man who made obstacles into challenges and challenges into legends. This would be the greatest yet. He would cut a bloody swathe to rescue his bride. Times were changing, and the pendulum was swinging back toward humanity. Soon New York, Chicago, London, Paris, Munich, and all the rest would be free. The vampires would be annihilated, or at least driven underground to exist as the inconsequential parasites they had been for millennia before.

This would be the first battle of the Great War. The history books would read "The Battle of Bordeaux was the opening blow struck by humanity to retake the Earth. Senator Clark led the victorious allied forces in a brilliant audacious strike." With thoughts of glory in his head, thoughts he had nurtured his entire life, the senator drifted off into his usual deep comfortable sleep.

The next day, he was well rested when the time came. His American frigate led the two Equatorian ships out of the light clouds, venting buoyants rapidly and taking in sail as fast as possible. Chief Montoya's science and art were dead-on. The air was warm and the wind was still. Only a few vampires were aloft in the sunshine. At the sight of the warships some of the creatures sluggishly drifted away. Others dropped to the crumbling town below, no doubt to warn their fellows.

As *Ranger* veered hard alee, the Equatorian cruisers opened their keel ports and made a slow bombing run, laying stacks of incendiaries on the town. Flames sprouted in the predatory shadows of the two warships.

Soon a swarm of vampires rose in the light air. Some used the updraft from the fires, but others were covered in flames and soon spiraled down like burnt embers. A group of vampires tacked for *Ranger*, which wallowed low without sail. Gatlings at the rail and in nests aloft swung out. Cranks turned and the guns roared, sending a wall of steel into the drifting vampires, pounding their feather-light bodies, shoving them back, and ripping some into pieces.

Senator Clark gripped the quarterdeck rail and waved a gloved hand in a circle, indicating he wanted another bombing run. Flags went up on the yards to signal the squadron. The Equatorians came around smartly and passed over Bordeaux again, dropping line after line of bombs. The old town erupted in flames and smoke. Dilapidated buildings burst into fire and crumbled to pieces. Small figures scrambled through the havoc; vampire or human, it was impossible to tell from the decks of the attacking ships.

Senator Clark drew a hand across his throat, and the signals for bombing came down. The Equatorians drew off as *Ranger* dropped to near treetop level leeward of the smoke roiling from the city. He raised an open hand and the bugler sounded "Lines Away." Boarding cables dropped, and Clark's Rangers took positions at the gunwales between the smoking Gatlings. Clark seized his own line and raised a gloved fist. The bugler sounded "Charge!" and his boys plunged over the side.

Clark plummeted toward the green earth far below his feet. He loosened his grip on the clamp to fall faster; he intended to be first down. The wind whipped through his clothes and pounded in his ears. It was like flying. Just like the vampires. He relished the brutal irony of attacking them from the air. It made the killing sweeter.

Black shapes circled in the sooty sky. A figure loomed up in front of Clark, scrabbling with its claws as he slammed against it with his shoulder. The vampire spun away above him. Clark scanned the air beneath him and breathed with relief to see no other creatures moving toward him. But he heard a faint choked scream over the rush of the wind and strained his head around just in time to see one of his men clawed from his drop cable.

Clark felt rather than saw the earth coming up; his drop timing was impeccable. He couldn't help grinning with anticipation as he squeezed the clamp to slow himself. His feet touched down, and he pulled pistol and glowing saber to cover his boys.

Commandos landed and quickly formed ranks, unslinging their gas-powered Winchester carbines and kneeling in defensive formations. Clark had no intention of moving a step closer to burning Bordeaux. Between the Americans and the outskirts of town lay a decrepit orchard in which dark figures darted from ragged pear tree to ragged pear tree, lurking among the fresh green leaves and grey boughs. The Rangers waited, guns poised, eyeing the trees. When the enemy came, they would have to cross two hundred yards of open ground with no cover.

Clark paced and patted men on their shoulders, making heroic small talk. His sharp eyes caught the creatures gathering behind the distant brambles. The vampires watched from the shadows, showing more restraint than normal. Typically they would have rushed headlong at the humans. The Americans couldn't stand here forever; the imperials might get the glory of cleaning out Bordeaux.

Clark felt an unusual pinch of worry and checked the position of the sun. He had barely two hours of maximum temperature. His meteorologist had predicted a cool breezy evening. Surely there was no way the vampires could know this, but if the creatures did wait to attack, once the sun set, they would have all the advantages.

"All right," Clark said to his second in command. "I'm not waiting for them to decide what to do. Let's smoke 'em out."

Nodding, Major Stoddard shoved his hand in his rucksack, and a shudder went through the ranks as he pulled out two canisters. Blood grenades. They dispensed smoke with the scent of blood. Unlike shroud gas, blood grenades were designed to play into the vampires' animalistic craving. Normally the grenades were used to distract and divert vampires away from humans, but this time Clark intended to goad the creatures into a fighting rage. The smoke from two blood grenades should drive the vampires mad with hunger. Major Stoddard checked the light wind, twisted the top of one canister, and heaved it toward the orchard. The canister flew a strong seventy-five yards, hit, and rolled. There was a loud pop, and reddish smoke boiled over the grass. Stoddard hurled the second canister a bit wide of the first, then quickly took up his rifle as more smoke poured aloft.

Hissing strengthened from the orchard, proving that the vampires were getting a massive whiff. Dark shapes coursed frantically onto tree trunks and bounded from limb to limb. Some scuttled like lizards into the unkempt canopy and rustled through the green. The hissing changed to weird sounds like growling cats that came from deep within inhuman throats.

Then they came. First one, then more. They streaked unbelievably fast into the open, running and leaping, landing and crouching in the high grass, then up again. They never stopped moving, like a wave of locusts.

"Steady, boys," Clark said, and Winchester barrels rose.

His men waited as the creatures loped toward them. It seemed like hours watching the growling figures scramble through the sun-dappled meadow, but it was mere seconds. Several vampires bounded high off the ground, spread their arms, and caught the air.

"Fire!" Clark bellowed.

The front rank opened up at ground level with their carbines. The second rank raised muzzles in practiced style and blasted vampires from the air. The Americans' chemical-fueled cartridges threw off a greenish smoke. The commandos worked their lever-action rifles, keeping up a murderous roar. The vampires fell. Some rose, only to be hit again. And again.

The air was choked with smoke as several of the tattered and bloody beasts reached the square. They flailed with their clawlike nails, but only against bayonets. The Rangers thrust and slashed, tearing through the vampires' bodies. The creatures collapsed when muscles, tendons, and organs were destroyed. They dropped to the ground writhing and spitting.

One vampire dropped inside the square and seized a trooper. Before the man could shout, his head was nearly torn from his shoulders. The vampire lashed out, and a second soldier dropped with savage wounds to his side.

Clark whirled with his saber merely a blur of light and slashed deep into the thing's face. The monster showed little pain as Clark wrenched the sword free. Clark then fired his long-barreled Colt revolver, punching a hole in the vampire's left cheek and staggering him. A second well-aimed blow with the searing sword severed the vampire's head, and he fell lifeless to the grass.

Rifle shots were tapering off. The Rangers stood with guns poised, watching for shapes moving in the mist. Slowly, the light wind shoved the emerald smoke away to reveal the field. Wounded vampires wriggled hissing in the grass. Some dragged themselves forward despite horrendous wounds. They wouldn't stop until they were destroyed.

The field medic reported six Rangers down. Two dead. Two more soon would be. Clark hefted his saber, reveling in its constant sizzle. He would make the vampires pay for every one of his men lost.

———∿∿∿———

The female vampire thrashed against the chains. She rolled on the cobblestones and fought the heavy irons binding her ragged arms and legs.

"This is the clan chief?" Clark muttered as he glared from under an upraised eyebrow at the ragged thing at his feet. It had been a decidedly quick fight against such primitives. It was akin to cleaning rats from a cellar.

Captain Eskandari nodded. Around the Persian officer, his marines leaned on their long, bloody pikes, watching the thing struggle. "War chief. These Bordeaux vampires are nothing. Throwbacks almost."

The American sneered and stamped his boot on the female's chest. He lowered a torch close to her face. "All right. Talk. Where is Princess Adele of Equatoria?"

The vampire gnashed her teeth.

Clark tossed the torch to Major Stoddard and snatched a pike from one of the Persian marines. He lowered the wicked blade against the vampire's throat. "I know you understand me! No clan mounts an action so large as the one that took the princess without all you animals being aware. Where is Princess Adele? Tell me or I'll take your head!"

The creature eyed the pike. Her voice came out as a gargle. "Dmitri."

Captain Eskandari whispered to a fellow marine, "King Dmitri, lord of London. His son is Cesare. The Slaughterer."

Senator Clark could hear fear in Eskandari's voice that chilled him. The American pushed the blade against the vampire's throat, slicing skin and drawing thin watery blood. "I am Senator Clark from the American Republic. You are the last of your clan. I have killed every other vampire in Bordeaux. The only reason you're still alive is that I want you to deliver a message to old Dmitri. Tell it that it has five days to release Princess Adele alive and well. If it fails to do so, I will come to Britain and kill every vampire there." Clark tossed the pike back and stepped off the vampire's torso. "Release it."

The Persians and a few Americans aimed their weapons at the female as two wary marines unsnapped the lock and scrambled away. The vampire flailed free of the chains and crouched in the middle of the soldiers. Clark refused to cower, but did place his hand on the butt of his pistol. In the silence, he could hear the last of the creature's wounded brethren being put to death in the night. The vampire glared around her and then seemed to disappear, trailed briefly by the sound of her moving off through the rubble-strewn streets. The soldiers all sighed with relief, knowing that she certainly could've killed several of them before the other troopers could have stopped her. But apparently even vampires wanted to live.

"Senator," Major Stoddard asked, "do you think it will really take your message to Britain?"

"Doesn't matter." Clark strode down the ash-strewn cobblestones. "I delivered my message here in Bordeaux. Those things in Britain will hear about it." He stepped past scorched bodies, both vampire and human. He kicked his way through a pile of vampire heads. Some of them were from children. "They'll know I've been here, and they'll know I will not be trifled with."

CHAPTER 12

CESARE SAW CONFUSION descending across his father's face again, and it was all the young prince could do not to groan aloud with annoyance. He leaned forward in his chair next to King Dmitri's tarnished throne and regarded the ragged war chief from Bordeaux with uncommitted boredom.

King Dmitri's chin quivered as spittle drizzled onto his wispy beard. "Is she right? Is she here?"

Cesare understood his father to refer to Princess Adele. "Yes. I have her." He indicated the Bordeaux visitor. "She is correct in that matter."

A murmur of alarm spread through the clan council as Cesare adopted a look of amused disregard, making it clear he felt there was no cause for dismay and that he was firmly in charge of the situation. He raised a lazy hand to quiet the elders. "Please. I have had her for several weeks now."

The king went wide-eyed. "What? I did not know."

"No, Sire. I am your right hand. There is no need for you to concern yourself with minor matters."

"Minor?" shouted the bearded Lord Ghast of Cornwall. "Didn't you think the humans would fight to get her back? What have you done, Cesare?"

Prince Cesare said in a steady voice, "Are you afraid of the Equatorians, Lord Ghast?"

The elder snarled. "You have no right to start a war!"

The old king began to fidget uncomfortably. He rolled his hands together, his cracked and yellow claws permanently extended due to age.

Cesare replied, "Isn't it better that *they* fight *our* war rather than us fighting theirs?"

"*Our* war?" Ghast protested. "How is this *our* war? Bordeaux has been destroyed because of your actions, and the first we hear of it is from this pathetic trash dragging herself into our presence! This is how the elders hear of Cesare's war? There has been no clan gathering!"

Cesare grinned. "Oh, my war has not yet started. Don't trouble yourself about that clump of degenerates in Bordeaux. My seizure of Princess Adele has sapped the Equatorian initiative. Now we can fight them when we are ready. I don't have to explain my plan. And frankly I'm concerned that you have the temerity to question me here in my father's chamber." He rose menacingly.

The Lord of Cornwall paused. He gave the prince a curt nod and sat. The other elders were pleased enough by the spectacle of Cesare handily folding the haughty Lord Ghast into the calming embrace of clan hierarchy that they forgave the prince's high-handedness.

King Dmitri, completely out of the flow, muttered, "Are we at war?"

Cesare made a show of considering the king's comment as if it meant something and replied, "Not yet, Your Majesty. That is why I have done what I've done. You recall that I told you Equatoria and America were gathering their forces, awaiting the alliance of those two people?"

The elders again broke into dismayed murmuring. This was the first they had heard of these actions by the human kingdoms. The king's brow furrowed with dismay. He did not remember it either. Of course, the king could no longer be sure what he'd been told or not. Cesare knew this, and that's why the prince never told his father anything. Still, the aged king preserved some semblance of control by nodding his head as if recalling a conversation.

"Should we call the clan?" The king rubbed his wispy chin. "The attack on Bordeaux . . ."

"Is nothing." Cesare pointed toward the filthy female war chief from the Continent. "Look at her. The humans obliterated Bordeaux with three ships and a few men. In fact, if we act boldly, the attack on Bordeaux gives us the chance to move this game even more in our favor. We can bring other clans into our fold." The vampire prince stretched out his long fingers and closed them into a fist. "Then we can strike the humans at our convenience. But only because I had the foresight to take Princess Adele into my power. One day, my actions will be remembered as the turning point of our clan, and our kind."

—⁊⁊⁊—

Cesare floated toward the Tower, followed at some distance by Flay. He had been deeply troubled by the pathetic showing of the king in council. Cesare had to guard against the doddering old relic's natural tendency to panic and call the clan at the first sign of trouble. A clan gathering was not in Cesare's plans at the moment because he could never be sure which direction the mob would jump. Cesare preferred to rule by whispers in the king's ear.

In addition, a clan gathering might draw his brother, Gareth, into the game. Gareth was a terrible wild card who would have to be eliminated at some point. Destroying him required the most careful preparation given that his older brother was the rightful heir and that vampires, being creatures of time, loved nothing so much as tradition in their governance. Cesare would certainly finish his brother and rule the clan after feeble Dmitri, but it would take skill. And he wanted time to relish it all.

Nearer to hand, Cesare already had a plan to turn the Bordeaux massacre to his advantage. He had heard tales of Senator Clark, a man who had turned one battlefield victory into a reputation as a "vampire killer." Now the human had a reputation to preserve. Clark was no doubt deluded enough to think that humans could defeat vampires. Stupid, yes. But dangerous. For all the excuses that Bordeaux was a pathetic clutch of ferals, the sudden and brutal success of the human forces caused Cesare to worry. There would be no taking the humans by surprise like the Great Killing. This was a delicate matter, and men like Clark were enemies of delicacy.

Cesare and Flay settled onto the crumbling stone roof of the central tower and went down the dank steps to find the princess huddled near a glowing brazier. She didn't glance up. Her clothes were dirty and beginning to show prison wear. Plus her hair was in danger of becoming a great tangled hive despite her best efforts.

"Princess," Cesare said quietly, "I fear there is bad news."

Adele kept her eyes locked on the glowing coals.

The vampire prince continued, "Your beloved fiancé has killed several hundred of my brethren. Without provocation or reason."

Now Adele did look up with real interest, and a smile.

It infuriated Cesare. "Yes. How proud you must be. Your brave Senator Clark massacred the poor population of Bordeaux. Women and children included. And humans. Hundreds slaughtered. It is a frightful outrage, and all the clans have justifiably taken great umbrage."

Adele remained stoic.

Cesare said, "There is, of course, no hope of releasing you now. Unless you can provide me with some useful information with which to distract the clans from their bloodlust for revenge."

The princess returned her eyes to the fire.

"Tell me about your spies in Britain," Cesare repeated for what seemed like the thousandth time.

There was, again, no reply.

The vampire moved closer, letting his iron-laden breath wash over the woman. "Your people obviously have no regard for your welfare. Why should I keep you alive if they are going to start a war against us anyway? You afford us no protection. Tell me about your spies in Britain."

Silence.

"I'm wasting my time with negotiations for peace. Your people have no interest in peace. I should just prepare for war."

Silence.

"I should just kill you. Your brother is dead. And after I assassinate your father, your people will fall apart."

Silence.

"Is that what you want? The end of your kind? Your silence will cause it. Tell me what I want to know and you can go home to keep your people safe. It's just that simple! Talk or your people will all die!"

Silence.

Cesare drew back his clawed hand with a guttural roar.

The blow did not fall. A figure appeared over Adele, grasping Cesare's wrist with a firm hand. The tall vampire then released Cesare, who staggered back a few steps.

Adele stared up at the newcomer. He was dressed in a long black frock coat over a white shirt and black trousers. Long-limbed yet powerful, with long supple fingers. His hair was dark and a bit unkempt, unlike Cesare's close cut. His pale, icy blue eyes darted quickly and intelligently about the chamber, piercing Adele for a long moment before slipping away. His face was strong and his lips curled into a slight wan smile, which seemed unusual.

The new vampire's sudden appearance changed the emotion of the room. Flay stood transfixed. And Cesare was angry, but not playacting this time; he was truly furious. But more, he was surprised and confused because he was no longer in total control, like a vicious animal suddenly finding itself in a cage for the first time.

Cesare glared at the new arrival. "How dare you lay hands on me!"

The tall, dark vampire gave a slight bow. His movements were spare and reserved. "I apologize, Cesare, but I was afraid you were going to kill her."

"What's it to you, Gareth?"

"Everything. She is my prisoner now."

"I'm sorry?" Cesare stared with narrowing eyes as his jaw worked back and forth.

"I am the heir. I claim her. In fact, I feel that I've neglected clan affairs too long now. I intend to take a greater interest. If you will excuse me, I wish to interrogate my prisoner."

Cesare brushed the sleeves of his coat roughly and raised his eyebrows. He turned and left without another word or gesture. Flay paused at the door, looking at Gareth with a gaze that caught Adele's attention. Then the war chief followed her master.

Gareth waited, listening to the sounds of his brother's exit that weren't audible to Adele. Then he studied the princess for a long moment.

Adele stared at Gareth. Something about him seemed familiar, but she didn't know why. She had never encountered a living vampire before this voyage, but now she'd seen far too many to suit her. Maybe they were all starting to look alike to her.

The vampire bowed slightly. "I am Prince Gareth, Lord of Scotland. Are you well?"

Adele almost responded, but then shut her mouth and turned back to the brazier. Gareth waited for a long minute before realizing no reply was coming. He exhaled in disappointment. "Very well. I will have you moved to more comfortable quarters. You are under my care now. Cesare won't trouble you again."

Adele assumed this was just some interrogation ploy. One brother treats her harshly. The other brother steps in to treat her kindly. In gratitude for the respite she breaks down. She found herself eyeing Gareth surreptitiously as the vampire turned away and disappeared through the door.

The young woman didn't move for several minutes. It was typical for Cesare to leave and then abruptly return to throw her off. But clearly Gareth wasn't coming back. Adele stood and went to the window. A few shadows flitted across the cloudy sky in the distance. Just another night in dead London.

She dug her fingers into a niche in the stone wall and pulled out a thin length of rock about six inches by three. The edges were sharp. She tested it with her thumb. Not sharp enough yet. The young woman sat on the floor and spat on the stone, working the edge of the makeshift knife patiently across a whetstone placed on the floor.

Now she had another vampire lordling to kill.

CHAPTER 13

JUST AS PRINCE Gareth had promised, Adele was moved to
better quarters away from the treacherously decrepit central tower
with its vast open spaces that invited stinking breezes from the river.
The new rooms had ancient but serviceable coal heaters. There was furniture to keep her aching body off the cold stones, but the bed was so ill
used and foul that Adele contented herself with using the cleanest of the
blankets and sleeping on the floor near the warm grate of the heater.
While bugs and rats were still constant companions, her existence was
made gentler by the fact that Cesare's frightening and debilitating inter-
rogations stopped.

Over the course of the first week, Gareth came once to check on
Adele's comfort and haunted the chambers, inspecting her accoutrements, seemingly eager for gratitude or conversation. She refused to
acknowledge him when he asked about her welfare. He contented himself to stare at her in a fashion that unnerved her, neither aggressive nor
angry, but instead unnaturally attentive and curious. There was an
attempt at personal connection in his gaze that frightened Adele and
threatened not her person, but her personality. Even though he never
asked for any sort of political information, he wanted something from
her. She stared hard into the corner until Gareth sighed and departed.

Adele had seen no one since Gareth's visit until the day she spotted the figure walking across the yard in the direction of her rooms. She froze in amazement at the window. He was clearly human, a free human. There were differences in how vampires and humans moved and carried themselves. Bloodmen usually had a soulless slump, but this man strode with head up, alert, quick on his feet. He wore his sandy, grey-streaked hair long and tied in a ponytail behind him and had a beard that was heavy and unkempt. He was clad in the fashion of an outdoorsman, but looked more like a scholar forced into the wilderness than a true Ranger like Greyfriar. All he carried was a rucksack over one shoulder and some peculiar device dangling from his belt that looked like a combination sextant and astrolabe.

Vampires crouched along the crumbling slates of the Tower complex and flitted through the air. Surely they could see the man; he was in plain view. Yet they didn't react. The presence of the dark fiends crouching around him concerned the man, because he glanced toward them frequently as he trod across the yard, but he came all the same, with his face tense and lined with effort. He was concentrating to the point of being in pain.

A geomancer. Mamoru had told her that it was possible for people to master certain arcane arts that let them go unnoticed by vampires. Even Greyfriar had dismissed them as myths. Incredibly, this man appeared to be the very thing. So there were spies roaming Britain, just as Cesare feared. That thought made Adele smile.

When the man looked up at the window and saw Adele, he placed a finger to his lips to beg her silence before he began to climb the pile of rubble that crowded the wall. His foot dislodged a stone and it clattered loudly. Several vampires turned, with heads tilted like alert dogs. Their eyes locked on Adele at the window rather than on the man. He stayed perfectly still, and the princess felt it was important not to look at him. The vampires soon turned away with disinterest, and the man began to climb again, slower and more carefully, testing handholds and footing before putting his weight behind them.

When he reached a point only a few feet below Adele's window, he whispered in a smooth Alexandrian accent, "Your Highness, don't speak.

Forgive my impertinence, but I can't afford for you to attract attention to me. My name is Selkirk. Look here quickly and then look away."

Adele glanced down furtively. Selkirk held up one hand to reveal a tattoo of a sinuous dragon on his palm. Mamoru had a similar tattoo on his left palm, along with a tiger on his right. Adele felt a great thrill at the familiar and comforting sight so far from home.

The man said, "Mamoru is my teacher. I am his geomancer here in Britain."

Adele was confused. Geomancer or not, Mamoru had no students other than Adele. He was an imperial tutor, exclusively employed by the court. Maybe this man Selkirk had been Mamoru's geomancy student in Java. She knew Mamoru took an inordinate interest in that topic. He had instructed her in some of its rudiments even though she hadn't really taken to the subject; it seemed a bit vast and distant, sometimes even silly. Adele always preferred subjects that had a more human dimension, such as martial arts and ethics.

Selkirk's whisper shook her from her thoughts. "Don't despair. I will send word to Mamoru that you are alive and well. We will bring you—"

"Princess?" A voice came from behind her.

Adele spun to see Prince Gareth standing in the doorway with raised eyebrows.

"Is someone out there?" The vampire moved quickly toward the window.

Adele met Gareth halfway and blocked his path. "No. I talk to myself because there is no one here I deign to speak to."

The vampire slipped around her and leaned out the window. Adele froze.

Gareth drew back inside and asked, "Was Cesare or Flay here?"

Adele paused. Had Prince Gareth not seen Selkirk? Was that possible? Her head shook slowly in response to Gareth's question.

"You can tell me without fear of retribution. I will deal with my brother. He has no claim on you now that I'm here."

Adele thought he sounded almost sincere, but that was impossible. Vampires had no emotions except hunger. Still, this one had mastered the mimicry of sympathy. He knew how to incline his head just so and peer at her out of crystal blue eyes, but he was merely hiding cruelty, and she saw the razor edges of his teeth when he spoke. She shook her head again and, to pull his attention from the window, she crossed the room with pantomime frailty.

Adele cleared her throat loudly. "I want to thank you. For your kindness. These rooms. The food." She feigned a near swoon and held herself up on the door frame. "Cesare was so brutal."

Gareth merely watched her curiously.

Adele swallowed the bitterness she tasted in her throat. She toed the stone floor with a dirty boot. The life of an imperial heir had given her very little practice being coquettish.

Gareth seemed unmoved by the tattered young waif. "If you're weak, you should eat more. Don't worry about the meat. It is cow. And some horse. That is acceptable to humans, yes?"

"Horse? No! Civilized people don't eat horses. We ride them. Oh God, have you fed me horse?"

"Cow is fine, then?"

"Yes. Cow. No horse. No dog. No cat. Just cow. Or sheep. Or goat. Do you know the difference between animals?"

"Yes. I know the difference. What about clothes? Do you want new clothes?"

"No. I won't wear rags torn from some cadaver."

Gareth seemed insulted. "As you will."

"Do you intend to release me or keep me as some trophy?" Adele surprised herself by dredging up that hopeless question. But she might as well call this charming monster's bluff now and get back to her sullen self.

"I don't know. Senator Clark's attack on Bordeaux has given Cesare an excuse to raise a furor, as if he needed one. It will be hard for me to free you now." The vampire seemed to be talking more to himself than to her. Then he leaned back against the window embrasure; his elbow couldn't have been more than inches from Selkirk's unseen head.

Adele suddenly threw her hands against her face and began wailing. She fell to her knees and even called up tears from somewhere. After a few moments, she peered through parted fingers to see Gareth still leaning and staring at her like a man watching a play. And not a particularly well performed one.

There was a small sound from outside the window. As Gareth started to turn, Adele sprang forward.

"Listen to me!" the princess shouted desperately. "I can't take it anymore! I will tell you about the spies in Britain!"

Gareth flattened against the wall and held up calming hands. "I don't want to know anything about spies in Britain."

"What?" Adele abandoned her swooning burlesque and glared. "What's wrong with you?"

"Was that Cesare's interest? Spies? Well, my only interest is seeing you safely home. I have no wish to involve myself in Cesare's affairs."

Adele said angrily, "So you're afraid of Cesare too? Is everyone afraid of that little creature?"

"Yes," Gareth replied. "It would be ignorant not to fear him. He's capable of anything. And his packs are numerous compared to mine. Which number exactly one." He laid a hand on his chest and smiled.

"Aren't you the elder brother?"

"Yes. But politics are complicated, as you well know."

"If you release me, it will earn you goodwill in Equatoria."

"That's nice, but to what end? There are no politics between vampires and humans. To us, you are food. To you, we are parasites. There is no ground where we can meet. You want your territory back. We won't give it back. It's life or death between us."

"It doesn't have to be. You will be a . . . king and I'll be empress. Together we can take your brother down. . . ."

Gareth's face fell. "Please stop. If only you truly believed that. But don't worry. I intend to free you, Princess, while Cesare does not. There is no need to sway me. And it won't serve you to catch me in some treacherous utterance, thinking you can gain your freedom by selling me out to Cesare. There are no secrets between me and my brother. When our father the king dies, I will kill Cesare. We both know it; it only has to play out someday."

Adele felt a wave of weariness and misery crowd out her desperate scheming. It all seemed so pointless to argue with a vampire. This was why she had refused to speak to Cesare in the first place. If it weren't for wanting to protect Selkirk, she would never have let herself be drawn into conversation with this one. She thought about going for her stone knife. At least one of the things would die. But that was foolish. It could bring every vampire in the vicinity and doom Selkirk.

Gareth continued quietly, "All you need do is wait. Don't do anything foolish like trying to escape. And pray your countrymen don't attempt to rescue you by force." He extended his arm out the window, causing Adele to start. But he was only pointing to the vulturelike sentries perched across the yard. "They are waiting for a signal to kill you. They won't ask questions. They won't wonder about the reason. They'll just kill."

"They can try." Adele gave a sarcastic grin, wondering why those assassins, if they were truly so fearsome, couldn't even see a man hanging right under their noses.

"Indeed. I'm sure you might take a few with you. You're quite extraordinary."

Adele was taken aback by Gareth's praise, faint though it was. He must've heard that she had killed vampires in France. The young princess actually felt pride that Gareth, one of the creatures himself, would recognize her skills. Cesare, on the other hand, had done nothing but harangue and berate her, always reinforcing her role as part of an inferior species.

Wait, Adele thought abruptly. This was just a sham. Gareth was only toying with her. Winning her confidence with gestures of goodwill. She wouldn't be so easily swayed, though.

"Would you go now?" she said as forcefully as she could muster.

Gareth gave a half bow. "I beg you to believe what I say. I am your only chance to get home alive." The tall prince pinned her eyes with a fierce stare.

She dropped her gaze to the floor as Gareth's faint tread passed her and faded from the room.

Adele let out her breath in a rush and hurried to the window. Selkirk was gone. She frantically scanned the grounds and decaying structures. She thought she saw a figure slipping behind a pile of rubble, but couldn't be sure. Adele gripped the damp stone and wondered if he had been there at all. Perhaps she had conjured him out of desperation for freedom.

The princess thought with manic irony how peculiar it was that so many people seemed intent on securing her release from captivity. Cesare claimed it. Now Gareth too. Her Intended was busy slaughtering every vampire in Europe to effect it. Yet the actions of each made it impossible for the others to act. Such was diplomacy. It would've been hilarious except for the fact that she was pondering the joke while standing in a chilled vampire prison wearing filthy clothes and eating horse.

"My only chance to get out alive," Adele muttered scornfully, repeating Gareth's words as she turned away from the window. Maybe Mamoru's uncanny reach, through Selkirk, could pluck her from her prison. And somewhere, she believed, Greyfriar was slipping through shadows in pursuit of her freedom. A brief bubble of hope rose in her. "We'll see."

CHAPTER 14

"**Y**OUR IMPERIAL MAJESTY, may I present the *ambassador* from Dmitri, king of Britain.*"

Lord Kelvin's unbelievable words rang in the great vault of the Suez Hall of Victoria Palace. His manner was bland and formal to diminish the inconceivable nature of his announcement. The members of the Privy Council, despite the pomp of their dress, looked as hostile as a lynch mob. Lord Aden stood quietly to one side, observing this bit of history with an air of curiosity.

At the far end of the hall was Emperor Constantine II, the Empire in person. His robes of state were adapted from the British pattern with the addition of a tiger skin shoulder throw as a nod to India. His crown was forged from Egyptian gold and weighted with sapphires and rubies from India. The scepter in his grasp was topped with a fist-sized diamond from the Cape. His massive throne was carved with symbols of the Empire, including Indian elephants and lions of Africa. Two golden Egyptian sphinxes crouched malevolently at his feet.

Senator Clark stood like an angry bearded statue at the foot of the throne, arms clasped behind his back. Lord Kelvin had argued vehemently against the American being near the dais during an official state reception. It simply wasn't done. But since Clark's return from Marseilles bearing young Prince Simon on his broad American shoulders, followed closely by his blood-soaked triumph in Bordeaux, the emperor was compelled to show deference to him as he would his own son.

Emperor Constantine motioned for the newly arrived "ambassador" to proceed up the long aisle between row after row of empty seats. This "damnable" reception was advertised and attended by only his closest advisors.

Gas lamps flicked dramatic shadows on walls covered with bold murals, painted figures of war, gigantic and vital, with faces fixed in red concentration. Horses reared. Cannons vomited fire and smoke, and forests of lances flashed. All the painted soldiers and weapons seemed to issue forth from the living figure of the emperor poised on his throne. The ceiling hosted a magnificent sweep of the Imperial Navy airships streaming out triumphantly over the heads of all who came into the Presence.

The mousy ambassador appeared suitably awed by the vast chamber. He stopped ten feet from the dais and gave a curt bow. His clothes were mismatched and poorly patched. Lord Kelvin had tried to provide him a proper suit of clothes, but the ambassador refused. The ragged outfit only made the imperial councilors more scornful of this diplomatic mockery. The grandees hated to see their emperor brought so low as to meet with a representative of vampires. It was ridiculous. It was unthinkable. It seemed to many of these political oaks that whenever the honor of Equatoria was damaged, Adele was at the root of it. Fortunately, Senator Clark would make the monsters pay for this terrible indignity.

"Your Majesty," the human ambassador croaked, "I bear a message of greeting and goodwill from King Dmitri, sovereign of Great Britain."

Lord Kelvin squirmed with annoyance from his shadowy place near the great doors. He had expressly forbidden the word *sovereign*. If these vampires and their lackeys couldn't follow a few pages of simple rules, they shouldn't pretend to be members of the world community.

The emperor's frown deepened into a scowl of hatred. Constantine was a large man, once a stunning physical specimen with a life full of military exploits. But that was years past. A relatively easy reign in the last ten years had softened and enlarged him. He had been handsome when young, but his face had grown jowly, which his bushy muttonchops and his relatively weak chin only exaggerated. His thinning hair was hidden from view by the jeweled crown. His left eye drooped, the souvenir from a Zulu assegai, and the last few weeks living in fear for his children's lives and his Empire's future had left him sallow and with dark, sleepless eyes.

"At least you can speak," the emperor snapped. "We will hear you, Bloodman. What does your master want?"

The ambassador had the gall to silently upbraid the emperor for such undiplomatic directness by raising a bemused eyebrow. "His Majesty Dmitri is regretful of the current state of affairs between our nations."

"How nice." Constantine clamped his scarred hands on the arms of the throne. "We feel that it's simple enough to bring this *current state of affairs* to an end so he can stop being regretful."

"It isn't as simple as it sounds."

"No?"

The ambassador exhaled. "Your daughter's fleet entered vampire territory without permission. We had no idea of your intentions. We defended ourselves, as is the right of any people."

The emperor's face reddened. His drooping eye began to twitch. "Vampires are not people. They have no rights. They have no territory. They are animals."

The envoy continued, "Now your forces have made an unprovoked attack on Bordeaux. King Dmitri is wary of being attacked himself."

"He's one smart vampire." Clark rattled his saber.

The wiry ambassador extended a trembling hand in Clark's direction. "There. That is my king's point for all to see. King Dmitri has no desire for war. He desires the goodwill and friendship of Equatoria. And America."

Constantine shouted, "Get to the point, you insufferable toad!"

"King Dmitri wants a peace treaty."

Senator Clark laughed. "I'll write terms on a bullet and you can take it back with you in your skull."

Constantine leaned forward angrily. "Are you insane? Some vampire dresses up its pet as a human and sends it to me? To ask for a peace treaty? A peace treaty with vampires? Would we make a treaty with a mad dog?"

"Perhaps if the dog was holding your daughter captive."

The chamber erupted. Many of the privy councilors shook their fists and shouted scorn. Clark drew his sword with a steely whisper, but Constantine was faster. The emperor bounded off the dais and grabbed up the ambassador by the jacket and neck.

Lord Kelvin raced up the endless aisle shouting, "Gentlemen, gentlemen, please!" as the emperor lifted the squealing envoy off the floor. Kelvin didn't dare lay hands on Constantine, so instead he grabbed the British ambassador. "Your Majesty, this is not proper! Please, I beg you!"

The emperor threw the little man down on the marble floor, where, fortunately, Lord Kelvin cushioned his fall. Constantine towered menacingly over the tangle of diplomats while Senator Clark stepped forward with his sword glinting red-hot in the gaslight.

The emperor's voice was a hoarse whisper. "Get this maggot out of our sight before we kill it."

"By which," Kelvin added hastily to the ambassador from underneath him, "His Imperial Majesty means that negotiations are concluded for today."

The envoy sat up slowly and disentangled himself from Kelvin. He said matter-of-factly, "You are making a mistake, Your Majesty. You should think of your daughter."

Lord Kelvin scrambled to his feet and blocked the furious Constantine, struggling to maintain his professional manner while laying hands on his emperor. "I suggest we adjourn until tomorrow, Sire. I will escort the ambassador to its quarters."

The emperor glared at the bloodman with chest heaving and fists clenched. "You're a filthy animal. They bred the human out of you!"

The little man straightened his mismatched suit and without looking up muttered, "I am as human as you, Your Majesty. We all are in the north. How could you know from here?"

Clark stiffened with anger, but Constantine raised a hand to still him. The emperor's furious breathing slackened, and his sunken, red eyes drifted over the little man before him. His brow knitted with rational thought for the first time in this incredible session.

"You're descended from humans," Constantine allowed in a strained voice. "We will pay you handsomely for any help you can render us. And you can stay here in Equatoria."

"I'm here to sign a peace treaty. There is nothing more I can do."

The emperor clenched his teeth and reached out an imploring hand that trembled from both shame and fear. "Please. Help us save my daughter."

The ambassador's eyes shone with the hint of tears. "I have a daughter too. And a son. And they are both in the hands of Prince Cesare. If I don't return with the peace treaty, they will be killed."

"There can be no treaty," Constantine said simply.

The man didn't react. There was no reaction suitable.

Lord Kelvin said quietly, "Your Majesty, I suggest we adjourn the council for today. Everyone needs time to reflect." He led the ambassador back down the aisle without waiting for a response. Lord Aden stepped from the ranks of the Privy Council and fell in beside the prime minister and the British ambassador. After they slipped out, the massive carved doors closed with an unsatisfying click that echoed through the shadowy chamber.

Constantine climbed wearily to his throne, where he collapsed with his face in his hands. The remaining Privy Councilors paid silent obeisance as they filed out.

Senator Clark sheathed his saber. "You should have let me kill it, Your Majesty. There's no point talking to that useless rag."

Constantine nodded sadly, but stayed silent.

"Don't worry. I'll get Adele back if I have to slaughter every vampire in Europe to do it." Clark began to ponder the outline of his attack with restrained glee. "A strike on Bruges will give them something to think about and let them know our intentions are serious."

Although the American frightened the emperor, Clark's intense confidence stemmed the old man's objections. At least the senator was doing *something*.

"Your Majesty, if I may." The words came from the shadows.

Both Constantine and Clark looked sharply into the corner. Even the imperial guards started. Mamoru stepped from the darkness wearing long silken robes with full sleeves and a lavish brocade pattern of cranes and bamboo in red and gold. He walked with a slow tigerish tread that betrayed strength and power.

Constantine relaxed. "Did we send for you?" He was genuinely unsure.

"No, Sire. I apologize for coming unbidden."

"You saw, then. What did you think?"

The samurai rested a hand on the hilt of his ornate katana. He rubbed his chin as he eyed Clark with frank openness and a faint smirk on his lips. Then he turned back to Constantine. "I admired your restraint in not killing the man. But I feel pity for the ambassador as well. We all have our duties."

Clark bristled. "Pity? For that toad? Who are you, sir, if I may ask?"

"I am Mamoru. I am Princess Adele's private tutor."

"Really, Your Majesty, I see no reason for a schoolteacher to be here."

Constantine was weary. "We value Mamoru's opinion. Or we wouldn't have him as Adele's tutor."

"But these are affairs of state and war."

The emperor said, "Mamoru led the Japanese assault on Kyoto to recover their imperial relics. He's familiar with both affairs of state and war. He chooses to teach."

"But still, he's—"

"Enough, Senator!" Constantine shouted, red-faced. Then he fell back into his chair with a narrow and impatient gaze, gnawing distract-edly on his knuckle, like a father exhausted by bickering children.

Mamoru offered, "Senator Clark, we have the same goal—the safe return of our beloved princess, Adele. And I believe I can help you."

Clark put one booted foot on the dais and smiled sarcastically, inviting Mamoru to continue.

The samurai priest made a slight bow. "I believe another unfocused assault by your forces will cost the princess her life."

"Do you now?" Clark retorted. "Well, I believe different. Those creatures know what would happen to them if they harmed Adele."

"More likely they do not care. If you attack, Senator, the princess will die. You must instead go directly into London and take her away. Quietly. Without pomp. If that is a possibility for you."

"Well, here's a lesson for you, schoolteacher," Clark scoffed. "London is a big place. Maybe you know where she is?"

"I do." Mamoru pulled a scroll from his sleeve. "And I have a map."

Clark threw up his hands in disgust over this foolishness.

Constantine sat up with a hungry gleam in his eye. "Mamoru, are you sure?"

"Yes, Your Majesty. My sources are excellent."

Constantine stepped down past the American and took the scroll. "The Tower of London?"

"Yes, Majesty. She is kept in these rooms."

Clark rolled his eyes. "How can we trust this? What are his sources?"

Constantine said, "If Mamoru says she's here, she's here. When did you get this?"

The samurai replied, "Only today it arrived by courier. The intelligence is barely days old."

The emperor smiled. "Magnificent! We'll have her back right out from under their noses. Thank you, Mamoru. Thank you."

Mamoru bowed deeply. "It is my honor to serve you and Princess Adele."

Constantine slapped the map against the senator's brass-buttoned chest. "Go. Go today. Take whatever you need."

Clark was nonplussed for the first time. He stammered, "Your Majesty, I need more than this scrap of paper to commit my boys to a mission so deep inside vampire territory. I don't know this Jap from Adam."

Constantine glared at the American. "We could easily send our own troops. But we're giving you the honor of rescuing our daughter, the future empress and your future wife. Either go or don't. That is your judgment as a commander. But if you refuse, sir, you'll see the Second Coming before your wedding."

"I have a treaty with Equatoria."

"You are looking at Equatoria." Constantine closed his eyes for a few seconds as his aggression melted. He reached up and dragged the heavy crown from his head, standing bareheaded with his wispy hair askew and sweat-tipped. "And a father. Son, you can trust Mamoru's intelligence as you would the sunrise. So, I pray you, give me your answer. Will you help me?"

Clark studied the emperor, who was now just an old man worn down by the loss of his daughter. No man could look into that worried face, the eyes filled with terror and faint hope, and not be moved. The senator was not made of stone, he reflected on himself. This was just a man asking another man for help. Plus, to have the greatest ruler in the world beg for his help was more than Clark could've hoped. If he brought Adele back from London, there was nothing he could not ask of the Equatorian court.

Senator Clark had long known, for a certainty, that he was the only man who could accomplish the miracle of destroying the vampirs. To do so, he had agreed to marry a woman for whom he cared nothing. He needed to control the power of Equatoria to forge a war machine sufficient to aid him in liberating mankind. It was a terrible burden, but he bore it selflessly.

The American slapped the emperor on the shoulder. "Oh, never fear! I'll go, by God. I'll go. And I'll bring her back, if she's there. And if she isn't, I'll be back." He grinned and winked at Mamoru. "I'll be back to see you, schoolteacher."

CHAPTER 15

"COME WITH ME, if you please."

Gareth was not asking, despite his pleasant formality. For the first time, he was insisting. Still, unlike his brother, he did not brandish his claws or make a hint of violence toward Adele, but the princess had little doubt Gareth would seize her and take her if she refused to go. For a perverse moment, she contemplated forcing him to follow through on his implied threat. If she made everything difficult, Gareth would enforce his demands only when it was most important and merited the exertion. However, his manner seemed to pose no danger for her. And she needed to choose her battles carefully.

Adele went to gather her cloak, although it was not cold outside. The sun was bright and the day warm. She felt hints of spring even through the constant aura of death. Perhaps she was growing accustomed to that aura now. She hardly smelled the decay.

As she took the cloak from a hook, she quickly seized one of the razor-sharp stone blades she had chiseled and slipped it into her blouse. With her cloak around her shoulders, she charged past the waiting Gareth. The vampire caught up with her at the door and led the way across the yard, which was now carpeted with lovely yellow flowers. A few daffodils and crocuses waved in the shadows of the walls. One of the sentries lifted into the air and drifted away on the spring breeze.

Gareth strode out the dilapidated main gate and into the city. Adele followed his black frock coat as his long legs ate up the cobblestone streets and muddy lanes. Occasionally, he turned to check on her, but she was always a few steps behind, maintaining a look of bland detachment although she was busy studying the street layout. Adele caught sight of a dark shape as it swooped between crumbling buildings and caught hold of a rooftop. It was Flay.

Gareth saw the lurking war chief too. A small chuckle escaped the prince as he said over his shoulder, "Cesare's afraid you might escape from me."

Adele felt the blade resting hard against her stomach. "Hilarious."

Gareth laughed again and openly stared up at Flay as they passed beneath the vampire's perch. Several more times over the course of the silent stroll Flay appeared outlined against the bright blue sky like a gargoyle. Eventually, Gareth and Adele passed between two wrought iron gates and stood before a large domed building with a great colonnaded portico.

Gareth asked, "Do you recognize this place?"

"Should I?" Adele replied sharply.

"It's the British Museum. My home in London."

"Hmm. I imagine it is more pleasant than the crypt or hole in the ground where you lived before."

Gareth smirked at her retort with real amusement, his angular face softening.

The thought of a vampire making its nest in this great museum chilled Adele. This was a place that had been dedicated to preserving the valuable past and learning from it, a uniquely human activity that the vampires could never understand.

She asked, "Do you intend to hold me here?"

"You're welcome to stay here," Gareth replied very quickly, then added, "But you're also free to keep your rooms in the Tower. Come."

Adele followed his tall, straight back along the gravel walk. Flay drifted high overhead as Gareth pushed open the massive bronze door, stepped aside for Adele to enter, and then closed the door behind them.

His voice echoed in the empty space. "Don't worry about Flay. She won't dare enter. To violate my rights would mean her death. Not even Cesare could save her."

Gareth stretched out his arms in a shaft of sunlight. He looked around the vast entryway with something like pride. "Come, walk with me. I have questions."

Adele stood rooted to the floor. Was this it? Would he begin the interrogation proper now?

Gareth pointed to his right, like a tour guide. "The books were through there once. Rooms full of them. Quite amazing. I didn't realize you had created so many." The vampire seemed apologetic suddenly. "They are gone now, I fear."

"Yes, I know. Your kind destroyed them all."

"We did." He nodded gravely. "But not completely. Many of them were used later by humans for fires. Still, no matter. There are other things I want to show you, and ask you about."

"I have no intention of telling you anything. Ask your brother; I'm capable of prodigious silence."

The vampire looked disappointed, then brightened. "And I told you I have no interest in the affairs of your state. Or your spies. Or the numbers of your ships or soldiers."

Footfalls rang in the emptiness as Adele followed Gareth through dim chaotic galleries. She stepped carefully through the detritus of ancient societies, as well as the remnants of furniture and fixtures from the time of the Great Killing. When their path was blocked by toppled and smashed statuary, Gareth reached back to assist her, but she ignored his out-stretched hand. He sighed softly but respected her independence.

Great mute heads and muscled arms and torsos of marble lay useless all around them. From cracked wooden panels and terra-cotta vessels stared faces of peoples from distant lands, many now part of Equatoria, and Adele's future subjects. There were dusty clumps of shredded tapes-tries and portraits. Bronze helmets and weapons stood in piles. The princess noted several greening daggers that would serve her, but she didn't dare stop. They paused before a great winged lion, human-headed, with a long curly beard.

"Magnificent." Gareth ran his hand slowly along its massive stone flank. "But why make such a thing? I understand making tools and weapons. There is a purpose in it. But this? It must've taken enormous effort. To what end?"

Adele didn't answer. Was he actually interested in human culture? He seemed sincere, and it was difficult for her to believe a vampire could pretend so well. It just wasn't in them. It would be like a cat feigning interest in intricate needlework techniques for the ultimate goal of getting its paws on the ball of yarn.

Gareth didn't seem disturbed by her silence. The prince had too many questions to worry about one. He quickly cut through another doorway with Adele in his wake. As they stepped around an enormous stone head facedown on the floor, Gareth pointed up at a colossal Egyptian figure of a man, a red granite trunk and head, partially sheared off.

"There," he said. "See? *That* is extraordinary. Why make it so large?"

Adele recognized the monument instantly. An ancient pharaoh of her homeland, wasted here in London. It had no power in this place. It should be standing in Victoria Palace in Alexandria. After all, her father was the heir to the pharaohs. As was she.

Gareth asked, "What was his name? Do you know?"

"Ramses." Adele couldn't help herself. There was a certain amount of family pride involved. "He was the greatest ruler of his time. One of the greatest of all time. The king of Egypt."

"Ramses was from Egypt," Gareth mused. "Why is his statue here? Did the British hold him in esteem? Did he rule here too?"

"No. He is long dead. When Ramses ruled, Britain was peopled with savages. Like now. But when the British were civilized, they found the statue in Egypt and brought it here. All this material was brought here by Englishmen with an interest in mankind."

"The Egyptians then had become savages?"

Adele didn't answer. She stared at the immortal statue. Then she noticed on the stone pedestal, in faded red letters, perhaps even scrawled in blood many years ago, were the words "Look on my works, ye mighty, and despair." How odd. How sad. And true.

"How old are you?" Adele suddenly asked Gareth.

"What?"

"How old are you? Do vampires live forever?" She started to touch the granite base of the great pharaoh, but hesitated. "Were you alive when he was alive?"

"Of course not. This stature is three thousand years old. There are no vampires alive from his time."

"How can you possibly know how old it is?" Adele's eye fell upon a mildewing label posted on the stone pedestal, with the only legible information being a date listed for the colossus. "You can read!"

Gareth replied defensively. "We know more about your history than you suspect. We know more about you than you do about us. Humans think that vampires are their own dead, risen to life. It's grotesquely vain."

"Don't change the subject," Adele retorted. "Only ignorant people believe that fairy tale about the undead. We know what you are. Parasites. And I know your kind couldn't care less about human culture or history. Your brother, Cesare, made that clear. He wouldn't know Sulayman the Magnificent or Julius Caesar if he fed off them. But you're different, aren't you? You *can* read even though your kind holds reading and writing in great disdain. Cesare said so."

"Perhaps you shouldn't believe everything Cesare says."

Adele raised a bemused eyebrow. "I wonder what your brother would think if he knew the heir to the clan could read human writing? That doesn't sound like proper behavior for a king of vampires."

Gareth stared at her for the first time with a look that scared her. Then he turned away, the long hem of his frock coat snapping with the movement. He strode off through collapsed funerary accoutrements, heels clicking loudly in the silence. Adele followed as the prince kicked his way through mummies without care.

"Wait!" Adele called out. "I won't use it against you."

Gareth kept walking.

"Listen to me." She grabbed his arm. "Didn't you bring me here to talk?"

Gareth spun around in a blur, his face angry at first, but quickly subsiding to mere annoyance. "Very well. You're right. I can read some of your languages. I do have an interest in your culture. And yes, there may be very few of my people who share my interest. Well, none most likely. We hold writing in disdain. As we do all things your kind has made. Art. Agriculture. Cities. Weapons. They're all nothing to us."

"You mean like those clothes you wear?"

Gareth heard the sarcastic edge to her question. "We use your clothes because your skin is too fragile to wear." Despite the savage words, his tone was melancholy. He knelt and dug into a pile of detritus, lifting a tiny figurine made of translucent alabaster. Gareth rolled the lustrous white object along the tips of his long fingers with a tenderness that surprised Adele.

He said, "We make nothing. We create nothing." He pushed his other hand deep into a mound of shattered clay fragments. "And we leave nothing behind."

The vampire stood and tossed the figurine back onto the waste pile. "We *are* parasites. Which is fortunate for you. It would have taken little effort to make your kind extinct. But we need you to survive."

"Yes. But we don't need you."

Gareth inclined his head graciously. "Among our greater failings, vampires are notoriously slow to appreciate irony. We have grown lazy and decadent, with no desire to go back to living in crypts and holes in the ground. We like the houses and the clothes. Not enough to make them, of course, but enough to want slaves who will make them. And we like having meals that don't require hunting or danger. It seems that we aren't even good parasites anymore."

"So *you* don't care about the survival of your kind?" Adele's voice was incredulous, perhaps slightly sarcastic.

The prince wiped dust from his hands. "I think only the valuable should survive. It remains to be seen where my kind falls. I'll take you back."

Adele watched his lonely figure as it disappeared among the toppled magnificence of ancient humanity. Then she stooped to recover the precious figurine. It was a washabti. In ancient times they were placed in tombs to be vessels where the wandering souls of the dead could rest. She blew the dust off its lustrous surface and followed Gareth.

CHAPTER 16

ESARE STARED ANGRILY as Flay concluded her report. The
vampire prince let his twitching meal slide to the filthy floor of
the empty House of Commons. His appetite was gone. Feeding meant
little to him these days. Merely sustenance. He remembered the dark
days hunting humans in forests and sleeping in catacombs, but those
days were gone, and it was his duty to see they never returned.

Cesare asked, "How long were they closeted together in that
museum tomb of his?"

"Not long," Flay replied. "An hour at most. Then he led her back to
the Tower."

Cesare wiped blood off his face and absently licked his hands. The man-
shaped lump at his feet fumbled feebly at his throat in a vain attempt to
stanch the flow of blood. His pitiful moan attracted Cesare, who indicated
the wounded man to his war chief with a brief nod of invitation.

Flay smiled a polite decline, but when Cesare looked away she shot
him a fierce glare. As if she would deign to feed after him. It took a conscious effort to remove the disdain from her face, but when Cesare
looked up she again appeared the ever-patient retainer awaiting orders.

Cesare was bare-chested; he often removed his coat and shirt while
feeding. He claimed it reminded him of the old wild nakedness of pre-

Conquest times, but Flay suspected it was because he didn't want to stain his clothing.

Cesare put on his white shirt and pulled suspenders over his shoulders. Flay held out a long grey morning coat for him to slip into. He tugged at his cuffs and inspected his dark trousers for blood spots. "I'm going to have King Dmitri call the clan."

"What? But you didn't want the clan lords interfering with your plans."

"Plans change." Cesare buffed his shoes on his dying dinner and muttered angrily to himself, "What is wrong with that Clark? Doesn't he think I would kill her? Doesn't he know who I am?"

Flay watched Cesare's face. The young prince was obviously annoyed by the situation, but there was something more. Cesare had assumed his fearful reputation would terrify the humans into inaction. Senator Clark's attack had been unexpected. For the first time, Cesare had lost the initiative, and he seemed mired in doubt.

The prince continued, "That attack on Bordeaux is meaningless, just a symbol for the people at home. Clark wouldn't dare start a major offensive. Even he isn't that idiotic. I will certainly kill her!"

The war chief didn't respond. She was occupied watching Cesare fidget. The careless movements made him seem small and worried. Then a thought occurred to Flay—a thought that astonished her. Cesare was afraid of Clark. The senator was an unpredictable human.

Like Greyfriar, Flay thought sourly.

But no, it wasn't the same. Flay dreamed of destroying Greyfriar with her own hands. Cesare seemed to want to avoid fighting Clark. He would rather isolate the human than kill him. Clearly, the prince did not relish the idea of coming to grips with the great vampire killer.

Flay sensed a gnawing emptiness in her stomach where her duty used to burn. Cesare had never been her ideal as a male, but at least he had seemed powerful and determined.

Until now.

She thought back to the Great Killing. She remembered seeing Gareth in a frenzy, driving a regiment of human soldiers before him through the gory snows of the Great Glen. Magnificent. Not a wasted move, not a lost opportunity. He was a machine of blood and claw. Flay had dreamed of being Gareth's war chief.

Those had been heady days for the clan. Dmitri still had some sense and was the most respected king in Europe. The future of the British clan had seemed bright. Dmitri had two sons who were both capable in their own way. Gareth had an aura of power and superiority. When the Great Killing began, he threw himself into battle in his father's name and showed his mettle with violence, demonstrating that he was in line to be the next great king. Cesare, on the other hand, was a chilling manipulator and a political strategist who would make a perfect advisor to his brother. Over the last century, though, civilization had drained the soul of the clan, of all the clans, and Dmitri had spiraled into senility. The two brothers, who had never been close, gave up any hope of coexistence. Surprisingly, it was Gareth who abdicated his natural role as leader, wandering into his solitary wasteland of Scotland, barely deigning to attend clan gatherings unless he was compelled to do so. Cesare filled the void and became the king's right hand, which served Flay well, as Cesare's war chief. The younger prince was cunning and completely ruthless. He could be a skillful king, but he was no Gareth.

Cesare's voice snapped her back. "And why would Gareth choose this moment to show his miserable face in London?" It was almost as if he knew she was thinking of someone else.

Flay found herself secretly enjoying Cesare's discomfort as she reclined on one of the long benches lining the Commons. The prince settled into a thronelike chair at the end of the chamber and crossed his outstretched legs at the ankles. Several bloodmen dragged his bleeding meal from the chamber as the vampire drummed his claws on the chair. He began to pontificate, as he always did, thinking of himself as the brooding lone genius, but in fact he found the sound of his voice intoxicating, no matter which language.

"If my brother had just stayed away, I could've maneuvered the king into naming me heir. Father listens to me. And the lords fear me. I can work the clan to my advantage. I had the princess to my credit and the attack on Bordeaux to panic them, but now Gareth is here. The king and the old lords are too spineless to shove my brother aside while he is looking at them. They pretend to respect tradition." Cesare paused, his mind flicking through images of the outsider Gareth among the bloody old clan lords. It was a jarring picture, but one he could twist to his advantage. His brother had no proficiency in politics, and that would be his undoing. Then a long, toothy grin spread slowly across Cesare's face.

"If I allow Gareth to reveal himself to be the coward and failure he is, the elders will all see that he couldn't be their king, and the only choice is me." Cesare looked at Flay and laughed. He pounded his hands down on the chair arms with a thud that echoed through the chamber. "Think of it! Played properly, I can destroy a century of progress by the humans, throwing them back so far it will be another century or more before they dare threaten us again. I will be the savior of our kind. I could soon lead every major clan in the world." He rubbed his hands together in expectation and leapt off the dais, settling to the tiled floor with feather lightness. He was almost giddy. "How amazing! It's an absolute boon that Gareth bumbled in here. This is the beginning of the end for him. And the beginning of a new era for me. For us, Flay. Bring my packs to order and lay them close by. I want the city firmly in my hands when the clan gathers and I start the war chant."

As the prince passed, he reached out and stroked Flay's cheek. She flinched with surprise, but managed an uncomfortable smile.

Cesare held her eyes with his. "Come. I'm off to tell the king what to do. Believe it or not, Flay, it's possible to be too cunning. There are times when killing is the only thing for it."

Flay smiled, but this time it was real. She believed much the same thing.

———✦———

After Gareth left Adele alone in the Tower, she was startled by a sound from the corner of her room. Her hand went for the stone blade, but she saw Selkirk detach himself from the shadows and step forward. He held a finger to his lips and waited, giving Gareth time to withdraw.

After a moment, he dropped to one knee and bowed his head. "Your Highness."

Adele's whisper was barely audible. "Can I speak?"

"Quietly, if you please."

"How do you do that? Walk around in broad daylight without fear!"

Selkirk's blue eyes sparkled. "I assure you it's not without fear. But as long as I stay near a ley line, I can shield myself from them. Of course, it isn't foolproof. They could still tumble into me and I'd be dinner."

"Ley line?" Memories of some of Mamoru's more eclectic lectures in geology and geomancy came back to Adele.

"Yes. They are lines of power that run along the surface of the Earth. Dragon spines, they're sometimes called in the Orient. They're troublesome to vampires; they interfere with the creatures' senses for reasons we don't quite understand."

Adele pointed at the odd astrolabe on his belt. "Does that instrument manipulate the power of these ley lines? Is that how you move safely?"

"No." Selkirk paused. He looked hesitant. "I'm not at liberty to say more. I'm sorry, Your Highness."

"Are you Equatorian?"

"Yes, Highness. I was born in Aswan. Educated in Alexandria and Siwa."

"Then I could command you to answer my questions."

The man glanced at the ground, embarrassed. "I cannot. I'm sorry, Highness. But I can tell you that I sent word of your location to Alexandria. It should be in Mamoru's hands, and no doubt the emperor's by now. A rescue mission is on its way. Do you have your talisman?"

Adele touched her neck where the crystal pendant used to hang. "No. The vampires took it."

Selkirk tried to suppress a look of concern. "I wish I had the power to fashion a replacement for you, but I suspect you won't be here much longer in any case."

Adele took a deep anxious breath at the thought of home. She smelled the lemon tree in the courtyard outside her antechamber in Victoria Palace.

"Why can't I go with you right now?" Adele asked anxiously. "Can you hide me from the vampires too?"

"No. That's impossible, Your Highness. I can cloud my presence from vampires, but only with great difficulty. But I couldn't hide you at all. I assure you, if it was possible, Mamoru wouldn't have suffered you spend one extra minute in this place. But no, it's best to wait for a proper rescue. In this case, trust your army to get you out."

Adele smiled to assuage the man's discomfort. Selkirk's belief that she would soon be rescued buoyed her feelings. Adele realized with delight that apparently Cesare was right to be concerned about "spies" in his country. The power to hide in plain sight would be an invaluable weapon in the coming war.

Selkirk said, "Your Highness, I must go. I don't dare remain in one spot for long. It becomes more likely they will detect me with each second. Hopefully you will be rescued before I see you again."

"Thank you, sir, for your help." Adele took Selkirk's hand, causing him to start with surprise. "If you are ever in Alexandria, I hope you will call on me. You will be welcome."

The man lowered his head with gratitude and slipped quietly from the room.

—⟨ঞ⟩—

When Cesare reached the throne room, he found the king already in conference—with Prince Gareth. Flay made a soft trill of surprise as Cesare shook himself slightly, recovered his wits, stepped over several bloated footmen sleeping by the door, and strode into the vast throne room.

King Dmitri squinted toward the approaching blur. Gareth sat back slowly and crossed his legs, posed in the chair next to the throne, the chair usually occupied by Cesare. The king demanded who it was that neared, and the elder prince murmured to him.

"Greetings, Majesty." Cesare bowed to his father and then swept an arm low to the floor in Gareth's direction. "And Prince Gareth. At least I assume that is who you are, since I've so rarely seen you here. What a delightful surprise. Father, I have something to discuss with you."

The king merely sat blinking furiously at Cesare.

Cesare said to Gareth, "Would you excuse us?"

Gareth didn't move. "Speak. There should be no secrets between brothers in times of trouble."

"You couldn't be troubled to appear at court for nearly a century. Father, we haven't time to explain details of state to him. Why should we waste our time when he will simply return to Edinburgh when it suits his whim?"

Gareth peaked his fingers at his chin. "I'm here, Cesare. I've taken my rightful place at father's right hand. I am the heir, and have been since before you were born." The elder prince smiled. "If you have something to say, say it."

"Father?" Cesare extended his hand at Gareth. "This is ludicrous."

"Stop this!" Dmitri shook his head irritably. "You are brothers. The clan depends on both of you. I don't have time to create more to replace you, although I would if I could. You both exhaust me."

Gareth chuckled comfortably at the old king's wit. Cesare stared, annoyed as much by his father's sudden ability to jest at his expense as by Gareth's presence.

Dmitri snapped, "What do you want, Cesare? Speak!"

"Very well." The younger prince inclined his head passively. "I believe you should gather the clan."

Gareth stirred while trying to maintain an aloof calm. Cesare noted the consternation with mute pleasure.

The king said, "But didn't you recommend against calling the clan just the other day?"

Cesare tried to hide his surprise that his father could remember back that far. This burst of reason by the king was distressing. Without missing a beat, he replied, "The situation has changed, Your Majesty. You were correct when you suggested gathering the clan. I wasn't wise enough to see as far as you. I now believe, as you do, that war is imminent and we must gather the clan to prepare."

King Dmitri sat up with alarm. "War imminent?" He looked at Gareth with eyes that were now cloudy with confusion. "Why was I not told?"

"Because it isn't true, Sire," Gareth said slowly. "Cesare is panicking. He claimed his entire reason for capturing the Equatorian princess was to forestall war. Surely he won't admit that his plan was so far off the mark?"

Bristling but keeping his voice even, Cesare said, "I only admit underestimating the viciousness of the humans. The Equatorians apparently don't care that we have their princess. They attacked Bordeaux, and they continue to gather their forces."

Gareth asked, "But what about the ambassador you sent to Alexandria? We should wait to see if there is any movement toward a peace treaty."

"No," Cesare retorted. "The ambassador was a failure. Flay's spies report that he was murdered by the Equatorians and his head displayed to the mob." The young prince turned to his war chief for confirmation.

Flay added quietly, "As Prince Cesare says."

Her face was stern, but her eyes flicked briefly to Gareth's, and he knew she was lying. Anything to support her master.

Cesare continued, "Equatoria's goal is clear. They want us all dead. There is no doubt about that. Their threat to attack us if we don't release their princess is unambiguous." He regarded Gareth. "Do you deny that?"

Gareth replied in a matter-of-fact tone, "Then perhaps we should release the princess. That will remove their excuse for aggression."

The younger prince scowled. "As if they need an *excuse*. How extraordinarily naïve of you, Gareth. Why don't we just give them London in the bargain? Why don't we just kill ourselves to save them the trouble of doing it? I won't give them the princess because I was right to take her. She was in our territory! I am trying to save our kind. Did you learn nothing from the Great Killing? When we have the chance to crush them, we must!"

Gareth stirred uncomfortably in his seat, but said nothing more. He avoided the triumphant glare of his brother. His suggestion to release Adele, although glib, was a terrible misstep and made him look weak. To argue further, or to seek to set the record straight on the Great Killing, was pointless and would merely put him deeper under his hawkish brother's thumb.

The king now leaned toward Cesare, body language making it clear that he had slipped back into his comfortable place following his younger son, as he always did. Cesare sighed with relief now that his father's moment of lucidity had passed.

"Just so," Cesare said with obvious contempt for his brother, then regarded the king with a renewed aura of a wise man. "The Equatorians are coming. Would you try to prepare for war while their ships are bombing us? We must ready the clan, as you wisely suggested in council. As king, you can do no less. Would you have your people taken unaware?"

"No," King Dmitri muttered. "No. I am their king. I must act, yes?"

"I will see to it, Majesty," Cesare replied. "I will call on the lords, and they will gather here in two days. I will see to everything."

"Yes." The king was relieved to have the burden of decision taken from him. He reached out with a feeble hand and patted Gareth on the knee. "Yes, thank you, Cesare. You're a good son."

Gareth felt the gnarled old claw stroking the wrong son. He would've liked to take comfort in his father's touch, but he felt only rage at the king's impotence. Cesare bowed with a smile and withdrew.

The older prince glanced up at his father, who was now hunched forward on the throne, chin trembling and hands shaking. Gareth shook his head angrily. The king was lost again somewhere in eight hundred years of memory that sprouted brambles to prick and trap what was left of his old mind. Gareth fought back bitterness for the wizened, drooling figure as he recalled the many years at his father's side in cool forests and frosty glens, listening to ancient tales of battling rival clans. His father had taught him to hunt human prey. The pleasure of it was to savor each kill, not wallow in countless slaughters. Blindly destroying the source of your nourishment just to demonstrate superiority was prideful insanity. King Dmitri had seemed the most noble and fierce and wisest father imaginable, and Gareth had once wanted to be just like him.

However, now old Dmitri was nothing more than a regal skin that Cesare put on to govern a clan of gluttons. Soon they would all come to London and, despite the fact that Gareth was heir, Cesare would rule the gathering. If Cesare wanted war, he'd have war.

Gareth rose and paid obeisance before the cloudy eyes of the king. Perhaps he should have stayed at court the past century, if only to protect his father from Cesare. But it was too late for those thoughts now. Gareth left the palace to prepare for what was coming.

CHAPTER 17

ADELE EXERCISED IN the yard of the Tower, where flowers pushed up around the rubble. Her arms weaved a slow pattern around her body while she breathed deliberately and shifted from one foot to the other. She brought her hands together and then pushed them apart. Mamoru had taught her a wide variety of kata, for martial arts and fitness and meditation. It gave the young woman great satisfaction to hone her killing skills under the unsuspecting eyes of her watchers. She wondered what Greyfriar would think of her training routine. Adele thought about the excitement of dueling him, crossing blades with that master swordsman and basking in his praise for her style. He could teach her more practical fighting skills than Mamoru had ever attempted.

Mamoru. When Adele thought of him, she was increasingly confused. She respected her mentor, even loved him in a way, but he was withdrawn by nature and she knew very little about him. There was only a certain level of connection they could ever make, separated as they were by culture and position. She had had no idea Mamoru had a secret network of mysterious geomancers such as Selkirk. Was her father aware? Adele intended to know more about geomancy and this ability to cloud the minds of vampires once she returned home.

She surprised herself by how matter-of-factly she entertained the notion of freedom now. The possibility had seemed so distant a few days ago that she had refused to allow it into her mind because it might soften her mad resolve to assassinate the clan royal family. But now she knew she had to return home. Sacrificing her life for the pipe dream of killing King Dmitri and his dreadful brood was ridiculous. With Simon gone, Adele was now sole heir to Constantine II. With the Reconquest imminent, this was no time for a succession crisis in Equatoria.

Out of the corner of her eye, Adele saw her watchers suddenly turn to the north. She had known them to perch motionless for hours, but today they had seemed agitated, constantly craning their necks and peering off into the distance. Now the watchers glanced briefly at her and seemed to consult with one another before lifting into the orange sky to join a growing flock of black figures gathering over the city.

The princess discerned weird background noises that she realized she had been hearing, but ignoring, for hours. Sounds of celebration mixed with screaming, like the fantastic sound of a distant unwholesome festival. Adele hastily concluded her exercise. The sun was sinking and the air cooling, and she wanted to find the fireside. As she turned toward the doorway to her prison, several vampires dipped sharply from the crowd overhead.

Three horrible figures surrounded her—two males and a female— thin and dirty, clad in filthy rags, with claws extended. They hissed to one another, which Adele understood. They were apparently strangers to London and hungry from traveling, and pleased with themselves for happening on a bit of unprotected food—meaning Adele. They decided to celebrate their trip to the big city by sharing her.

Adele launched herself at the larger male and slammed the palm of her hand into his nose. The creature roared in shock and fell like a sack of wet laundry. The other two stared in surprise. Adele took the female by the back of the head and gouged her eyes with thumb and forefinger. The princess felt pain in her shoulder and was pulled backward into a flurry of nails and teeth, which tore her clothes and skin with mercury-fast strikes. Adele kicked out at the knee of the vampire attacking her. She heard a solid crack, and the male glanced down at his leg, now bent backward like a bird's, flailed at the air for support, and dropped. The blinded female sniffed and felt the air with her clawlike hands. Adele looked around for some weapon to dispatch this trio of horrible cripples.

A tall, dark figure settled to the ground in front of the young princess. She drew up her fists in desperation, ignoring a warm droplet of blood drizzling down her cheek. Then she realized the looming figure was Gareth, and for a mad instant she was grateful for his presence. His face was a mask of anger, but it wasn't directed at her. He spat a few harsh sounds at the three vampires in which he identified himself and condemned them to death.

The three froze with looks on their faces like naughty children caught in a prank. They attempted to flee, climbing unsteadily to their feet and preparing to rise into the air. But Gareth was on them, and in less time than it had taken him to pronounce their deaths, they lay dead in the grass. The large male was decapitated, his head torn from his shoulders. The female and smaller male both had their entrails steaming in the cool early evening.

Gareth briefly inspected the eviscerated intruders, as if coolly comparing them to plates in an anatomy book. Barely winded, he then scanned Adele up and down. His penetrating azure gaze gave her chills. "Are you hurt?"

"No. Who were they?" The sight of the prince amazed Adele. He was so nattily attired in black mourning dress with shined leather shoes, but dripping wet and red. She was both horrified and thrilled by the ease with which Gareth had slaughtered those vampires, as well as by the satisfaction he had seemed to take in it. His attack had been swift and brutal, yet almost elegant.

Gareth replied, "They're bumpkins. They wanted a meal and didn't know you were under my protection. They know it now." He smiled haughtily. "The dead can never infringe on your rights. That's a bit of vampire politics."

Did he just make a witticism? Adele wondered, eyes wide.

The vampire extended his arm toward the door to her rooms. "Collect your things and come with me to the museum. For your own protection."

"Why?"

Gareth looked up into the darkening sky. A loathsome multitude swirled in the air like black snowflakes caught in the wind currents. Writhing fliers touched and intertwined in disgusting congress, then rejoined the mindless mass. Adele shivered in horror and said a prayer.

"The clan is gathering," Gareth said.

———⟨∿∿⟩———

Gareth watched Adele as she went about arranging her new quarters at the museum. She had not noticed his arrival, which pleased him because she was uniquely attuned to the threat from vampires. She was straightening a few Egyptian objects she had rescued from the rubble, including a small bust of Ramses. Gareth was struck by the juxtaposition of the timeless face of a king and the fragile life of the future empress. He suddenly understood the value of such objects. One day there would be statues of Empress Adele that humans generations from now would see. They would know something of her from the mute stone. Part of her would transcend time, perhaps even long after Gareth was dust.

Humans lived a short time compared to vampires, but *humanity* remained immortal. Vampires would never understand that. And it would be their downfall. Humans swoon and falter, they often died off in great swathes—Gareth remembered the days of plague when the vampires took advantage and killed many thousands across Europe—but the vampires' wave crashed and slid away, as it always did, and the humans recovered. As they always did.

The Great Killing a century and a half ago was more than just another wave. The humans had been uniquely vulnerable—losing the magic of faith but not yet masters of steam and steel. In the ensuing century, the humans had made their choice to embrace technology. Rumors from the frontiers spoke of new weapons—gas that blinded, cannons that deafened, and guns that spewed bullets at great rates—which would allow a single soldier to kill many vampires, no matter their speed. Human armies everywhere were showing greater skill in fighting vampires and, even more significant, the petrifying fear that had served the vampires so well during the Great Killing was diminishing with familiarity.

Even shut away in his refuge, Gareth could hear the sound of riot. London was alive with celebration. Thousands of humans had been driven into the city to feed the gathering revelers. He imagined the floors of the palace would be slick with coagulating blood by now and his father likely would be bloated and incoherent, as he would stay for the remainder of the gathering. Cesare, on the other hand, would be the ever-alert stand-in for the king. Gareth intended to pass the festivities closeted here in his museum. He refused to lend his presence to the monstrosities occurring across the city.

Gareth was comforted by the thought of Adele making a home here with him. Despite a myriad of choices for lodging in the vast building, she had chosen a small plain room and surrounded herself with a few items, perhaps because they reminded her of home. She had appeared comfortable and appreciative, even chatting in what seemed to be an unguarded fashion for the first time while they shifted the Macedonian refuse into the corridor.

Now Gareth watched with fascination as Adele made some sort of tea with herbs she had found around the grounds of the museum. Her hands astonished him. Her skin was so much darker than his alabaster flesh. And she used her fingers so effortlessly for intricate tasks. He was mesmerized by their gentle dance as she nimbly plucked small leaves from the stems. The scent of the herb clung to her fingertips, which were smeared with its oil, mixing with her normal scent to create a tangy, almost spicy aroma. He breathed in the heady fragrance.

Adele heard Gareth inhale deeply and said without starting, "It's mint. I find it soothing."

He took that for an invitation and stepped into the room to stand beside her. "So much preparation."

She scoffed. "All it takes is some leaves and a little hot water. Not much work at all. It's not as if I'm cooking a banquet. But I suppose it looks like far too much labor for a vampire."

Water boiled in a bronze helmet, but his gaze slipped again to her hands as she readied a small cup. They were so gentle handling a piece of porcelain, but he had seen her use those same hands to dispatch many a vampire.

"How did you manage to disable the three vampires who attacked you in the Tower yard, without a weapon?" The question seemed simple enough. But Adele merely shrugged and smiled at him. Then she settled back onto her mat with her cup of hot herb water. The princess wasn't going to answer. Gareth knew there would be no further conversation. He could watch her all he liked, but she was intent on drinking her tea.

In France, the princess had possessed a softness—perhaps the shock from the attack and her brother's death had caused her to need Greyfriar for sanity. That was gone now; she was an empress now. Distant. Aloof. Mysterious. Commanding. Even her scent was different. While with Greyfriar, she had smelled sweet, although tinged with fear. The undertone of fear was still present, but the dominant scent was spicy and harsh and defiant. It was a scent he rarely got from humans in vampire territory, and he had only smelled it this strong in very few humans anywhere. It was intoxicating.

If Gareth hadn't seen the frightened girl in France from behind his mask, he would never have suspected this princess was ever anything other than her imperious self. It made her more appealing. She had her own mask, it seemed. He longed to see that delicate other side of her just once more.

He slipped away to the ground floor and the gallery that led to the large chamber with the huge statue of Ramses, Adele's ancestor. Odd that Gareth had wound up wandering here. He was thrilled at the prospect of spending time with Adele during the clan gathering. The festivities would last for days and consist of endless hours of blood-drunk chest thumping and threats against the humans. The lords would swear fealty to Dmitri and promise to come whenever he called, but when the king's herds ran dry, the bloated guests would totter into the sky and depart. During the gathering, Gareth and Adele could wander through his museum home at their leisure. The lonely Prince of Edinburgh now had someone to share it with.

However, as much as it pained him, Gareth would then take advantage of the stuporous, sluggish days after the gathering to spirit Adele out of London and back to the Continent. He would slip her into the hands of the human underground that he knew as Greyfriar, and they would ensure she made her way safely home. Then he would return to Edinburgh and renew his efforts against Cesare and his peoples' blind savagery.

The sound of a bird flitting in the rafters drew his attention. He immediately sensed coldness seeping down from above, and smelled stale blood in the air. Something moved on the granite shoulders of Great Ramses, writhed around the massive head, and slid into the dim light filtering through the broken windows.

Flay.

Gareth lightened and pushed off, silently floating up into the air. He settled onto Ramses' crumbling other shoulder, gripping the stone with the talons of his left hand while with his right he seized the surprised Flay by the throat.

"How dare you," he hissed at her. "Did Cesare send you? I could kill you, if I wished."

The war chief looked down in obeisance. She wasn't here to attack, or she would have struck before he saw her. She had given her life to Gareth in the instant she allowed him to grab her, but she knew full well that the moment he might have slain her out of instinct had passed. Unlike most of their kind, Prince Gareth rarely acted out of instinct.

For his part, Gareth had no wish to fight Flay. While he had no doubt he could kill Cesare in a fair fight, if Cesare ever engaged in such a thing, Flay was another matter. Every day of her long life she had been a warrior; she did nothing else and cared for nothing else. He had matched her well in France, but Flay had been interested only in capturing Adele, not in drawing out a fight with Greyfriar. She normally would not have suffered Gareth to seize her without striking back, prince or not. So clearly she had a purpose coming here.

Gareth loosened his grip. "Talk."

"I am not here from Cesare. I am here for you. You must move now if you wish to stop him."

Gareth stared at her. He tried to decipher what her message meant. What was his brother trying to trick him into doing?

Flay saw the dark prince pondering and insisted, "This is not a trap.

I risked my life coming here. You could've killed me. Or you can leave me to Cesare's revenge should you refuse my offer. If you don't move now, he will take control of the clan. If you ask me, I will betray Cesare. Most of his packs would follow me to your side. But you must act now! Once he begins his war, you'll have only two paths—serve him or oppose him. Either way, he wins."

"The lords won't go to war now. They are too fat and lazy."

"The attack on Bordeaux has fired them up, and the prospect of a human alliance frightens them. Once they're feted, they'll do whatever the king tells them. And the king will do whatever Cesare wishes. I tell you, Cesare will have his war. Unless you stand up."

Gareth released the female and floated to the floor. "Why would you betray my brother for me? What am I to you?"

"You are the heir." Flay massaged her throat. Then she slid languidly down the pharaoh's naked torso. "I will make Cesare's army yours. You can kill your brother and take the clan. Let me help you." She clutched the statue's massive chest with her thighs and reached out a thin strong hand. "Let me serve you."

"So you, of all people, want me to stop this war?"

"No!" Flay's eyes burned with cold blue fire. "I want you to *lead* the war. I remember you serving Dmitri. You were magnificent. With me at your side, there is nothing you can't do." Her voice was hypnotic, her words full of smooth poison.

The opportunity to use Flay as the tool to destroy Cesare was something Gareth had never foreseen. But here it was, an extraordinary gift, waiting to be grasped. Cesare would never suspect Flay might betray him. And once Cesare was gone, Gareth would have no rivals for clan leadership. He could halt the war drums. Perhaps he could even begin to negotiate for some future where both species could survive. Gareth felt as if he were suddenly on the edge of a great precipice.

The sinuous Flay was beginning to look quite inviting, exuding an aura of power and allure. Her bloody exploits were legendary; it was no surprise that Cesare had made her his war chief. Gareth had often wondered if there was anything more between those two. It could be nothing official because Flay was too common to birth a prince's child.

She was enormously attractive, a physical specimen that any male would covet. And she couldn't possibly make it any clearer that she would welcome Gareth's advances. He stared at the hard muscles of her stomach and the smooth hollow of her throat as she clung to the stone colossus like a spider.

Then he asked, "Are you sure you could seize Cesare?"

"I can." Flay licked her lips. Gareth watched her with an interest, even approval, that she had never seen from him before. His blue eyes softened, and Flay saw the cloudy warmth of desire that she saw in all males. "I know where he is at all times. And I can place my most loyal packs around him. Once I take him, you will kill him."

"I will deal with my brother in my own way."

Flay drew back against the chest of Ramses. "Let's be clear, my prince. Cesare must die, and it must be by your hand. To do less means none of us are safe."

Gareth scowled, playing the lord annoyed by an underling. "Don't overstep yourself, Flay. Leave it to me. I'll deal with him."

"Good." Flay smiled with excitement, unfazed by Gareth's rebuke. She enjoyed his show of authority; she expected nothing less from the future king and her master. "But there is something you must do before I can move against Cesare."

Gareth inclined his head and breathed out sharply through his nose. Here, finally, was her bargain. Various propositions floated through his head—some ridiculous, others vaguely attractive. Would she ask for a lordship? Would she ask to be queen? Would she ask for some profession of love?

Gareth asked, "What do you want?"

"The death of Princess Adele."

"What?"

"Kill your prisoner. Her presence adds to Cesare's prestige, and the information he believes she has is part of his war plans. Take her out of the equation now. I will kill her if you wish. I'll go now. And once she's gone, you will accuse Cesare of playing with the security of the clan for his own purposes. I will seize him and you will parade before the clan with your brother's blood on your hands. The most savage of the lords will be delighted at such a coming-out. You'll be the belle of the ball."

As Gareth listened, his thoughts moved from surprise to rage. When she paused with a horrible sly smile on her hard face, he snarled, "Now let *me* be clear, Flay. If you dare lay a hand on Princess Adele, I will dismember you." The fury of his response surprised even him, but it rushed out before he could stop it. It was pure instinct.

Flay was taken aback. She lowered her eyes again in supplication. "I meant no disrespect. I merely offered to kill her for your convenience. You may feed off her. Kill her yourself if you wish."

"Get out!"

Flay stared in dismay. Her mouth hung open in shock. Her plan had been complete. She was to serve Prince Gareth. They would fight side by side and rule the clan together, just as she had always dreamed. Now he glared at her with hatred and disdain. Could it be because of the Equatorian prisoner? Surely there was just a misunderstanding. She had stepped over some unseen line. She had gone too far too fast, and triggered his natural princely scorn for an upstart commoner.

She attempted another explanation. "I didn't . . . I don't . . . ."

Gareth cut her off with a booming, "I told you to get out! Crawl back to Cesare. I'm sure your usual place at his feet is still vacant."

Flay hardened visibly at his slur. "If I go, Gareth, I will never offer myself to you again."

He shrugged. "We've always been enemies, Flay. And we always will be."

Her shock and embarrassment turned to rage. She drew back her lips. "He will never believe you if you tell him I was here."

Gareth merely looked at her. He had no intention of telling Cesare anything, but he wouldn't give her the satisfaction of knowing that, preferring for her to wallow in confusion and doubt.

"I hope you die, Gareth!" Flay shrieked. "You're weak and worthless. I hope you die!" She threw herself into the air, rising slowly through the turgid air of the museum until she caught a draft and vanished abruptly through a broken window. The faint echo of her anguished cry could be heard mixing with the bloody screams and cheers across the murderous city.

CHAPTER 18

FLAY RETURNED TO the museum the next night.

This time she came to the front door, and she had others with her: five red-jacketed members of Cesare's honor cadre called the Pale because of their role in slaughtering so many of the Irish. Gareth stared at the grim-faced war chief, who refused to look him in the eye.

"What now, Flay?" Gareth's voice was tired.

She replied flatly, "Your prisoner is required at the palace."

"Tell Cesare I think not."

Flay raised her head, briefly caught his eye, then glanced away. "This is directly from King Dmitri."

Gareth had no choice but to agree. "Then I'll come along."

"Do as you wish." She paused, then added, "Great Lord."

Gareth went back inside, where he found Adele staring enthusiastically at a wall of marble carvings. She turned easily, but quickly noticed the stern look on his face and went grim herself.

He said, "You must come with me. The king has asked for you at the palace. You will see things no human has ever seen, and lived. Terrible things. In a feeding frenzy, my kind is unpredictable and very dangerous. Do not get isolated. I will protect you so long as you stay near me."

"I will."

"You'll be safe."

"I'm sure. Can I get my cloak?"

"Of course."

Adele ran to her room, where she grabbed her heavy cloak. She touched the washabti in her pocket and was grateful that Gareth would be with her in the wretched palace. Clearly, though, he was worried about this summons; it was something out of his control. His promises of safety were weak.

The Rosetta stone was propped in the corner. Behind it, she had hidden two stone blades. She slipped the knives into her blouse.

———⟨∿∿⟩———

The walk to the palace horrified Adele. Mobs of vampires with their faces and torsos stained red wandered the streets or flitted overhead, feeding on naked and ragged humans with blank cattle faces. Men, women, and children. Sometimes they were chained or hobbled, but usually they stood motionless without restraint or squatted quietly on the cobblestones waiting for their devourers to collect them at their whim. It angered Adele that the humans didn't at least try to run, but she knew they were no longer humans in any real sense; they were bred as food and they acted like food.

Gareth stayed close, which Adele found comforting. Still, frenzied ruby-faced vampires occasionally surged at her from out of the crowd in hopes of tasting something new. The Pale shoved interlopers back with annoyed rebukes, although Flay trudged on without apparent interest. Gareth, however, was not so lenient. He seized several vampires who reached for Adele and put a quick and savage end to their evening festivities. Soon the black-suited prince was as bloody as the sodden revelers, and the growls that came out of him reminded Adele of a trapped, vicious dog. Even so, she found herself pressing closer against him as the air grew thicker with shrieks of pain and delight with every step.

Soon the old Buckingham Palace loomed in the darkness. They made their way up stained steps, past columns of veined marble, and into a great corridor once bright and lavish with intense colors and golden fixtures but now drab and caked in filth. Ragged remnants of carpet clung to the floor of the wide gallery. The palace's decrepit decorations were overwhelmed by piles of bone and hundreds of skulls staring down from broken chandeliers. Vampires slouched along the walls, drunk with blood, sometimes with red hands resting on humans who still showed signs of life.

The princess and her escorts passed out of the main gallery and through a series of smaller rooms crowded with vampires not yet drunk and bloodmen quickly herding humans from one place to another. They all cleared the way for Flay and her red-coated entourage. Heads turned as the Pale passed, and hundreds of curious blue eyes locked on Princess Adele. In a small grim room, a tall vampire wearing an odd checkered jacket and striped trousers met them and conferred with Flay.

Gareth leaned down to Adele. "That's Cesare's bailiff, Stryon. It's rare to see him outside of Dublin."

When Stryon concluded his discussion with Flay, he bowed to Gareth. "My lord, won't you join His Majesty and Prince Cesare?"

Gareth received the homage with a bare nod. "I'll wait here with my prisoner."

"Very good." The bailiff's eyes flicked between Gareth and Adele without emotion before he withdrew.

"We wait until we're summoned," Flay said wearily. Then her gaze settled on Adele, and she studied the princess with a severe curiosity.

Several of the Pale began to chat in low hisses, wondering if the royals were going to share the princess with the lords of the clan. Flay didn't bother to quiet her troopers, and in fact an impertinent smile twitched at the corners of her full mouth.

None of them realized that Adele understood what they were saying. She managed to keep her face calm while their chatter became bloodier as the soldiers waxed on about how delicious she might be. Behind the folds of her cloak, Adele plunged one hand into the deep pocket of her heavy skirt, feeling for the hard, smooth washabti. She found a sense of serenity as her fingers slid over the supple facets of the small figurine. Gareth glanced at the young woman and shifted his feet subtly, as if to put a few more inches between them. Flay's eyes narrowed and dropped to Adele's skirt, as if the vampire sensed something peculiar.

Abruptly, Stryon the bailiff summoned them with a long crooked finger. Flay stood aside with a look of disgust as Gareth motioned to Adele. The bailiff led Gareth and Adele to massive double doors where he paused to listen. Raucous but muffled sounds drifted from the room beyond, led by Cesare's rabble-rousing hiss and complemented by guttural responses from a sizable crowd. He was listing the many triumphs of the clans over the humans, extolling the strengths of vampires versus the weaknesses of humans. He exhorted the clan to greater victories in the future in the face of growing threats from the grasping humans. The lords cheered at the appropriate times.

Cesare's topic changed to Equatoria and the growing threat of an alliance between two ambitious human states. He explained that the leader of this evil alliance had already massacred the clan of Bordeaux. But Cesare had succeeded in scoring a significant victory; he had seized the mate of the Butcher of Bordeaux.

At this, Stryon motioned Gareth forward, threw back the doors, and stood aside. Gareth paused, hoping to score a minor victory of his own by throwing his brother's stage show off its timing. He was amused by the thought of Cesare standing before the throne with his arm extended toward the empty doorway, watching and fuming impotently as no Equatorian captive was dragged screaming into the throne room. Stryon touched the prince's elbow and pressed him forward with a look of alarm. Gareth freed himself and glared back as if ready to rip the bailiff's arm out of the socket for his temerity.

Gareth whispered to Adele, "Stay near me. Don't be afraid." Then he added after a moment's thought, "And don't do anything to antagonize them."

The Prince of Scotland swept into the vast chamber, his heels clicking loudly in the expectant silence. The waiting lords stared, surprised first by the delay and now by seeing Gareth when they expected the delightfully demeaning spectacle of a free human royal in chains. Then followed the human woman, but she was unbound, with her head up, staring back at them in disdain. The vampire lords parted reluctantly for Gareth. They hovered around Adele with wild eyes and wet grins, but none reached out to molest her. Adele was reminded of a hideous version of her father's Privy Council lurking through a state event at Victoria Palace in Alexandria.

The throne room was very large and had once been lavish enough to befit the greatest ruling family in Europe, as it still did. Cesare stood on a raised platform at the far end of the room with an arch above and columns on either side. An ancient rag doll that Adele took to be the fabled King Dmitri slumped in a chair behind the vile prince. Gareth mounted the royal dais, and Adele followed.

Cesare extended his hand toward the princess and spit in his vampire tongue, "Here is our enemy! This is the future mate of the one called Clark, who slew so many of the American clans and our kin just days ago in Bordeaux."

The lords began to rumble with outrage.

"But I," Cesare continued, "have her now!" He laughed, and the lords laughed with him. "I took her because she came with her army into clan lands. I believed we could negotiate a peaceful settlement with the human warlords. I believed the humans would care for their own enough to talk to us. But I admit now that I was wrong. Ask the dead in Bordeaux about peace! Ask the children who were slaughtered by the human fires about peace! There can be no peace with the human warlords. They do not understand the concept."

Unabashed hatred grew in the chamber as a tall grey-haired lord shoved to the front of the crowd. He dragged a filthy young human woman by the hair as any partygoer might circulate with his wineglass in hand. The woman slapped at his strong forearm, forcing the clan lord to frown with distracted annoyance and shake the woman as someone might a misbehaving puppy.

"So what now?" this old lord boomed. "What would you have us do, Cesare?"

"Lord Ghast," the young vampire prince muttered at the elder with unconcealed contempt, "what would you expect us to do? We must fight! We must strike now before we are taken unaware! Would you have our herds taken from us?"

Ghast snarled. "Don't try to demonize me, Cesare! My history of killing is well told! I welcome war with the humans!" He searched the room with fierce eyes. "But I won't have your upstart as clan war chief! Flay is not noble. I demand the role." There was a murmur of agreement among some of the lords.

Cesare raised a calming hand and gave a cynical grin. "One thing at a time, please, Lord Ghast. Can we begin the war before you begin demanding your position? The king will name the war chief. Not you."

Lord Ghast growled and reached for the woman he dragged. It was only then that Adele realized the captive woman had a small baby clutched close to her body. The vampire seized the child. A wave of sickness overcame the princess, instantly replaced by righteous murderous rage.

Adele reached into her blouse and took a stone knife, while her other hand unconsciously grasped the washabti from her pocket. She leapt from the dais with a shout. Lord Ghast stared at her uncomprehendingly, with the woman in one hand and the baby in the other. The princess felt heat surge through her body. Ghast started to shout, but his throat was already cut. Adele spun, and drove the blade up through his chin into his brain, then grabbed the baby before it dropped to the floor.

The room went silent. The bloody mob stared at Adele cradling the baby as Lord Ghast's body collapsed to the floor. She looked down at the child and saw that it was dead already, and probably had been for days. The mother, driven to insanity by her lot in life, could not understand. The wretched woman pleaded for the tiny cadaver, and Adele placed it in her hands.

Adele was pulled back with tremendous force. Gareth quickly released her and held his hand as if injured, staring at her with shock and anger. His eyes locked on the washabti in her left hand. Growling, he smashed it out of her grasp. The little figurine shattered against the tile floor.

"What are you doing?" he snapped. "Are you insane? Attacking a clan lord?"

"I thought he was going to—"

"Keep quiet! We'll be lucky to get out of here alive."

The dense silence was pierced by singular laughter.

Both Adele and Gareth turned to see Cesare doubled over with uncontrolled hilarity. This incredible tableau left the already surprised lords exchanging glances of confusion. Gareth placed himself between his brother and Adele as Cesare turned to face them.

"Well," Cesare said quietly with a broad grin, "that couldn't have worked out better if I'd planned it. Poor Ghast. Killed going for a snack."

The doors burst open, and Flay stormed into the chamber. Behind her stood a small male vampire, looking quite frail. The lords all turned to see what new surprise lay in store.

Cesare was not pleased by the look he saw on Flay's face.

"My lord," Flay shouted as she shoved through the clan lords, nearly dragging the vampire behind her. She approached the dais and pushed her baggage to the foot of the steps.

The little vampire trembled from the collected greatness around him. Flay prompted his recovery with a stern blow to the back, causing him to stammer, "I . . . have news, my lord. Humans."

Cesare folded his arms and waited in cold anticipation. Gareth eyed Flay, wondering what game she was playing. Her face seemed quite intense and involved in the moment; there was no furtive scheming behind her eyes. She seemed almost breathless for the small visitor to speak.

Cesare did not prompt him, so the stranger glanced at Flay for approval and then continued. "We are under attack."

The room broke into an uproar. A thought of escape flashed through Adele's mind. She could take advantage of the confusion and slip away. She shifted her weight to move and immediately felt a vise on her arm. Gareth glared down at her. He seemed to sense her thoughts, and his mirthless stare was enough to make her still.

Cesare held up a hand for silence, which was partially granted, and demanded of the newcomer, "What are you blathering about?"

"I was near the water this early morning. The ocean." He pointed southward. "I was with my brother. We saw an airship. A warship. Flying north. We watched and then started to go, but one of the humans climbed into the rigging of the ship. He had a gun. And he killed my brother." The vampire put a finger to his forehead. "A hole here. I fled."

He pulled his threadbare shirt up and turned to reveal a jagged hole in his back. "He shot me too, but I escaped."

The appearance of the occasional human warship over the southern sea was not unheard-of, although it was unusual. Typically it meant they were off course. No captain would wish to stray so close to a vampire stronghold. Still, Cesare knew he had to appear as if this was momentous news.

So he announced, "No doubt it is a scout ship for a coming invasion. Or perhaps it is the beginning of the invasion itself. The Equatorians—"

Flay interrupted, "Not Equatorians, my lord."

Cesare intoned frostily, "No?"

"No. The ship's flag was American."

Adele gasped with sudden elation and exchanged a startled glance with Gareth. The vampire prince's expression was unreadable, but she sensed that he was once again jockeying for a new strategy.

Flay pointed a clawed finger up at Adele. "It is her mate. Clark. He is coming for her."

The clan lords began to rumble again with dismay and confusion.

The war chief continued in a lower voice to Cesare, "Kill her, my lord. You must kill her now."

Cesare drew Flay close. "Take Princess Adele back to the Tower. Keep her alive. Do you hear me? Keep her alive."

"But this is the Butcher of Bordeaux coming to—"

"I said take her back. Now! You do it yourself. And if she's hurt, you will answer for it! Then dispatch my packs around the city. If the American dares set foot here, I want him dead no matter how many it costs you."

Flay nodded unwillingly. She crossed in front of Gareth without looking at him and took Adele by the arm.

Gareth said to Flay, "You heard your master. Keep her safe or it's your life."

Adele blurted out with unexpected alarm, "Aren't you coming?"

"No," Gareth replied. "I have much to do here." He looked again at Flay with a silent warning before slipping out.

CHAPTER 19

ADELE TRUDGED THROUGH wretched London with Flay as her sole overseer. The manic pace of bloody celebration had slowed. The air was warming, and the city's stink hung heavy with a filthy fog. The war chief vented frustration on the princess with harsh sounds and firm cuffs. The princess wasn't sure if Flay would protect her from aggressive passersby despite Cesare's warnings, but the two moved through the streets so quickly that most of the slothful vampires in the street barely had time to stare, much less accost them.

Gareth's abandonment hurt her, but she shouldn't have expected more from him. He was a vampire, and she chided herself for dropping her guard as much as she had around him. Now, Adele thought about the possibility that Senator Clark was indeed sailing northward. Selkirk's information apparently had made its way to Alexandria, and now her medal-chested Intended was roaring in to drive this rabble before him and bring her safely home. She grudgingly allowed that this was the kind of man many women would justly crave. After all, how many men would take on a country full of monsters for his fiancée? In this day and age, there was nothing wrong with having a husband willing to spill blood to ensure his wife's well-being. Adele's thoughts were broken by a blow from Flay that knocked her hard to the cobblestones.

"Get up!" the war chief snarled.

The princess struggled to her hands and knees. Flay had no patience for the human's weary pace, so she reached down and gripped Adele by the neck, pulling her to her feet, and slammed the woman into an iron lamppost. The breath whooshed out of the girl, and she grunted in pain.

Flay smiled at the noise and raised a clawed hand. "Maybe if your face was disfigured, Prince Gareth wouldn't find you so fascinating."

Adele had a sudden revelation about Flay. Pain and hurt showed in the flicker of Flay's gaze, quickly obscured by despair and a feverish recklessness. The vampire was jealous. Adele could hardly believe the startling concept that vampires had emotions, but this emotion in this particular vampire was even more horrifying. Flay was eager to harm Adele in spite of Cesare's warning.

So Adele plunged her other stone knife deep into Flay's abdomen.

Flay screeched with fury. Blood oozed through the vampire's fingers as she pulled the knife free and studied the weapon.

Adele raced down an alley, but the soft pads of Flay came up fast behind. A weight fell on her and slammed her down in a tangle of arms and legs. Hissing was close in her ear, and she lashed back with an elbow. She caught something solid, but Flay's claws sank into Adele's soft shoulder and lifted her up. Adele struggled, but there was no escape this time.

A sliver of steel slid from Flay's chest. The vampire looked down with surprise at the sword point dripping with her blood. Her mouth tightened into an annoyed scowl as she leapt forward off the blade, tossing Adele aside. A heavier blade whispered through the air where her neck had just been.

Greyfriar surged past the prone Adele, tossing something white over his shoulder that hit the ground at the princess's booted feet.

"Run!" he shouted as his cloak filled the narrow alley. The sound of swords cut the air.

Adele grasped the small bundle. It was paper wrapped around her own Fahrenheit khukri that she had lost in Riez. Glancing hurriedly at the paper, she saw it was a yellowed old map of southern England with a black X scrawled over the town of Canterbury.

Adele drew the glowing blade. "Let me help you."

Greyfriar took a second to turn and stare through smoked glasses. "Run! Fast!"

In that split second, Flay fell on the swordsman like a hawk. The two became a blur of arms, steel, and teeth. Flay surged, fell back, and surged again. Greyfriar dropped the wide-bladed scimitar and worked the tip of the rapier. His blade was a blur, and its sharp hiss filled the air, competing with Flay's own snarling.

The war chief parried with her claws, taking awful gashes across her hands but blocking Greyfriar's killing strikes each time. The need to spill blood surged through her. This was the moment she'd waited for, the moment when she could kill the Greyfriar and feed on him. But she knew she could not. The princess was her charge. The princess mattered.

And the princess had fled.

Despite Flay's need to kill this man, he was merely an impediment preventing her from going after Cesare's vanishing prize. He seemed to know it and revel in his ability to delay her. Flay tried to slither past in a swift shadow, but he blocked her with a skill and agility that was extraordinary for a human. Each passing second carried the princess away into the chaos of London. The desperate vampire lifted herself only to feel Greyfriar's grip on her ankle. She kicked him across the face, but his steel grasp refused to lessen.

Enough, Flay thought. *I have no time to duel this lucky wretch.*

The war chief threw back her head and screeched. Greyfriar flinched at the sound. Within seconds, the alley began to fill with vampires. Some responded to the old war call. Others were merely drunk and hoping for some bloody street burlesque. The sight of a human and a vampire in battle sparked an instinct that pressed them onto the swordsman.

A flood of bodies tumbled into Greyfriar. Their claws and teeth ripped into him while he strained to hold Flay's ankle. She took hold of an iron fixture high on the wall and pulled with all her strength. His fingers slipped from her foot and, through a web of arms and legs, he saw Flay rising into the sky.

With a frantic burst of strength, Greyfriar surged to his feet, shedding revelers like a trapped bear sheds dogs. He rushed out of the clinging mob and leapfrogged up from side to side between the narrow alley walls. Pausing on a ledge, he pulled his pistol and fired all the cartridges one after another. The barrage hit the airborne Flay and tumbled her like a pinwheel. But none was a kill shot, and she righted herself quickly. The vampire slipped out of sight among the rooftops.

Greyfriar tore frantically at his gun belt and scabbards, needing to jettison his weapons and baggage to go after Flay. He had to stop her from finding Adele at all costs, even if it meant abandoning his precious masquerade. But countless sharp hands pulled him down. He battered helplessly against the surrounding rabble, only hoping Adele had enough time to escape.

⁓∾∾⁓

Adele felt like a coward, but she ran anyway, racing into the street, where drunken vampires watched her pass. Some pointed and laughed at the spectacle of someone's meal running away. She quickly turned off the crowded thoroughfare and slipped into a canyonlike alley. It was empty, but in the narrow slot of pale light overhead figures glided past.

If her Intended was coming for her, where would he go? Selkirk knew she was in the Tower. Should she go there and wait for rescue?

Adele felt the crumpled map in her hand. Canterbury. Would Greyfriar meet her there? Was he part of the rescue attempt? Was her Intended waiting there? She had no idea if the ship that had been seen was really his. One thing was clear: London was teeming with vampires. The only solid chance she had was the X on the map. Greyfriar. He was the answer.

Adele moved silently down the narrow lane. The enemy could emerge from any of the doors lining her path. One of the doorways was open, and she crept to the side to see or hear if there was activity within. She heard nothing, so she slipped past, but a glint of light inside caught Adele's attention. She was amazed to see piles of metal inside the room. Weapons! Perhaps she could find another weapon to add to her dagger. Something longer and deadlier.

Adele rummaged as quickly and as quietly as she could in the steel debris. Finally it was mere providence that made her stumble. A glance toward her foot and she saw a weapon of distinction. It was the blade of a halberd with the handle snapped, so its length was no more than four feet. It was a weapon designed for crushing blows and powerful thrusts. Even without the long wooden haft behind it, the halberd had an edge that would slice through the flesh of vampires.

Adele looked out into the lane and her courage trembled, but she had no choice. She tightened her grip on the halberd and stepped out into the street, where she was greeted by fog and shadows, which worked in her favor. Adele racked her memory and decided the river was to her left. She set off, hoping that her instinct was correct; there might be no time for a second chance. Soon the sound of lapping water indicated to her that she had made the right choice.

The entrance to a massive bridge came into sight, and her heart sank. Vampires crowded nearby. She prayed that she could find a second bridge farther on. Stumbling across rocks and brambles on the shoreline, Adele found a small path along the river that she followed with legs numb and aching, her eyes darting toward every shadow.

The morning fog was beginning to thin. Through the grey mist above, Adele saw blotches of red. Her heart leapt with thoughts of her own White Guard. Then she realized it was Flay's Pale. They were searching for her, and they were very close.

She darted into the underbrush, where sharp thorns easily tore through her garments. Abruptly she ran headlong into a brick wall, long forgotten and hidden from view by vines. Reeling back, the young woman looked up to see a small circular building. Surely no one lived in there. It was far too tiny. It must merely cover something from the weather, but it would serve to hide her. With one eye cocked to the sky for signs of approaching Pale, she searched halfway around the building before she found a door. Her shoulder shoved hard, but it resisted. Desperation drove her, and the wooden door eased inward. Debris built up inside scraped back as she wrenched the door back enough to slip inside, where she put her back to the wall and waited. Her frantic breathing sounded loud, so she tried to quell it, but it only increased the ache in her chest. Nothing sprang at her from the darkness and she heard no sounds, so she took the chance and closed the door. Immediately her small sanctuary plunged into complete darkness. It was so ebony black inside that there wasn't even enough light to form the dimmest of shadows. And silence infused the room like a tomb.

Like a tomb.

Adele dropped her hands to her sides and fumbled along the floor, reaching out to touch anything that would give her a clue where she was. Stiff fingers touched things barely recognizable: metal scraps; silky, mold-covered material; and more. She had no idea what they were.

She struggled to her feet carefully, keeping a hand on the wall. The small structure wasn't very wide, and she decided to traverse it keeping close to the wall. With one hand out for protection and the other bracing her against the wall, she followed the curve of the structure. Shuffling forward slowly, she thought she'd be prepared for anything.

She wasn't.

Soft wood gave way beneath her, and she fell farther into darkness.

CHAPTER 20

PRINCESS ADELE WAS gone, Flay thought.

The miserable little wretch was somewhere in London. Most likely she was dead, enjoyed by some drunken rube unaware that he was drinking Prince Cesare's possession and killing Flay with the same act. The cooling body of the bothersome girl probably lay twisted under a tree or jammed in a gutter crowded with corpses where she would never be found.

It was a fate richly deserved, Flay thought as she clung to the dome of St. Paul's, staring into the misty grey morning. The muffled sound of the diminishing bacchanalia reverberated below her. Several members of her Pale perched near her. At some point, she would have to alert Cesare to the princess's disappearance. And it would mean her death. Too bad. Flay would have liked to have seen Gareth's face when he learned that his precious trophy was gone. The war chief considered the possibility of assassinating Cesare and throwing herself on Gareth's mercy. If the elder prince were handed the *fait accompli* of his brother's death, he would have to take control of the clan.

Or she could kill Cesare and flee Britain. Her reputation was vast and celebrated. But no clan would accept a traitor with hands dark from her master's blood.

Flay caught her breath and tried to think. She was feeling the effects of the warm weather combined with exertion and hunger. She had not fed for two days thanks to Cesare's constant demands on her time.

There was no proof the princess was dead. Perhaps she had escaped with the help of Greyfriar. Flay had broken the fight with the Greyfriar to chase the girl, but had ended up losing both of them. If any human could secure the captive's freedom it would be that hateful swordsman.

Perhaps Cesare would not blame Flay for such an unexpected complication. Greyfriar was well known across Europe for doing the unexpected and unpredictable. Flay had never encountered a human who fought so well, and she had fought and killed thousands of them over her lifetime. He was different. Therefore he had to die.

Flay had to act fast. She would leash her finest hunters and track the princess. She would find the prisoner before the end of the day. And perhaps she would get Greyfriar in the bargain. She smiled at the thought.

One of the Pale whispered and pointed eastward. Through the humid mist Flay glimpsed a small warship as it slipped from a low cloudbank. She had run out of time.

Flay snapped an order to gather the packs and assemble at the Tower. Then she launched herself into the air, angling toward the river, as the ghostly ship drew back into the clouds. She felt a tremor of delightful anticipation. Senator Clark was actually coming into the heart of vampire London to retrieve his mate. It was a grand gesture that Flay could applaud or deride equally, and it was completely futile, even if the princess had been waiting in the Tower for him to rescue.

Now Flay had the opportunity to present Cesare with the head of Clark, and hopefully return the princess to captivity and perhaps finish the Greyfriar too. The hearts of the alliance and the resistance broken in one night.

It was turning into quite a clan gathering after all.

———✦———

Adele couldn't survive alone. He had failed her.

Greyfriar crouched under a bridge strut listening to the river and the cry of birds growing louder with the rising sun. His besotted brethren were dragging themselves back to their dark holes for a day of sleep after a night of gorging.

The drunken mob that Flay set on him had been troublesome to escape. Greyfriar had spent the next few hours of thinning darkness frantically trying to track Adele through the bloodbath, relying on his vampiric skills again, and those skills were very rusty. He did take in tantalizing whiffs of her, sending him scampering one fruitless direction then another.

Greyfriar had seen Flay tracking the princess too. The war chief had been a brief shadow, and he had no chance to strike. He was relieved at least that Flay didn't have Adele. But that didn't mean the poor frightened girl had not been slaughtered by passing revelers. The vision of Adele dying, calling his name in vain, nailed him in the heart.

She couldn't survive alone. He had failed her.

Nothing was going according to plan. He had hoped to come to Adele in her prison quarters as Greyfriar and spirit her away from London. But as he had shadowed Flay and Adele from the palace across London, he saw that the war chief had become enraged and was ready to kill the princess. Intervention was his only option.

He pulled the cloth wrap away from his face and scented the air, taking in the wet clotted smell of the river, the rusting iron of the bridge, and the ever-present aftertaste of blood in the wind. None of it was Adele's blood. Her scent was so familiar he could almost taste it.

Greyfriar growled and leapt to his feet. Once again, the cloth covered his fanged mouth and his human weapons felt heavy on his hips. He made a show of touching and adjusting them as no vampire ever would, comforted by their shape and weight.

He would work his way east, toward Canterbury. Perhaps he would catch Adele's scent and find her safe. That was all he wished. To find her safe and keep her safe.

She could not survive alone. He must not fail her.

———

Clouds drifted across the deck of *Ranger*, winding through the shrouds and ratlines, softly caressing the men and brass. In the grey silence, masts creaked like trees snapping, gas vented with a roar, and the crew shuffled over the wooden planks as if they wore iron boots. Senator Clark stood at the rail clutching a drop line in his gloved hand, cringing at every noise and glaring at every movement.

This was the type of fight that had made him famous. Flying wildly into enemy territory on the wrong side of the odds, trusting to surprise and boldness and his innate invulnerability. But this was not the type of situation Clark wanted. He only had intelligence from scouts he didn't know or trust. And his goal this time was not his usual favorite of slaughtering the enemy's population or crippling their ability to fight, but to seize a target and escape.

Major Stoddard appeared at Clark's side. He saluted to confirm that shroud canisters had been loaded in the deck carronades. The major's eyes betrayed uncertainty.

Clark nodded confidently and fingered the brass-and-leather gas mask hanging around his neck. It was designed to allow humans to operate normally inside the dark pall of the shroud gas cloud. While the gas wasn't poisonous, it was harsh on human lungs. The goggles were designed with a special gas layer so vampires appeared in the black smoke as a blue aura, whereas humans appeared red. This operation in a well-defined space suited the deployment of shroud gas, however, and Clark had ordered the cannons loaded with the canisters to fire into the Tower precinct.

Major Stoddard's voice was barely a whisper, but he felt the risk of speaking aloud was warranted. He had to make Clark see reason on this matter. "Sir, shroud gas is a dangerous gamble with Princess Adele in the target zone."

Clark's gaze stayed focused on the barest glimpses of the ground he could see through the mist, but his mouth grimaced tightly. "Thanks to that Jap schoolteacher's map we supposedly know exactly where Adele is. She's on a high floor of the central tower. The gas should hang low. The princess will be fine until I get to her, which should be quickly." The senator touched a second gas mask, hanging from his belt, that he had brought for Adele.

He then pinned a scathing glare at Stoddard. "Now get back on the line, Major. You worry like my grandmother, and she annoyed the hell out of me. And if you break operational silence again, I'll see you drummed out of the service."

Stoddard stiffened, his lips pursed. He saluted sharply and returned to his squad at the far rail.

Meanwhile, Captain Root huddled with the ship's officers studying an old map of London by the pale light of the binnacle. The frigate had slipped out of the clouds briefly to take bearings and had then drawn back above cover. The captain glanced at his gold pocket watch and motioned to the senator that he had five minutes before the suicide drop into the Tower grounds.

Clark passed the word by hand signals to the ghostly grey Rangers in the mist. Gas masks were quickly fixed in place down the ranks of soldiers. At least the chief meteorologist had been accurate on the front again. They had patrolled off the coast for two days waiting for prime assault weather. And now the morning air was warm and wet. Fog was settling in at just the hour he had predicted. The shroud gas would hang for a long while. The commandos should be able to drop, retrieve the princess, and escape under cover.

If this gamble succeeded, and Clark was confident it would, he would become the unquestioned leader of the American-Equatorian alliance. His name would go on top of a short list of men who had changed the destiny of civilization.

Clark smiled.

The warship's gasbags vented with a roar, and *Ranger* plummeted. Hearts leapt into throats and hands tightened on weapons and drop lines. The fog thinned, and grey stone buildings appeared perilously close to the airship's hull. Sails luffed and more gas jetted. *Ranger* went hard over to starboard. The grimy Thames rose into view above the rail.

There was the Tower of London. Clark instantly noted the structure where Princess Adele was supposedly held. He was committed to the intelligence, but he still doubted the Japanese schoolmaster. If Adele was not in the right place, this drop would go very bad very fast.

Ranger righted and nearly scraped the Tower's crenellated outer wall as it inched over the courtyard. Cannons along both sides fired with low thuds, sending canisters spiraling downward. The large cartridges exploded almost noiselessly, and a greasy black smoke began to roll out along the ground, winding around rubble and sliding along walls. The ship's fore and aft anchor guns whoomed and sent heavy spiked grapnels slamming into ancient stone walls. The frigate jolted to a dead stop.

"Go!" Clark shouted, with his booted feet already on the mahogany rail. The whining of drop pulleys screamed through the heavy, moist air as American commandos with robotic faces plummeted to the occupied British soil.

Senator Clark hit the ground, unbuckled and armed as he ran with tramping feet following him. There was no sign of vampires yet beyond distant blue figures bobbing lazily in the misty sky. Clark signaled one squad of red shapes to follow while the other held the base of the tower. Troopers swept through the doorway, hit the stone stairs, and curved upward.

Now above the shroud gas, Clark smelled coal smoke. Good. Fire was a sign of captives. Maybe the schoolmaster was right after all. In which case, Clark would have to dig into Mamoru's intelligence network. It would not do to have such resources outside his control.

The senator reached the top of the narrow staircase and kicked open the heavy plank door. He pulled down his gas mask. A dark, slender shape stood in the corner.

Clark struck a pose and grinned. "My dear, I am your husband. Pleased to meet you!"

"I think you're mistaking me for someone else," came the oily sibilant reply. A female vampire inched from the shadows. Other creatures came forward. "Your lovely has fled—"

Her words were drowned out by a barrage of gunfire as the senator leapt out of the room.

"Withdraw!" Clark yelled—unnecessarily, since his men were already shoving their way down the stairs with sharp shouts and cursing.

Gunfire came from outside too. It was a trap.

As he ran, the senator reached into his ammo pouch and drew out a metal egg shape—a shrieker. He fumbled with his finger and popped a ring away from the shiny surface. He pulled out a long, thin strip, launching the egg into a piercing scream. Clark dropped it on the steps and reached for a second one.

Several commandos did likewise, and soon the close air of the Tower was electric with an ear-aching whine. It was uncomfortable to the men, but it was painful and disorienting for vampires. The female and her cohorts paused in their pursuit, confused and confounded by the sounds, their heads twisting in pain.

The little devices were already winding down as Clark bounded from the Tower. The wreckage-strewn courtyard was chaotic with vampires dropping from above, striking and tearing at the soldiers. His men tossed more shriekers. Part of a squad had formed a square, firing up and out. Others ran for position, shooting and flailing with bayonets. The popping of marksmen's guns came from *Ranger* overhead.

Cooling bodies of men were visible all around.

"Withdraw in order!" Clark shouted hoarsely through the smoke.

A high-pitched metallic scream began to pour from *Ranger*. Crewmen were wrestling the handles of massive shriekers bolted on the deck, slowly at first, but then turning them in a rhythm. As the screams grew, vampires whirled in the air as if hit by a concussion.

Major Stoddard was struggling to maintain his ragged square as his squad shuffled in some order toward the tangle of drop lines. Guns fired. Green gunsmoke blended with the heavy black. Clark shouted orders from inside the formation. Shapes flashed past. Claws raked. Bayonets flashed. Men fell.

Clark reached through the shroud gas cloud and found a drop line. He slung his carbine and clipped the pulley onto his belt. When he tugged the cable, he was instantly yanked off the ground. Other troopers around him flew up, trailing black mist. Even with the shriekers, vampires slipped past, banging into him, hissing and raking with their hands. He pulled his pistol and fired at the fluttering things around him.

Strong hands lifted the senator over the rail back onto the deck of *Ranger*. He gagged from the shroud gas, and his ears throbbed as he watched the ship's surgeon asking him a question and reaching out for him. He shoved the doctor aside and resumed firing.

Bloodied commandos flowed over the gunwales, assisted by airmen.

Many fell to the deck unable to move, staining the wood red. Major Stoddard struggled back on board and gave a cast-off sign. Every soldier who could return had returned.

Clark felt sick, but signaled to make way. Mooring lines were cut. Gas vents rumbled under the knife-edge squeal of the shriekers. The airship shot straight up. The senator's knees almost buckled from the jolt, but he kept his eyes locked on the female vampire on the roof of a tower below. She waved jauntily with one hand, but with the other she clutched the twisting body of one of his men.

Ranger climbed above the clouds, where the unfurling sails bit the wind. The ship bucked and raced for the open sky. There was halfhearted pursuit, but vampires could not match the frigate's sleek pace.

Major Stoddard came to Clark, who stared out into the orange clouds with a revolver dangling from his hand. "Sir, you should go below with the surgeon."

"How many did I lose?"

"Not sure yet. I'd reckon fifty."

"Fifty!" Clark glared at his trusted junior officer. "Out of two hundred! Impossible, Major. How many vampires attacked us?"

Stoddard replied, "It wasn't many, sir. I didn't count more than twenty or thirty. But they were good. If we hadn't had shroud cover, we'd have lost more."

"Dammit!" The senator spat in disgust, but nodded in agreement. "This didn't happen, Major. I do not intend to return to Equatoria until I make this not happen."

"Do you think Her Highness's mentor misled you?"

"I don't know. I think the princess was there, and recently. That room was set up for a human prisoner."

Major Stoddard buckled against the railing and repeated in a strained voice, "Sir, you should see the doctor. Let him check you out. You could've been injured."

Clark wiped gloved hands over his spotless tunic and laughed. Then he noticed Stoddard wavering on his feet. The major's tunic was shredded across the midsection. Bloodstains covered his chest and trousers. Deep incisions laid open the flesh of his stomach.

"Doctor!" Clark snapped. "Lend a hand to Major Stoddard here. Slap a bandage on that. We've got work to do."

—————

Pain was the only sensation available to Adele. Her world was black. She couldn't be sure if she was awake. Dust clogged her nostrils and caused a coughing fit that made her body ache all over. She shoved a hand out to right herself. It slipped on something round and smooth and wet. Stifling a groan, she pushed it aside and sat up in a couple of inches of water. Her limbs were still attached and not broken thankfully, though they all throbbed fiercely.

Looking up, she tried to determine how far she had fallen, but only the barest of shadows showed above her. Her hands fumbled and grasped rotten wood that disintegrated into near pulp in her fingers: the remains of stairs, decayed with the passing of time, that had fallen with her, coating her clothes. She was lucky she hadn't broken her neck.

Hands flung out again, searching for her halberd, scattering both ball-shaped and long, thin objects, but finally Adele found what she sought. A small gasp escaped her as her finger pressed too hard on the blade's edge, causing a small slice into her flesh. She drew back immediately and stuck the finger in her mouth till the dirt made her gag. She was about to wipe the blood on her skirt when she paused. Vampires smell blood, even as little as this. Smearing some on her clothes was folly. She ripped a bit of her undergarment and used the small piece to wrap her finger. She could discard the scrap once the bleeding had stopped.

Adele was desperate to know where she was so she could keep terror at bay. Survival wasn't just about knowledge and skill; it was about sanity. Mamoru had impressed that on her. Cold, stiff fingers found one of the round objects that littered the ground nearby. Blindly, she gently caressed the features of what she held, her brain trying desperately to puzzle it out. She peered closer at the object as her fingers found hollows and breaks, as if by sheer willpower she could bring this thing to light.

Then a cold chill of fear found her that displaced the numbness drawn from the cold water around her. She knew what she held in her hands—a human skull. There were a great number of them all around her. She had stumbled into a tomb. Only it was more than a tomb; it was a mass grave.

The skull tumbled from Adele's hands into the water. The young princess didn't want to be down here another minute. There had to be a way out. She began to explore the small dimensions her world had been reduced to. Hands reached into the dark in an attempt to gather information. She felt more of the objects that she recognized as human debris. Skulls and femurs and smashed rib cages were all around. She didn't know which terrified her more, touching something solid or touching nothing at all.

Long, agonizing moments of effort gave Adele what she needed to know. She was in a tunnel of some sort, about seven or eight feet in diameter. She could stretch out her arms and almost touch both sides. The walls were made from overlapping circular pieces of iron.

Adele had fallen into one end of the tunnel and had no way back up. The stairs were gone, and the walls didn't seem to provide handholds for climbing. Her only option was to follow the tunnel wherever it led. There was no help coming.

The water at Adele's feet was icy, but shivers racked her body and, along with the tremendous amounts of adrenaline, warded off the worst of her chills. A stroll should warm her further. The water grew deeper as she traveled the tunnel. She surmised that she was walking under the Thames. This must have been a foot tunnel that fell out of service long ago. Humans had been trapped inside when the vampires invaded and were slaughtered. Or maybe they had tried to hide here during the occupation and had died waiting for salvation that never came. Adele longed for daylight. Her every sense was straining to see, hear, or feel. She endured an oppressive fear, as if something were just about to seize her, but she knew she must either find an end and escape or go mad in the darkness with the dead.

Something long, cold, and sharp brushed against the side of her face and pulled gently at her hair, like a cobweb's sticky touch. She flung an arm out wildly. Something skittered on the ceiling like nails on chilled steel. Abruptly Adele felt the touch again on the other side of her cheek; this time it drew a nail sharper across her flesh, extracting blood.

She screamed and struck out with the halberd. The blade whistled through the rancid air and elicited a hissing from a large object above her, though she knew she had not struck it. A vampire. But its hissing was not language like other vampires. It was guttural and formed no words. Adele froze in the ankle-deep water. There was more scuffling above her, and she slashed again without connecting. She strained to see in the blackness. This thing was toying with her. It could kill her at any time. It had all its senses, even in this night.

Suddenly two long bony hands seized her neck from above, lifting her off her feet. With choking breath, she twisted and kicked, hoping to break its grip. Its nails dug deep into her throat, cutting any sound she could utter save a strangled whimper. With both hands clutching the halberd, she stabbed up in a straight thrust. This time blade met bone.

The grip on Adele's neck lessened. One rough hand still clutched her, while the other pulled at the halberd stuck in the beast's belly. The princess twisted the handle so that the blade tore through the vampire's innards. Suddenly she was falling, and she hit hard. The halberd tumbled from her grasp. With a desperate cry, she fumbled through the garbage-filled water for her weapon.

Then there was a splash behind her and her hair was roughly seized, sharp nails scraping her scalp. Her head was jerked back, exposing her throat. Adele screamed, and listened to the echo of her voice as it resounded through the tunnel. Instead of fighting to pull away, she thrust herself back into the vampire and landed atop the thing. They rolled in the water, clawing at each other. To her shock it was naked. It was hairy and terribly lean. It was a savage, not at all like the "civilized" creatures that lived off the remnants of humanity. This was a true animal.

The princess drove her elbow into its face; its fang ripped into her skin, and a grunt showed that the blow had some effect. She leapt to her feet, but it grabbed her skirt and flung her off her feet once again, her chest slamming against the floor. A strong yank pulled her back through the water, her open mouth filling with the sour stuff. Her hands scraped at the floor, desperate for a handhold. What she found instead was a divine providence.

Adele twisted onto her back and swung two-handed the recovered halberd with all her body strength. The invisible arc of the weapon sang in the tunnel. Only a sickening squishing sound and the slightest hint of resistance on the blade told her she had struck true. Then something splashed beside her, and she could feel a round object bob beside her leg.

The creature's head. At least part of it.

A moment later the torso collapsed on top of her. Adele thrashed wildly to be free of it, but its dead weight and her exhausted muscles made it difficult. The way it flopped around seemed to give it new life, though her brain insisted that it was truly dead. Finally she pushed free and scrambled to the side of the tunnel, where she sat gasping. The dripping water from her hair felt like cold tears on her face.

Adele shivered uncontrollably. Her hand lifted to gently touch her burning cheek and slid down to check her throat, which ached horribly, especially when she swallowed. She could feel raw skin, but the damage didn't seem major. She counted herself as fortunate to have survived at all. The vampire had had every advantage being able to see in the dark, while its victim could not. It had underestimated her, which was the sole reason she still lived.

Adele's strength was gone; exhaustion beat at her, and every bruise and wound ached within her. She had to escape this place now, while she still had energy. If one feral vampire had found refuge here, so might a dozen more. Rising unsteadily, she balanced herself against the wall and took shuffling steps forward. Then she stopped. She didn't know which direction she'd been heading. The fight had twisted her around so many times that she was no longer sure. A curse dropped from her lips.

Calm down, she thought angrily. *You've got a fifty–fifty chance at worst.* There was no light in either direction. *Pick one.* Adele took a deep breath and started off.

Hours seemed to pass. To Adele's relief the water began to recede a bit and she seemed to angle slightly upward. Finally she bumped into something solid. Grime-crusted fingers felt a wooden structure.

Stairs. She had found stairs. The path she had chosen had been the right one. There was no water at her feet, so she hoped that the wood had not rotted through like the other end. It held her weight as she slumped against it, without so much as a shiver or a scattering of dust from above. Perhaps luck was still with her.

Trembling hands grasped the handrails. With a deep breath she took her first step, and it held. Then another and another. It took every ounce of patience not to rush up to the top. She kept her pace slow and steady, listening all the while. Her fingers felt every nuance of the stairs in an effort to predict if the structure would fail under her.

It took a few minutes before she realized the blackness was turning grey. Shapes formed in her vision. The darkness was receding. Daylight crept in through cracks above and cast its rays in her direction. Her blindness was at an end.

CHAPTER 21

ADELE CLAWED HER way into daylight. The lifeless air outside was almost clean after the cloying stench in the tunnel. As she got her bearings, she saw vampires were moving about. The princess could only hope that she looked as ragged and dejected as she felt, because she needed to appear like the rest of her subjugated kind. She stumbled, partly on purpose and partly in true exhaustion, as she trudged eastward.

Slowly green displaced the dull dead grey of London. Adele made it out of the city. She would never have believed she could make it this far. The green called to her, lightening her footsteps as the hours passed. It was clean and alive, so unlike the city behind her. She touched the leaves and trunks of the trees, relishing the feel of living things beneath her fingertips. It seemed like ages since she had been around such things. She pushed her way though hedgerows and groves, sometimes with the tree canopy so heavy she walked through a tunnel of green. She kept to heavy cover and skirted the edges of open fields. Patches of berries helped her stave off growing hunger.

In the growing dusk, Adele spotted ancient stone monoliths, worn short and smooth with time, in the middle of an overgrown field. The two parallel slabs of stone immediately fascinated her. Against all reason, she dared the open ground to walk over to the grey monoliths. She placed her hand on cool stone and felt an unexpected sense of warmth and protection.

Shadows crossed over the field in front of her—vampires hunting, silhouetted in the sky. Adele almost bolted for the forest's edge, but it was too late for that. Any movement would betray her presence, though there seemed no way they could miss her.

She shrank between the two stones, praying, cursing. She could feel her heartbeat through her hand pressed against the monolith. The vampires paused in their flight, their pale forms like wraiths floating in the air directly above.

Exhaling slowly, Adele held herself motionless, melting into the stone and vines. She gazed up into their eyes as they looked down, but to her amazement they could not see her. They turned away and drifted to the west, leaving her to stare after them in disbelief. There was no rational explanation. She had not been hidden; she was in the open.

There in the stillness of the glade, she felt a vibration through the stones, humming from below the surface. It wasn't her heartbeat. It was something else—a power of some sort. And it had kept her safe. Perhaps this was the energy that Selkirk tapped to walk unseen among the vampires. Somehow, she had the same ability. Perhaps Greyfriar did as well. He seemed like a creature of shadow. When last Adele had seen him, he had been fighting for his life against Flay. And she had left him. Her heart sickened at the memory. He had come for her across the whole of vampire territory. He had dared bloody London. For her.

So had her Intended, of course, but he had an army at his disposal, and more than likely he was more interested in not losing his claim to a powerful throne. She could never be sure of the senator's motivations. Not like Greyfriar. He had no claims on her or her throne. He had placed his life on the line over and over again. He spoke to her not of politics but of books and simple people. He never gave up, even when all odds were against them.

The strange power of the stones rumbled to a halt and was silent beneath Adele. Immediately she missed its presence. It had spoken of things she had almost forgotten: warmth, safety, and relief from her weary reality. But again, she was alone and unprotected. She had to move on.

Greyfriar, please don't be dead, she pleaded.

———⁓∿∿⁓———

Greyfriar's map led her to the outskirts of little Canterbury.

The town was so much smaller than London. Buildings were overgrown, covered in vines, and trees grew out of collapsed roofs. The tower of a great central church rose out of the red-roofed morass like a mountain above the jungle. There was something orderly and clean here. The air didn't stink of blood and offal. Her feet didn't crunch over the skeletal remains of long-discarded meals. Adele felt comforted as she walked under the bright starlight. And the sky was empty of dark figures.

As she made her way into the outskirts of the wise old town, Adele recaptured the same sense of security she had felt clinging to the monoliths. She had a strange awareness that some vague protection seemed to waft from the ground, from the grass-choked cobblestones under her sore feet. Perhaps it was just the fact that less blood had been spilled here than elsewhere. Perhaps it was just the knowledge that she was not under the eyes of vampires that gave her an irrational sense of freedom.

Adele didn't know where to go. There were no notes on the map—just a mark under the word "Canterbury." It made sense, though, to choose the main landmark, the church tower, as a rendezvous spot.

When Adele reached the magnificent cathedral, she began to feel a sweet heaviness in the air, ancient and inexplicable. Pleasure tingled through her. She entered the massive church slowly and was nearly overwhelmed by a surge of emotion that felt like a sheet of warm water rushing up. She couldn't understand it, but she knew it was natural, something that she was meant to experience. It brought a peace and contentment she had expected for so long and had been missing, although she had never experienced it before. At the same time she was burning; every nerve was shimmering. Adele dropped to her knees and clutched her hands before her, hoping for some guidance to help her understand this thunderbolt that racked her exhausted but energized frame. She was enveloped by the glory around her and she was lost.

Then Adele found herself standing in the sunlight with her hands on the peeling wooden door frame for support. She had no idea how long she had been inside the cathedral. The young woman staggered out and settled on the stone steps in magnificent exhaustion and tried to collect her thoughts. Her clothes were drenched in perspiration, and she could feel tears still running down her dirty face.

A hand reached for Adele. She saw it out of the corner of her eye and recoiled, but the gloved hand snagged her cloak. Her blade glinted.

"Don't struggle, Princess."

Greyfriar!

She gasped and fell against the swordsman as he knelt at her side. "You're alive!"

He took her hard by the shoulders, holding her for a long moment without speaking as her fingers curled in the material of his thick jacket. They both silently rejoiced they had found each other. Then his masked head tilted as he regarded her soaked, shaking frame. "What happened to you?"

Adele wasn't able to discuss the "event" in the cathedral because it didn't seem real now that she was again beside him. Back in a world of masks and swords and guns and blood. And she was more concerned by the distress she sensed in him. He was tense and stiff, as if in pain. His voice was strained, even though the sound of it exhilarated her.

She shook her head. "I'm fine. I'm just tired. Lack of food. Light-headed."

Greyfriar released her and stood back. "I'm grateful you made it here. I'm sorry I couldn't find you in London." He handed her a canteen.

Adele drank greedily, then wiped her mouth and eyed him with a slightly curious smile. "You sound as if you didn't expect me to make it without you."

"No, not at all."

"You just tossed me a knife and a map and sent me off. Didn't you think I could survive alone?"

"Yes, Princess. Of course. I'm just grateful that you did survive. Were you followed?"

"Not so far as I could tell. I saw a few vampires along the way. I thought two surely saw me, but they didn't. I was standing next to some stones. Like monoliths."

Greyfriar nodded. "That was fortunate. Vampires don't like those places." He indicated the towering church behind them. "This place too. They never come to Canterbury if they can help it."

"Why?"

The swordsman shrugged and ran a trembling hand over his masked face. "I don't know. The place disturbs them."

Adele touched his arm. "Are you okay? You don't seem well to me. Did Flay injure you?"

He pulled farther back. "Nothing to worry about. Come. I know where you can hide and rest. But only briefly. We must move fast if we're to keep you out of Flay's hands again."

"Of course. Lead on." Despite his apparent illness or injury, she couldn't hide her joy, so happy she was to see him alive.

They left the center of tranquil Canterbury and returned to the rolling green ruins. Adele didn't feel as safe away from the cathedral, but she noted with relief that Greyfriar seemed to have recovered his energy and stamina. He moved with his normal lithe ferocity.

Soon they topped a low rise, and Adele drew in a sharp gasp at what lay before them. A farm. A small house with a few rude outbuildings surrounded by freshly plowed fields. A couple of cows and pigs wandered the dirt yard around the house. And beyond it were more farms just the same. There were humans working. This picturesque glade could have been anywhere in the world. The Nile Valley. Cyprus. Adele couldn't believe it. The humans of the far north were ignorant animals. This village was impossible.

At the farmhouse, Greyfriar knocked gently on the door. An old man with silver hair opened it. The man's crinkled eyes widened in surprise and delight, and he opened the door even wider and gestured for his guest to enter quickly. He was dressed shabbily and was very ill kempt, but his humanity remained.

"Greyfriar! It warms my heart to see you again and that God has kept you safe." The old eyes paused on Adele for a moment, and even in that brief span of attention, she felt as if her whole soul had been weighed and judged. He smiled kindly at her and then returned his gaze to the swordsman.

Greyfriar said, "It is good to see you well too, Alphonse." His voice lowered even further, as if he was ashamed to ask a favor of this man. "I need shelter and food for my companion."

"I figured as much. It is rare that you travel with anyone." Alphonse turned to Adele. "Greetings. Our humble abode is at your disposal."

"Th-thank you," the girl replied with a small bow, feeling as if she was doing a poor job of hiding her shame at a lifetime of dismissing poor gentle souls like this man as cattle.

"We don't have much in the way of food, but it is yours to share." He waved a hand behind him, and a small frail form came into view. She was an elderly woman whom Adele assumed was Alphonse's wife, with snow white hair to match his.

The woman said to Adele, "Come, little one. You look done in. Sit here. My lord, you're injured. Look at the blood on your clothes. You need tending!" She glared at Greyfriar. "Men!"

Adele smiled at the silent swordsman as she collapsed onto a three-legged stool. "No, I'm fine. Very little of this blood is mine. What may I call you?"

"Nina."

The old woman disappeared for a moment and brought back a steaming bowl of soup. Soup! The wafting aroma encircled Adele with soothing warmth. She briefly wondered what it was made of, but when Nina slid a spoon in front of her, Adele dug in with relish. It was a vegetable soup, thin but delicious.

Nina held up a second bowl for Greyfriar, but Alphonse waved her aside. After all this time, the swordsman had never eaten with them, as if he knew they had little enough and had no wish to place more burden on them. Greyfriar inclined his head politely toward Nina, acknowledging her graciousness. Nina smiled and returned the bowl to the pot bubbling on the fire.

The old woman sat beside Adele and observed the young girl as she ate. A hesitant hand reached out and touched the once-fine cloak that hung in tatters over Adele's shoulders.

"I'm sorry about my appearance," Adele said through a mouthful of soup.

"I've never seen anything so fine as that garment must have been. Are you a free human?"

Before Adele could answer, Greyfriar informed Alphonse, "She needs a change of clothes."

"You are being hunted," the older man said.

Greyfriar nodded. "She was in the Tower in London."

Nina's hand flew to her mouth. "They could follow you here."

Alphonse looked sharply at his wife while he said, "Of course they could. And it doesn't matter. They have asked for help and they shall have it."

Nina straightened a bit, ashamed, and glanced askew at Adele. Then, drawing a gentle sigh, she announced, "I'll get some clothes."

When she returned, she handed them to Alphonse. He patted her frail old hand and then offered the bundle to Adele.

"They aren't pretty, but they will serve to hide you, make you one of us."

The clothes were rough homespun, like the attire of practically every human she had come across since entering vampire territory.

Adele pulled Greyfriar aside and whispered, "We must go."

He replied quietly, "We'll go soon enough. You need to rest."

"No! We have to go. Flay will come again. I won't have these people killed because they harbored me."

"They know me. They accept the risk."

"So did the people in Riez," Adele snapped. "The risk is too high."

"These people live with the constant threat of vampires, Princess. They could be struck down any day. Helping you will give their lives a purpose. You must see that."

Adele rubbed her face in exhaustion. She nodded against her will.

"Change now and then rest," Greyfriar told her. He stared out the window, as if anxious to be gone. "We'll only stay a few hours. Then we will be on our way."

Nina showed Adele where she could change behind a blanket stretched across a corner of the cabin. When the princess emerged, she was dressed like any other human in the north. If Greyfriar hadn't known her to be royalty he would have thought her only a mere farm girl except for her poise and the determined expression on her face. Even dressed in rags, she was powerful and beautiful. She regarded him curiously, a silent smile in her eyes. He half expected her to twirl for his inspection.

Adele placed her original garments on the table. "Nina, you may have these if you wish. Perhaps you can sell them. A little money could—"

"Burn them," Greyfriar commanded.

"What?" Adele retorted with angry surprise.

"Flay will have her hunters out. They know your scent."

"Hunters?"

Nina's whisper was laced with so much fear it sent chills up Adele's spine. The princess looked at Greyfriar with fearful curiosity.

"Hunters are raw vampires," Greyfriar explained. "Throwbacks. They have changed little since the dawn of time. They are more primal than clan vampires. They are true to the animal nature of the race. They are trained to track and kill prey."

Adele flashed back to the tunnel under the Thames. That creature had behaved more like an animal, but it had the same twisted sickness she had witnessed with vampires.

"What do they look like?" Adele's voice was no louder than Nina's now. "I think I saw one."

Greyfriar immediately turned to her. Even through the smoked glasses she knew she had alarmed him.

"I doubt it. If you had seen one, you'd be dead."

"I killed it in the tunnel. Under the Thames."

"You came through a tunnel?" He stepped up to her and grabbed her shoulder.

"I—I was trying to lose Flay's soldiers. There was someone, some-thing in there along with the . . ." She glanced at Nina and Alphonse nervously, but couldn't find the words to describe the encounter. The very memory of its touch and breath made her ill. "It was hairy and . . . like an animal. It didn't speak. It just growled."

"You say you killed it?" The disbelief in Greyfriar's voice was evident.

"Yes." Adele straightened determinedly, pushing back her dark memories in the face of Greyfriar's impertinent doubts.

"You . . . are amazing."

That shocked her. "What?"

"You killed a vampire when your ship crashed. And now a hunter. I know of no human who has managed that."

"She killed a vampire?" Alphonse's response was a mix of awe and dread.

"Indeed." Greyfriar squeezed Adele's shoulder. "Get some rest."

"What about you?" Adele was worried about him. He never seemed to rest when she rested.

"I'll rest in a bit. But I want to check the area first."

She couldn't control the swell of anxiety that flooded her as she watched him leave. She felt safer with him than without him; bad things happened when he wasn't around.

Greyfriar walked beside the freshly turned fields, observing the valley's farmers as they settled for the night. One young man was putting away his herd, two cows. His farm was near the edge of the woods, where it was dark and remote. He was ideal.

Greyfriar slipped into the woods and removed his glasses, relishing the moment when he could look upon the world with unshaded eyes. It was much brighter, with much more color. He unwound his head wrap, letting the breeze dry his heated skin. Then he pulled off his gloves and unstrapped his human weapons.

The young farmer was in the process of closing the gate of his cattle pen and had his back turned to Gareth. A cold hand fell upon the man's shoulder, and he spun around and saw the marked features of a vampire. There was no scream from his throat, almost as if he were expecting it.

Gareth's fingers brushed along the man's jaw. "Do not be afraid. You will not die tonight, but I need sustenance." Gareth wished there was some other way, but the fight with Flay had drained him, and there was still a long flight ahead. He could not protect Adele if he did not feed.

The human cast his eyes to the forest's edge, and his throat lay exposed in the moonlight.

"Close your eyes."

The human swallowed hard, and Gareth watched the man's Adam's apple bob wildly for a second. Then Gareth took the man's hand, bared his fangs, and sank them into the wrist. The man shuddered as his energy and life's blood was siphoned. Gareth kept his wits about him, monitoring the victim's heartbeat, taking only enough to see him and Adele safely away. When they reached Edinburgh he could feed more fully, spreading his hunger over more of his flock.

Finally the farmer's heart raced, struggling to pump his draining blood supply. He grew limp in Gareth's arms. The vampire prince released his hold and drew back his fangs. He took some blood and rubbed it over his chest and arms to renew his olfactory disguise. Then he lifted the unconscious human, entered the lean-to, and placed the man in the straw meant for his cattle. The man moaned slightly as Gareth closed the makeshift gate behind him to keep other predators from the farmer.

Wiping the excess blood from his lips with the back of his hand, Gareth strode back into the forest to his human clothes. Adele would wake soon, and then they would move on. Soon he would have to reveal himself to her, and he knew what her reaction would be.

His numb heart broke at that realization.

CHAPTER  22

ADELE SMELLED THE sea before it came into view. Greyfriar led them to the coast, and for the first time the air tasted salty like in Alexandria.

"It's wonderful," she remarked to Greyfriar, drawing a deep breath.

"You like the sea?"

Adele smiled. "I do. I live near the sea."

Greyfriar didn't reply, but he was relieved to hear such things. It gave him hope for her tolerance of the next stage of their journey.

Adele asked, "How about you?"

Greyfriar merely regarded her strangely.

"The sea," she said. "Do you like the sea?"

He shrugged. "I don't have time to consider it, although I have a home near the sea too."

"Really?" Adele exclaimed, delighted. "I think it's nice we have something in common, in addition, of course, to hating vampires and fleeing for our lives."

"I do also," he replied.

They followed the coast road for a bit. Greyfriar had an unerring sense of direction, and it wasn't long before he veered abruptly down to the water. In front of a shrouded grove overgrown with vines and thick hedges, he started hacking his way through until he revealed a fifteen-foot sailboat with a mast and moldy canvas inside.

"I've had it hidden here for many months. We must now travel by sea."

"We'll be more visible to enemies in the air," Adele pointed out.

"Perhaps, but it will provide us a better opportunity to escape. We need distance fast." With a few hard tugs the two of them maneuvered the boat over the rocky beach to the water's edge.

"By the way, do you know how to sail?" he asked her.

The question took Adele by surprise. "Yes. Don't you?"

"Not really. I've never liked being on the water." In fact, he didn't like flying over it either. Most vampires were plagued by uneasiness when drifting over water. The thought of falling in and being weighed down, and finally drowning was terrifying to them. "You will need to operate the sails."

"How did you get from France to Britain? Fly?"

"No!" he retorted a trifle strongly. "I have allies in the underground with boats."

Adele hid her small grin as they set the mast, grateful that she could do something he could not. The man was almost infallible, and it pleased her to be needed. They manhandled the boat into the slim surf, and with practiced hands she raised the ragged sail. It immediately caught the breath of the wind and puffed out as full and tight as the mildewed old canvas could stand. They put out to a mercifully calm sea.

Greyfriar said, "We appear to be sinking already."

Adele scanned the scummy water sloshing at their feet. It wasn't rising rapidly. She shrugged. "No. We're fine. You may have to bail later. But we can stay ahead of it. We're lucky this old boat is afloat at all. But I've seen worse. Trust me."

"As you say. Turn north when you can," Greyfriar informed her, still eyeing the water in the bottom of the boat with some alarm.

From her place in the stern clutching the tiller, Adele playfully said, "I realize you're no mariner, but the Continent is south. As is Equatoria."

"Small steps, Princess. We must go one way first to eventually reach our goal. North. There is sanctuary there. Trust me."

"I do." Adele offered him a broad smile. As the sea wind buffeted her, she relaxed for the first time in many weeks.

Greyfriar stopped looking at his water-soaked boots and stared at her. It was almost a full minute before he responded. "That's good. I might need that trust more before we're finished."

"You'll have it. You've always had it." She leaned forward and placed her hand over his gloved one.

He imagined the warmth of her hand as she squeezed.

—◦◦◦—

Alphonse sat in a chair as Nina cleared the dishes from their simple meal. His worn pipe was in his hands, and his thick fingers gently packed it with the last of his tobacco. He'd have to go and see whether Maize had more in his storehouse that he might be willing to trade for some of Nina's preserves. It was a foolish indulgence, he knew. But Nina even claimed she liked the smell in the little hut. She said it covered the stench of their existence.

The old woman cast a smile to her husband over her shoulder, and he smiled back.

The door smashed open. Nina spun around with barely time to grasp the edge of the table behind her before she was thrown to the floor next to her husband. Three red-coated vampires stood over them. The hut filled with stench as two snarling animals with elongated fangs entered, naked and dirty, crawling on all fours. Taut straps of leather attached their straining necks to the corded arm of a tall female dressed in the remnants of royalty. Flay surveyed the room, then released the hunters.

The two things scuffled to the table, grabbed items, smelled them briefly, and threw them to the side. They were going to find out. They were going to know that the escaped girl had been here with Greyfriar. The hunters touched Nina's thin white hair with their claws. They both sniffed the base of her neck as she huddled over her knees. Her shiver was a violent thing.

Their master said nothing, not even bothering to speak to the lowly humans. She stood idly, waiting for the creatures to find a scent. The hunters could kill the elderly couple and the female wouldn't care. Her total disregard for the humans cowering at her feet was chilling.

One of the hunters drew its gnarled hands over Alphonse, picking at the edge of his shirt with its skeletal finger. Alphonse groaned as the hunters scuttled to the door. He heard Nina weeping faintly as the two things left the hut, followed by the other vampires. Alphonse's hand slowly covered Nina's. It was inevitable that they would return. What they searched for was outside.

Mere moments passed, and Alphonse experienced a shard of hope. Perhaps the creatures would find nothing. Perhaps the couple's efforts at deception had been adequate. Then the hunters let loose a ghastly screech.

"They found it," Nina moaned.

"And if they did, then that is our fate. We will face it together and know that we did the right thing."

Nina nodded, unable to speak in the face of her fear.

A vampire soldier entered the hut.

"Stand," he commanded, his unconscious hiss dragging out the word.

Alphonse assisted Nina, who barely had the strength of will to make it to her feet. They followed the red-coated vampire outside and were led directly to the pit where Alphonse had burned and buried the clothing of the girl with Greyfriar. The hunters crouched in the middle of it, covered with dirt and ash. They were hissing and moaning, snuffling in the ash. The vampire soldier shoved the two humans to their knees in front of Flay.

Flay's lips broke into a cruel smile. "They actually believed they could fool us."

Alphonse made no effort to respond. It was useless.

Flay slapped her thigh, and the hunters shambled against her legs like pets. She caressed the beasts' heads with affection before quickly grabbing handfuls of the hunters' hair and flesh. "Find the princess and this entire village will be your reward."

The hunters licked their fangs, staring hungrily at Alphonse and Nina, who both whimpered against their will. With a shriek, the hunters shook loose and ran toward the northeast, the direction Greyfriar had gone barely two days before.

Flay towered over the two trembling humans. Nina collapsed to the ground, and Alphonse fell with her, grabbing Nina's arm tighter in a vain attempt to give her his strength. Death was only hours away, and there was nowhere to run.

—⁓—

Days passed with fair wind the whole way up the coast. It was fine sailing weather, and Adele actually enjoyed herself. They put into land a few times for food, water, and to camp for the night. They sailed by day because it was still usual for vampires to prowl the night. Greyfriar, though obviously uneasy about being at sea, grew more relaxed, or at least Adele imagined him to be so. After several days, he offered to take a turn at the tiller, for which she was grateful. The minute she stood, the boat rocked and Greyfriar grasped the sides nervously.

"Sorry," she offered, moving forward.

Only when she had settled did he ease to his feet and inch past her. It was odd to see the man who had faced vampire armies quail at the thought of falling overboard. He reached the stern and clutched the tiller with a relieved sigh. He unstrapped his longsword and laid it across his lap.

Adele asked, "Is it possible you don't know how to swim?"

"Very possible indeed."

Adele grabbed the small pail he had been using to bail and began to scoop water. "So swimming isn't considered a requisite skill for a master swordsman folk hero?"

Greyfriar replied, "Not so far. But the day is young."

She laughed and noticed how his grip never lessened on his sword. "Is that blade special to you?"

"It is exceedingly sharp. And it bites clean."

"I mean, does it have special meaning? Was it . . . your father's sword?"

"Oh no. Nothing like that. But the sword is such a remarkable creation. It's an extension of one's self. Unlike the pistol, which is clumsy and impersonal. There is no skill to firearms."

"I agree with you. I learned how to shoot quite quickly. The sword took a long time. I'm still learning."

Greyfriar leaned forward. "But don't you find the challenge incredibly satisfying? Using your hands." He extended his arm and worked his gloved hand as if manipulating a sword. "I never tire of it."

"Yes, definitely. It was worth every aching muscle and reprimand." She raised her eyebrows in mock conceit. "I was taught by a master swordsman from Japan. And I fancy myself an excellent swordswoman. Or I did until I saw you in action."

"No, don't think that. I've told you before. You are most extraordinary."

Adele blushed.

Greyfriar said, "Your instincts are excellent, but your blade work needs more control. That is merely a matter of practice."

Now she pursed her lips in mild annoyance. She hadn't been expecting criticism.

He continued, "Still, I have spent many years among vampires, and among those who wish to kill them. I have never seen anyone like you. You sense the world around you in a way that is . . . unnatural." He laughed. "Like a vampire. You feel rather than see."

"I'm not sure that's a good thing."

"It's neither good nor bad. I marvel at you. I have from the beginning. I can tell you were born to it. With some final honing, you will be fearful to behold."

Adele couldn't catch her breath at his words. "Well, I . . . uh . . . thank you. I wonder why my teacher has never told me anything like that."

Greyfriar replied, "Perhaps he doesn't know. Or perhaps he's afraid that if you realize what you can be, he'll have nothing left to teach you."

"Well, who taught you?"

"I had a very poor instructor. Myself."

"What? You're self-taught? That's remarkable."

"Not so. My skill is merely a product of time. And I have time. I spend a great deal of time alone. As you might imagine." He took a breath. "It's a great pleasure to have you with me now."

Adele ran her hand through her tangled hair, frowning at its wretched condition. "Thank you. I've told you, you can come to Alexandria and spend as much time as you like."

"That is unlikely. For my sake, I'd have you with me much longer. For your sake, I'm sorry that I can't take you home immediately."

She felt an ache. "So can you tell me what is in the north for us?"

"Temporary safety. It will buy us time while Flay scours the south for you. Do not worry."

"I'm just curious, that's all," Adele reassured him. "I do have an interest in this affair. And I still know so little about you or your plans."

He nodded. "I think you will like it in the north."

The young woman accepted his deflection of her comment. For the moment. She was happy to have a conversation that wasn't about pure survival. "I've never been this far north. I've only read about it."

He paused a moment, and his voice grew rich. "Where we're going is wild and rugged. It is a place of dark lochs and mountains covered in heather. It's cold and it smells clean. I love it there."

"I figured you were the outdoors type."

He shrugged. "If it were up to me I'd spend all my time outside rather than in the bowels of a building. To live as my ancestors once did, off the land and traveling the open road."

"You're a romantic."

Smoke-covered glass turned toward her. "Is that bad?"

"No. Not at all. Quite fetching, actually." She smiled shyly at him. "And you come complete with a dashing cape and sword. What's not to like?"

"Are you a romantic, yourself?"

Adele considered, pausing a moment from the chore of bailing. "I'd like to be. It's hard when you're a princess. I have an enormous amount of responsibilities at court. It doesn't leave much time for being a romantic. But when you were talking about the north, about how wild it is, it reminded me of the open desert. I was always overwhelmed by the desert, although I never spent much time there. Unfortunately."

"When were you last there?"

"Years ago. I went on a trip with my brother and Colonel Anhalt.

And about forty members of my court staff. But one night, I slipped away with only dear Colonel Anhalt as my bodyguard. He told me I needed to experience the desert, to see its loneliness and its beauty. He said it had much to teach me. He is such a wonderful man. A constant presence in my life." She sighed, a bit melancholy, and gazed out over the waves. "We rode to an oasis, where he named the stars for me. It was so beautiful. So open and wild. The stars and the moon. The wind. I can't even describe it. Have you ever been to the desert?"

"No."

"Colonel Anhalt told me that the desert is like a person. You can never know it completely. If you think you do, you are playing a dangerous game. You can never trust the desert, because the minute you do, it will kill you." Adele laughed. "I didn't really understand what he was telling me. I think he was warning me that, as a princess, I could never completely trust anyone. Or maybe he was saying I shouldn't be seduced by the wild side. That I had to put girlish dreams aside. I have a duty to my people, and I shouldn't even think about running off for a life of adventure and romance."

"I'm sorry," Greyfriar said.

"For what?"

"That something you love can't be a source of comfort."

"It's the way life is, I suppose. There are some things you can trust, and some you can't. You just have to figure out what they are. Listen to me. I'm a philosopher."

The swordsman turned to the sea, almost melancholy. "Indeed."

Adele watched him start to withdraw. Desperate to change the mood, she cast about for something new to say. "Do you know how to fish? I might be getting hungry."

"No." His posture relaxed. "If I can't swim, what are the chances I fish?"

She chuckled with relief. "True. Fish were a staple of my diet. My brother and I would go fishing with Colonel Anhalt when we were younger, though that's a luxury we no longer have. Plus, Lake Mareotis is too polluted to fish now."

"Did you enjoy it?"

Adele paused to reflect. "I enjoyed the time I spent with my brother, now more than ever." Her sad eyes turned to him, only to soften with a small secret smile. "But I don't miss the fish themselves. They stink. I don't know how cats stand them."

Now it was Greyfriar's turn to laugh. It was such an odd sound to hear. Adele loved it. It was strong and low. Her skin shivered with goose bumps at the sound of it. She immediately longed to hear it again.

"Of course," she said, "we don't smell so good either right now, I'm sure."

"You'll be able to clean up once we reach our destination," he told her.

"I suppose that will have to do." Adele sighed and watched the slate coast. She knew Greyfriar was staring at her. She liked it.

He suddenly stood. "Take the tiller, if you will." He started making his way forward.

"Is everything all right?" she inquired as she settled at the stern.

From the other side of the fluttering sail, he said, "Yes. I just want to clean up a bit."

Adele smiled. He was doing it for her, most likely. She probably shouldn't have said anything about the smell, but she delighted in the fact that he was making himself more presentable for her. No man had ever lavished such consideration on her except when there was an underlying reason for it, like her hand in marriage or a plea of forgiveness from her father on a matter of state.

Greyfriar removed his tunic and shirt. Adele saw his arm dip into the cold seawater. Biting her lip, she leaned over the rail a bit, angling for a better view. Perhaps he had removed his mask. She just wanted to see what he looked like. After all, she had followed him, a stranger, based only on his word. It would be a small reward to place a face to the myth.

Greyfriar's back was to her, broad, muscled, and scarred. His flesh was pale, not tan like she had thought. He probably spent far too much time cloaked. Dried blood caked his skin, and Adele saw his wet hand come away dripping red.

"Are you hurt?" Adele stood up abruptly, causing the boat to rock.

Greyfriar grasped the edge of the prow and almost looked at her, but stopped. "No. It is not my blood." There was almost shame in his tone.

"Oh." Adele sat down and held the tiller steadier. "Do you need any help?" she asked nervously.

His answer came back fast. "No." His voice settled after a few seconds. "I'm fine." He donned his clothes again, masking his identity from her once more.

"I'm glad you're not hurt." Adele could not hide her disappointment that he had shoved her concern aside. But he was a warrior, and proud. She knew his type from her time spent with Colonel Anhalt.

As another day, and then another, passed on their northward cruise, Greyfriar studied the shoreline. When they camped ashore, he was restless. They were nearing their destination, and most likely he felt pangs of worry that something would go wrong at the last minute. Adele hoped he would confide in her, but by the next day at sea, he was still silent.

"So," she said plainly, "we must be off the coast of Scotland by now. Yes? I wonder that there is somewhere safe in Scotland. That's Prince Gareth's territory."

Greyfriar started. "Yes, it is Scotland. But you have nothing to fear from Prince Gareth."

"How do you know?"

"Didn't you meet him in London?"

"Yes. So?"

"What . . . what did you think of him?"

The princess shrugged. "I don't know. He was odd. He seemed to have an interest in human culture."

"Yes. He is not your enemy."

"Well, in any case, he certainly seemed better than Cesare."

"Thank you."

"What?"

"Nothing. Humans are safer in Scotland than anywhere in Britain." Before Adele could ask any further questions, he pointed. "There. Turn into that inlet. Careful. I'm told the sea is rough. We'll put ashore and walk the rest of the way."

Adele obediently adjusted the tiller and trimmed the sail. She guided the boat around a rocky promontory. There were signs of a town along the shoreline and the caustic scent of smoke in the air. After many minutes of careful and strenuous sailing, she coaxed the waterlogged old boat to the shore. When they drew close, Greyfriar leapt into the freezing water and wrestled the boat until it scraped onto the rocky bottom. Then he gave a hand to Adele. The footing on the rocks was precarious, but Greyfriar did not let go of her hand as they made their way dripping wet onto the jagged shore and away from the sea.

Eventually the ground evened out and they crossed what looked to be an old wagon-rutted road. Adele hesitated, instinct immediately warning her to stick to areas not so well traveled, but to her surprise Greyfriar shook his head.

"We will be safe enough. I know this area well."

Alarms were beginning to sound in her. How could a lone human be so at ease so deep inside vampire territory? She saw the distant grey skyline of a city. A forest of smoke rose from many chimneys.

"What is that place?" Adele looked around with increasing distress.

"Edinburgh."

"Edinburgh? Are you insane? Why go there?"

"You must trust me, Princess. What I do is for your safety."

Adele stopped dead in her tracks. She could see clearly a brooding castle rising in the distance, crouched on a bare rock face overlooking the grey city. Its black stones hovered like shadows in the dispersing fog. She knew what monsters lived there.

Greyfriar had hoped they'd be closer before he had to show himself. They were still out in the open and therefore still vulnerable. But he knew that the trust he had garnered with Adele was rapidly dissipating. His shoulders slumped ever so slightly. "I once told you that your trust would be tested."

"But this seems a trifle extreme," Adele snapped, glancing about for the enemy. "How could this possibly be a safe haven? I'm no better off here than I was when a prisoner of Cesare!"

"I'll explain everything soon. We just need to go a bit farther."

Defiant and fearful, she refused. "I want answers first. I've followed you blindly long enough. I need to know what our plans are, right now!"

Greyfriar laughed quietly, but there was no trace of mirth in it. His chest rose and fell with a shuddering breath. The camaraderie they had shared these last days ended now.

Greyfriar looked into her eyes, knowing that it would be the last time he would see familiarity and warmth in them. He drew in one more tantalizing breath of her subtle scent. Then with his arms he threw back the cape and drew a sword. To her surprise, he handed it to her. Adele's face was a painting of curiosity and shock, her mouth held in that perfect O shape. He pulled his pistols and then his daggers. He laid them at her feet. She held the sword with one end cradled in the crook of her arm.

Completely unarmed, he reached out a gloved hand and slowly drew down his mask, and with the other he pulled away the glasses from his eyes to reveal himself as Prince Gareth, the heir to the vampire clan of Great Britain. And in those few seconds her scent changed again. Sweetness gave way to acidic spice.

After a few heartbeats, Adele attacked him. His own sword whipped at him with finesse and swiftness. He used his natural speed to slip her strike, feeling the air as the steel sliced inches from his face. Her cry of fury carried after, and it cut through him far more effectively than the blade could.

She sidestepped quickly and spun, catching the shoulder clasp of his cape. It snagged the sword, and Adele shoved the blade hard into his shoulder. He surged toward her, capturing the blade in his muscle almost to the hilt, barely feeling the coldness of the steel. She tried to flee, but his arms snaked around her.

"Princess! Please! I do not wish to harm you!"

"You . . . you can't be . . . Let me go!" she shouted struggling against his grip. "What have you done with Greyfriar? You . . . you killed him . . . took his place!" Her voice was hoarse with wrath and terror.

"You know that's not true. I am Greyfriar, and have been from the beginning."

Adele sobbed against his arms. Of course she knew it. There was no way this vampire could have pretended to be Greyfriar. He was Greyfriar.

Oh merciful heaven, she had placed her trust and her . . . How could she have been so blind!

His voice was low in her ear. "I feel deeply for the plight of humans. I swear it. I regret how my kind has treated your people. I want to help."

"Liar!"

"To what end, Princess? I've only tried to keep you from Cesare's hands."

"You hide behind a mask, pretending you're a human, like it's a sick game!" Adele could barely breathe. Her struggles ceased. It was no use to fight against the strength of this vampire. Her freedom had been snatched away again like a terrible joke.

Gareth's arms slipped away from her, and he stepped back. His face was cold and pale, his eyes as colorless as frost. He lifted a hand to the hilt of the sword and pulled it free of his shoulder in a single tug. Adele stiffened, ready for a fight, but he merely tossed the blade at her feet.

"You may not believe me, Princess, but it is my hope to succeed my father's throne and begin reforms. But such a thing takes time, and until then, I can only help humans from disguise."

"Why should I believe anything you say? Stop using his voice!"

Gareth shrugged and drew Greyfriar's cloak around him. He consciously altered his voice to his normal deeper tone, the voice of Prince Gareth. The voice that spoke to Adele of London and death and horrific violence. "Keep my weapons for safety, but you must follow me to the castle."

Adele cautiously knelt and picked up the sword, still wet with Gareth's blood. "What do you expect of me?"

"Nothing, but to stay safe until I can return you to your home." Gareth indicated the castle. "Please."

Adele rubbed her face with a tired hand. All her energy had drained away, leaving her confused and helpless. She stated wearily, "I hate you."

"I know."

The prince gestured again with Greyfriar's hand for Adele to go ahead of him. She dropped back to gather the rest of his weapons, placing them in her belt and pockets until she was a walking armory. She straightened with his blade held firmly in her one hand and his pistol in her other. "After you."

He studied her a moment and then turned and strode toward the ominous castle. Adele stood alone on the cobblestones, staring at the bleak city and empty streets. Then she followed him.

CHAPTER 23

THE STREETS OF Edinburgh were soulless and damp. Adele remained fixated on the back of the vampire walking before her, his dark cloak floating behind. The smell of smoke filled the air, and homey yellow windows glowed in many of the dark slate buildings.

"Where are your herds?" The acid in Adele's voice burned her own ears.

Gareth didn't flinch. "I have none."

How easily the vampire lied.

As they entered the courtyard of the great castle, the gaping maw of a door yawned open before Gareth. A dark figure stood just inside. Startled, Adele stepped back. The man bowed low to Gareth and then to the princess.

Gareth inclined his head to the man. "Allow me to present my oldest friend, Baudoin, the only other vampire in all of Edinburgh."

Adele pointed a pistol at him in warning. Baudoin's eyebrow rose and he regarded Gareth a moment, studying his prince, noting his blood-soaked shirt.

"Are you all right, my lord?"

"Have rooms and a hot meal prepared for the princess, Baudoin." Gareth's hand rose to touch his shoulder. He swore the wound pulsed with each beat of his heart, as if his flesh was freshly raw.

He waved Adele inside, but she still refused to go first. With the barest of defeated sighs, he went in, gesturing Baudoin after him, expecting and hoping the princess would follow. To Gareth's relief, she did, leaving noticeable distance between them. He couldn't blame her, really.

Adele's eyes bored into the back of the vampire. She couldn't believe that she hadn't been able to tell the difference between human and vampire, that a mask and dark glasses were enough to fool her. Gareth had used a different stance than the Greyfriar, and his voice was wildly different. But still. Now, every gesture appeared so obviously similar. What an idiot she was.

Baudoin disappeared into a side door, and Adele almost didn't notice, so intent was her attention on the vampire prince. As her gaze shifted about she noticed other inhabitants of the castle, dark shapes that slinked from shadow to shadow as if uncertain.

Cats, hundreds of them.

They swarmed around Gareth, but he seemed to pay them little notice. Their small heads rubbed against his legs in a desperate attempt to attract attention. Finally he reached down and scooped up a black-and-orange cat that immediately began to purr loudly and settle in the arms of the vampire. He stroked it absently as they continued down the hall. Empty suits of armor lined the walls like silent sentinels, many with living feline sentinels perched on their shoulders. The cats seemed almost happy to see their master. Adele had never heard of animals that could abide the company of vampires, nor vice versa. Every living thing was food to vampires.

The chill of the castle infested the young girl. Adele shivered but refused to draw her arms about herself to ward off the cold. The sword clutched in her hand trembled, catching the ambient light, casting it onto the dark walls in bright little slivers. The quick darting beams of luminosity excited the cats, who vainly tried to catch them with their paws. Adele sought to keep her attention on Gareth instead of on the antics of the cats, but she was so weary and the long journey was taking its overdue toll. Her eyes kept darting to the side, and her blade dropped lower as she stumbled along.

Abruptly, Baudoin appeared in front of her, holding a hissing torch. She started, pistol and blade slicing up quickly in front of her.

He kept his distance. "If you will follow me, Princess, I will show you to your quarters."

The thought of going off alone with a strange vampire repelled her, but she had no choice. She no longer felt safe with Greyfriar or Gareth or whomever he chose to be.

Adele gestured with the blade that Baudoin should precede her. He bowed slightly, his face grim, and slipped through a doorway. Gareth had paused and was watching her, still holding the dark-coated cat. Their eyes met; while regret infused his eyes, only smoldering resentment flared in hers. She turned abruptly away from him and disappeared after Baudoin and the yellow glow of the torch.

The servant stopped in front of a massive wooden door etched with geometric designs and with an ornate metal handle twice the size it needed to be for a human hand. Opening it with little difficulty, Baudoin entered. The room was huge and appeared clean and comfortable. There was a sitting corner with a chair and a table, and a huge sleigh bed with layers of thick blankets. A fire already roared in the corner fireplace, flickering warmth into the room.

Baudoin stepped up to a wall sconce and fixed the torch into it. "If there is anything you need, use this to call me." His hand fell upon a thick cord beside the bed. "I'll send you a meal in a short while."

The princess bolted the door solidly behind him. Shuddering, she moved closer to the fire so the warmth could seep into her aching bones. The weight of all the weapons dragged at her. Her shoulders throbbed and her legs trembled. A beautiful white rug in front of the fire warded off the chill from the stone floor. She meticulously removed each weapon and set them within reach before easing her body into a large, straight-back chair ripe with cushions. She left the loaded pistol in her lap just under her hand.

Adele hadn't realized she had drifted off to sleep until there was a knock at the door and she jerked in her chair, the weapons rattling as she twitched. She would have sworn that it had been only a few seconds, but the fire was now only embers and the heat was fading. Her vulnerability frightened her.

The knock came again, gentle and almost hesitant.

Adele picked up the pistol and aimed it at the door. "Who is it?"

"My name is Morgana, miss. I've brought your dinner."

"Are you alone?"

"Yes."

Adele stood, and every muscle cried out in pain. She limped to the door. Standing to the side of the door frame, she threw the bolt and then stepped back with pistol raised. After a few seconds, the latch clicked and the door opened slowly to admit a young woman. A human, dressed plainly, but better than the humans in London. She was tall and sturdy, with short blonde hair. The girl's eyes quickly locked onto the pistol in Adele's hands. Her eyebrows rose in astonishment, though Adele could not determine if it was the shock of being threatened or the mere sight of a human holding a gun.

The woman's hands held a tray heaped high with food. Adele's stomach immediately betrayed her as she breathed in a nose full of the wonderful scents. It smelled of stew and bread and beer. It took all her willpower not to leap on it like a starving animal.

"Are you another of Gareth's prisoners?" Adele asked, trying to keep her attention off the food.

The young woman laughed softly. "I'm no prisoner. No more than you." She placed the dishes on the table near the sputtering fire. "You best eat now while it's hot." Morgana emptied the tray and set it on the bed. Then she moved to the fire and stirred the embers before adding more wood, making it roar once more.

Adele sat almost against her will. She didn't want any of Gareth's kindness, but she needed her strength if she was going to find a way to escape, and the serving girl seemed harmless enough. Adele watched the dance of the flames as she devoured a piece of warm, crusty bread.

Morgana gestured to the pistol still in Adele's hand. "You have no need to keep holding that."

"That's sweet, but I like having it while there are vampires lurking."

"You have nothing to fear of Prince Gareth."

"Did he write that for you to say? Oh, that's right. He can't write. He's a vampire!" Adele ripped into a soft chunk of stewed pork.

Morgana smiled as she watched Adele chew. Then she rose, brushing her skirt of ash and sawdust. "Rest tonight. Tomorrow you may see for yourself." The girl retrieved the tray and left.

The room became silent once more except for the snapping of the wood in the fireplace. Adele ignored her vulnerability for the moment and concentrated on eating. She didn't even care if it was poisoned, although she doubted Gareth would go to all the trouble of dressing up and bringing her to Edinburgh just to murder her.

Eventually empty plates were pushed aside and Adele wiped her greasy face with a stained linen napkin, hunger satisfied for now. She dragged a chair to the door and jammed it under the latch before bolting the door securely again. Only then did she remove the dirtiest of her outer garments, like her shoes, cloak, and skirt. Those she folded onto a nearby chair, then crawled under the bedcovers still dressed for the most part.

Shadows crept along the walls. Adele tried to still the fear that grew inside her. The thought of giving in to her exhaustion terrified her. But she knew that eventually her body would betray her.

Suddenly a shadow moved in the wrong direction.

Adele jumped up, grasping the pistol. However, she didn't fire. Her instincts held true. It wasn't a vampire creeping in the darkness. It was a cat.

The furry little beast stretched lazily, as if it had been woken from its sleep. The cat didn't even question who the stranger was in its room. It hopped onto the bed and came over to her without fear, immediately purring its contentment at finding company this evening.

Adele warmed to the cat's affections; after all, it had no concept of its circumstances. It was not to blame for being in the house of a monster. Its fur was grey and white, with little white paws and a white spot dotting the left side of its face.

Adele reclined. The cat's body was warm and it curled against her, its tail encircling its feet. Such unconditional trust eased Adele's own anxiety a bit. She reached out with her other hand and pulled the long blade close, her fingers wrapping around the cold metal. Before she realized it, she fell asleep, clutching Greyfriar's sword.

Adele woke alone in the bed. Her dreams had been filled with vampires and screams. The cat that had kept her company through most of the night had disappeared somewhere, although the bedroom door still remained locked and barricaded. Pale daylight streamed through the thin curtains, dispelling the darkness that had so frightened her during the night. She threw back the warm covers and opened the curtains to see a bare castle courtyard. Not so very different from her view in the Tower of London.

She turned from the window with her breath misting and lifted her ratty cloak from the back of a chair. It was stained beyond measure, and there were rips and tears over most of it. The cloak was hardly worth mending, but she had to try anyway. She had no idea how long it would be until she could find another to replace it. There was no thread and needle in the room, so it would have to wait. All she could do was brush it as clean as possible. Perhaps the girl Morgana could supply the necessary items to mend the cloak properly.

It was easy enough to restart the fire to ward off the damp morning chill. Then she strapped on the weaponry and sat by the fire. However, it didn't take her curiosity long to get the better of her, and she wondered what lay outside the door.

The hall was quiet, with a few cats moving in the shadows. No one seemed to be watching her; even the cats gave her only the occasional glance. Adele couldn't help but wonder who else lived in this sprawling castle besides the three people she had already met. Well, one person and two vampires.

The hallway wound through the castle, and she passed many doorways, open and closed, on either side. The majority of the rooms were unoccupied, but all of the doors were unlocked. Nothing was forbidden to her.

She heard sounds and cautiously approached, finding Gareth and Baudoin as the source. The former sat alone at the head of a great table. Cats mewled around the two vampires as if looking for handouts, while Baudoin prepared a place at Gareth's left.

Gareth turned to her, although she had yet to step through the threshold. "Good morning, Princess Adele. I told Baudoin to expect you up early."

It annoyed her that Gareth knew even that much about her. "I'm surprised you allow me to wander around alone. I could have walked right out the door."

Gareth leaned back into his chair. "Yes, you could have."

Baudoin gestured for Adele to join them. She remained rooted to the stone floor. The servant brought plates of sizzling eggs and warm bread with fresh jam and thick rich coffee. The smell of it was overwhelming to her.

A cat jumped into Gareth's lap and immediately curled up. It was the grey-and-white cat that had spent the night with her. It presented its chin for him to scratch. He obediently obliged the feline, which began to purr.

"I hope you slept well," Gareth said to her.

Adele turned on him angrily. "No! I didn't! Did you? Did you laugh yourself to sleep? If your kind even sleeps."

Gareth drummed his long fingers on the table. "There is no danger here to you. You may rest easy."

"Why should I believe anything you say?"

"I can't ask you to. But I tell you again, I will see you home in time. Just as Greyfriar promised."

Adele resented the pain that struck at the name of her onetime hero. "Why? Why the charade?" she exclaimed abruptly. "The mask and the glasses and the voice."

"I want to help."

"Help me feel a fool? Congratulations. Well done!" Adele strode over and grabbed a long loaf of bread. "Am I free to go back to my room?"

"Yes." Gareth drew in a deep breath. "You are free to walk anywhere here in the castle. I beg you please not to leave the grounds, however."

"What? No chains?"

The vampire flicked a glance at her from beneath clenched brows. "You are not my prisoner. I can only tell you so many times. You will go home. When the time is right. Go where you will. But please be mindful that there are dangers about. I depend on your native intelligence to stay safe. I do not intend to follow you around like a jailer."

Adele glared at him and stalked out the door with bread in hand and a sword in her belt.

The cat jumped down from Gareth's lap and followed her out, tail in the air.

Baudoin appeared from the shadows. "Should I follow her?"

"No."

"What would happen if she left the castle and Flay found her?"

"I don't believe even Flay could've tracked her here by now. Even if she did, everything would remain status quo. I would merely say that I recaptured her from Greyfriar."

"Would your brother really believe that?"

"Of course. What's the alternative? That I *am* Greyfriar?" Gareth laughed harshly.

"I did not mean any disrespect, my lord."

Gareth waved a hand at his servant, dismissing the issue. "I know. This is just not how I imagined it would be."

"My lord?"

"I don't like that she feels betrayed. She is very angry and hurt."

"You are not in danger, are you? Surely she's not powerful enough to strike you down. You mentioned she had skills."

"No," Gareth emphatically assured his servant. "I'm not afraid of her attacking me. It's just that she's . . . far more pleasant when she is not angry."

"You like this human female's company?" Dismay rather than surprise filled Baudoin.

Gareth was lost in his own musings, unaware of his servant's horrified expression. "I find her most interesting. Full of life and vigor."

"I gather you're not referring to her as a delicious meal."

Gareth gave him a scathing look. Then he stood.

"Are you going to follow her," Baudoin asked, "like a jailer?"

"Yes I am." Gareth slipped from the room.

CHAPTER 24

Adele stormed out of the castle. She had no plan; anger propelled her. She had no idea what awaited her outside the castle walls, but she had every intention of leaving and making her way somewhere safe. There had been so many lies lately that she couldn't trust anything anymore.

She followed the same path that had brought her here, heading north toward the water and the boat. The city had been empty when she arrived, but she now saw people. Lots of people. And what amazed her was that they were performing everyday duties: cooking, cleaning, and bartering. Adele had seen none of that in London. The humans there were repressed, as if having no will. People here seemed content; some even smiled. The only other time she had seen a northern human show a happy emotion was the couple in Canterbury, Alphonse and Nina. They hadn't known Greyfriar was a vampire. She wondered if the people here knew the truth about him.

Adele finally reached the lonely sea and scanned the shoreline. The boat was gone. Of course, he would hide it from her. She was a prisoner, after all. Her anger seethed at Gareth.

As she slowly trudged back into town, people eyed her curiously, and a few lifted a hand in greeting. Adele hesitantly returned their waves. Then hurrying down a street was Morgana, carrying a bundle in her arms. The princess called out to her.

Morgana stopped and smiled. "Ah, there you are, miss. I went to your room, but you weren't there."

"What's wrong?"

"Nothing. I collected your cloak to be mended."

"You shouldn't do that. I can sew. I just need a needle and thread."

"No bother, miss. I'm just bringing it to Ol' Mary. She'll fix it up right."

Adele hesitated, then asked, "May I come along with you?"

"Of course, miss."

The two walked quietly for a bit until Adele's curiosity got the better of her.

"How did you get here?" Adele asked. "To Edinburgh, I mean. Were you born here?"

"Have you ever heard of Greyfriar? Human wonderworker. He rescued a number of us from the slave pens in London and brought us here. He must work with Prince Gareth or something."

"Or something."

Morgana laughed loudly. "I'd most likely be dead by now in London, a meal for the royal court or worse, if not for Greyfriar. And Prince Gareth. They are gluttons there, and not one of them would stop before they drained a soul dry."

Adele couldn't help sneering. "So everyone is safe and happy here? Then what does Gareth eat? Dirt? Angels?"

"No. We offer ourselves to him."

Adele's expression of horror was raw and open. "You let him feed off you?"

"Prince Gareth asks for only sips and none from the same person within the year." Morgana bared her wrist. There were long-healed puncture marks. "It's a small price to pay not to be murdered in your sleep."

"My God! I would die before I let him feed off me!"

"I doubt he will ask it of you. There are too many who would give it willingly."

"You're all insane. This place is insane." Adele pointed north toward the water. "And the boat is gone! He took it away! He knew I could use it to get home."

"Where are you from, miss?"

"Alexandria." A sigh escaped the princess.

Morgana nodded knowingly. "That's near Berwick-on-Tweed, isn't it?"

Adele laughed. "No. That must be another Alexandria. I'm from Alexandria in Egypt. In the Equatorian Empire."

Morgana whistled low. "That sounds far away, wherever it is. No wonder you're out of sorts. But I'm sure there is good reason for you to be here."

"Greyfriar brought me here from London." Adele's voice was laced with sarcasm.

"Well, isn't that something, we both having that in common?" Morgana smiled warmly again. "Things will feel less strange if you know your way around."

Adele eyed the servant critically. "Tell me the safest route out of the city."

"Out? There is nowhere much to go that is safe."

"So in essence we're trapped here."

"Well, I'm not trapped. I live here. I'm content. But I wouldn't suggest you try to make your way through any realm not under Prince Gareth's protection."

"That isn't much use to me. I refuse to remain a prisoner."

"You don't seem much like a prisoner, if you pardon my saying." Morgana jutted her chin at Adele's arsenal.

The princess scowled. "A prison can be more than four walls."

Morgana waved to a man with a flirtatious smile. "That's Thomas. He's a butcher."

"A butcher?" Adele was noticing shops of sorts in the buildings that weren't demolished. And her stomach rumbled. "I'd buy you a meal, but I don't have any money."

"Money? There's little money here. Most of us here have a talent or we lend services, like gathering wood for fires or repairs. Any such thing, really. You'll see when we get to Mary's."

"But I don't know what I could offer."

"Can you cook or clean?"

"Cook, no, but I suppose I could clean."

"Well, Ol' Mary will let you make use of the tubs and soaps. Just wash the clothes yourself and then perhaps you could just assist Mary with some of her duties. That should compensate her."

Ahead of them rose stately spires with little crowns on them. The architecture was markedly different than those surrounding it. It was a massive structure.

"That is the High Kirk of St. Giles," Morgana pointed out.

"Kirk?"

"Church."

"Is it safe to go in?"

"Aye. There are meetings there every Sunday."

"Meetings?"

"Services."

"Worship services? Gareth allows such a thing?"

Morgana regarded her oddly. "Of course. Why would it matter to him?"

Adele was surprised Gareth did not suppress religious rituals. A sudden coldness drew Adele's eyes up to the lofty spires of St. Giles, where she saw a dark shape.

The servant looked up, protecting her eyes against the glare in the slate grey sky with the flat of her hand. "It's Prince Gareth."

Immediately Adele's anger flared. "I told you I was a prisoner."

Morgana let her hand drop. "I'd wager he's keeping an eye on you so you don't place yourself in danger. I'm surprised he didn't warn you about wandering about outside the city."

"He did."

Morgana raised an eyebrow. "You are a headstrong one, then. Probably giving him fits about now."

"Good."

"Miss, I don't know why you've come to hate him so."

"He made me a promise," Adele voiced softly, unable to hide the pain of it. "I found out it was all a lie."

"I don't know about that, but I'm sorry if he did."

The princess took the young woman's arm and squeezed with affection. Maybe that was why fate had chosen her to be captured, Adele suddenly thought. Perhaps she was to witness these people and bring back word of what was really going on in Europe. This was not a continent of cattle. Adele swore when she became empress she would try to help these people and free them from the tyranny that repressed them. That one good thought cheered her as the two women wandered on through the city.

———✦———

Cesare's eyes were closed. His breathing was shallow. His bony fingers clutched the arms of his thronelike chair. His voice was slow and icy. "It's been nearly a week."

Flay didn't respond. She waited in the center of the Commons.

Cesare continued, "She could be back in her father's embrace by now."

Flay said, "She has not left Britain, my lord."

The prince opened his eyes. "Do you wager your life on that?"

"Yes." If Flay did not find Princess Adele, she would certainly die. It was simple. "My hunters are widening their circles. We know she left Canterbury with the Greyfriar and went to the shore."

"To a boat," Cesare growled. "To cross the Channel."

"No, Sire. My networks on the Continent are excellent. She has not landed there. And I had scouts over the Channel within the hour of her departure. While it is very difficult to track over water, my hunters are the best in all the clans."

Cesare stood suddenly. "You have ruined me, Flay! Why should you live another minute?"

"I shouldn't if you will it. But I can find Princess Adele. She sailed north with the Greyfriar."

Cesare pursed his lips in annoyance. "Greyfriar. How often will that human shame you? Perhaps *he* should be my war chief."

Flay stared hard at her prince.

Cesare stepped down from his dais and said with a mocking humor,

"Why would they go north? Is there a free human settlement somewhere you don't know about? Is this Greyfriar operating out of Whitby under your very nose?"

"There is no free human settlement, my lord. It is possible they merely went north to lose the pursuit—"

"And it worked!"

"—to lose the pursuit. And now they are ashore and in hiding. I will find them."

Cesare inclined his head with doubt.

Flay said suddenly, without fanfare, "I believe they went to Scotland."

The prince narrowed his eyes. "Are you suggesting, in your pathetic desperation, that Gareth is in league with this Greyfriar?"

Flay pressed on with her conclusion. "No, of course not, but attend, my lord. There are fewer of us there. Gareth is protective of his territory. Adele could hide there for years without encountering a vampire. Scotland. The daring choice. It's what Greyfriar would do."

"Flay, you are quite dangerous. You rightly say that Gareth is jealous of his barren little territory. Do you honestly believe I could just barge into Scotland checking behind draperies for Princess Adele? I dare not give Gareth any excuse to raise some stink over protocol. The clan is still on edge after the attack on the Tower."

Which I beat back, Flay thought, snarling that Cesare neglected to mention her successes.

The prince resumed his seat. The human attack, small though it had been, on the clan capital had put concerns in some of the lords' heads over leadership. Some of Cesare's enemies had suggested moving the king into hiding and turning the management of the clan over to the "heir." By which they meant Gareth. Cesare had managed to calm the storm and was prepared to calm it further by assassinating troublemakers.

Flay asked, "Do I have permission to send hunters into Scotland?"

Cesare took a deep breath. Flay's theory that the princess might have fled to Scotland had some merit. It was possible that a human refugee could slip into that barren territory unnoticed and make her way with Gareth's neglected herds.

"Seek the princess where you will." Cesare paused, making it clear he was not giving explicit permission to enter Gareth's territory.

Flay bowed in acceptance. Scotland. It had to be Scotland. She was sure that the princess had not made it to the Continent. As sure as she could be with Greyfriar in the mix.

Greyfriar.

Flay growled deep in her throat. Cesare had placed his thumb on her rawest wound. The man had taken her prize twice. It was inconceivable. How did he do it? She was the most feared war chief in Europe. She turned to leave.

Cesare murmured, "Flay, I will prepare a ship to retrieve the prisoner. And I will come north with it. Remember, your life is being counted in days."

"As you will, dread lord."

"Just so."

—◦◦◦—

Adele spent the day with Morgana and Ol' Mary, who was delighted by the company. The older woman helped Adele clean her clothes and mend them as well. She loaned Adele a change of clothes, another set of homespun. The princess had long since forgotten about style and silk. In return, Adele refilled the washtubs. Her hands were red from the hot water and the cold air. Thankfully her palms were calloused enough from hours of swordplay not to blister from lugging pails.

When they took a break for lunch, Ol' Mary brought out a hunk of cheese and Adele eagerly shared the bread from Gareth's table. Morgana had brought some apples and sliced them up. It was a fine meal. This method of barter was more fulfilling than Adele would have thought.

Mary tottered off to check on the tubs, leaving the two younger women alone. Morgana was good company. And Adele couldn't help her curiosity over a life in Gareth's Edinburgh.

"Does it hurt when the prince feeds off you?" Adele asked.

Morgana raised her head slowly, unsure what answer this woman was looking for. "At first, like a sharp prick of a sewing needle. The rest is rather odd—warm almost. He always permits us to look away if we wish. He's actually quite embarrassed sometimes."

"That's disgusting," Adele muttered without thinking.

Morgana rose abruptly and gathered the dishes.

Adele grabbed her hand. "I'm sorry. I didn't mean—"

"You wanted to know what it was like here. Now you do. What you think of it is your business, of course. But don't judge us too harshly. Life is hard anywhere, and we make do the best we can."

"I didn't mean to look down on you. It's just . . . I'm not . . ."

"Different folk have different customs."

"I had no idea what life was like up here. I've learned so much already. Humans do thrive here, in a way, at least better than we all believe. I just wish so much more for you."

"Someday, perhaps that will be so." Morgana smiled genuinely. "I may even be alive to see it if Gareth gains the throne in place of his brother."

"You have that much faith in Gareth?"

"More than most." She looked Adele in the eye before departing for Mary's kitchen.

Near dusk, with all the chores finished, Adele and Morgana walked up Castle Hill again. Adele was tired. She was looking forward to a hot meal and a warm bed.

Gareth's shadow flew past her toward the ramparts, a black spot against the grey sky. He had watched her all day, staying on the rooftops. She certainly hoped she had inconvenienced him.

The temperature dropped as Adele entered the stone walls of the castle once more. Morgana retired to her own quarters, leaving Adele to walk empty halls—empty except for cats, of course. The animals welcomed her, so she took a moment to kneel and greet them. The grey-and-white cat was among the crowd, and he pushed his way to the front. Smiling, she picked him up and carried him to her room. He purred all the way.

CHAPTER 25

THE SUN WAS breaking through the clouds for the first time in the many days since Adele's arrival. She was pleased to feel the sunlight on her face, warming her cheeks. The windows of the castle only allowed narrow shafts of light to pierce the gloom of the interior, so she decided to take a walk around the grounds.

She came out in a quiet, solemn courtyard. Her footfalls were the only sound that walked with her until a rush of birds fluttered away at her approach. Adele leaned over a wind-torn rampart, gazing out on the city far below. Nearer to her left she spied a strange tiny cemetery, far too small for a human cemetery. There were numerous gravestones, all very diminutive.

"Pets. Of the garrison."

Adele spun about to see Prince Gareth about ten feet away standing on the parapet edge, unafraid of the height. He was looking down at the small cemetery also. There was an expression of sorrow on his face.

Damn him! He was still following her.

He continued without looking at her. "In the old days, the soldiers here were allowed to bury their pets in this small graveyard."

"And where are the soldiers buried?" Adele inquired bitterly.

Gareth let out a slow sigh. "Perhaps in a cemetery as well. One can only hope for the sake of their families."

"You talk as if you care."

"What makes you think I don't?" He floated to the stone walk with the wind filling his long frock coat.

"Since when do you care about family?"

He glared at her. "Don't pretend to judge our families or politics. My quarrel with Cesare is far more than a mere filial squabble. His war will upset the balance of all the clans."

Adele smiled at him. "Then it is the perfect time to strike, while your people are weak and conflicted. My father's victory will be assured and legendary."

Gareth shook his head sadly. "No. War will destroy both of our people. Our back will be at a wall and we will fight to survive. We will be at our most vicious. The losses on all sides will be horrific."

Adele did not dignify him with a reply. They stood in silence, staring at the small graveyard. There was fresh dirt in one corner.

"That grave looks new," she noted.

"I bury some of my cats there."

"Why?" It did not seem to be a thing a vampire would concern himself with.

Gareth shrugged. "I thought they might enjoy the company of others. I would not want to die alone, nor lie alone. Why should they?"

Adele took a sudden deep breath. At this moment Gareth appeared to be almost human. She was still prone to humanize him. Hundreds of Mamoru's lessons were on this very subject. Vampires looked human, acted human, wore human clothes, but it was all a façade.

She struggled to recover her cynicism. "Thank you for removing the boat, or I might have injured myself escaping."

The prince's brow furrowed. "I'm having the boat repaired. It was unsafe and leaking, if you remember. And we will need it to get you to the Continent."

Adele retorted, "I will never return home and you know it."

Gareth's demeanor changed in one swift stroke, not angry but full of ice, his patience at an end. "Enough. There is so much more at stake here than your imperial well-being. Just look around you." He turned away from her and strode down the cobbled path.

Adele watched him and, inexplicably, felt her heart ache.

Some days later, Adele walked through the dark castle halls with a dripping candle as her main light source. Exploration diverted her attention from thoughts of home. The rooms were all surprisingly tidy; at least there were no skeletons nor debris littering the corners. Just cats. This place was such an antithesis to what she had seen in London.

Adele had seen little of Gareth since the morning in the pet cemetery. He went about his solitary business, as did she. There were times she would watch him talking with people from the town, his "subjects." He was earnest and intense. He seemed to listen to them and ask them questions. On those occasions when their paths did briefly cross, she found him less infuriating. He wasn't a storybook hero come to sweep her off her feet. He was a prince with duties and responsibilities. She understood that part of him, despite herself.

Memories of those contented moments with Greyfriar, and the ease they had shown with each other, washed over her at the strangest of times. And, oddly, they weren't as bitter. She liked to remember, actually, if only to study her memories, to discover why she hadn't been able to see Greyfriar as the vampire he was.

Adele passed another door, this one slightly ajar, and her candle guttered. The room was murky inside, but silhouetted against a window she could see a figure hunched over a table, moving his hand back and forth in a painstaking motion.

Greyfriar. *Gareth*, she corrected herself.

If he noticed her, he gave no indication. At first Adele thought he was holding a pistol, cleaning it perhaps. Surely that was something his human servants would be doing. Suddenly she realized he held a pen in his hand. He was writing.

A vampire was *writing*.

With a grunt of frustration, Gareth pushed back in his chair and wadded up a piece of paper, which he then threw across the room. Adele's eyes narrowed when she saw the wad fall among numerous others in a corner.

Gareth finally saw her and shoved a pile of paper on the desk to the side as if to hide it. "Princess?" He seemed almost embarrassed.

"What in heaven's name are you doing in here?" she demanded, walking purposefully to the crumpled papers. "Drafting a ransom note?"

Gareth rose from his chair but made no move to stop her, though his pale face seemed mortified by her discovery.

She smoothed out one of the wadded papers, fully expecting to see a detailed note of her capture and a demand for ransom, and instead she saw only poetry. The language was archaic English, and the script was old-fashioned with large ornate illuminated letters opening each line. Everything was so perfectly proportioned, it appeared to have been typeset on a printing press. But the ink was still wet, and it smeared under the pad of her finger. Looking up, she spied an old book open on the table in front of Gareth.

Confused, she regarded him. "What is this?"

"It's writing," Gareth said plainly, and raised a contrary eyebrow.

Adele peered at him through one of the holes ripped in the paper. "You're holding the pen a bit too hard, I should think."

Gareth nodded, slumping back into his chair. "I know. It's hard for me to feel the instrument." His fist clenched.

Looking at the book on the table, it was easy for Adele to spot the section of page he had copied. The mimicry was perfect. The enormous detailed illuminations were duplicated to the last curl.

Adele said. "You're quite a draftsman."

He shook his head. "I'm writing."

She pushed the book back toward him. "Well, you're copying. But the way you've re-created the text is remarkable. It's so precise. Very artistic."

"So this is . . . art?" Gareth took the torn sheet from her.

"Well, no. Again, this is copying. Art is creation, like writing. The man who originally wrote these words was a writer, but all others after who copy his work are not considered writers." She paused and smiled. "Plagiarists, actually, but that's a completely different topic."

"I'm confused." He set down the pen. "Explain it to me. What is the difference between this book and what I wrote? They look exactly the same."

Adele sat. "You must learn to write your own words, your own thoughts. Here"—she indicated his piece of paper—"you only spoke in another's words, like reciting history. You wrote, but did not create."

"But I did." He held up the crumpled paper in frustration. "I wrote this with my own hand. I've seen humans do it thousands of times. As Greyfriar, I tell them messages to send. And they write them. Just as I've done here." He seemed confused and angry. "That's creating. The message is mine."

"It's close. You know these letters and you know how to read them, so now you can create your own words with these letters. Think of something and write it down. It's that simple."

"What are you talking about?"

Adele sighed with exasperation. "If you record your thoughts personally it will allow your true voice to be heard by others rather than diffusing it through someone else. The spoken word always has a habit of becoming distorted. Particularly when moving from person to person. If your kind wrote, you could keep a permanent record of events. Others could read your ideas as you meant them."

"Vampires would never bother to learn to read my words. They only understand the sound, the spoken word." Gareth's tone was bitter.

Adele leaned toward him with her elbows on the table. "You know, humans at one time had strictly an oral tradition. It wasn't until the invention of letters, like this alphabet"—she pointed to the book—"that writing came about. We used to have poets and bards journey from one town to another to tell us news and stories. But writing liberated the life of the text from the moment of performance. Now everyone can enjoy a poet's stories whenever they wish, rather than wait for the poet to come around again."

"Why did your kind create writing?" His long fingers brushed the letters of the book with awe.

Adele wished she had paid more attention to her ancient history, but she soldiered on. "Cultural changes, I guess—social, political, economic mostly. A need to record commercial transactions."

"My culture deems themselves above all that," he remarked resentfully. "We have no economy. Therefore we have no need to create a written language."

"It takes only one, Gareth, to beat the drums of change."

He raised his head to look at Adele directly with his pale blue eyes. Passion and determination haunted his gaze. The woman suddenly realized that Gareth was jealous of humans. He wanted so badly to be something other than a vampire. She found it hard to swallow for a moment.

He asked a question in a low voice. "Would it insult you if I used your alphabet? I don't think I could start from scratch."

Adele laughed, amazed by his polite request. "Gareth, you are without a doubt the most perplexing vampire I have ever known."

"Do I have your permission?"

"To use my alphabet? Yes, absolutely. It's all yours."

"So what should I write?"

"Anything that you think is important. What have you been longing to say? Perhaps to someone far out of your reach."

Gareth lowered his head and shrugged.

"Think about it. Then send me your work later this evening after dinner. I'll look over it and we can discuss it tomorrow."

He straightened with excitement. "Yes? You would do that?"

"I would." The young woman rose from her chair and picked up her flickering candle. She left the way she had come, with Gareth's gaze upon her.

Adele spent the rest of her evening helping Morgana in the kitchen, cleaning, cooking, swapping tales, laughing. It was curious how much easier laughter came to her lately among the people of Edinburgh. Perhaps the sense of threat was easing a bit. Her life had become a series of lows and highs, flashes of terror and moments of peace. She had learned to relish those small gaps of serenity amid the chaos.

The serving girl grinned as she put various plates into the tall cupboards and then indicated the grey-and-white cat twining around Adele's feet. "I see he has taken a liking to you."

"Seems so."

"That's good."

"Why?"

"He used to be quite the greeter, but that was before."

"Before what?"

"Before his companion passed. After that, he kept to himself. The two used to play all over the castle. Knew each other since kittens. Now he keeps only to himself and hides in your room. It's nice to see him take an interest in something again."

"Animals don't grieve."

Morgana shrugged. "I don't know if it is grief. But he was different. That's all I know."

"Where did all the cats come from? There are so many."

"They took up residence here when all else was ruin and slaughter."

"Are they food for . . . him?"

Morgana looked aghast. "He would rather starve than harm a single cat within these walls. He is quite smitten with them, though for the life of me I can't understand why."

"Does this one have a name?"

Morgana shook her head. "Name it as you wish. There's too many to name. I've just called it Pet, though that's what I call each and every one of them. Much easier for me to remember." She chuckled at her own joke.

Adele rubbed the cat's jawline, and it angled its head so that she could rub all the harder. She would ponder a name for this particular cat. It had to be a good name, because it had brought her comfort during her dire predicament.

Hours later, sitting in her chamber with Pet curled on her lap purring, there was a knock on the door. At her behest the door opened and Baudoin was there with a silver tray awkwardly in his hands. He stood silently.

Adele nodded him in.

Baudoin bowed ever so slightly. "My lord has bid me bring this to you."

For a moment she couldn't think of what it was, but then she suddenly remembered and her excitement grew. "Oh!" She stood quickly, gathering a disgruntled Pet in her arms. Stepping toward Baudoin's stiff form she eagerly regarded the folded paper lying on the tray that glittered in the firelight.

Baudoin stepped back, almost as if reluctant to relinquish the note.

His expression was bitter, but then the servant caught himself and pushed the tray toward the princess. She claimed the note with a grateful inclination of her head and moved to the fireside for better lighting.

Baudoin lingered a bit, and Adele realized he did not know the contents of the note and was most likely curious. But he knew his place like any good servant. With a straightening of his spine, he spun on his heel and departed without so much as a "by your leave." How positively frustrating for him to witness the interactions of his master and the prisoner and have no say in the matter, Adele realized with a grin. She returned to the note, which had her curiosity on pins and needles. What could Gareth have written? It was incredibly exciting to watch his creative awareness growing.

She unfolded the paper quickly. Her breath caught, and she almost dropped the note into the crackling fire. Pet squirmed to get a better grip on her, with a plaintive meow, but Adele did not hear it. Her eyes were glued to the words on the note.

I am sorry Adayla.

She had to reach out and hold the mantel. Pet dropped to the floor under protest, but coiled around her feet inquisitively. The implications of the note astounded her. A vampire understood a concept such as forgiveness, and craved it!

For the first time in so many weeks, Adele heard the voice of Greyfriar speak to her. Her eyes slipped closed as she remembered his masculine tone that once whispered of rescue and hope. The joy she had known in his presence flooded her again. She recalled the weight of his hands on her shoulders in Canterbury, and the utter concern for her well-being above and beyond the rescue of an heir of Equatoria. She had not imagined it.

Her fingers brushed across the letters of the note. She smiled at his attempt to spell her name. He had never seen it written, so he had no idea how to emulate it. Such gentle precision had been given to each letter. Only the letters of her name betrayed a slight tremor in his hand. There was such power in names.

She had been wrong about him, so very wrong. If there was even a remote chance that he was sincere and true to all he had told her, she had to see it through for the sheer possibility of peace and for her own wishes for it to be genuine.

Perhaps there was as much Greyfriar in him as Gareth.

Perhaps even more.

CHAPTER 26

ADELE LOOSENED THE blanket around her shoulders as she approached the great hall. She could feel a rush of warmth and saw a great glow in the distance. For a moment she wondered if the castle had caught fire. Her footsteps quickened toward the radiating heat that filled the hallway. There was so much light blazing through the door at the end she could have sworn it opened out to the daylight, although it was evening and deep inside the castle.

The door swung back even as she reached for the wrought iron handle. Baudoin stood there. She always expected him to bow deeply to her like any manservant, but as always he only gestured her inside. Eyeing him critically she could see he seemed a bit stiffer than usual, the creases in his forehead furrowing deeper.

Puzzled, Adele stepped inside. Fires were roaring inside the three massive hearths in the room. Gareth stood at the long table that was set in elegant fashion. He was dressed in a fine waistcoat with no shirt underneath, though his pale skin could match any white linen. The breeches were black and tight, disappearing into equally ebony high boots, shined to perfection. Gareth's wardrobe was an eclectic mix of periods and styles. He stood regal, his eyes bright with excitement. The moment she approached, he stepped to a chair to his left and pulled it out for her. Politely, she took a seat, marveling at how well he knew human courtesies.

The table was laden with wonderful foods. Automatically her mouth watered. Even though she ate regularly, this feast was far beyond the normal fare.

"I trust you are warm," Gareth said as he sat to her right at the head of the table.

"Yes, I'm wonderfully warm. Thank you." In fact, she felt beads of sweat on her neck from the roaring blaze. Studying him openly, she saw tenseness to his smile. "Aren't you awfully uncomfortable?"

Gareth shrugged. "I can tolerate it."

"This is a lot of food."

"Eat what you like. I'll have the remainder sent to the people in town. They prepared it. I wasn't quite sure what you liked."

"You arranged all this?" The myriad of meat and vegetables must have taken days to collect and prepare. "It must've been a great deal of work for everyone."

"It was a challenge. We actually enjoyed it."

"Thank you." It seemed strange to say, but Gareth's efforts warranted it. In a way she was honored that she was worth the endeavor. Reaching for venison that was nearest her, she piled food on her plate. Food always seemed to be a primary need. It was Greyfriar who had drummed that into her. Eat and drink when you can, as much as you can.

Glancing at Gareth, she noticed he wasn't eating. With a sigh she sat back. "I don't particularly like eating alone."

The vampire prince turned his gaze to the food on platters in front of him. "But I don't eat. . . . I mean to say . . . I don't . . . ." Words failed him.

Adele understood all too well. In an instant he became a *vampire* yet again. It was still disconcerting.

Gareth realized he was losing her. He reached for a tray and served himself a piece of steak. "But if it means something to you, I'll be happy to join you."

"Can you actually eat?"

"It doesn't provide any nourishment, but I can go through the motions."

"It's all right. It doesn't matter."

"It does matter. To me. I want you to feel at ease." He studied the hunk of meat on his plate. He had chosen a rare piece of flesh so that at least he could taste some blood. But the blood was dead. The meat itself held little taste, like eating wood pulp. "It has been several weeks since you came here. I've seen no sign of Flay or hunters. I want you to know, you are getting closer to returning home."

"How close?" Adele asked quickly.

Gareth held up his hand. "I don't know. I just wanted you to know it is going to happen. As I . . . as Greyfriar promised."

"Why don't you contact my father? He will send ships for me."

"I tried that in France. But here in Edinburgh, there is no one to send with the message. Baudoin would be killed instantly if he went, and I cannot go without leaving you unprotected."

"My father would not kill Baudoin."

Gareth's eyes rose to meet hers, cold as steel. "I am not prepared to risk it."

His natural distrust stilled Adele into silence. Her appetite waned, but she forced herself to eat a bit of everything. So many people had labored to cook this meal that she refused to let their efforts be wasted.

"Is this food considered good quality?" Gareth asked, chewing methodically and ignoring the bland texture in his mouth.

Adele nodded. "It is very good. You did well."

"I had nothing to do with it. Everyone was excited to cook once I told them it was for you. They did it of their own volition."

"They are wonderful people here." Adele felt a warmth course through her. She brought her gaze up to study him. "And they seem to care for you very much as a sovereign."

"Humans deserve to be treated well. They have the power to give us life."

"Could it ever be possible that your humans leave here and come with me to Equatoria?" It was a foolish question. Adele knew it immediately and regretted putting Gareth on the spot. It looked as if she was spoiling for an argument, which she wasn't. She waved her hand, dismissing the question before he had a chance to answer it. "Ignore me. I've become fanciful thanks to a blazing fire and a full stomach. I know what I ask is impossible."

Gareth nodded. "Not impossible. Maybe someday."

Adele resumed her meal with more interest. She reached for the wine, but Gareth lifted a decanter. He filled her glass and then his. It was dark ruby port, and she tried not to imagine what it resembled in the firelight. She sipped it generously and held back a cough as the peppery taste hit the back of her throat. It warmed her inside as much as the roaring fire warmed her skin. In truth, she hadn't felt so content in a very long time. Reclining in the high-back chair with her wineglass, she sighed with satisfaction, which brought a small chuckle from Gareth.

She arched an eyebrow at him. "I enjoy good port."

"I'm glad. This was a gift to Greyfriar from the free people of Lisbon. I've been saving it for a special occasion."

Adele allowed a gentle smile. He was trying so hard. "Thank you for sharing it with me."

Gareth smiled at that, his sharp teeth showing ever so slightly before he clamped his lips tight once again, lest the sight disturb her. His frost-rimmed eyes glinted, the pallor of them both haunting and mesmerizing. Despite the fact that his entire race possessed them, his alone shone with something akin to warmth and life.

He stood and offered her his hand. "I would like to show you something, if you please. It would mean a great deal to me."

Adele's hand lifted to his, and he pulled her to her feet and led her to the eastern door. The princess wondered what was so important for her to see. Her curiosity grew deeper as he led her through the castle like a man with a secret. Her excitement grew with his. Finally they came to a room she hadn't seen yet.

"My library," Gareth whispered respectfully with his hand on the half-open door. "I have long wanted you to see it."

"A library!" Her delight was physical. She knew such a castle as Edinburgh must have a vast library, and what better way to pass her time here than by reading mysterious books long thought lost.

"It isn't much, but the collection is my most prized possession. In this room I feel most human."

The door swung open to reveal broken and empty walls. There were no towering bookshelves and endless rows of books inside. The crackling fire in the hearth cast light on a room that was vacant save for a lone leather chair and an ancient trunk.

Gareth, still excited, showed her to the chair. She slumped into it while he opened the trunk with care. The lid lifted to reveal a stack of about fifteen books. His *library*. Adele could not find the words to respond to his exhilaration. She only stared at the musty books, packed with great care inside the trunk.

Gareth realized something was wrong by the expression on her face. Confused and embarrassed, he slammed the trunk shut. He stood and backed away.

Adele stopped him with a touch of her hand and, without speaking, gently reopened the trunk. She saw the volumes on top, the most well read, were an elementary grammar text, a book of French poetry, an etiquette pamphlet, two adventure novels for young readers, and the anatomy text she had seen in Europe. So of all the books in the world, these were books he treasured. Suddenly she understood so much more about him.

"How long did it take you to collect all these books?"

"Since my first excursion to the mainland as Greyfriar. Some thirty years ago."

All that time and he had gathered only these few? It was a sad statement of how rare books had become in the north.

She told him softly, "There was a time when I would have never believed this. A vampire with a library. Yet here you are."

"Perhaps the world isn't what we think it must be. Perhaps someday our species do not have to be at war."

Adele told him dubiously, "Nice thought, but your brother will never change."

Gareth shook his head. "No, he will not. He will have to die instead."

Adele was taken aback by his frankness. "That's quite cold."

Gareth shrugged.

Her hand reached for one of the books. It was a boy's illustrated adventure novel. Apparently it told the story of a young man who fought injustice by stealing through the night, rescuing damsels, and foiling villains with swords and pistols. Her eyes widened as she saw the melodramatic watercolor of the dashing young hero in a cape and mask.

Adele slowly regarded the tall vampire standing beside her. His head was cocked as he watched her curiously. There was a trace of anticipation in him as she held a book he obviously prized.

Gareth realized something was amiss by her expression as she stared silently at him. "Are the books not to your liking? Are they offensive to you? I can only guess at—"

"Are you so desperate to be human?" Adele's finger traced the heroic figure on the cover.

"That can never be. But there is still so much about you that I want to know."

"Like what?"

Gareth grinned, his eyes gleaming at the prospect of answers. "Like why do humans nurture their children for so long? Why do you create music? Why are your bodies so heavy?"

The questions kept coming until Adele stayed him with a gentle hand on his. "So many," she noted. "And so few I can answer since I have never thought of the answers myself."

"So you can't answer them?" Gareth appeared crestfallen.

"Some I suppose I can." Adele pondered for a few moments. "I guess we nurture our children for so long because we love them. We want to see them grow up strong and proper." She paused and regarded him quizzically. "Do vampires . . . have children?"

"Yes, of course."

Adele sat back. "Really? You see, we always believed vampires created more of their kind by infecting humans with your bite. Or at least we used to. Now, we just don't know."

"No. We . . ." Gareth fell silent. "I understood it was improper for a male to discuss such personal topics with a female in your culture."

"Such personal topics?" The princess sat forward. "Do you mean sex?

Vampires have sex?" She felt her face flush with excitement, and tried to cover it by glancing at the books again. She was discussing a forbidden topic with a forbidden man.

He remained quiet.

Still, the young woman continued, "So female vampires get pregnant?"

"Yes." He knelt on one knee and took the book of French poetry. "I had a question about a particular phrase that—"

"Don't change the subject," she scolded. "Does it happen the same way as humans? Pregnancy, I mean?"

"I assume so."

"Have you . . . fathered a child?" There was no way to be coy about a question like that, but she was curious.

"Princess, please!"

"I'm sorry, I'm sorry." Adele felt a wonderful sense of satisfaction that she hadn't felt in a long time. He was very uncomfortable, and she took a peculiar delight in tightening the screws a bit in a teasing way. His appalled expression at her boldness was endearing.

Gareth heard the rush of her heartbeat, and the sharp tang of her scent shifting again from soft toward something very pleasing with a sharp bite. How could he not give her the answers she wanted? He touched his chest. "I have not. I mean, not yet."

Adele wasn't sure if she was relieved or not. "So how do vampires care for their young?"

"After birth, we feed off our mothers for a few months until we can hunt."

"Feed? Do you mean blood?"

"Of course. Like any infant."

Adele cringed and tried not to picture Gareth as a feeding baby. But she was unsuccessful. "Not quite like any infant."

"Of course, these days our child rearing has changed like everything. Many newborns feed off bloodnurses, humans who provide food. Since the Conquest, our females have lost the taste for the danger of motherhood."

"Danger?"

"Well, newborns could well nurse their mothers to death." Gareth waved a dismissive hand. "Things happen. When we are strong enough to hunt, we are placed in packs with others our age."

"Is that how you grew up? In a pack?" It sounded so savage.

"Within the royal family it is somewhat different. We were not placed with common children. I grew up in a pack of clan leaders."

"And you think that's a good way to do it?"

"My duties as a prince could best be explained by royal tutors." Gareth made himself more comfortable. He closed the lid of the trunk and used it to sit closer to her. "And you, as a princess, who taught you?"

Adele leaned back in the chair with the books cradled in her lap. "Most of my studies were with a tutor too." Then she smiled at a distant memory. "But some things were taught to me by my mother. I can remember being in her arms while she read to me. And dancing lessons! I used to twirl about the room while she played the *ney*."

Gareth interrupted her reminiscences. "You knew your mother?"

"Yes. Only for a while. She died when I was young. But I remember everything about her." Adele touched the hilt of the khukri still secure in her belt. "This was hers." She regarded Gareth. "You didn't know your mother?"

"No."

"Did she die?" Adele was afraid to ask directly if Gareth killed her as a newborn. She prayed it wasn't that.

"No. She deemed not to take the risk. Cesare's mother, on the other hand, elected to let him feed."

"And?"

"And he killed her."

Gareth seemed about to stand, drifting into his own darkening thoughts, so Adele quickly asked, "Were you and your brother ever close?"

"No. Never."

"Do you regret it?"

"My only regret is that I didn't destroy him when he was a baby."

The room had become shadowy and frightening. Gareth was cloaked in morbidity now, and Adele wanted desperately to lift the pall. She struggled for something to say. "Tell me about your father, the king."

Gareth smiled and straightened. "Ah. He was everything to me. He taught me how to hunt and fight."

"Is he a great fighter too?"

"He was indeed. The finest I ever saw." The prince pursed his lips. "He is nothing now. He lost his senses during the Great Killing. Or that was the end of him, anyway; his mind had been in decline for some time. He is well over eight hundred years old."

"Is that old? For a vampire?"

"Yes. Quite. And he didn't father children until late in life. Only managed Cesare and me. Not exactly the legacy he deserved. One son a monster. And the other a traitor."

That saddened Adele. Her eyes fell back to the adventure book. Gareth had never heard any stories from his mother. Yet he had such devotion to his father, who was a great hunter and warrior. Was it no wonder that he had become obsessed with stories of adventure from human books?

She mused, "My mother used to read me these sorts of stories often."

His hand lightly touched the books in her lap. "Are the stories true? Were there such people?"

Adele smiled once more. "Some are based in truth. Others are fairy tales. They're all meant to teach a lesson of sorts."

"Then I think I have learned the lessons well." Gareth turned to a page with an illustration of a man in a flowing robe who held twin pistols and protected a young woman from fierce pirates.

"That's true enough." Adele noticed that the young woman in the picture had beautiful flowing hair. She reached up self-consciously to touch her own hair, which was still a tangled horror despite her best efforts. She sighed, wishing for one day with her maids to correct the matted mistake that was her hair.

"What's wrong?" Gareth asked.

Adele gave him a wan look. "Nothing important. Just my hair."

He stared at it without comprehending.

She continued, "It's a mess. It used to be so . . . pretty. Now . . ." Her voice trailed off.

"Now what? What's wrong with it?"

"You wouldn't understand. You're a man." Adele looked around the room. "Don't you have mirrors?" She glanced back at him, a bit embarrassed. "Oh sorry. Vampires don't like mirrors, do you? You don't cast a reflection."

Gareth raised a surprised eyebrow. "What? I have nothing against mirrors. There just aren't any here because they've been broken over the decades." He laughed. "We cast perfectly fine reflections."

Adele laughed too. "Oh. Another beloved myth destroyed. Anyway, my hair was like my mother's, thick and curly. But now it's just a tangle of knots back there. It's a mess. A hive. I'll never get it under control again."

"Then cut it off," Gareth suggested.

Adele started to roll her eyes in dismay, but stopped. It was an idea. And the more she thought about it, the more she liked it. Why not have new hair for her new life? She closed the book and hummed in thought. Her fingers drummed on the leather cover.

Gareth interrupted her musing. "You mentioned once that you have a library in Alexandria. Is it a magnificent thing?"

"Oh yes. I spend days in there often. It's my place of solace. Of course, I never know what book to choose first, so I spend hours just browsing."

"Hours?"

"Alexandria's library has thousands of books," she explained.

Gareth was stunned. "Thousands?"

"Alexandria is one of the oldest cities in the world. Its library is one of the most complete."

"I can't imagine it."

Adele took his hand in hers, an impulsive gesture that surprised even her. It was cool and gentle. But it felt right. She hadn't forgotten his species this time, nor confused her hero with her supposed captor. His long fingers curled around hers, and her heartbeat raced as he softly squeezed. Her breath caught at the force of his gaze now upon her. It was no longer icy and cold, but warm and inviting as the blue of her Mediterranean Sea.

"I'd like to show it to you someday." Her quiet words were sincere. There was more of a kindred spirit in Gareth than she would have ever imagined.

His eyes shone with gratitude. "I would like that."

CHAPTER  27

"AIRSHIP, SIR."

"Where away?" Senator Clark shouted.

The bosun's mate pointed over the rail and downward. "Four points starboard, sir. Running deep three fathoms."

Clark muscled his way through his officers on the quarterdeck and waded amidships, then grabbed a spyglass from the bosun's mate and leaned over the rail. He jammed the glass against his eye, swaying dangerously with each unpredictable burst of wind.

Clark spoke to Major Stoddard, whom he correctly assumed would be at his side. "It's a derelict. Dammit! I can't see clear."

Before the trusty Stoddard could reply, the senator threw a leg over the rail and clambered onto the network of trailing lines and slid down a heavy cable to the keel. The wind pounded him as he twisted an arm and leg around the line and pressed the spyglass back to his eye, staring intently at the wretched airship below wallowing at barely treetop level. The crew of *Ranger* would have stared at him in amazement, normally, at such a feat. But this was Senator Clark.

The senator's mad laughter was nearly lost in the ferocious wind as he slipped the brass spyglass inside his shirt. He climbed back to the deck as easily as if he had been finishing an exercise rather than clinging precariously thousands of feet above the earth. Major Stoddard knew better than to offer an arm as his commander lifted himself onto the deck with a masculine grunt.

"Bloodmen ship." Clark leaned against the mahogany gunwale and pursed his lips in ostentatious thought. "Vampires don't fight with them. So I doubt it's looking for us." He grinned. "They're a transport ship, Major. Such as they use to move bulk. Or prisoners. Follow me?"

"I believe so, sir."

"What prisoner means most to them?"

Stoddard knew the answer but stayed quiet so Clark could supply it.

"Princess Adele." The senator backhanded Stoddard on the chest, raising a wince. "If they already had her, they'd be heading south. Toward London. But they aren't, are they?"

"No, sir. North."

"North. So they're still chasing her."

Stoddard inclined his head and smiled too. He wasn't sure why. It seemed the thing to do.

Clark said, "So we follow them. They'll lead us right to my wife."

Now the major frowned. "That's pretty thin evidence, sir."

Clark wasn't fazed by the criticism. Stoddard was allowed token resistance to the Great Man on occasion, though it was occurring more and more often. That was something Clark would have to remedy soon. The senator glanced back down at the tattered airship. "What else have we got, Major? We've been floating out here for weeks doing nothing."

"No, sir. But we are low on supplies. And our nearest base is still days away."

The senator raised his iron eyes. "Base? We aren't going back without her, Major. I thought I was clear on that. If we do not find my future wife, no man will come back alive."

"Yes, sir."

"So what's your thought now?"

"North, sir."

"Quite right, Major Stoddard. Please instruct Captain Root to shadow that airship. And if we are spotted by them, I will personally throw every man jack of *Ranger's* officer corps overboard."

"Yes, sir."

"Exactly as I said it, Major. I'm dead serious."

"Yes, sir. Overboard, sir."

Clark laughed and gripped the rail in excitement. Now this was living.

———&———

The morning after the conversation in the library, Adele sought out the beckoning soft glow of the kitchen fires. It was easy to understand why Morgana loved being down there. Adele wanted to thank the servant for helping Gareth orchestrate the dinner, but she also needed her help with a simple matter.

The kitchen was empty. Morgana was nowhere to be found. Disappointed but not undone, Adele looked for the implement she needed for her chore, but after minutes of fruitless searching she came up empty. Huffing with mild frustration she closed yet another drawer, so caught up in her search she failed to see the dark figure to her left. It startled her.

"Baudoin."

The servant stared at her. "Do you need something?"

"Is Morgana here?" Adele didn't really want Baudoin involved in the matter.

"No. A human is ill and she has gone to help."

"Oh." This news was upsetting. "Who is sick?"

"I do not know."

Adele stifled a sigh at the vampire's seeming disinterest in a sick human. Baudoin possessed only rudimentary manners. He was no Gareth, that was for sure. "Do you know how long she'll be gone?"

"I did not ask."

"I see." Adele gave in. "I'm looking for scissors."

He stared blankly at her.

"Scissors. You use them for cutting things." She demonstrated the action with her fingers. "You know, scissors." His obvious incomprehension spoke otherwise. "No matter. I'll find some eventually." She darted past him and back into the main part of the castle. By the small itch on her back she knew he stared after her.

Her hunt for scissors continued for hours; she ventured into every room. She searched through dusty piles, rifled in cabinets and wardrobes, and shifted mobs of cats who inhabited every cranny.

Adele entered a vast room with weapons and armor standing along both walls like a bizarre receiving line. The space was bathed in sunlight streaming through many tall windows decorated with colored glass that cast wonderful surreal works of art on the walls and floor. She loved this room. Lifting her skirt a little, she spun around in a circle and danced a small minuet with an imaginary prince before noticing Gareth watching her from the frame of the door. She stumbled to a halt.

His head was tilted to the side, and he seemed fascinated with her girlish glee. "I was told that you were in need of this." He held aloft a pair of shiny scissors.

Delighted, she approached him and took them from him. It came as a surprise that Baudoin had bothered to relate the small request to his master. "Thank you! These will do splendidly."

"Do what?"

"Cut my hair," she responded, and turned back into the room.

Gareth stepped forward. "Here. Let me."

"No, I think I can manage. I don't suppose Morgana has returned."

"Not yet. It would be easier for me to do it."

Gareth's hands were at the back of her shoulders, arranging her hair. She immediately stiffened as a wave of chills washed over her. He hadn't been so close behind her in many weeks—not since his time as Greyfriar.

Gareth sensed the change in her. He took a slight step back. "I only wanted to help."

"I know," Adele assured him, drawing in a steady breath. Her hands on her hips, she studied him up and down, in particular his long fingers. "Do you even know how to use scissors?"

"I imagine I can handle it," Gareth said confidently.

Adele thrust the scissors at him. "Show me."

One of his eyebrows steadily rose, and at its highest apex, he snatched the implement. He studied the oval holes in the handle, trying to recall how he had witnessed humans use them over the years. With a smirk of triumph he slipped his fingers through the holes and held them up.

Adele pursed her lips, not convinced. "Now snip."

"What?"

Bemused at his fuddled expression, she demonstrated with her slicing fingers exactly as she had shown Baudoin earlier. "I just want to see you operate them."

"Oh." It took all his concentration to mimic the correct action. To his relief, she wasn't laughing at him. "Do you trust me now?"

Adele's smile faltered as she realized that this event had come down to that simple question. Her playful little game had suddenly turned to something else. To say no to him could undermine how far they had come together. In truth, she did trust him. Her fear of him had been lost long ago, and her anger had faded too. She hadn't expected this simple act of cutting her hair to go this far, however. Suddenly she had a choice to make.

"I see." His humor fell away. "I presumed too much."

Adele straightened with resolve, presenting her back to him. "I do trust you. Cut it short."

Her body trembled slightly as he once again moved close to her. It was not the fear of him standing behind her with a sharp implement that drove the breath from her lungs; it was Gareth's proximity alone. Her tangle of hair lifted, and even though she was prepared for his touch, she gasped faintly as his gentle fingers brushed the nape of her exposed neck. His breathing was strong enough to blow a temperate breeze across her bared skin, while his cool touch skimmed quickly after it, bringing rise to waves of chills.

Then his head bent to the task at hand. Awkwardly, he struggled to angle the scissors and keep them far from her skin. The scissors would not obey him as his swords did. This called for his fingers to work in unison and opposition at the same time. He yanked Adele's hair several times as he jockeyed to angle the scissors properly.

She tried to turn around, but Gareth caught her head with his hands and pushed it forward. "Hold still," he commanded, intent on his work.

A glimpse showed Gareth with his elbow at a ridiculous angle, practically over her head, as he attempted to cut. It was as if a left-hander was trying to use scissors. Adele wanted to laugh but thought it prudent not to for the sake of her haircut. He cursed in vampire, a sharp hiss practically guttural.

"Maybe I should just do it," Adele offered. Again, she tried to turn around a little more urgently, a little more unnerved.

Gareth maintained a stern voice and grabbed hold of her head once more. "No. It's fine. Almost have it."

Her eyes closed, willing the panic to subside. Then suddenly there was the metallic sound of scissors, and the weight began to drop from her head. It continued for what seemed like hours.

"There!" Gareth held a handful of her shorn locks like a trophy. "It is done!"

Adele's hand instinctively touched the back of her neck, as much to feel the difference as to still the goose bumps still running rampant. The cut was ghastly short. Her neck was cold.

Her gaze lifted almost shyly to Gareth's. "Thank you."

"Do you need more?" His fingers flicked the scissors.

Laughter burst out of her at his enthusiasm for this new skill. "No, no. I think this one haircut is quite sufficient."

"What do I do with this?" He eyed the lock of hair in his hand quizzically.

With a shrug of her shoulders, she ran her fingers through her remaining hair. It felt very odd to her. "Throw it out, I guess. I don't need it. Though I would kill for a mirror right now."

Gareth instantly wrenched a battle shield from the wall and held it up in front of her. "Will this do?"

The shield had once been shiny from chrome plating, but it was tarnished grey now. Even so, Adele could see clear enough the travesty that was her hair. It was still tangled on top, but cut straight just above the nape of her neck. She ran her fingers over the rough ends.

Gareth asked, "Is there a problem?"

"No. No. It's . . . delightful."

"Don't move." He stood close by her side, touching her shoulders and hips, and held up the shield before them. "See. I cast a reflection. I am real."

Adele saw herself with Gareth for the first time. She wore the rude homespun outfit from Canterbury with a haircut that looked like she had caught her head in a wheat thresher. Gareth was tall and slender in his typical stylish grey and black. Their images were both distorted by the slope of the shield and obscured by the patina. But still, she smiled.

He was real. He was not a monster.

CHAPTER 28

AN EARLY MORNING fog enshrouded the city of Edinburgh, casting it as a surreal and eerie kingdom. But Adele was not afraid of the dark closes or the leaden skies. Gareth walked at her side, her personal guide. Where once she had shuddered to see his shadow on the ramparts, now she was grateful for his presence. Though she had been bold and obstinate when she ventured out into the city those early days, there had always been some fear in her heart. She had defied it, but that didn't mean it wasn't present. Not today, though. Today seemed to be a new experience for Adele.

Gareth had something else new to show her. They were going steeply downhill, away from the towering castle, and the fog deepened around them. A few figures strolled past them through the mist, going about their business as if a vampire wasn't within reach. As if no vampires had ever come here more than a century before.

Soon they began to head up again, still walking south along a road once called Candlemaker Row, where Adele had not ventured before. The tendrils of fog slipped around their legs as they trod up the cobblestones. Adele did not see the tall iron gates until she was almost on top of them. Beyond the wrought iron lay a magnificent structure of old stone. All around it were gravestones topped with crosses and magnificent monuments to bless and honor the dead. It was a churchyard.

"What is this?" Adele asked.

"The people call it Greyfriar's Kirk," Gareth answered with a gentle smile.

She turned to him, pleased. "This is your namesake!"

"Yes. I like this place. It has history, and I like the stones."

"It's a graveyard."

"I know. The irony does not escape me." He pushed open the heavy iron gates, and they entered the churchyard. Some graveyards were filled with dread and superstition, but to Adele, and even to her brother, they were places to explore. Her homeland was famed for its tombs and homes for the dead. They captivated Adele. Strangely enough it was something else she had in common with Gareth.

The stones of Greyfriar's Kirk were old and dark with age, some worn almost smooth, but the ornate carvings on many of them were still pronounced and beautiful. A majority of them were large and situated right up against a stone wall that encircled the small churchyard.

Gareth gestured to a tombstone. It was scribed in Latin. "This is the same language as the anatomy book I have. I can see names. But do you know what the rest of it says?"

"I do." Adele had been taught Latin. "This is the person's name—the person buried here." Her finger brushed over the surname at the top in large bold script. "The rest gives the family's lineage. A husband, a beloved wife, and three sons, aged two, five, and seven."

"It says all that?" Gareth touched the deep etchings that had withstood the passage of time.

"What's inside the church?" Adele asked him.

"I don't know," he replied absently, still studying the tombstone. "I've never been inside."

"Why?"

"I'd prefer not to enter."

Adele stared at him. "So it's true, then, that vampires are repelled by religious symbols? You intimated as much in Canterbury."

Gareth gazed out over her head. "I would simply prefer to stay outside."

She didn't believe him. But she couldn't expect that he would confirm his species' weaknesses to her. Even though they had forged a unique relationship, she was the future leader of his kind's greatest enemy.

"May I go in?" she asked.

"Certainly. I'll wait for you out here."

Adele headed for the church's main doors. One hung off its hinges, but the other stayed straight and true. She grasped the heavy iron handle and gently pulled the door open. It was dark inside at first, but as she made it past the first archway, the chamber opened up into a wide, long cavern with high-set windows. Most were broken, allowing more light to shine down on the vast stone floor. There were shards of colored glass on the cold stones, and she bent over, trying to determine what picture they had depicted at one time. She could make out a face or a symbol.

Finally she straightened and walked to the altar, where a glint of silver caught her eye. It was a small cross on a chain, almost camouflaged by grey dust. Smiling, she lifted it from its hiding spot. Deciding that it was a sign, she knelt in front of the altar, offering up a small prayer of thanks for the sanctuary afforded her throughout this trial, and a prayer of hope for the future, wherever it led her.

Outside, Gareth reared back. His flesh crawled. He couldn't remember feeling such power here before. Sometimes during the people's rituals at the other church, St. Giles, he could feel waves of warmth emanating, which he found uncomfortable. But nothing like this. The power scorched him, and he found it hard to draw breath. Pressure grew in Gareth's head until it forced him to retreat from the churchyard. As soon as he stepped outside the gate the distress waned. He took a deep breath. Unconsciously, he began pacing, waiting for Adele. After several minutes, when she had not come out, Gareth stepped toward the large gate once more, only to feel the harsh discomfort rise again. He paused, a low growl passing from his lips. He was about to plunge over the threshold regardless, worried at Adele's long absence, when finally she emerged into the hazy sunlight.

She looked around anxiously, but calmed when she saw Gareth outside the gates. It took her by surprise when he shuffled back at her approach.

"Is something wrong?" she asked.

"No, no. Everything is fine." He turned his head slightly. Her scent was acrid, just as it had been in Canterbury when he found her barely sensible on the cathedral steps. "You were gone a long time. I was . . . concerned."

"Oh, I just stopped to say a small prayer." She fingered the silver cross tucked in her pocket.

"I see." There was a trace of pain and agitation in his stance.

"Are you all right?"

The prince nodded curtly. "Yes."

"Would you like to read more of the tombstones?" She stepped toward the graveyard, but he didn't follow.

"No," he said, anxious to be away. "Let's go elsewhere."

Adele smiled. "I don't mind." She took his hand before he turned away.

With a hiss of pain that bared his teeth he yanked away from her. His skin smoldered with red welts left by Adele's fingers.

"Gareth," she cried in alarm, instinctively reaching out for him again.

"Please, Princess, stand back. Please do not touch me just now."

"How? What did I do?" Then Adele comprehended. She had prayed. Her eyes widened in amazement. "I'm sorry. I didn't realize . . ."

"Nor did I," he responded. "You wield great power, Adele. More than anyone I have ever known."

"This comes as news to me," she admitted.

Gareth's brow furrowed deeper as the waves continued rolling off her, and he tried not to reel back. "Let's return to the castle."

"As you wish. Perhaps we can come back another day and I'll read more of the gravestones to you."

He graciously inclined his head, grateful that finally the discomfort was beginning to ease. He wanted to be near her, but he kept his distance. They walked quietly for a bit, both absorbing the magnitude of what had just occurred.

Adele was torn between feeling guilty about hurting Gareth and the amazing revelation that she had discovered an exploitable weakness in the vampires. Her crystal talisman. The standing stones in England.

Canterbury. And now this cross. They were all related. It was magic. Or religion. Or both. It was as Mamoru had taught.

"How am I doing this?" Adele asked. "Is it prayer? In the old days, we thought religious objects repelled vampires. Do they?"

"No," he told her honestly. "The icons of your faiths are nothing to me. The people of Edinburgh hold their religious services. Their prayer troubles me slightly, but if it pleases them, so be it. It is no great problem for me. But you are quite another matter."

"I feel bad about your hand."

"It is already healed." He showed her his hand, and the welts had indeed all but faded.

"That's good. I'm glad."

That simple statement pleased Gareth.

Adele asked, "Aren't you at all concerned as to what this means? Aren't you worried what I could do? What I might do?"

"Why? What can I do about it?"

"It could be a way to fight vampires, to destroy your kind."

Gareth stopped. "I trust you."

"Maybe you shouldn't." His complacency was exasperating.

"If you decide that this is the best course of action for your people, then I concur."

"Gareth, remind me to explain to you about power and politics."

"I prefer diplomacy." Adele laughed and Gareth smiled at her. "So what did you think of Greyfriar's Kirk?"

She struggled to follow his example and bring her thoughts back to mundane matters. "It must have been beautiful once. A lovely place for weddings. But it's small compared to the palace I will be married in." She sighed. "You know, I've lost track of time, but I think I might've been married already if your brother had not kidnapped me."

The lines around Gareth's mouth tightened. In the beginning of this adventure, he hadn't given much thought to Adele's impending marriage. Now that he knew her, it weighed on him. For just a moment, he imagined a different life, one without the constraints of duty, politics, and prejudice. That was foolish and he knew it, but still, the thought of Adele not marrying that braggart of a vampire killer warmed him.

The princess rolled her shoulders back so she stood a mite taller. Her sad expression lifted and she regarded Gareth. She gave a smile as if to banish her gloomy thoughts. She must be the only woman ever to be depressed about her wedding to a great hero, but oddly it seemed like a part of her past and not her future. A lifetime had passed for her in these last weeks, and her old life was so very distant.

Adele said, "I'll tell you the truth, and you're the first I've admitted this to, but—from all I've heard of my Intended—I am not enamored of Senator Clark."

"Oh yes?"

"But our union is important for Equatoria. So my happiness doesn't really matter."

"I'm sorry."

"It's not your fault. In fact, I'll have to say that you are the only person trying to set things right." Greyfriar's pistols suddenly felt heavy on her hips. They had offered protection and assurance when she had needed them, but now with deft fingers she unbuckled the rig and handed it to Gareth.

"I gave them to you," he said in confusion.

"I don't need them. I'd like to keep one pistol, though. For my own protection. But the rest are yours. Thank you for the loan."

He reached to take the gun belt, gently brushing her soft, gloved hand. He felt another shock of pain, lighter, more a warning than damaging. The power was still coursing through her, taking its time subsiding. He covered the shock and inclined his head graciously as he took the weapons and tossed the belt carelessly onto one shoulder. He couldn't help but smile; the bond between them that he had thought lost forever had returned. Her scent was intoxicating.

Then another scent drifted on the wind and Gareth stiffened sharply, the leather belt sliding from his shoulder and dropping from nerveless fingers to the ground. Adele reacted in kind, her own hand slipping to the pistol in the pocket of her skirt. She had learned to read both Gareth and Greyfriar when they sensed danger. She swiveled her gaze about, but saw nothing.

"Run to the castle," Gareth commanded. He took to the skies in a single leap. "Hunters are coming," were the words that trailed back.

Adele grabbed his gun belt from the ground and fled. Her eyes continued to look up as she ran across the cobblestones uphill toward the looming castle. She saw no dark shapes in the sky. If she ran faster, maybe she could send Baudoin to help. Her fear was back, and she grasped the pistol rig tighter to her chest.

Soon she couldn't even see Gareth's silhouette. How far away could he sense the hunters? Far enough out so that the hunters couldn't sense her?

It took forever to get to the castle. Adele shoved open the great doors, letting them bang loudly against the stone wall. Only guessing where Baudoin was at this time of the day, she ran for the kitchen. He wasn't there, but Morgana was, and together they ran until they found Baudoin. His face was like granite when they told him.

"Stay inside," he said.

"How can we help?"

"Stay out of sight. It's up to His Lordship now."

Adele and Morgana exchanged anxious glances. Morgana grasped the princess's hand and squeezed. Adele's first instinct was to look out a window, but she resisted the urge. Instead she made sure Gareth's pistols were loaded and ready. She could only imagine what was happening over the skies of Edinburgh.

—⌘—

The air currents were fast, and Gareth rose quickly. Two distant specks marked the arrival of hunters to his domain; the creatures were not tracking vampires, so they would see him and discount him. Of course, the hunters might be following the scent of the Greyfriar, but that's why he wore human blood on his skin as the Greyfriar to mask his true scent to his fellow vampires. Then he had a terrible thought. Perhaps he carried enough of Adele's scent to attract them. Sure enough, the hunters veered and glared at him curiously as if trying to puzzle out why a vampire had a scent with faint resemblance to their prey. Finally they continued their flight toward the castle. They had Adele's scent. These were well-trained hunters. Flay used the best.

Gareth waited until they flew beneath him. Then he drew his arms in to his sides and descended at an incredible rate of speed. He slammed down onto the back of one of the unsuspecting hunters. It screamed in surprise and pain as its spine cracked. The wind rushed as they tumbled out of control. Even mortally wounded, the hunter tried to twist and claw his attacker.

Gareth struggled to hold the hunter close to him. If he gave it room to strike, he would be eviscerated. Gareth grunted as his skin was ripped across his shoulder practically to the bone. The second creature was on him already, but he had to ignore that. Gareth extended his fangs and buried them in the back of the hunter's neck, ripping through its rope-like tendons and sinking into the spinal cord. Digging deep, he tore at the base of the thing's brain. It thrashed before he felt a satisfying snap and the creature shuddered.

Gareth gave a maniacal shout at his victory as he released the limp hunter. Then he whirled to face the second creature, eager to destroy another brute. But this one was cunning. It could smell the power surging in its target and refused to be taken by it. The hunter soared up to gain distance and then turned to face Gareth. There was no glare of surprise or anger. A hunter was too simple for that. It was a killing machine, trained specifically to hunt and kill its target.

Now that it had regained some position of dominance, it came at Gareth.

The prince wrenched aside as long claws sliced the air where he had once hovered, but the hunter twisted its agile body, and one of its clawed feet stretched out and ripped an open gash the length of Gareth's thigh. He grabbed the hunter's hairy leg and pulled it toward him. He wouldn't allow it to circle and strike again, slicing him until he weakened. Gareth was no match for its agility and speed. The only way to take down the beast was to stay close, where his strength, before it faded, was the advantage.

The hunter screamed in protest as it was captured. It slashed again and again with claws and teeth. Gareth could feel blood loss weakening him. It was hard to command his limbs to hold this furious beast. He was losing the fight to protect Adele.

The fear of this creature attacking her gave him a renewed strength to endure its savage mauling. He wrapped his arms around the head of the creature, ignoring the fact that he left open his chest to the beast's attack, then summoned the vestiges of his fading strength and twisted. The beast let out a wail that abruptly ended with a dull crack, and its body went limp in Gareth's grasp.

The battered prince let it go and watched it tumble to the earth far below as drops of his blood followed after. He was badly wounded, he knew. His vision greyed; he needed to descend to the ground before he lost consciousness, but there was a voice behind him.

"Strange how the hunters led me to you." The words were laced with suspicion and spite.

Flay.

Wearily, Gareth faced her. Members of the Pale were with her. It showed her utter gall in bringing so many of her soldiers into his realm.

He snarled through blood-flecked lips, "I don't allow vampires in my land. Particularly my brother's underlings."

Flay sneered in anger, but she fought through it with feigned deference. "I am pursuing an escaped prisoner, the princess Adele. The hunters tracked her here, Great Lord." She stared down to the earth far beneath them at the crumpled cadaver of one of her pets. "I know she is here. Somewhere."

"Leave. Now."

Flay smiled cruelly over her sharp canines. "Though she is technically your prisoner, Cesare has graciously offered to retake responsibility for her."

"How kind. I decline."

"Cesare is coming with an airship to transport the prisoner once I have located her." Flay waved an elegant hand toward the distant castle. "Perhaps you will lend me your hospitality while we wait for your brother."

"You will not set foot on my land. Withdraw!" Gareth was stalling with the only weapon he still had strength to wield, playing the outraged nobleman. He had to buy precious time before Cesare arrived with reinforcements.

The war chief resented his haughty tone. Her every gesture said she wished to attack and be done with this foolish charade of respect. Gareth had had his chance with her, and he had spit on her proposal.

Flay kept tenuous rein on her anger. "You are making a mistake."

"Probably the worst I've made since failing to tear your head off in London." He could feel the blood draining from his failing body. He held himself erect, lest she suspect his weakness. "Go! I won't tell you again."

Her eyes simmered into steel. She turned abruptly and flew southward with her retainers following after.

Gareth remained where he was till they were distant spots in the sky. Then his strength left him and his density increased. He drifted helplessly to the ground far below, his dripping blood reaching the destination before him.

CHAPTER 29

BAUDOIN WAS AT Gareth's side as soon as he staggered into the castle. The servant dipped a shoulder under his lord's arm. Gareth was already throwing off orders, his mind occupied by only one thought: flight.

"Cesare is on his way. We don't have much time."

"Your wounds are—"

"Nothing. Where is Adele? She must be kept out of sight till we're ready to leave."

"She is waiting in her room."

The prince nodded gratefully.

"Gareth!" Adele ran to him, her face flushed with anxiety.

The prince cast an inquisitive eye at his servant, who was glaring at the princess.

"She *was* in her room," Baudoin intoned.

Adele wrapped her arm around Gareth's side. Even though she was no longer on hallowed ground or invoking her power, a harsh electricity buzzed through the contact. It mattered little to Gareth. He was comforted by her physical presence, and he relished that she felt no fear around him. The pain paled by comparison.

"You're hurt!" she exclaimed as she saw his torn frame.

"It can keep. Cesare is on his way. You must get to safety."

"How soon?"

"I don't know. But we must be gone from here before he arrives."

Her eyes were shining. "You're coming with me?"

"Of course, I trust your safety to no one but myself."

"Thank you." Adele returned her attention to his injuries. "We need to bind your wounds first. Or we won't get far."

"My wounds will heal. There is no time. Gather your things. . . ."

"Morgana has already taken care of that for me. Besides, I don't have much, and I expect we will be traveling light. I have enough food for several days, then we may have to forage. Anything else I haven't covered?" At the end of the hallway stood a small pile of satchels and supplies.

The corners of Gareth's mouth lifted in a pained smile. "No. I see you've met every contingency."

"Exactly."

Baudoin asked, "Shall I pack Greyfriar?"

Gareth replied, "No. I have him hidden in various places if we make it to the mainland."

"You mean *when* we make it to the mainland, don't you?" Adele noted. "I have no doubt we'll reach Equatoria."

"I do," he answered, reaching down for a satchel, but Adele quickly picked it up and eased it onto his shoulders.

"You do?" she asked anxiously.

"It will be very difficult."

"We'll fight as hard as we can." Adele's demeanor altered again to the strong-minded princess he had come to know. She quickly distributed the supplies between them both, taking the heavier load for herself, and left her hand lingering on his. "That's all we can do."

Baudoin observed the tender touches between his prince and the human female. Such concern for Gareth's well-being on her part was disturbing. Even more distressing was the gentle look on his prince's face, almost thoughtful and even grateful. Perhaps it was a result of his weakened state.

"My lord?"

"My friend." Gareth straightened with weary resolve and motioned to Baudoin. "I want you to leave Edinburgh before Cesare arrives. It would be safer for you."

"No," was the simple reply.

"What?"

"It is best I stay. I can mislead Cesare and direct him away from you."

Gareth shook his head resolutely. "No. He is my brother. You won't be able to fool him. It is too dangerous."

Baudoin adjusted a strap on one of the packs, easing the strain on Gareth's wounded shoulder. "I know Cesare quite well. I did raise both of you. I have never shirked my duty before. I will not now."

"This is much more than just covering my masquerade as Greyfriar. Cesare will stop at nothing to regain the princess."

"Then why not give her back to him?" Baudoin simply asked, perfectly willing to sacrifice the human female to safeguard his prince.

Adele stiffened beside Gareth, her eyes darting between the two vampires.

"Because I don't want to," was Gareth's simple reply.

Baudoin heard exactly what he didn't want to hear in that one straightforward remark. His lord cared for the human princess, and there was nothing Baudoin could do to stop it. No vampire had ever dared place a human life before a vampire's. If nothing else would start a civil war, that would.

The servant did not know what future lay before them, but he would not abandon his charge. The prince had always been headstrong and unusual, causing great strife within the clan. Perhaps with any luck, the prince's inconvenient infatuation would fade over time, and this would all become just an annoying memory.

Baudoin shrugged his shoulders. "Then I don't want to leave the castle. If I can stall your brother only an hour, it's useful. It is my decision to make, not yours."

Gareth glared at his faithful friend, but he knew that he had already lost the battle. Baudoin had always accepted risks without question. But that did not mean the prince worried less for him. Cesare would strike him to hurt Gareth.

Gareth gave an answering sigh. "So be it. But don't let my brother use his influence to march his forces into Edinburgh. He only wants the princess and me. If he tries to occupy the city, just send him toward us. We will make do as best we can. All servants need to leave the castle. And send word to all my subjects to go into hiding."

"Where will you go?"

Gareth said, "North."

"The stones?" the servant asked, but Gareth didn't answer. Which was his answer. Baudoin eyed the bloody state of his liege. "You won't make it. It's too far."

Gareth's mouth opened in surprise at the bluntness. Baudoin was never one to mollify, but this defeatist attitude was new. "I don't have much choice."

Baudoin withheld a disparaging comment. There was no solution to this problem. Gareth couldn't hope to outrun Cesare overland, and he couldn't take to the air for any length of time with the girl. But the prince would not abandon Princess Adele. "You had best leave immediately, then. You're wasting time."

Gareth clasped Baudoin on the shoulder. "We will see each other again."

"Of course." Baudoin could feel the weakness in the grip of his charge.

Gareth and Adele made their way through the castle and into a cramped, ill-used stairway. After descending far through the darkness, they reached a small barred opening set at the rear of the castle. They were hundreds of feet above the tumbled buildings, with a sheer cliff face between them and the ground.

Adele said, "I seem to remember a front door on the castle."

Gareth took out a rusty key and unlocked the iron door, swinging the heavy grate back until it slammed against the rocks. "This way is faster. I don't know how close Cesare is."

Adele took one look down and grimaced. "It's not that I'm afraid of heights, but that's a long way down without a rope."

"Hang onto me."

"But you're weighted down already! And wounded!"

"I can manage you. It won't be a leisurely fall, but we'll survive. Come on. Wrap your arms around me."

Adele obeyed, mindful of his injuries. She was relieved that he did not wince in pain as he took her weight and stepped off into the air. They dropped. Adele screamed, but they lurched and slowed into a more controlled plummet. The stones raced upward beside them at a dizzying pace. Adele's clothes flapped loudly as the strong crosswinds buffeted them. Gareth managed to keep them upright as they sank toward the overgrown lane below. They were coming down too fast. He was struggling. His gasping breaths near her ear were agonizing.

They landed hard on the cobblestones, and Gareth slammed down onto his knees. Adele held him tight as he slumped. He felt as light as air for a second, but then his density returned full force and she couldn't hold him.

"Gareth!"

It took a few moments before he responded. He struggled to his feet, easing his weight off her. "Let's go."

"Are you sure?"

"Yes. We have to go now."

Adele's concern for him outweighed everything else, even her own safety. She couldn't doubt his determination, but a knot in her stomach grew tighter as they ran. The front of her coat was soaked in Gareth's blood, slapping warm and hard against her chest. They headed north, through the quiet orderly new city of Edinburgh. Glancing back at the dark castle she realized that she had not had the chance to say farewell to Morgana or even to Pet, and the pain of that struck her hard for a moment. She swore she would someday return to Edinburgh and take them both back to Equatoria.

Gareth constantly scanned the sky above them, but to Adele's relief it remained clear. They left the city behind and entered a forested countryside. The terrain was uneven and overgrown, with only a few paths and cart tracks cut north through the tangled woodlands. The ground was muddy, making it a crueler and more unforgiving struggle for Gareth. Still, he set a grueling pace, covering miles of countryside. Adele did not argue because she knew what was at stake.

As the long hours passed, Gareth's usual tenacity faded. He faltered twice only to catch himself at the last moment and push on. Adele saw the etched lines of determination on his face and knew that this man would put himself into a grave before he would stop.

Finally, encroaching darkness made the footing more treacherous. When Gareth went down for a third time and stayed on his hands and knees, his panting breath spraying the ground with bloodied spittle as it hissed from his straining lungs, Adele prevented him from rising.

"Enough, Gareth. You have to rest."

"No time." The words rasped. His body ached as though from a great distance, and weakness plagued his bones. Far too much of his life's blood had seeped out.

"At least let me sew your wounds so you don't lose any more blood. Please!"

He tried to stand, but her hand all too effectively kept him grounded. Closing his eyes, Gareth fought to stay conscious as he licked at his lips before croaking with a voice as defeated as his battered body, "If Cesare catches us out here in the open . . ."

"Then so be it. But you won't make it to the end of the hedgerow, much less into some wild countryside in the north in this condition, and you know it." Her hand brushed his check, drawing his gaze up to hers. "Even Greyfriar must accept he has limitations."

Gareth watched with dull eyes as Adele efficiently shoved off her pack and gathered what passed for rudimentary medical supplies—scissors and a simple needle and thread. He struggled to remove his coat, and she quickly moved to help. Then with scissors in hand she cut away his shredded shirt. She gasped at the vicious and ugly wounds.

"Oh, Gareth," she whispered. She threaded the needle quickly, but when she turned to sew his torn flesh, she faltered.

"I won't feel it," Gareth assured her even as he grimaced at the touch of her hand. "Quickly now, do what you must. Stop the bleeding, and I'll do the rest."

Adele paused, still hesitant to add to his pain. "Should I remove my cross?"

"It doesn't matter. Just don't say a prayer for me."

Huffing at his odd humor, she remarked, "Better safe than sorry." She laid the silver object aside and bent to the task, jaw clenched. Gareth did not flinch or gasp, so her confidence grew until she realized she was quickly stitching as if he were merely a tailored shirt. The allusion made it easier to bear, though no less dreadful.

Gareth tingled at her touch even without the cross, although without the same overwhelming intensity. He watched her with attentive eyes. Her steadfast nature through adversity was calming. Exhaustion nagged at him, his vision tunneling at times as his body threatened to shut down. He was loath to admit it, but he needed to feed. Baudoin's scolding frown was in his mind's eye, as if the servant was bidding his master to eat and build strength. Gareth smiled.

"Gareth?" Adele's worried voice called to him. It took a moment, but then the prince concentrated, feeling a low ripple of fire along his nerves. He hadn't realized his eyes had slipped closed. Her hands were at his shoulders, anxiously attempting to rouse him.

"I'm fine." Straightening, he placed a hand on hers to reassure her. Again, the current in her passed to him. It felt like a dull thumping against the back of his skin.

"You're so pale," Adele whispered as she reluctantly sat back.

"I was born pale." He released her hand and the current faded. He tried to rise but still lacked the strength. "Help me up."

But she didn't, studying him, her eyes teeming with concern. "You need to feed, don't you?"

He sighed. "Eventually. It will restore what I have lost. But there is no time for it now. Come, get me on my feet." He drew his long legs under him but couldn't find the strength to straighten them.

Adele felt a sense of shame. Morgana and other humans were willing to spare some of their life's blood to help Gareth and didn't find it strange or repulsive. Adele had known Gareth only a short time, and yet she already understood this bond.

He had given so much of himself to keep her safe, to keep everyone safe. And still he refused to falter. Her heart pounded at her chest as the impact of what this vampire, this man, had endured for her sake washed over her. The human princess of Alexandria knew what she wanted to do.

She bared her arm to Gareth and met his pale gaze.

His eyes widened as he realized her implication, and he reared back. "No, I cannot. . . . I'll feed from someone else."

"There is no one else around. Gareth, you don't understand. I *want* this." Adele couldn't bear to see him suffer one minute longer, not when she could ease his hurt.

"But there's no reason!"

"There's every reason! I caused this pain." Her fingers dropped to gently brush against his hideous wounds. "So it should be my blood that eases your suffering." She shifted closer to him, preparing herself.

Gareth exchanged a panicked glance with her and again tried to sway her from this venture. "You can't afford to be weak, Princess. Our flight will be long and arduous. We'll pass a settlement eventually. It will be wiser to let me feed from—"

Adele cut him off with an exasperated sigh. "Good God! You're wasting valuable time. Now, drink." She lifted her arm to him, her voice softening, "Please. Let me heal you."

Gareth's instinct cried for him to grab her arm and sink his teeth into her veins and drain her dry. That hunger was always with him, but his will had always been stronger. That was what set him apart from his kind. Through this act, he would come to know Adele more intimately than she could imagine. The desires and emotions that combined to make her who she was would slip tantalizingly across his tongue. Humans had no way of absorbing another on such a profound level. Or so Gareth assumed. He wasn't a human. He had never "loved" anything before. He protected the human inhabitants of Edinburgh. He cared for the cats that shared his home. But Princess Adele was the first being that he wanted to please, with every gesture or word.

His strong graceful hands took her arm as if it were the most delicate of instruments. He brushed his lips against the warm skin at her wrist, and her breath drew into her lungs in a small gasp. He could hear her heartbeat race, and the flow of blood in her veins rushed beneath his lips like a river. He needed to dip into those waters and ease his pain.

"You may turn away if you wish," he said, almost in rote fashion, his concentration solely on the blood just the skin's depth away from his mouth.

"I won't turn away," she promised him softly.

"Adele." Her name slipped like a prayer from his lips. He opened his mouth and extended his fangs and bit her swiftly.

Adele reeled, reaching with her other arm to steady herself against the cold damp ground. The pain quickly faded, and all that remained was a pleasant warmth created by the heat of Gareth's lips on her skin and the rush of blood that sped to the source of his gentle bite.

The thick rich liquid flowed into Gareth, bringing with it a torrent of knowledge that nearly overwhelmed him. In that instant, he knew all that Adele was—and it terrified him.

Death.

She tasted of death.

Fear flooded his brain. Princess Adele would kill every vampire that walked the earth. Her hand would sweep across the land, purging all of his kind. There would be no place to hide. Even for him.

Instinct demanded he kill her now. Save his people! Save himself!

But he couldn't.

Beneath the horror of her power he could sense her kindness, her rebellious spirit, her sense of wonder. All the things about her that thrilled him. And he tasted her profound feelings for him. She trusted him. She needed him.

Adele's breath quickened. Gareth's gaze lifted, and his light blue eyes locked with her dark ones. She was desperate to convey to him she was all right. She was speechless, but she wasn't frightened. Where once his vampireness had terrified her, now she saw the eyes of Greyfriar nestled in the face of Gareth: tender, caring, and filled with wonder about everything human. Her gaze softened, a tender smile tugging at her lips.

She released her hold on the rooted grass and touched his hair, silky and long between her fingers. Her contact was gentle and soothing. His wounds were terrible things to behold, and she wanted him to heal, needed him to be whole once more. She could never repay his sacrifices for her. He had turned his back on his kingdom, all for her. That devotion sparked in his eyes every time she looked into them. May all of mankind forgive her, but she cared deeply for him.

Finally he withdrew. It was a quick motion, not so much painful but more a chill as the heat of his mouth left her. Gareth quickly placed a strip of his torn shirt over the small wound and tied it with a tender touch.

Already there was a blush on his pale cheek as he wiped his lips clear of her dark rich blood.

"Did I hurt you?" he asked almost shamefully.

It took a moment to find her voice. "No, Gareth, you didn't," she reassured him, her voice soft. "But was it enough? Your wounds still look ghastly." She had no concept of how long it took for vampires to heal. She knew little about vampires other than how to kill them. And even if he could feel no pain, she did every time she looked at his raw injuries.

"It was enough," he told her. "Thank you. I'm very grateful."

"You are welcome to more if it would help."

"Any more would drain you too much to travel. Trust me. In an hour or so, my flesh will close. Your blood has healed me." Gareth bowed his head.

He had always known there was something special about her, but he had never expected the revelation he felt while feeding. She was terrifying in her power, yet he was unafraid. He had craved absolution from her and it had finally been granted; she was no longer afraid of him. He would forever be loyal to her, and now he was damned because of it. His whole species was damned, but he didn't care.

Adele kissed his head softly, resting her cheek against him, relishing the relief she felt at his words.

He looked up, his breath a shuddering inhale. "I will always protect you."

For a brief moment, Adele forgot her own impending marriage to a man she did not know or care for. Instead she reveled in the moment she shared with Gareth, the Greyfriar. Her heart sang with the simple joy that fact brought.

"We must keep going," Gareth cautioned, the fear of losing her again weighing heavily.

"I know." Adele rose and pulled Gareth up with her, supporting him. But his vigor was already replenished, and his strong hands steadied her more than she him. They pulled away from each other reluctantly. Adele picked up her cross again and adjusted the Fahrenheit dagger and Greyfriar's revolver in her sash.

She was ready.

CHAPTER 30

CESARE'S AIRSHIP MUSCLED into the air over Scotland. The ship flew low and slow, but with the confidence of superiority. There was no chance it could be attacked by an enemy. It was the king of the sky, despite the fact that it was an unpainted hulk with splintering wood and tattered sails. It looked like a ghost ship. The bloodmen slaves cared little for naval discipline or maintenance.

Cesare paced the bow. A cruel smile flittered across the prince's thin, bloodless lips. No doubt Gareth would be livid that his younger brother had the audacity to challenge him on his home ground. If Gareth had been a true noble, he would have set his own packs, if he had any, on Cesare by now. Cesare would have loved a fight; his brother needed to be put in his place. The black stones of Edinburgh Castle finally slid beneath the hull of the ship. And still no challenge had come from Gareth.

Cesare leapt over the rail, followed by Flay and a cadre of the Pale. They lit in the main courtyard. The place was empty—in fact, dismally barren. Except for cats, some of which stared openly at the vampires as they entered into the castle. The little beasts unnerved Cesare. Their constant mewling bored into his sensitive ears. How typical of Gareth to live among such vermin.

"Show yourself, Gareth!" Cesare shouted. "I have no time for games!"

From out of the shadows stepped a lean, tall vampire.

"Baudoin," snarled Cesare. "I haven't seen you in ages. How comforting to know you're still coddling my brother."

Baudoin bowed to his other nursery charge of long ago, out of duty rather than courtesy.

"Take me to Gareth," Cesare demanded, done with feeble pleasantries.

Baudoin droned an official reply, "Prince Gareth has urgent business in the west. I do not know when he will return. I must convey his enormous regrets."

"He knew I was coming!" Cesare roared.

Baudoin struggled to hold back the small smile at Cesare's childish tantrum. It was all very familiar. Apparently age had not tempered the young prince's self-important indulgences.

"Then no doubt he will return soon." Baudoin bobbed his head in deference to Cesare's logic. "Surely he would not keep you waiting."

Flay was not amused. She stepped close to Baudoin, her lips near the servant's neck. Baudoin stood straight, refusing to show fear to this fierce warrior, though he knew that she might kill him in an instant.

"You're toying with your life, butler." Flay's tone was whisper low.

"I only speak the truth."

"Where is my brother?" Cesare asked.

Baudoin shrugged. "One human settlement is like any other to me. I have no way of knowing which one he went to."

Furious at the delay, Cesare kicked his way through the curious cats. Suddenly he spun to Flay. "Search the road to Clava in the north. There are places humans might hide from me there."

Flay's lips split into a merciless grin. "It will be my pleasure." Her long fingers slid along Baudoin's neck, drawing a thin red line of blood as they withdrew.

With a shrill hiss, she commanded three of her Pale. They slid into the air and left the castle's confines.

—◦◦◦—

Adele and Gareth ran across the countryside. He moved as if he had never been injured. The terrible wounds he carried were already losing their raw and horrible aspect. The thought that it was her blood that had healed him so quickly thrilled Adele. She did an admirable job of keeping up with his brutal pace. They moved as a well-oiled machine. She even flashed him a broad smile, enjoying their return to flight, just the two of them again. For a moment he was caught up in her exhilaration and belief that they would escape.

"Where are we going?" Adele asked with labored breath.

"North. There are stones there. Remember how you hid near stones on the road to Canterbury?"

"Yes."

"Well, there are many stones to the north. Vampires never go near them. It may help hide you from Cesare until I can make arrangements to get you out of Britain."

Adele thought back to Canterbury. Her heart pounded with anticipation, a palpable desire to have that amazing surge roar through her again. Plus she felt, she knew, that such a place would keep her safe from any vampires, even Cesare and Flay. Then Adele remembered how Greyfriar had reacted to Canterbury. "Can you go to these stones?"

"Yes. I can stay for a short while. It won't kill me."

"Is there some other place? Some other way?"

"No. We are in a corner, Princess. The stones are your best hope now. There is nothing else."

Adele didn't question further. They moved on relentlessly by day and night. They rested only when Adele could move no more. Skies grew grey, and rain spattered them constantly. Mists hid their footsteps along mossy pathways. The air grew colder, and the fierce Scottish wind howled hard around them. Gareth didn't notice, even though he had only his torn, long-sleeved frock coat over his bare chest. Adele longed for a fire and warm food, but she knew that was impossible.

The terrain grew even more difficult. Valleys deepened, and sharp rock faces slashed up from the green hillsides. Ground turned wet and boggy. Heavy forests hid them from spying eyes overhead, but also made their path harder.

Gareth paused under the boughs of great trees, staring out over a long open glen. They would need to sprint across the rolling moors to reach the next stand of trees. Although Adele made no sounds of weakness, he could tell she was failing from the chill and damp, and sporadic meals. The stones at Clava were still days away. He wanted to move so much faster, but Adele simply couldn't.

Gareth took her by the hand and started out across the wet ground. The pain of her touch was almost minuscule now. She still gave off a fierce heat, but it wasn't searing. The strong wind slapped at their clothes. The soft turf squished beneath their boots. Adele could barely feel her feet as they fell one after the other over the muddy earth.

Suddenly, Gareth stopped and stared back up into the sky. Three dark shapes dove for them out of the misty clouds. "They found us!"

"Good. I couldn't run another step." With a scrape of steel, Adele drew the Fahrenheit blade. Her other hand pulled a pistol.

Gareth found himself grinning at her fighting visage. She was a marvelous sight, hood flung back and her traveling cloak swirling about her as she spun toward the attackers.

Gareth lifted into the sky to confront his kindred, relishing the fact that he could fight now as a vampire and not hide his abilities behind a human mask. His claws and teeth elongated as he drew close to the Pale. One vampire's head snapped back abruptly, and he went spinning backward as Gareth heard the report of Adele's pistol.

Then he was in the thick of battle, colliding with the next vampire at such speed that their impact sounded like a clap of thunder. His teeth sank deep into the jugular of his foe, and a twist of his jaw ripped through the tendons and sinew. The Pale gurgled and clawed, but the prince flung him aside as the third vampire dove past him for Adele.

Gareth propelled himself after his last foe. Adele stood ready, the dim sunlight unable to match the glow of her drawn dagger and her other arm outstretched, aiming with steadfastness at the vampire barreling toward her. Gareth saw the puff of smoke and watched her hand jerk as the pistol fired. With frightful anticipation, the vampire twisted to the side, and Gareth felt rather than saw the bullet tear through the Pale's red tunic and then rip his own coat.

The Pale dropped toward the princess, hissing a terrible screech. His arms reached for her. Adele stepped forward, and there was a brilliant flash as her khukri arced up and over. The vampire screamed as one of his hands fell to the ground. Adele followed the motion of her blade and ducked low as he flew over her. A moment later a second shadow passed over her as Gareth grasped hold of the vampire's shoulders and let momentum draw them up. There the prince made short work of his opponent, snapping his neck and nearly wrenching it from the torso in his rage.

Gareth looked around to see the vampire with the torn throat sprawled on the ground, nearly dead. Adele was running for him with her wide-bladed dagger drawn back to deliver the coup de grâce. The first Pale she had shot was trying to escape, so Gareth flew after him. It took only seconds to catch up and dispatch him.

Gareth settled to the ground next to Adele as the blood boiled on her blade. She was breathing heavily; her eyes danced with animalistic exhilaration. With a smooth flourish the dagger was back in its sheath, and she reloaded the pistol before it found its home back in her belt.

"We beat them!" she exclaimed.

He smiled at her. He hadn't dared to hope they would ever fight side by side again. But his smile didn't linger. Behind Adele he spotted more black dots in the sky. Adele gasped when she turned and saw them too.

Cesare, Flay, and more vampires approached. There was no chance to flee now.

Throwing off his tattered frock coat, Gareth prepared to fight the small army.

"What are you doing?" she cried, grabbing his arm. "You can't stop them all!"

"They will not have you!"

"But if you're killed, then what happens to me?"

Gareth hesitated, looking down at her pleading face, her eyes wide with fear and determination. The vampires were almost upon them, and Gareth knew he had no choice. This was the end, his last gambit.

Suddenly, Adele's eyes tightened with determination. Even an insane plan was better than suicide. She threw herself away with a small cry and fled wildly. "I will not be taken by you vampire scum!"

Taken by surprise, Gareth stared after her. To his horror, Flay swooped at Adele and grabbed her.

"No!" screamed Gareth, as he smashed into Flay and drove her into the sodden ground.

Adele rounded on Gareth with a fist and slammed it into his face, forcing the stunned prince back.

"Get away from me, you wretched slime!" She scrambled away from him with her face full of disgust and fear reminiscent of when she first came to Edinburgh.

Bewildered, Gareth stepped toward her with his hand out. But her gaze was only on the shadows coming up behind them. Gareth knew Cesare had arrived.

Adele collapsed at Gareth's boots. "I surrender!" she gasped. "No more!"

Flay angrily gained her feet, dripping mud. She stalked toward Gareth, but Cesare motioned her aside.

Cesare studied his older brother and his human prisoner with astonishment.

Abruptly, Gareth understood. "I have captured the escaped princess."

Cesare stammered, "Why . . . ? How did she come to be here?"

Gareth's response was to grab Adele roughly by her upper arm and drag her to her feet. She seemed limp and frightened, but not quite resigned to her fate.

Adele snarled, "It was Greyfriar who rescued me!" She met the gaze of Flay. "Don't you tire of being bested by him?"

Flay raised a clawed hand, which Cesare slapped down. The war chief glared silently at Adele and worked her toothy jaw in anger.

Gareth said to Cesare, "Apparently you cannot keep hold of your prisoner. So she will remain in my possession. I am taking her to Edinburgh."

Cesare snarled at his brother's barb, but then his face twisted into a sneer. "I don't believe that will happen. Our father has decreed the prisoner be returned to London. He will decide what is to be done with her. Surely even you do not have the audacity to disobey our king."

Gareth desperately tried to think of a solution to this matter that wouldn't result in Adele being taken from him. His father's word was law, and to openly disobey it would be fatal.

With a stiffening back, he conceded. "So be it. But before relinquishing *my* prisoner, I will consult with our father." Through eyes narrowed to slits, he regarded his brother. "Unless you wish to invite a clan war over this affair."

Flay brandished a clawed hand again and surged at Adele. "I have no compunctions about starting one."

Gareth shoved her back, keeping Adele behind him.

"Enough!" Cesare boomed. "For the moment, I'm willing to play your little game." His words were punctuated by a meager bow. "Let us return to your home, by all means."

With a cold stare, Flay followed after her prince as Cesare strode off. Gareth turned toward Adele. He couldn't comfort the fear in her eyes because he knew it was echoed in his own.

CHAPTER 31

EDINBURGH CASTLE WAS filled with vampires.

It made Gareth ill to see it. He had given strict orders to his brother to keep the Pale confined to the wretched airship hovering over the courtyard. A bristling Flay had gone to deliver the message.

"You live like a pauper here." Cesare sneered at Gareth over a goblet of rich thick blood. "You are more foolish than I believed. Here I thought you had the life of a god in this desolate kingdom. Your herds live better than you."

Gareth hid his vehemence with nothing more than a flush of pink on his linen cheeks. "I prefer them to present company."

"You are no more a prince than that ridiculous creature." Cesare waved a hand at a slinking cat.

Gareth forced a cold smile for his brother, drumming long fingers impatiently on the tabletop.

"You know, Gareth, I've been thinking about the princess." Cesare leaned back in his chair.

Gareth's heart skipped, but he didn't miss a beat in his finger patter, and his face remained tired and bored. "Do tell."

"I think her usefulness is at an end. London has already been attacked by the humans." He now smiled at Gareth's raised eyebrow. "Oh yes. Apparently you were away or hiding at the time. The princess's mate dropped out of the sky and slaughtered a few helpless wanderers. Flay drove him away with little trouble."

"She didn't kill him, then?"

"No. He was obviously looking for his female. But she was running loose by then, thanks to that . . . that . . . man."

"Greyfriar," Gareth offered a bit quickly.

"Yes. Greyfriar." Cesare took another long draft of blood. He swirled the vintage with disapproval. "Bit thin, I think. Still, Greyfriar. Did you encounter him when you found the princess?"

"No. The princess was alone." Gareth laughed derisively. "Perhaps Flay killed him."

"No, she didn't." A bitter look crossed Cesare's face. "She didn't."

"Mm. Well, I never saw him."

"How fortunate that you happened on the princess wandering alone in the wilds."

"Quite."

Cesare straightened. "As I was saying, the war has begun, for all intents and purposes. We have been bloodied, first in Bordeaux and now in London. Obviously the madmen in Alexandria will not hesitate to pursue their war. So their precious princess means nothing to them." He stared at his brother. "Therefore, she now means nothing to me."

"And so?"

"And so she needs to die."

Gareth stopped drumming his fingers and stopped breathing for a moment. Then he recovered his blasé countenance. "Interesting logic. Unfortunately, she is my prisoner. So I say what happens to her."

"For now. Once in London, she is the king's property and he can dispose of her as he wishes. I wonder who he'll give her to? You or me?"

Cesare laughed like a wicked child as Gareth stood abruptly and went to the cold fireplace. He could face his brother no more. Traces of ash remained in the hearth from the dinner days ago, the first time it had been used in over a century. It seemed like a century since that exciting evening. Baudoin attracted his prince's eye as the tall servant strode from the room bearing an empty tray.

Gareth followed him out. "What is it?"

"Prince Cesare's pack won't stay on the ship for long. They'll want to prowl soon."

Gareth nodded. "The townsfolk have been warned to remain in their homes. But I'm afraid you are right. Eventually they will be hunted."

"The longer the delay, the greater the risk."

"We should be gone by morning."

"What will you and the princess do?"

Gareth regarded his old friend and saw nothing but sincere concern. A weary shrug was the response. "I'm not sure yet."

"I will stay with the princess tonight to watch her."

Gareth smiled. "Thank you. Though I suspect she may be the safest one of us all. Cesare won't dare harm her here in this place. One thing Cesare still respects is protocol."

"Protocol." Baudoin spat. "I will stay close to her. You may need to help the rest of your subjects, should any of our brethren steal away for a late-night repast."

Gareth chuckled despite the grim situation. Baudoin always had a succinct way of stating the obvious. "Thank you. I don't know what will happen after I return to London. I leave my realm under your care."

Baudoin bowed deeply.

Gareth climbed to the ramparts of his castle. He glared angrily at Cesare's dilapidated airship moored to his home. He thought he saw Flay wandering the deck. The sky was overcast, as was the norm in this land. Dismal and dark. The clouds hung low, almost to the parapets. His home was enshrouded like a cocoon, safe from the outside world.

So it came with some shock that another airship dove out of the clouds, flying the American flag and unleashing a thunderous salvo from its cannons. The ground shook, and vampires scattered. Flay flung herself toward the nearest cover, one shot coming close enough to leave her trailing smoke.

Cables dropped from the sleek frigate like jungle vines, and heavily armed commandos poured forth. The soldiers were out for blood and vengeance; they cut through Flay's disoriented guards. The Pale fell back from the humans' fury.

As the fight on the ramparts raged, Flay left the ship and rushed to Cesare's side. "We are under attack!"

Cesare had heard the booms of cannons, but he still found it hard to credit such unbelievable audacity. Then a terrible thought struck him. "It's Clark! How is that possible? He's come for the princess!"

Let the Butcher have her, Flay thought. The human female had been nothing but trouble from the start. But her lord still deemed the prisoner important to the future of their kind, so the war chief only nodded and they started for Princess Adele's room.

A small squad of human commandos appeared in the way, surprised to encounter the onrushing female. Flay extended her claws in twin arcs and killed them all. Cesare smiled as he waded through the corpses in her wake. The rest of the way was clear. Flay kicked open Adele's door and Cesare stepped in. The room was empty.

"Where is she?" Cesare shouted, incensed that his prey was gone.

Flay stood to the side, her fingers dripping red onto the pristine white fur rug by the fireplace that still glowed warm. "She's gone. Let me go and I'll destroy the Americans."

Cesare heard her but did not respond, lost in thought. Flay grabbed her lord's arm to pull him from the room. "Release me! You dare!"

She snarled, hoping to break through to his fearful reason. "Forget the princess! The human war chief is here. Now! Let me go and I will decapitate the human war machine!"

Cesare muttered, "I can't lose the princess. Then I will look foolish to the clan lords. You must find her, Flay, and we will escape to London. This is no time to worry about the humans."

"This is the perfect time! They are far from home. They have no reinforcements. Let me destroy them! The war will be over now!"

Cesare raised a fist. "Do as I say! Find the princess. Do you think I care about killing humans? I won't have Gareth making a fool out of me!"

Flay bowed her head in defeat and slammed out of the room with a fierce growl.

Prince Gareth and Princess Adele ran along the ramparts. The moment the attack began, Gareth had raced to Adele's room. He knew this castle and all its hidden passageways. It didn't take a tactical genius to realize Cesare would try to secure the princess. As they ran, Adele caught her first glimpse of the sleek American warship that floated over the great castle. *Ranger* had come for her. From the deck, riflemen and machine-gunners poured a murderous fire into the courtyard. The port cannons raked Cesare's ship with a deafening broadside. The high pitch from shriekers sliced through the air, causing Gareth to wince.

His grip on her hand tightened, and he shouted over the pain, "You must escape with Senator Clark. I will keep my brother from pursuing."

"But . . . I . . ." A concussive blast shuddered through Adele, and thick, oily gas enveloped her. With her ears ringing, she instinctively covered her mouth and nose with the inside of her elbow. Harsh smoke stung her tightly shut eyes.

Something knocked Gareth back against the stones. Through the roiling smoke appeared the indistinct figure of a man wearing a blue uniform with bright buttons. His face was a leathery mask with lifeless round brass eyes. He had a rifle to his shoulder, aimed at the prince.

Adele instantly turned and jumped in front of the rising Gareth. She felt a hard punch to her shoulder that slammed her into Gareth's arms. They tumbled to the ground together. She was lying on her back, staring up, gasping for breath in the purplish smoke. Gareth rose and placed a hand on her. Through the haze, she saw his confused, terrified face staring down at her. She wanted to tell him she was fine, but couldn't speak.

The smoke clung to Gareth like a second skin. He could barely see or smell, and the distant shriekers ripped at his ears. But he was near enough to Adele to scent the blood oozing between his fingers from the wound in her shoulder. He seized her slumping body, sensing her life leaking out over his hands. Amid the chaos, horror gripped him at the realization that he would lose her. After everything they had been through, she could be taken in mere seconds.

A sturdy wind parted the stinking smoke, and now Gareth saw the faceless man. He knew it was Senator Clark, who had shot him and then Adele as she tried to protect him. Gently, Gareth lowered Adele's body to the flagstones. Then in a blur that no human eye could track, the vampire prince charged.

The senator fired point-blank at the grey motion, then felt as if a cannonball struck him. His rifle shattered, still clutched in his hand, as the senator slammed against the stone battlements.

Gareth's sharp talons shredded flesh and cloth; he was desperate to take retribution because nothing else was left for him. A devastating blow brought Clark to his knees, but he swung the smashed rifle barrel, snapping the prince's head to the side. The unfazed vampire spun back, teeth bared. The senator had never seen such an expression on a vampire's face; it was almost emotion and not hunger. For a second Clark knew something akin to fear.

A rigid claw of a hand darted out for Clark's throat. Nails that had turned into razors dug deep into frail human flesh, and Gareth lifted Clark, who writhed in a desperate attempt to dislodge himself.

The prince stepped to the battlements' edge. Far below were dark rocks to dash this murderer's bright blood upon. Gareth wanted to see it. Maybe that would take the pain away for a second.

A voice called out—one he had never expected to hear again.

"Ga . . . eth . . . stop."

He froze in his killing. A glimmer of hope retraced its path to his soul. He turned.

A bleeding Adele reached out toward him as the last tendrils of smoke slipped away from her. "Please . . . don't."

Gareth cast the man roughly aside and rushed to Adele's side. He held her once more, burying his head against her cheek.

With his hands Gareth tried to stanch the blood that slowly leaked out. He gently pushed hair from her eyes.

"You mustn't . . . hurt him," she murmured.

Gareth couldn't understand what he was hearing. Was it love? Loyalty to her kind? Mere kindness? It didn't matter anymore. The princess was dying. He spared a glance at the crumpled man on the stone path, knowing what had to happen.

"You have to go with him," Gareth whispered to her. "He can save you."

"Gar . . . eth . . ." She reached a shaking hand to a face no longer savage and cruel.

"I wish we had more time. . . ." His voice trailed off. He brushed his lips over her cheeks. "I'll never forget you. Promise you'll never forget me."

Gareth stood. Adele tried to cling to him, but he pulled away, and the edge of his coat slipped through her fingers. The prince regarded the miserable Clark with his inhuman false face, sitting up now, holding his bleeding throat. Clark's other hand was fumbling for something at his waist, but he was still too dazed to move with any true coordination.

Gareth drew in a deep breath and addressed the senator. "Take her and leave." He turned around quickly and disappeared into the wrecked heart of the castle.

Senator Clark staggered to his feet. The vampire had had him at his mercy and failed to follow through. Instead, the vermin had returned to feed on the princess. Typical cowardly beast. Straightening, he pulled his pistol from his holster. He debated going after the creature and making it pay, but Adele caught his attention. She was trying to crawl to the castle door, toward what she perceived was shelter. He adjusted the filter on his goggles because Adele appeared in a whitish glow, which was not natural for humans. The mask must have been damaged in the fight.

"Easy now, darling. I've got you." Clark's voice came thick and muffled from behind the gas mask as he gathered up the princess in his arms. "I'm taking you home."

Senator Clark raced for *Ranger*. Adele's head lolled against his shoulder. His troopers were scattered about the castle, searching for the very thing he had cradled in his arms. As he neared his ship, the crew—all glowing proper human red—smartly ceased their fire and a bugle sounded recall.

A blue shape landed effortlessly in front of Clark, interrupting his daydream of a successful hero's return. The vampire soldier straightened its tall frame with a cruel smile and even had the audacity to hiss at him.

Clark never even heard the second vampire swoop down on him, its claws ripping into his shoulders. He was lifted off his feet and lost his grip on Adele. He swung his pistol and fired wildly above him. The lithe female vampire tossed him forty feet to the side.

Clark tumbled halfway over the precarious edge of the battlement. Even as he clutched at the stones for his life, he snapped his head wildly about, searching for Adele. He saw her in the grip of a slim male vampire who dragged her toward the decrepit bloodmen ship. Clark scrambled back onto the rampart of the decaying castle, but he knew he would never make it in time to rescue Adele. He shouted in rage as the sails of the enemy ship gathered wind. He would break his gunners for not turning the vampire ship into unflyable kindling.

At the same instant, Flay bulleted toward *Ranger*, easily eluding the regrouping commandos as they converged on the drop lines hanging beneath the frigate. She settled aloft to shatter some of the ship's spars. She propelled off a mast and ascended, raking billowing sails with her clawed hands, leaving them fluttering loose in the wind.

"Kill it!" screamed Clark, dragging his mask from his face as he limped toward his ship. "Blast it out of the sky!"

His answer was a volley erupting from multiple barrels in a cloud of green smoke. Flay glided from the airship's rigging into the open air as bullets whipped around her. Some troopers heard her laughing over the sound of the gunfire. She spiraled away from *Ranger* as the crew made the crippled ship ready for a desperate launch.

The princess was thrown at Cesare's feet on the deck of the bloodmen airship. It didn't matter to the prince if she was alive or dead. He was pleased enough with the victory. He was going to win, despite Clark the great human vampire killer, despite the human hero named Greyfriar, and despite his treacherous brother.

As the bloodmen ship rose into the twilight sky, a streak of grey and steel flashed across the battlements. Greyfriar leapt from a crumbling tower in a desperate grab for a trailing mooring rope.

Flay approached the bloodmen vessel and actually paused in midair, staring in disbelief at the figure dangling from the airship. Her face grew sharp and hard. Her eyes slitted with hate. She gathered speed and flew at Greyfriar. Incredibly, even while flailing on a wind-blown rope, he pulled a pistol and took a shot. She eluded it all too easily and came in like a banshee, raking him across the shoulder and back. The sheer force of her attack knocked the pistol from his hand and almost made him lose his grip on the line.

Greyfriar immediately drew his sword, but he was in an awkward position. Flay took full advantage of that, her clawlike hands ripping as she darted past him. Her delighted laughter flashed loud and then faded as she flitted in and out of range. He couldn't release and meet her in battle. His burden of arms would slow him down, and he would lose the ship, and lose Adele. If the princess returned to Cesare's domain, she would never be seen alive again.

Flay arced against the skyline as she turned, and Greyfriar let his sword droop as if he were near defeat, as any human would be with his terrible injuries. With a smirk of glee she dove for the kill, hands raised, claws dripping. When she came into reach, he swung the blade up, a solid strike, slicing her from hip to shoulder. Flay screeched. The blow sent her tumbling, screeching with her hand tightly pressed to her blood-drenched chest. She bolted up to the airship.

Adele watched Flay land on the deck and stagger as if badly hurt. It struck Adele as odd that the first thing the war chief did was seize the lashed end of a mooring rope that dangled off the side and begin to shred it with her claws. The sheer peculiarity of it compelled Adele to struggle to the rail and look over. She saw Greyfriar trailing far below, climbing as fast as he could.

The sight of Greyfriar spawned a surge of warmth spreading through Adele, similar to the Canterbury swell she remembered so fondly. The uncanny wave of comfort banished her pain and numbness, filling her with a euphoric strength that let her focus on action. She was shocked to realize her Fahrenheit blade was still in her belt. Cesare was too vain to search her, and the bloodmen were incapable of action without direct orders. With fingers tight about the hilt of the dagger, she straightened on unsteady legs. Then she shoved off and catapulted herself blade first at Flay, and the khukri sunk deep. Flay's snakish eyes dilated from the damage and darted to Adele. One claw slammed the princess back to the deck.

Adele cried out as darkness closed in. Pain flared in every nerve. She struggled to hold onto consciousness because Gareth needed her. As the war chief reached down for her, Adele threw all her strength into the sizzling blade and plunged it into Flay's throat.

The vampire staggered back, and blood gushed through her sharp fingers. Adele knew she wasn't strong enough for this fight, but she had to buy Gareth time. She struggled to her knees. Flay seized her by the neck, trying to throttle the remaining life out of her even as the vampire screamed from the touch. Adele didn't even try to grab Flay. Instead her instinct for survival directed her hand to the cross she had rescued from the dust in Greyfriar's Kirk.

Through her spiderwebbing vision, Adele looped the cross around Flay's neck with a fervent prayer on her lips. The princess felt a spreading warmth bringing strength and comfort while Flay screeched in pain. The vampire released the young girl and slammed against the side of the ship, frantically tearing at the object encircling her. Adele put her booted foot against Flay and shoved the vampire over the rail. Then the young woman collapsed across the gunwale, watching the vile Flay plummet like a rock and disappear screaming into the clouds below.

Then Adele's gaze drifted to Greyfriar, just below her. She grabbed the end of the rope just as it snapped.

"Don't let go!" Gareth shouted. "I can't keep up with you."

The hard cord sliced Adele's hands. The pain awakened her lagging senses, but it didn't give her any strength. She was going to lose him. Fresh blood welled from her hands and made the rope even slicker. She cast about for anything to assist her. All she saw was the bloodmen crew.

"Help me!" she pleaded. Surely there must be some sliver of humanity in them. But they merely gaped at her before returning to their duties.

A dark shape slithered on the deck behind her, its shadow crossing her.

Cesare.

He snarled and grabbed Adele, throwing her to the deck. He ripped the rope away from her and tossed it over the side.

"No!" she screamed, scrabbling futilely after the vanished rope.

Cesare regarded her emotional outburst for a rope with confusion. He peered over the side. A sword flashed upward and pierced his chest. Cesare fell back, stunned at the weapon protruding from his flesh.

Gareth struggled with one hand to gain purchase on the rail. His wounds were severe, and he had lost a great deal of blood. He was weak, unsure if he could climb the rest of the way up.

But suddenly Adele was there, reaching down with her good arm, desperate with hope. "Hurry!"

Gareth didn't hesitate, grasping her offered hand and lifting himself onto the deck. He climbed to unsteady feet as Adele slumped to the deck, her reserves finally spent.

Cesare yanked the blade from his chest. He saw no vampires around. None of the Pale had survived the American attack. Cesare screamed to the human drones about him, pointing at Adele and Greyfriar, "Kill them! Kill them now!"

They obeyed: no thought, no reason. They attacked as a surging mob.

Greyfriar didn't want to kill these humans, but he had no choice. Nothing must stop him. Adele must survive. Blood, flesh, and steel rose in the air until abruptly there was stillness, with only Greyfriar standing, drenched in the blood of the newly dead. Cesare stared in horror. He was alone now.

Cesare was wounded, but Greyfriar was worse. With a bellowing roar, Cesare charged his enemy.

He had never fought a human with such strength and quickness. Greyfriar dodged slash after slash of Cesare's claws. The human's forearm slammed into Cesare's stomach, doubling him over. Cesare righted himself with a wicked slash at Greyfriar's face. The human warrior dodged, and the claws ripped into his chest instead, staggering him. Vampire reflexes saved Cesare a nasty riposte of Greyfriar's blade. The human just kept coming, no matter what damage Cesare inflicted. Blood flowed from both of them, both scarlet in color, both a sign of their dwindling life.

The unmanned airship floundered in the wind, pitching to the side. The weakened Cesare dropped against the bulwark hard. He glanced at Adele. He needed only a moment to feed from her to regain the advantage. He started to scramble to his feet, but the shadow of Greyfriar came over him with blade raised for a killing stroke. Gareth was free to put an end to his brother's life, but he stepped back, his blade dropping.

"Go," Greyfriar said wearily. "Go now and you'll live."

Cesare stared, dumfounded. He contemplated taking advantage of the human's foolishness. But he was rational enough to know he didn't have the upper hand; it wasn't a sure kill. And Cesare never fought unless he believed he had a sure kill. Better to wait and fight again. And if this Greyfriar was giving him that opportunity, so be it.

Cesare sneered. The human called the Greyfriar was weak. He had the vampire prince at his mercy, but he couldn't bring himself to kill. The fool! Cesare decided he didn't need Adele after all. The die was cast thanks to the aggression of the humans, particularly Senator Clark striking the vampire homeland on three different occasions. The clan was Cesare's for the taking. The war would go forward with or without the wretched princess. Cesare leapt into the air, letting the air currents take him far out of the human's reach.

Gareth watched his brother flee. Adele struggled to stand beside him.

"Why didn't you kill him?" she asked, grasping Gareth's arm as the ship pitched again with a gust of wind.

"I won't kill Cesare as a human. When I kill him, I'll do it with my hands." Gareth slipped to one knee. Adele sank down with him. "And I can't move another step."

Adele squeezed his arm, offering her own dwindling strength. She understood. This was more than a battle between families; it was a battle between nations. When the time came, all of his kind would have to know that it was Prince Gareth who challenged their vile traditions. Then it would shake the vampire nation to its core and give it a chance to become something more. Killing Cesare as Greyfriar would only fuel the war between humans and vampires, not end it.

Gareth gripped her hand lightly and gazed at her. "You're alive."

"I've been better." Adele tried to smile wanly. "But I think I'll survive. A few of Morgana's meals and I'll be fine."

Gareth searched out his brother's diminishing form, and then he gazed in the other direction. The sails of *Ranger* were visible aft. The frigate was catching the foundering wreck of an airship.

"No," he said. "You have to go home." Gareth stood, pulling Adele up with him.

Adele turned to watch *Ranger* draw close. Her face drained of the exhilaration of victory. She exhaled and dropped her head in defeat as boarding hooks slammed against the rails.

Senator Clark swung across with a team of commandos, all flashing saber and revolver, white cowboy hat trailing behind. Gareth tensed for the fight. Senator Clark reached out and grasped Gareth's hand gratefully, shaking it with pride.

"The Greyfriar, I presume! I'm Senator Clark. Thank you for your help, sir. We got the devils on the run!"

"And the princess is safe," Gareth noted.

"Yes, yes!" Senator Clark turned to Adele. "Thank heaven for that." He pulled the fragile girl into his steely arms and delivered a powerful kiss on the blood-caked face of his future bride.

Adele grimaced as Clark's passion aggravated her wounds and his beard scraped her face. She fought not to squirm, and her return kiss was just above catatonic.

Clark immediately pulled back. "You were lucky, my dear, that you were not more seriously hurt when that filthy vampire used you as a shield."

Adele's eyes sought out Gareth's, but he had turned away.

"I'll have you transferred to *Ranger*, where our ship's surgeon will tend you." Clark lowered Adele to the deck and crossed to the gunwale, waving to his crew to rig a transfer basket.

Adele turned to Gareth and mouthed, "Don't leave me. Come to Alexandria!"

"I can't," he replied quietly as he came close.

"But I love you."

"You mean Greyfriar."

"No. It's always been you." She didn't care about the obstacles standing between them. Suddenly all she wanted was to be with him.

Gareth's head bowed low at this revelation; he touched her face reverently, consumed with regret, and his hand shook as it trailed slowly down her cheek. As quickly as his joy at these words blossomed it was replaced with sorrow. He knew what must be done, and he prayed he had the strength to see it through, struggling to keep his voice devoid of the fervor that blistered him. "We have to save our nations first. Someday we may meet again, but for now, it is best you return to Equatoria. At the very least, we can both work to prevent a full-scale war between our races."

She bit back her despair. "But I'll be forced to . . . marry." Her eyes tracked toward her Intended, who was still bellowing orders. With gentle hands, she lowered his mask just a few inches to reveal his mouth. She took his face in her trembling hands and kissed him hard.

The footsteps of Senator Clark echoed on the deck as he approached them. Gareth slipped his mask back on.

"We're ready to leave," Clark informed them with a quizzical glance.

Greyfriar nodded. He quickly lifted Adele in his arms and strode past a surprised Clark to gently deliver her into the basket. Greyfriar watched as the Americans carefully winched her out of his reach into the dizzying maw between the airships. Adele's gaze did not leave him even after the crew of *Ranger* lifted her from the basket.

His heart agonized as he watched her taken away, his eyes darkening with the sting of it.

Clark clapped an iron hand on his shoulder. "Come with us, Greyfriar. We can exchange a few war stories while your wounds mend."

Greyfriar shook his head, fighting the urge to sweep the hand off, but sadness weakened his limbs. "I wish you well, Senator Clark. But I leave you here."

"Look here, this ship is done for. We'd tow it as a prize, but it's not even worth breaking up for salvage. You can't stay on this wreck."

"Thank you, but my place is here."

"Well, I hope we'll meet again someday. Keep fighting the good fight!"

The big American laughed loudly as he grasped a line and swung across to the rail of *Ranger*. He waved farewell to Greyfriar as he placed his arm about Adele's shoulder. "I'll not let her out of my sight again," he shouted to Greyfriar.

Adele's eyes remained riveted on Gareth. The frigate gained headway and hove off.

With his keen vampiric eyesight, Gareth could watch Adele farther than she could him. She was crying at the rail, now alone, as her ship vanished into the clouds.

CHAPTER 32

"A MOST MARVELOUS day indeed," Sir Godfrey exclaimed as Mamoru entered the chamber deep inside the Great Pyramid. "Congratulations to us all!"

Mamoru bowed his head to the old gentleman. Even Nzingu the Zulu was smiling as she clapped her lace-covered hands. Sanah the Persian clung to the shadows and stayed quiet.

"We are fortunate," Mamoru said. "Selkirk performed magnificently. And we can, even against our better judgment, thank the boisterous Senator Clark as well as the mysterious Greyfriar."

"This Greyfriar chap needs to be brought into the circle, I should think," Sir Godfrey said.

"Perhaps," Mamoru replied. "If even half of what I've heard is true, he is more extraordinary than any other man alive."

"What of the princess?" Nzingu asked, a bit too abruptly to show true concern. "What is her condition?"

A calming breath helped Mamoru collect his thoughts before he spoke. "I am unsure. The senator's telegram from Malta indicated that Her Highness suffered grievous wounds, but he feels certain those will heal. He was, I'm certain, more concerned with the impending marriage than by Princess Adele's well-being. I am amazed by her strength of body." The samurai paused with a troubled sigh. "But emotionally, she cannot be unchanged."

"As we might well expect," Sir Godfrey consoled. "How could anyone endure what she must have in the north? But perhaps the ordeal has tempered her mettle, yes?"

"We can hope," Nzingu said. "She always seemed . . . insubstantial. Too weak to do what must be done. Maybe her tribulation will be a blessing. And it will bring out the true girl."

Mamoru cast a dark eye at the Zulu quickly. "It remains to be seen what Cesare has done to her. Certainly none of us have experienced what Princess Adele has."

Sanah said, "Do you fear that she has grown past the bond you shared?"

Mamoru regarded the Persian for a very long moment and considered the clarity of her question. "I only worry that she is not yet properly trained to accept the necessary knowledge. To direct it."

Sanah replied, "Perhaps she has a strength that even you did not perceive. There are springs in the mind from which others cannot drink."

"True enough." Mamoru gave a professorial tug on the cuffs of his jacket. "However, we are dealing with a power that can't be fully appreciated until the moment it is unleashed. And then it will be too late to realize it has been badly prepared. This is not a poem. This is a rigorous doctrine. And it will bring about the end of the world. For good or bad depending on how I . . . on how we remake Princess Adele."

Sir Godfrey chuckled and placed a hand on Mamoru's shoulder. "With a little time, I feel certain she will become your beloved student again. And we can get on with it."

Mamoru said, "That is my hope. It cannot end any other way."

———✦———

The ground crew at Pharos One roared out a rhythmic chanty as they drew USS *Ranger* and their beloved princess to the earth with each sinewy heave on the cables. The ship descended alongside the air tower, bathed in the chemical lights of the airfield.

Adele sat in a makeshift chair that had been rigged on the quarter-deck for the flight home so she could spend her days basking in the windswept majesty of her Intended. Tiring of this activity quickly, she had protested of constant chills and begged feebly to be returned to her private cabin. She became a master of the faint whenever Senator Clark felt compelled to visit her. Adele would smile, recalling how Gareth had merely stared at her swoon in the Tower, clearly unconvinced by her lampooned fragility. Thankfully Clark was not so savvy.

The senator brought *Ranger* to Alexandria at a time of Lord Kelvin's choosing, late evening and in the middle of the week. The court lied to the people about the time of Adele's arrival so no great crowds would be fighting to catch a glimpse of the returning heir. Apparently, the prime minister felt it was best if the residents of the capital did not see their frail future empress carried off the ship. Witnessing what was left of her after her frightful ordeal might shock them. No doubt Kelvin expected that Adele would be either catatonic or raving, with a head full of shock white hair.

The princess struggled from her chair and grasped the rail, staring down into the light-speckled crowd searching for her brother or Colonel Anhalt. Clark had related the joyous news of their survival. She could make out the uniforms of the Imperial Guard, but nothing more detailed. Perhaps her father was even present. The wonderfully familiar glow of gaslit Alexandria spreading out around her gave her goose bumps. However, the sight depressed her too. This was her city, the heart of a great empire that once seemed to encompass most of the world. But it seemed so small to her now, and crowded with people secure both in their power and in their ignorance about the world. Not just secure, but smug. This city wanted to rule the world, but it only saw the world through the haze of its own sand-choked surroundings. Just when she should be at her happiest, Adele was swallowed by an overwhelming sense of sadness. Perhaps, she wondered, it was the darkness and the cloying warm air. Maybe she would feel better in the morning after she had become accustomed to her own place again.

"Adele, take a seat," Senator Clark barked through the ruffling wind. "I can't have you tipping over the rail now!"

The princess served her Intended a sharp glare and held it until he added, "Your Highness." She considered snapping back that her sea legs were as good as his, but she didn't have the energy. Instead she returned to the chair with a pleasant smile and sat. Excruciating pain radiated through her frame. Adele would never admit it, but her body was recovering very slowly. She lived in constant agony despite the best drafts from the ship's surgeon. The inhuman exertions of her adventures in the north had caught up to her in the absence of the constant barrage of life-threatening dangers that had kept her frame empowered. It was all she could do not to collapse into a comatose bundle.

Still, Adele took comfort in the fact that she would soon see her brother. And Colonel Anhalt. And her father. She would be among her family. And there was much she wanted to discuss with Mamoru about his network of geomancer spies in the north, about Selkirk, and about the power she too seemed to wield. Clearly there was much more that needed to be learned than she had ever imagined.

Also, she had much to teach, and this gave Adele great satisfaction. She relished the idea of holding forth to the great minds of the court as they surrounded her, reacting to her matter-of-fact tales of adventure and horror with furrowed brows, tugged mustaches, and muttered admirations of her strength and courage. She was anxious to see Colonel Anhalt's astonished reaction with his wide eyes and white knuckles as she described her bloody exploits. But beyond those foolish conceits, Adele was most eager to set her countrymen straight on their knowledge of vampires and, even more, of human society in the north. There was so much the great leaders of the south didn't know, and needed to know before they started rolling their war machines across the European landscape.

Ranger touched down with a thud, and the air filled with sounds of bellowing longshoremen, heavy cables running through metal and over wood, and the vents above blowing the last of the chemical buoyants. The frigate was hardly secure before the gangplanks dropped and a mob surged aboard. They raced toward Adele, but then, overwhelmed by her mere presence, they all stopped and stared at her, waiting for something. Permission to approach? The screeching of a madwoman?

Adele recognized her own doctor and other members of the imperial medical corps. One of the nurses touched her own hair. Adele realized she was sporting Gareth's cut, which was nearly as short as the sailors surrounding her, rather than her former flowing auburn hair. The princess could see how different she looked now by the gapes on their faces. It wasn't just her shorn head. It was her whole self. They were terrified by the pain and violence that showed on the face and body of the royal heir. Adele had left them a soft, pampered girl, but returned a battle-worn woman. They were perplexed and frightened by the change, and the horrible imaginings of what could have caused it.

Adele smiled at them, hoping to relieve the tension. The nurse broke into tears, covering her face.

"Come now," Adele said, a bit more weakly than she would've liked. "I don't look that bad, do I?"

Her doctor shook his head vigorously, "No, Your Highness. Not at all. We just . . ."

Adele nodded with sympathetic understanding and lifted herself from the chair. They nearly gasped at her accomplishment. She rolled her eyes and laughed as best she could. When Senator Clark tried to take her elbow, she shrugged him off.

"Thank you, no," she told him politely. "I would like to try it on my own."

"As you wish." Clark inclined his head with stormy eyes. "My dear."

"Adele!"

Simon plowed through the line of petrified medical staff and raced across the deck. American sailors and soldiers tried to stop him, fearful that he would injure the battered princess, but they were too slow. The boy impacted his sister like a missile with arms, knocking her back into the chair as she shouted his name with uncontrollable joy and wrapped him in her suddenly pain-free embrace. She clutched frantically at his wonderfully solid frame and buried her face in his spiky, close-cropped hair.

Simon struggled partially free and looked up at her. "They say you met the Greyfriar!"

"Yes." Adele could barely form words through the tears that streamed down her face. Unwilling for him to be even a few feet away from her, she pulled him close again.

"Stop it," he muttered, wriggling up again. "What was he like? Did he kill vampires for you?"

"Yes. He did. Are you all right?"

"Did you kill any vampires?"

"Yes. All of them. Are you all right?"

Simon squinted at her suspiciously. "You did not. Did you kill even one? Did Greyfriar rescue you? From a castle?"

"As a matter of fact, he did." Adele choked back her sobs, smiling wildly. She pulled his head back to face her. "I'm so happy to see you."

He beamed broadly back at his sister. "I'm glad you're home, Adele."

A familiar voice cut through the air. "Prince Simon, stand away from your sister, if you please. She is injured and you can do her no good."

Adele opened her watery eyes. A stern Mamoru resplendent in a green silk robe embroidered with broad-winged cranes approached. She tried to argue that she was fine and that Simon could do her great good, but words failed her. She merely shook her head and clutched her brother harder so no one would take him away from her. Simon squirmed off her lap, but Adele refused to let go, squeezing his arm so hard he winced.

Mamoru bowed with hands clasped. "I am exceedingly grateful to see you, Your Highness. More than you can imagine."

"Mamoru," Adele breathed, reaching out to him with her other hand.

He was hesitant, but took her extended fingers. A quick glance over his shoulder to the medical staff urged them to move in and attend the princess. However, Adele ignored the questions and comments coming from the doctors and nurses as she tugged Mamoru closer. He bent low until his ear was at her mouth. His brow wrinkled in a very unaccustomed betrayal of surprise at her unusual familiarity.

"Thank you, Mamoru," Adele whispered. "For sending Mr. Selkirk. And for all you must have done."

Her mentor nodded quickly and said in a hushed voice, "Please, Your Highness, we can speak of these matters later when we are assured of your safety and robust health. Please allow the doctors to help you. There is time enough for us to talk later." Mamoru's eyes locked onto hers, studying her intently. It was almost as if he were scrutinizing a stranger. "I would like to learn all you know about the Greyfriar."

Adele stiffened and blurted out, "There's really nothing I can tell you. I don't know anything about him." She breathed out through her nose, clamping her lips shut and staring back at Mamoru without flinching. All she knew about Greyfriar was the truth, and she could never share that with anyone.

Mamoru's face gave a twitch of doubt, and his gaze searched her face. His eyes glittered with interest at her rushed exclamation. He wondered what she actually could know about Greyfriar that would prompt such a sudden and vigorous denial. But worse, he couldn't ignore a gnawing dread he felt that she needed to conceal something from him. It was as he had feared. This was not the same girl who had left Alexandria months ago. This woman had singular experiences that he had played no role in shaping. That could make for difficulties in the future.

The samurai stood slowly and said with deliberateness, "We shall speak of many things later, Your Highness. Your health is the Empire's only concern now."

Adele turned away, unwilling to watch his growing suspicion. Simon kept holding her hand as attendants lifted her from the chair onto a padded litter that floated on small gas bladders. They covered her with a blanket and held sweet-smelling ointments near her face to calm her. It was all she could do not to roll her eyes at their efforts as she was carried toward the gangplank. Mamoru eventually pulled Simon away so the doctors could engulf her. She protested, sitting up on the litter, but hands pressed at her, imploring her to relax.

"Stop it!" she shouted. "Simon! Come with me. Where's my father?"

Mamoru's calm voice wafted over her. "His Majesty was here to see the ship arrive, but he has pressing matters of state. He will attend your bedside soon enough."

Adele gripped the edges of the thin mattress and searched the wild scene around her. Doctors. Sailors. Dockworkers. Soldiers. But her own father could not be seen.

Then through the glare of the chemical lights that flooded the airfield she saw a group of men walking away. She noted the blue-clad straight back of Senator Clark and the black-suited Lord Kelvin as well as Lord Aden, dressed in formal wear with an opera cape and a top hat. In the midst of these great men, Adele saw a uniform greatcoat covering the hunched shoulders of Emperor Constantine. His pale face shone briefly as he turned back. The distance was too great for their eyes to meet, although Adele imagined they did. Her father paused and her pulse jumped. He was coming back. He would shrug off those three parasites and come to her.

Lord Kelvin's motions distracted Constantine, and he turned away from her. The four men disappeared in a mob of soldiers and politicians.

Adele lay back on the litter as she was carried back to her old life.

—◈—

The sunrise over the Mediterranean Sea cast a gold hue inside Adele's chamber. Many days had passed, and her wounds were healing. Her shoulder barely ached, at least in comparison to the ache deep in her chest.

Below her window the streets of Alexandria were ablaze with the celebrations that had reigned since her safe return in the arms of the great Senator Clark. The sound of people cheering her name and the union with their new champion echoed in her room until it hurt her ears.

Dread welled at the thought of the impending marriage. The ceremony had been blessedly postponed to allow Adele time to recuperate from her ordeal. Senator Clark was furious with the emperor for refusing to set a new date, but even he wouldn't dare force the issue with the poor princess clinging to health and sanity and battling the horrific memories of the bloody north. All she thought of was Gareth's arms about her.

The last time she had seen him he was standing on the ruined deck of Cesare's ship as it drifted earthward. He had looked so alone on the dying ship. She missed Gareth more than she had ever imagined possible.

There was a knock at the door. Adele looked at the ceiling with a long sigh. She didn't want to deal with any staff. But she was the princess. Wearing the royal mantle again for the sake of her people chafed more than she could bear.

"Come in," she muttered, with enough discontent that she hoped anyone would realize they were unwelcome.

The door eased back, and Colonel Anhalt stepped cautiously into the room. His face was etched with emotion, which was unlike the usually stoic Gurkha. He stood in the threshold with his arms tight at his sides and his head slightly bowed.

Adele grinned and left her place at the window. "Colonel Anhalt! How wonderful to see you finally!"

Anhalt seemed taken aback by her warm greeting. "Your Highness."

She tugged him by his gloved hand. "Come in. What's wrong with you? I'll send for tea. I requested you come several times, but they always said you were away. I was afraid you were cross with me."

He stared at her with his mouth agape in disbelief.

Adele laughed. "I'm joking. Of course I knew you were busy with war planning. Come in. I want to hear all about it." She pulled a cord for a servant.

The sturdy officer seemed completely confused. He struggled to recover his reserve. Before he could speak again, a maid stepped in and Adele ordered a tray of tea and sweets. She pulled the colonel to a low brass table surrounded by large pillows, rearranged the khukri that remained always in her belt, and flopped down. She glanced up, waiting for him to join her.

Anhalt stammered, "Your Highness, I fear I cannot."

"My dear colonel, I've been through too much to worry about protocol. You are welcome to sit with me. In fact, I command it."

The man took a deep, troubled breath.

Adele leaned forward anxiously. "What's wrong? Is it Simon? My father?"

"Oh no! No, Highness. There is nothing wrong."

She relaxed and slapped a pillow. "Ah. Good. Sit!"

The soldier made no move to join her.

The princess waved a hand dismissively. "Oh, I know you can't tell me war plans. I won't ask. I can find out those later anyway." As three servants entered with trays crowded with pitchers, pots, fruit, and sweets—a sumptuous feast—Adele said, "Do you want to hear tales from the vampire lands?" She gave a theatrical shudder. "Oh the horrors! The way they feed . . . watching you . . ."

The servants stiffened visibly with wide fearful eyes, and one turbaned man nearly dropped his tray. They settled the food safely, but with great rattling, and then quickly withdrew.

Adele laughed. "I love that! I've been doing that for days now."

The corners of Anhalt's mouth twitched up, but he refused to break his aura of distance. There was a pain in his eyes as they briefly settled on the young woman and slipped away.

He whispered, "I'm sorry, Highness."

"Sorry? For what? Will you please sit down before the tea gets cold?"

"I'm sorry for what happened to you." He stood at attention and focused his gaze on her like a soldier and gentleman. "I can never express my regret for failing you."

Adele paused in surprise. She set down the teapot gently. "Failing me? What are you talking about?"

"At the *Ptolemy*. I failed to protect you. I regret it bitterly."

Adele stood. "For God's sake, Colonel. We were attacked by an army. Led by the most vicious war chief of all the clans. I know. I saw her in action firsthand. There was nothing you could've done."

"I could have died. Protecting you."

He was a beaten man. Adele had never seen this side of the colonel. Anhalt was one of the touchstones Adele depended on. In a world that had been changed so irrevocably for her, she needed a few pieces of bedrock that would not ever alter. This new Anhalt was distressing, and it had to stop.

Adele snapped, "Enough! I won't have that from you! We lost a battle. We lost brave men. Mourn them. I do. But I survived. Simon survived. You survived. We'll learn from it. With what I know about vampires, we can build a new White Guard that will be the finest fighting force in Equatoria."

Anhalt took a deep breath, as if breathing in her fury. His eyes hardened. "No doubt you will, Highness. I shall not be part of it."

"What do you mean?"

"I have been reassigned. I will no longer command your home

guard. I came here, despite my misgivings, to thank you for the exquisite privilege of serving you over the years."

Adele stared at him for a moment. "What the hell are you talking about? Reassigned? I think not! Colonel Anhalt, you are the commander of my guard. You will continue to be the commander of my guard."

"Highness, Lord Kelvin has insisted that—"

"Lord Kelvin!" Adele clenched her fists and paused in silent anger. She whirled back to the table, seized a sliced pomegranate, and hurled the ripe fruit against the wall, where it splattered wet and red.

The princess turned back slowly with her face a mask of power and intensity. Anhalt took a step back. His princess had changed.

Adele said in a slow, gravelly voice, "That's what I care for Lord Kelvin. I will be empress. And that gives me power to remove both heads and pensions. If one doesn't scare Kelvin, the other surely will. You will not be reassigned. You are my commander. Do you understand me?"

Anhalt gave a quick half bow. "Yes, Your Highness."

"Excellent. Come to me tomorrow and we will begin to plan the new White Guard. Yes?"

"Yes, Your Highness."

Adele breathed heavily through her nose, trying to will the anger out. Her motionless body quivered with energy. Clearing her throat, she managed a smile. "Good. Would you care for something to eat? I believe I have another half of a pomegranate."

"I thank you." Anhalt's voice was thick with emotion. His eyes blazed as he inclined his head. "But I must crave your indulgence to withdraw now, Your Highness."

Adele clasped her hands together behind her with another breath of relief. "Very well. But I expect you tomorrow."

The soldier dropped to one knee before her and leaned forward. With a gloved hand, he reached out and took the hem of her gown and brought it to his lips. "I will serve you until my death."

She touched his shoulder and brought him to his feet, warmth filling her heart. He said nothing more, but they both turned sharply at a commotion in the hall. Alarmed, they prepared to rush to the door, but

Simon burst in. Adele laughed; the boy's vitality brought a smile to her face every time she saw him.

"Adele!" Simon shoved past her attempted embrace, but she didn't have the heart to reprimand his boisterous actions.

Simon leapt onto the large cushioned sofa in the center of the room. In his arms he carried a strange box.

"What is it you have there?" she asked as she settled next to him.

"A present! For you!"

Simon's joy was the same as if the present had been for him. He had such generosity in his heart, which would've been a worthy quality for a future emperor. If only he was the heir.

"From whom?"

"The Greyfriar!" His voice was dramatic and mysterious, a product of reading too many fanciful stories.

"What?" Adele's heart jolted. She stared at the strange box. It was worn and dirty, as if it had traveled a great distance through many hands. But it was obvious that those who had carried it had taken great care with their cargo. The box was made of wood and copper plate that was segmented as if there were slots, and she heard something shift softly inside.

"How did this get here?" Adele asked frantically. "Who brought it? Where is he? It couldn't have been Greyfriar! Is he here?" The thought that Gareth had come to retrieve her mushroomed in Adele's mind. She tightened her grip with both hands on a cushion, gazing at her brother in supplication.

Simon replied loudly, "No! It wasn't him! That would've been amazing! It was just a courier. I think Mamoru said he was from the Greyfriar's secret army in the north. But he left."

Adele sank back into the pillow in defeat. Since she had returned to Alexandria, gifts had poured in nonstop from every lord, lady, business interest, minor dignitary, and potential grandee throughout the Empire and across the periphery states. But she had had no great excitement in opening these gifts. After all, they were only reminders of her dismal future.

This time she ran her fingers over the carton with delicate, painful relish. As she lifted the lid, both she and Simon jumped as up popped the grey cat from Edinburgh, its paws clinging to the edge of the box. Her brother let out a squeal of delight.

"A cat!"

It couldn't be the same cat, Adele thought. She lifted the animal tenderly from the box. It was, though. Adele felt the familiar fur with a bittersweet shock. Edinburgh. The castle. That first horrible lonely night with only this warm animal for companionship.

And now, here he was. In Alexandria. Gareth had seen to it. For her.

Pet purred and rubbed against her. Memories flooded back to her as if they had happened yesterday, filling her with warmth and joy she hadn't felt since the day she left Gareth's castle.

"Now that's a wedding present!" exclaimed Simon, reaching for the cat. "This cat is from the Greyfriar?"

"Amazing." Colonel Anhalt shook his head. "I don't think even the Empire could find the resources to move a single creature across occupied Europe. The Greyfriar has an extraordinary reach, it seems. This poor animal has seen more of vampire territory than any Equatorian." He smiled at Adele. "With the exception of you, of course, Highness. Was this cat some part of your adventures together?"

Adele couldn't answer. Instead, she anxiously inspected the cat for injuries, but he seemed right enough. In fact, he was quite robust for an animal who had been halfway across the Earth. She placed her face against the cat's vibrating side and closed her eyes.

Anhalt murmured, "Prince Simon, come. Leave your sister alone for now."

The boy huffed, gave the cat one last stroke, and crawled off the sofa. Anhalt and Simon slipped from the room, and their whispered voices echoed away down the corridor.

The cat shifted with curiosity, but then quietly laid his paw over Adele's forearm and settled down for a nap. She went to scratch Pet's chin, his favorite itchy spot, and felt something hard.

A collar.

That was new. Adele opened her eyes. There was a thin leather collar around the cat's neck. She ran a finger inside it to make sure it wasn't too tight. She felt something sharp inside the collar, so she fumbled with the small buckle to remove it in case it might be worrying the cat.

As the animal fell asleep on her knee, Adele studied the collar. It was old and worn. Nothing special. But she noticed a slit in the leather on the inside. That's what had caught her finger. She picked at it with her fingernail. The slit widened. She continued to pull at it until the leather seams parted and something fell onto her lap.

Paper. A tightly folded sliver of paper.

Adele gasped and stopped breathing. She picked up the paper and began to unravel its intricate folds until it opened into a thin sheet of worn, frayed stationery. It was covered with an elegant script. With a shaking hand, she lifted it up to read:

Adayla,

This is the first letter I have ever written. That a few marks on this piece of paper can bring you my heart in my absence is a great magic. Life is now a constant source of wonder.

G

Adele scooped Pet up in her arms, squeezing him tight. He trilled with curiosity and slit open his eyes. She crossed to the window with him still purring softly in her embrace. Stepping into a shaft of budding sunlight, Adele leaned against the pillar, watching the sunrise. Her eyes strayed to a distant spot on the northern horizon.

———

Gareth stood on the ramparts of Edinburgh Castle watching his own sunrise. Cradled in his hands was the book he had acquired in Marseilles. He was struggling with the Latin language, but he wasn't going to give up. Currently, though, his mind was on something else.

Cats swirled at his ankles and sprawled languidly nearby. One picked that moment to jump onto the battlement, purring loudly, bumping his head into Gareth's chest. He smiled, wondering if his gift had arrived. The day Adele left, he had put the plan into action.

For days after, Gareth had wandered the castle. He couldn't think of anything but her. He had sensed his own death in her, the death of all his kind, but all he wished was for her to live. And perhaps one day to see her again.

His hand dropped and he stroked the cat. He was not a man of extremes. He was a creature of mission and duty. He had never loved nor hated, been passionate or jaded. But ever since Adele had come into his life, he had learned the joy of extremes.

And the despair of them too.

ABOUT THE AUTHORS

CLAY AND SUSAN GRIFFITH are a husband and wife writing team who have published fiction ranging from the dark fantasy novel *Banshee Screams* to the satirical comic book *The Tick*. They were married in Scotland, the country that provides much of the setting of *Vampire Empire*, and currently live with a cat in North Carolina.

Visit them online at http://clayandsusangriffith.blogspot.com/.